Love
and the
Silver
Lining

TAMMY L. GRAY

BETHANYHOUSE

a division of Baker Publishing Group
Minneapolis, Minnesota

© 2021 by Tammy L. Gray

Published by Bethany House Publishers
11400 Hampshire Avenue South
Bloomington, Minnesota 55438
www.bethanyhouse.com

Bethany House Publishers is a division of
Baker Publishing Group, Grand Rapids, Michigan

Printed in the United States of America

Library of Congress Cataloging-in-Publication Data
Names: Gray, Tammy L., author.
Title: Love and the silver lining / Tammy L. Gray.
Description: Minneapolis, Minnesota : Bethany House, a division of Baker
    Publishing Group, [2021] | Series: State of grace
Identifiers: LCCN 2021004783 | ISBN 9780764235917 (paperback) | ISBN
    9780764239182 (casebound) | ISBN 9781493431519 (ebook)
Classification: LCC PS3607.R39685 L68 2021 | DDC 813/.6—dc23
LC record available at https://lccn.loc.gov/2021004783

Scripture quotations are from THE HOLY BIBLE, NEW INTERNATIONAL VER-
SION®, NIV® Copyright © 1973, 1978, 1984, 2011 by Biblica, Inc.® Used by
permission. All rights reserved worldwide.

This is a work of fiction. Names, characters, incidents, and dialogues are products
of the author's imagination and are not to be construed as real. Any resemblance to
actual events or persons, living or dead, is entirely coincidental.

Cover design by Susan Zucker

Author is represented by Jessica Kirkland, Kirkland Media Management.

21   22   23   24   25   26   27   7   6   5   4   3   2   1

To my remarkable son, Christian

You are a treasure to me, and the only person I know who loves dogs nearly as much as Darcy does.

This one's for you.

ONE

MIDLOTHIAN, TEXAS

I'm supposed to be on an airplane, flying to Central America to teach children to speak English. Instead, I'm sitting on the couch and nursing my third pint of Rocky Road ice cream, watching a Telemundo soap opera in Spanish.

As if the woman on-screen understands my devastation, she cries out and slaps her now ex-boyfriend, who's cheated twice in the last six episodes. I wish my own heartbreak could be resolved with a hand slap. But I don't get the luxury of blaming a person. Only rotten circumstances.

"You tell him, girl!" I say as ice cream dribbles down my chin onto my wrinkled T-shirt. I grab for a towel, but I must have dropped it somewhere between my third trip to the freezer and my pity party on the couch. I check under the coffee table and spot it five feet away, right on the threshold where my living room carpet meets the kitchen tile.

"Piper." My three-year-old Maltipoo pops her nose in the air from the spot beside me, her ears keen to hear my next command. From that angle, she could be mistaken for a teddy bear, which is why her breed has been lauded one of the cutest in the world. And my gal is especially beautiful with her soft array of caramel-and-white fur, a little button nose, and a forever puppy face to match her 8.2 pounds. "Piper, fetch."

She jumps off the couch, her head swiveling to look for our usual play toy—a stuffed mouse she fell in love with at the pet store.

"Fetch the towel." I point to the crumpled blue cloth and give her the hand signal to retrieve it. She's a smart gal, so it only takes two round trips to the kitchen to find what I'm pointing at. "Good girl!"

She hops back on the couch and drops the dangling cloth on my lap. I reward her with lots of neck scratches and a few tasty chin licks before I wipe away the rest with the towel she brought me. If only people were as predictable as dogs. In fact, I would venture to bet that if the nonprofit mission organization I chose to partner with were run by animals, they would have told me months ago that the Guatemalan school was in financial crisis and not to spend every free moment I've had for the past year desperately raising money to fund my teaching salary.

"*Ugh . . .* Why?" I scream at the ceiling nearly as loudly as the woman did on my TV. It's not the first time I've yelled at God since getting the heartbreaking news three days ago that my one-year mission trip was canceled, and I doubt it will be the last time. That is unless I quit speaking to Him altogether, which is not off the list of possibilities.

I slam my head into one of my throw pillows, replaying the phone conversation again and again.

"I'm so sorry, Darcy," she had said. "If there was anything we could do, we would have. They raised our taxes again, and it crippled us."

"Rest assured all your money will be refunded."

"We're heartbroken, too, but when God closes one door, He usually has another opportunity just waiting for you."

Then she cried. My sponsor—the woman who walked me through every application, background check, and financial deposit—sobbed on the phone with me for five minutes while I sat there numb and unmoving.

Even now, days later, it still doesn't feel real to me.

After two years of preparation, one year of brow-beating savings and fundraising, quitting my job, ending the lease on my apartment, and giving half of my worldly possessions to charity, I have nothing except humiliation and a Facebook post with 143 comments. If I see another prayer emoji, I may just smash my computer against the wall.

Piper snuggles under the pillow covering my face and licks at my neck until I sit back up. She knows I'm upset, has sensed it since the moment I ended the worst call of my life, and she hasn't left my side since. I guess I should be grateful, especially considering I've had my phone on *do not disturb* for forty-eight hours now, so contact with the outside world has been nonexistent.

The screen flashes to a commercial, and I take the opportunity to stretch and use the bathroom. A mistake, considering the reflection in the mirror is as scary outside as the turmoil inside. My hair is matted, and my eyes are dark and puffy from too much TV and not enough sleep. I attempt to make some positive progress and gargle mouthwash. Yeah, it's no toothbrush, but it's all I have the energy for.

I flip off the light switch and shuffle back to my couch, now also my bed since I put my mattress in storage a week ago. That day was a celebration, every box a step closer to achieving my goal. We ate pizza, toasted with Dr Pepper and cinnamon cookies. I thought packing day was the first real movement toward the incredible journey God had planned. Who knew it would be the beginning, middle, and final leap off the cliff of disappointment?

The last commercial fades away and my favorite character is back in her living room, tears flowing down her face. She screams she will have vengeance and I believe her, especially when they zoom in close and show the determination in her gorgeous dark-chocolate eyes. I pick up my soupy ice cream container and spoon melting heap after melting heap of sugar into my mouth until my doorbell dings three times with persistence.

Ugh. I should have put that contraption on *do not disturb*, as well.

"Go away!" I yell, though it's likely muffled, since I'm trying to keep the ice cream from running down my chin again. Only one person would show up at my apartment unannounced, and I don't want to see him right now. Cameron Lee has been my best friend for nearly thirty years, and I have no doubt he will be there for the next thirty. But he's a lousy liar, and I know he's secretly thrilled I'm no longer moving away. "I told you I needed time."

"Well, your time is officially up," he yells back through the door.

I ignore him. It's rude, I know, but one has that luxury after getting the most devasting news of her life. The way I figure it, I can't be held responsible for any decisions made for at least four more days.

"Darcy." He pounds again.

I ignore him again.

Then it gets quiet, and right when I'm about to sink back

into my misery, the lock clicks and my front door swings open.

Crap. I forgot I gave him a spare key.

Cameron strides through my front door like a Spanish soap star, complete with the superhero determination and charming good looks, which he is fully aware of and uses to his advantage as needed. Luckily, I've never been swayed much by his sparkling blue eyes or rich brown hair that lies perfectly angled over his forehead.

"Holy cow." He waves a hand in front of his nose. "Your apartment smells like depression and stale milk."

And then there's that. The honesty that comes when you've known someone since sharing a crib and having your diapers changed at the same time. "What exactly does depression smell like?"

"Something rank." He shuts the door and flips on the ceiling fan. "It's a million degrees in here. Why isn't your A/C on?"

"I've been practicing getting used to the heat, since the school I was going to only had swamp coolers." I shrug, apathy and resentment rolling through each word. "I guess I succeeded."

He pauses halfway through the living room, the tough love, bang-on-the-door guy morphing into a soft mush of pity. "Ah, Darc, I'm . . . ."

I shake my head, not wanting to hear the word *sorry* ever again. It's too insignificant for what I'm feeling.

Cameron continues past me toward the hallway, where the thermostat's located. A click and then cold air rushes through my ceiling vent and down the wall behind me. Piper feels it, too, and snuggles underneath one of my throw pillows to stay warm. Not sure her choice of shelter is the best decision.

That pillow has more snot and tears in it than stuffing at this point.

My best friend appears in front of me and squats down so we're eye to eye. "You can't stay like this, Darcy. It's not healthy." When I turn away, he pushes aside my trash collection on the coffee table and sits so he's not having to maintain his balance. "Listen. It's time to pick yourself up, brush off this turn of circumstances, and return to the real world." He picks blanket fuzz from my unwashed hair and attempts to smile. "Who knows, maybe all of this will be for the best." Did I mention the dimples? He has two of them, deep and prominent on each side of his winning rock-star smile.

Yeah, even those don't work.

"You think me living out my worst-case scenario is for the best?" I cross my arms and sink deeper into the cushions. "Gee, thanks. Love the support. Really."

"I'm just saying that maybe you're missing the bigger picture here." He shifts closer. "Sometimes it takes having your perfectly planned life detonate right in front of you to discover what you really want. Trust me, I've been there."

I press my lips together because I don't want to admit he may have a point. Along with fundraising until I bled green, I've spent the last four months trying to support my friend through the hardest decision he's ever had to make—leaving the steady yet stagnant praise-team band he's been a part of for six years to join a secular rock band on the cusp of fame and fortune.

"Before I decided to leave it all and go on tour with Black Carousel, do you remember what you said to me?"

"Not really. I said a lot of things, most of which you didn't listen to."

He ignores my sarcasm. "You said that sometimes the answer to prayer is NO. And like it or not, we have to accept that answer." He spreads his arms. "This is your NO. And I'm sorry it happened, and I'm sorry you're so wrecked by it, but it's not going to change, no matter how many pints of ice cream you consume."

I look at the ceiling to keep the tears in my eyes from spilling over. I'm not typically a crier, and yet I feel like that's all I've done this past year. First with my parents' divorce, and now with the annihilation of my dream. "You don't understand."

"That's just it, Darcy. I do understand. I understand more than any person in your life right now." He cups my neck and pulls me forward until I have no choice but to use his T-shirt as a tissue. Sobs come fast and hard, but Cameron doesn't release me or pull away.

I guess there's one positive result of my chaos: at least I get to remain in the same country as my best friend. I'd call Cameron the brother I never had, except I do have a brother, and honestly, it hasn't been all that pleasant. If not burping, farting, or poking fun at my greatest insecurities, Dexter was tormenting me with his body odor and loud music. Cameron, on the other hand, has had my back since we toddled around at our church's Mother's Day Out program.

I finally come up for air, and Cam offers me my crusted blue towel. I wipe my eyes and nose before tossing it in my lap. "I think I ruined your shirt," I say, pointing at the massive wet circle in the middle of his chest.

He shrugs one shoulder. "No biggie. I have a drawer full."

"But that's your favorite," I insist, and finally he catches the joke.

Relief works through his eyes and relaxes his brow. "You

can't claim a shirt is my favorite simply because you bought it for me."

"I can too, especially if I scrimped and saved for two weeks to afford it."

"It was twenty dollars at Target."

"Which is a lot of money for a broke teenager." I smile through the mist in my eyes, and he squeezes my hand. "And look, it's lasted you twelve years. How can it not be your favorite?"

He nods. "You're right. It is my favorite."

I turn toward my little dog snuggled in the corner of the couch. "See, Piper. Give a guy some tears and they always cave."

Cameron snorts and stands, taking my pile of trash with him. "So, not to turn on the waterworks again, but have you made any headway with the landlord?" He disappears into the kitchen.

I groan and fall back into my new favorite slumped position. "Nope. It's like the old saying: 'I don't care where you go, but you can't stay here.' And my new apartment isn't available until September." Thank goodness for online applications or I wouldn't even have that.

I hear the snap of the trash lid, the refrigerator open and close, and then Cameron returns with two bottles of water.

He hands me one. "Does that mean you're definitely moving in with your mom?"

"Are you trying to make me cry again?"

He chuckles and joins me on the couch this time instead of the hard wooden coffee table. Probably a good thing, since it's older than I am. "Actually, I have been trying to come up with viable options to get you out of it, and I think I may have one."

I feel a spark of energy. "Do tell."

"Move in with us. I already cleared it with the guys."

The spark fizzles right away. "I thought you said 'viable options.' Living in that tiny three-bedroom apartment, tripping over you, Brian, and Darrel is ludicrous. Where would I even sleep?"

"I'll get a mattress to put on my floor, and you can have the bathroom. Brian's gone most of the time anyway, so I can use his."

The fact that I'm actually considering this idea instead of staying with my mom is proof that I've somersaulted into the Valley of Humiliation. Any minute now, Apollyon will begin slinging his arrows at me.

"Just promise you'll consider it." He falls back and mirrors my defeated position. "I need an ally in that apartment."

"The tension between y'all is that bad, huh?"

"It's been unbearable since I got back into town." Cameron's roommates are part of the praise-team band he quit to join Black Carousel in February. The tour they went on was only a small stateside three-month trip, but by the time he came home, resentment had ruined seven years of friendship. "And hey, it would only be until September. Then I could move in with you and we'd be roommates just like we envisioned as kids."

Oh, to have the luxury of being a kid again. When dreams and hopes and wishes don't die through the line of an 1,800-mile-away phone call.

"I guess we did have some epic sleepovers." Water-balloon fights, bike riding until dusk, Star Wars marathons. And then I turned eleven and my dad said no more. That was when Cam and I made a pact that when we became adults, we'd get our own place and stay up all night playing video games and eating junk food.

We turn our heads to face each other, and Cameron takes my hand. "I'll only say I'm sorry once for feeling this way, because truthfully I'm not sorry, which probably makes me the worst friend on the planet. But I'm relieved you didn't go. I need you here."

As young as I can remember, it's always been Cameron and Darcy, Darcy and Cameron. I suppose in a world riddled with failure and disappointment, that one security is worth its weight in gold.

TWO

I remember a time when I enjoyed going home. When my mom was my best friend and my dad was still my hero and the standard for all the men in my life. Now it's something I dread. Not just because there's been nonstop drama since the day my parents said the word *divorce*, but also because they've transformed into people I don't recognize.

We were a family that went to church on Sundays and prayed around the dinner table. We'd share our highs and lows for the day, listen to my dad as he'd give some funny anecdote from work while my mom would smile and shake her head because he likely said something inappropriate. My dad has always been the social one: handsome, funny, hardworking. A dreamer, some would say, mostly because he was always hatching some entrepreneurial plan to skyrocket his net worth. We'd be driving and he'd point to a house three times bigger than ours and say, *"One day we're going to own a home like this on the lake, and your mom and I will spend our evenings fishing until dusk."* He did eventually strike it rich, but instead of buying a lake house, he bought two new suits, a convertible, and an apartment in Dallas. But I'm pretty sure Mom got the fishing poles in the divorce, so there's that.

I trudge up the front steps of my childhood home and try to forget that my dad's car will never again be parked in the garage. Mom's called me four times in the last two days, and I'm not really in the mood for a guilt trip. One hour to fulfill my daughterly duty and then I can get back to my own depression.

"Mom," I call out as I open the front door. The house is clean, impeccably so. I shouldn't be surprised. My dad was the slob in the family.

"In the back, hun."

Her voice is coming from the master bedroom. The same room that once held a king-size bed my brother and I would jump on to snuggle with them on Saturday mornings. I can barely look at the smaller, more feminine bed frame that's there now.

I continue my path, down the hall, past my old room that was long ago turned into an office, and into the bedroom suite my parents added on when they first bought the property.

Mom's in front of the mirror applying eyeliner in just a bra and tight jeans. There was a time she wouldn't dare be so exposed, but the married weight was another thing that went away with my dad. She's now thinner than I am.

"Perfect timing. I need your opinion on my outfit." She drops the stick and blinks to dry her makeup. Then she's back in her closet pulling a silky tank top from a hanger. She slides it on, fluffs her blond hair, which is two inches past her shoulders, and does a pirouette. "Well, how do I look?"

Sad. Broken. But that's not the answer I'm allowed to give. "Beautiful, Mom. What's the occasion?"

"I have a date tonight." She smiles wide like it's a new thing. It's not. Mom's been actively dating since Dad carted his last suitcase to the car. I think it's her payback for my dad's infidelity. A way to show him she's still desirable.

I lean against the doorframe and try not to show my disapproval. "Is this another one you met online?"

"No, actually. A friend from work set us up. He's recently divorced, too, and is supposed to be tall and handsome."

Great. Divorced—check. Attractive—check. Whatever happened to all those lectures I got growing up about wise dating and finding a guy who loves the Lord first and me second? It's like all the rules and values changed simply because she is no longer married. How is that right?

"Anyway, I'm nervous for some reason." She presses her palms to her cheeks and sighs. "I think this could really be something."

I can't hold in my snort. "How? You haven't even met him yet."

"Trust me, dear. When you get to be my age, a man who has a steady job and isn't addicted to smut on his computer is a rare find."

Ah . . . another qualification. Not a loser—check.

If I'd held to the same standards, I'd be married with children already.

"Well, have a good time." There's not a whole lot of feeling in my voice, but that's not new either. This scenario is just one more thing I'm stuck with now that I'm not moving. My brother gets to live hours away in Oklahoma City with his wife. He's had exactly four interactions with our mom and dad since they broke the news, whereas I've had to be parent, girlfriend, and shopping buddy. And let me tell you, there isn't much worse than going to Victoria's Secret with my mom, knowing the items she's buying are not for my dad.

Mom flips off the bathroom lights and settles into one of the chairs by the French doors to slip on her heels. "And how are you doing? Any more thoughts about my offer to live here?"

I'd rather camp in a tent in the Amazon rain forest . . . and I loathe spiders. "I have. There's another option I'm considering, as well."

"Really? What's that?"

"Possibly living with some friends."

"Oh. Yeah, I guess that would be nice." Her voice holds a hint of hurt, but thankfully she doesn't say so. "Anyone I know?"

I'm not eager to share, but then again, Mom's recent choices pretty much guarantee I won't get a lecture on propriety. "Yes, actually. It's Cameron."

Instead of a warning on all the dangers of living with a guy, I get a smug smile. "Well, that's quite a turn of events. I was beginning to think the two of you would never take that leap."

"And we still haven't. Cam and I are strictly platonic."

"For now," she says in a singsong, overly romantic voice. "But you two aren't kids anymore. Moving in together is not the same as a Friday night sleepover."

I bite my lip because she just summed up the pressing worry that's been haunting me since Cameron threw his offer in the ring: could we take this risk and still remain friends?

The two of us are such different people that I've often wondered if we would be close friends if we'd met as adults. I'm a realist, the first to call a spade a spade. Cameron will turn a spade into a heart and then try to convince me it's

TAMMY L. GRAY

always been that way. It's irritating but it's also him, so I don't
stay mad for very long. In twenty-nine years, there's been only
one fight that's threatened to sever our bond, and I still blame
our parents for it.

When we turned sixteen, our parents began to see our
friendship as more, so much so that every time we hung out,
they'd start to talk about weddings and how cute our kids
would be. Cameron, being the dreamer that he is, bought
into the madness and went so far as to ask me out our senior
year of high school. *"We're perfect for each other,"* he'd said.
*"It's so easy with us, and isn't friendship the foundation of every
good relationship?"*

But I didn't want just an easy friendship. I wanted passion and flutters in my stomach. I wanted the challenge of
learning something new about the person I was going to
marry. I wanted more than I knew I'd ever get with Cameron. I told him as much, and he didn't speak to me for a
month. Then one day he called, and we never discussed the
issue again.

Truth is, even back then I wanted what I thought my
parents had, and now I wonder if maybe I've been the one
to confuse reality with fantasy because I still want what I
remember being so perfect. And deep down, I know he does,
too.

"Nothing is set in stone," I say, indecision being my new
best friend. "I still have eight days until I have to move out,
and who knows what may come up between now and then."

"Okay, well, just know you always have a place here. You've
taken the news of this trip so hard, I've been worried about
you."

Despite her tone of concern, I doubt it's true. Mom hasn't
been a mom in months. Seven to be exact. Sometimes I don't

know who I resent more for it. Her or my dad for making all this happen. "Well, no need to worry. I'm fine. Other opportunities will come."

"Or maybe this is God's way of telling you it's not your future."

I grit my teeth to keep from rolling my eyes. The last thing I want to hear from my mom is a sermon about patience and trust. She's shown neither.

"Darcy, like it or not, it's a mess out there, and you're going to be thirty soon. If not Cameron, then find someone else. I worry that if you continue to wait, there won't be any good guys left."

"Yeah, because getting married at twenty-two worked out so well for you." The harsh words come out before I can stop them, and I immediately wish I'd shown more self-control the minute my mom recoils. She's vulnerable, and I hit the tenderest nerve. "I'm sorry, Mom. I shouldn't have said that." It's not technically her fault my parents split up; Dad's the one who bailed, but deep down I'm still mad at her for giving up. Or maybe for moving on, I don't know, but it's there between us every time we interact.

She takes a deep breath and looks up at me. "I got thirty-five wonderful years and two beautiful children out of my marriage. You can't judge the journey simply by how it ends."

My throat burns because it's the nicest thing she's said about my father in months. And even though I've been too angry to speak to him since the divorce, her words make me miss him so much my chest aches.

She gets to her feet and walks toward me. "I know this has been hard for you, Darcy."

I swallow because it's all I can do to keep from crying. I know I'm an adult and shouldn't care as much as I do about the split, but I want my family back. Not this broken version of a mom and dad.

Her hands cup my cheeks, and she lightly kisses my forehead. "The worst of it is over. And in time, you'll see how all these disappointments work out."

I wish I shared her optimism, but I don't. I had it all figured out. Saved every penny for a year, beat the pavement to get support. Studied Spanish until I went cross-eyed. "It's just not fair," I say, more to myself than to her.

"No, it's not." My mom smiles the way only moms can when they've lived so much more life than we have. "But life rarely is." She clears her throat and drops her hands. "Anyway, I better get going. Michael is meeting me at the restaurant in fifteen minutes."

Ugh. I now hate the name Michael.

She grabs her purse from the bed and blows me a kiss. "Lock up when you leave, okay?"

"I will."

After one more check in the dresser mirror, she rushes out in a flurry of perfume and determination. I plop down on the chair she just vacated and close my eyes. Glimpses of the woman I've known my whole life are all I get now. Moments of authenticity before pain and bitterness bring her back to reality. I don't want to be that. I don't want to spend the next year being angry at God for allowing this to happen. I just want some kind of clarity as to why He gave me a path and then jerked it away before I could even step onto it.

What was the point?

As usual, I hear no grand answer. Just silence. I'm almost getting used to it.

I pull my phone from my pocket and text the one person I know will understand.

Me
What are you up to tonight?

Cam
Nothing really. You?

Me
Giving fashion advice to my mom before her 100th first date.

Cam
Yuck. Wanna come over?

Me
Be there in 5 minutes.

I stand, slip my phone back in my pocket, and catch a glimpse of my reflection in the mirror. Rarely do I see my mom when I look back. She's tall, while I'm fairly short. She keeps steady highlights in her hair, while mine is the same maple-brown it's been since birth. And my eyes are my dad's—a blue-green mix that have always been my favorite feature. Today, though, I see her in my eyes. The sadness, the defeat, the utter lack of any kind of positive future.

I've asked "why" too many times to ask again, so I simply walk away and count today as one more day I've managed to survive.

THREE

My refund check comes on Monday for every penny I sent in—six months' worth of salary. I should be relieved, especially since my bank account is quickly approaching zero, but mostly it's just the final confirmation that my trip was canceled. Cameron's right. No amount of ice cream is going to change that very real fact.

Only about a third of the money was my personal savings. The rest represented hours of PowerPoint slides and pitches to mission teams in churches all over Ellis County. The same teams that will eventually get all their money returned. Just not today.

Today I'm going to pretend that my life isn't completely spiraling out of control.

I park my truck along the curb and make sure to lock the doors before heading up the sidewalk. Bryson's one-bedroom rental is in what most would consider a rougher part of Midlothian. Public drinking and violence are common at the park down the street from his house, and every time I've come there's been at least one house with eviction furniture thrown on the lawn.

Cam says Bryson picked the location because he knew no one would complain about the noise coming from the house, and I guess he was right because it's been Black Carousel's practice space for the past three years. I don't normally watch them rehearse, or even perform for that matter, but today especially I'm finding it very difficult to be alone.

I finish my trek up Bryson's front steps and ring the doorbell. Cameron's car isn't here, nor is Jay's or Harrison's, but I don't really want to hang out in my car either.

"It's open," I hear through the chipping wood door and turn the handle.

Inside, Bryson pushes a large leather couch to the back wall. It's on sliders, as is the other furniture shoved into the corner.

It's remarkable how even doing such a menial task, Bryson can still carry himself with the cool confidence of a rock star. Even more remarkable is how little he's changed since high school. His clothes have adapted to the most current fashion, and the material gets heavier or lighter depending on the season, but every stitch is still a midnight-black.

He finishes his task and runs a hand through his wild, untamed hair. Also black. Bryson is Greek by heritage, though he's never known the father who gave him both his looks and his last name Katsaros. Maybe that's why he's spent a lifetime creating an image that screams *Back off.* The only thing mildly warm about his appearance is the one trait he can't change—his eyes. They're an intricate hazel and shine like polished granite. They're also the only thing I still recognize in the boy I've known since elementary school.

Finally, he turns, though his surprise makes it clear I'm not the one he thought he was inviting in. "Darcy?" He shakes his head like he needs a second to process I'm really here. "How have you been?"

"Wallowing, actually." That gets a rare genuine smile from him and makes my cheeks warm for some reason. "Can I help you with anything?"

He looks around. "Um, sure. You can grab the lamps and put them in the kitchen."

"Okay."

An awkward air of silence hangs around as I move to the end table. Bryson and I have an odd relationship. There's shared history and moments of friendship, but there's also this wall he projects. One that makes it impossible to be much more than acquaintances.

I unplug the lamp from the outlet. "I heard the tour went well."

"Yeah, it did. Lots of exposure, though I am happy to be home. The road gets weary after a while." He stops and tugs on the back of his neck, projecting the same uncomfortableness that we always seem to feel when alone together. Not that it's happened much. We shared many of the same friends growing up, yet Bryson always hung on the fringe of our group.

"Cameron's already geared up to go on the next one. He thinks Oklahoma could be another good market."

Bryson doesn't say anything, but his small grunt implies plenty. His and Cameron's is another relationship that's very hard to decipher. At times they seem like lifelong buddies; then other times there's such an edge of competition that it's hard to be in the same room with them. The only constant is the magic they make onstage together. Somehow, when the lights are on and guitars are pressed into their hands, they connect. The rest of the time is a crapshoot.

I set the lamps and other breakable items in the small alley kitchen, and by the time I return, the living room looks more like a recording studio than a home. Harrison's drums sit back in the corner, while electric cords and amps fill the perimeter. Cameron has also arrived.

"I saw your truck outside." He meets me halfway into the living room. "What are you doing here?"

"Looking for you." Instinctively, I exhale, feeling better simply because he's here. "My refund check came in today. And I was just sitting there, staring at the envelope and the boxes, and I don't know, I suddenly felt completely trapped." I look past him to Bryson, who watches our exchange until our eyes meet, and then he busies himself with some other plug. "I can go if you want me to. I didn't mean to crash your practice."

"No, of course not." He pulls me in for a much-needed hug, and I tuck my head into his shoulder. "Stay as long as you want to, though I can't promise it won't be rough. We're learning a new song."

I ease out of his embrace just as Harrison and Jay walk into the house.

"Hey, look at this. We have a new Alison," Jay says, winking at me. "I love cute groupies."

"Not funny." The edge in Bryson's voice is understandable. Alison and he didn't exactly part on the best of terms. So bad, in fact, that she moved two hours away and unfriended all of us on social media.

"Let's go, Cam," Harrison says before slamming his sticks against the drums. "I have a date tonight, and I'm not canceling again."

Cam hesitates to leave me. "You sure you're okay?"

"I'm fine." I push him toward his bandmates. "I'll probably just stay for a few minutes and then slip out."

"Whatever you need to do." He nods and joins Black Carousel in the center of their makeshift stage while I find a seat in the back corner and try to become invisible.

Life is ironic. While some things stay so familiar, like Bryson's black clothes and Jay's always inappropriate comments, other things completely turn upside down. Six months ago, Alison and Bryson were dating, Mason was the lead guitarist instead of Cameron, and I looked on the future of our group with wide-eyed hopefulness.

Bryson starts with a song I know, so I guess they're going to warm up before they get to the new stuff. His voice is edgy and dark, his eyes fixated on some invisible person in the crowd. This is usually when most girls would swoon. Bryson has that bad-boy allure. Sharp features, a smile that's more a smirk than anything authentic, and intense eyes that promise behind the persona there's a depth he'll never let you near. He is handsome, no one could deny that fact, but I miss the kid he used to be.

We were in the third grade when Bryson showed up in our Sunday school class with tears in his eyes. Mason was the first to talk to him, of course; he's always been the most inclusive. Within minutes they were laughing. Mason waved us over, and our little group of four became five. After that, we saw him every Sunday without fail. He didn't go to our school. Bryson lived in Mansfield, but his mom and stepdad would drive to Midlothian on Sunday mornings just to come to Grace Community. Back then he was sweet, shy, and always the first to make someone feel cared for; he even picked a dandelion for me the weekend after my hamster died and told me he was sorry I was so sad. I felt super special, until Cameron called it a weed and jerked it out of my hand. I think it might have hurt Bryson's feelings because he never gave me another one.

A wave of sadness hits, and not just for the changes in Bryson over the years, but for all of us. For Cameron, who quit inspirational music despite it being his first love. For Alison, who pushed friendship into more and got her heart broken. For Mason, who hasn't spoken to any of us since Bryson fired him from the band. And for me, sitting here, lost and afraid, clinging to bits and pieces of the past since my future is only a long road of unknowns.

I don't even make it through the end of the song before I feel the pressure in my chest that warns a breakdown is coming soon. It's one thing to cry and blubber in front of Cameron, but I'm not about to shed a tear in front of the rest of the band.

I disappear into the kitchen and out the back door. It's a small yard with only a waist-high chain link fence, but Bryson has made it somewhat of an outdoor space. Along an extended porch, there's a couch swing, two rocking chairs, and a metal fire pit. He definitely won't need that anytime soon. The temperature today is supposed to reach ninety-two degrees.

Carefully, I sit in the swing, not totally sure if it will hold me, and kick my feet back and forth. Time seems to pass slowly, seconds ticking like minutes, but that also seems to be my new normal—finding ways to kill time. I readjust and try to pull my shorts down on my thighs. Even in the shade, my legs are sticking to the lacquered wooden swing. Sweat trickles down my back, but I stay put . . . ten minutes, then twenty.

The backdoor screen squeaks as it opens and closes again. From my shadowed spot in the corner, I see my new guest faster than he sees me. Bryson stands with his hands on his hips, his shoulders slumped, his head lowered as if watching the trail of ants I noticed earlier.

It's an odd stance for him and makes my chest twinge with both compassion and curiosity. Bryson isn't the kind of guy who shows emotion. At least not that I've ever seen.

He lifts his head and blows out two long, intentional breaths, then lets out a frustrated growl.

"Practice not going so well?" I keep my voice nonchalant and direct, a default of mine when I'm not quite sure how to gauge a situation.

Bryson turns at the sound of my voice. "If Jay missing two lead-ins and Harrison fumbling through the beat is not going well, then yes, practice is abysmal." He rolls his shoulders and stretches his neck. "Cam's been on a tear writing music again, and he doesn't exactly know how to write songs for the common musician."

Cameron's a musical prodigy. He can play every instrument I know the name of and some I don't. But like most musicians, his creativity is directly linked to his state of mind, which has been jumbled for a while now. He spent months artistically blocked, writing and trashing every song or idea out of his head. But something changed when he got back from the tour. A dam broke and a flood of music has poured out ever since.

The swing catches and moans as Bryson sits, but it only takes a few seconds before our feet move in unison, pushing us lazily back and forth.

"We thought you left."

I assume the "we" includes Cameron, which is probably why he's not out here checking on me. "I was going to, but the backyard was closer."

"I'm guessing your escape act wasn't due to our tempo issues. You doing okay? I mean with everything that's happened?" This question is more tentative, like he knows it's potentially the unraveling string on a sweater.

"Oh yes, I'm fantastic. My future got blown to smithereens, but yes, I'm doing just fine."

Bryson turns to look at me, and I avert my eyes to focus on the skin around my cuticles. "Well, at least this setback hasn't ruined your ability to use sarcasm."

I shake my head. "This isn't a setback. It's a bolted coffin."

"Come on. All you have to do is find another school and you're back where you started."

"Where I started?" I look up, unsure if I feel more appalled or irritated at his lack of understanding. "I'm not doing this again."

When he gives me an eyebrow that basically screams *quitter*, the pressure I've barely been keeping at bay comes tumbling out in a massive verbal deluge. "Imagine asking a girl to marry you, and then, while you're all in love, you plan the wedding. Spend all the time and money picking out flowers and tuxes and invitations. You count the days on your calendar, so thrilled you will get to spend the next year with your bride. And then the day comes, and you stand at the altar waiting for that moment when all the planning and worry and stress becomes worth it. Only she doesn't come. Instead, she leaves you standing at the altar with a note that says, 'Sorry, but don't worry, there's more fish in the sea.'" I take a deep breath. "Now, tell me, how likely are you to go track down that girl and ask her to marry you all over again?" I stare into his eyes, daring him to argue with my logic.

Yet somehow he finds a way. "I can't answer that. Your analogy is flawed."

"It is not flawed; it's perfect."

"Hardly."

"Why?" I demand, my annoyance growing stronger the closer he gets to laughing.

"Because I'm never getting married."

"Shut up. You know what I mean." I close my eyes and seriously consider wringing his neck. "God said no. End of story. Now I just have to figure out what the heck I do with the next ten years of my life."

"Ten years? Maybe you should just start with ten days." He bumps my shoulder with his. "Overachiever."

I laugh even though I don't want to. There are times when Bryson's worldview is nice to latch on to. He keeps his circle small, his mind focused. People come in and out, but he never attaches. "Honestly, Bryson, I'd be happy just figuring out the next five days."

"What happens then?"

"Well, let's see. On Saturday, I will be officially kicked out of my current apartment, and since my new apartment isn't available until September, I'm left with two temporary living options. Move home and watch my mom date a bunch of men who aren't my dad, or move in with Cameron and share an apartment with three guys who are barely cordial to each other right now." I run frustrated fingers through my hair. "Believe it or not, Cam's offer is the lesser of the two evils."

He rolls his shoulders, and I notice how tense his body has become. It's probably the heat. He has to be catching on fire in those clothes, but I long ago quit teasing him about dressing like he's going to a funeral every day of the week. "Wow. You and Cam living together."

I don't know why hearing Bryson say it makes me feel guilty, but I do all of a sudden. "It's not like we'd be *living* together. It'd be more like a platonic slumber party."

"For three months?"

"Yep."

He pulls on his shirt, oscillating it to get some relief from the heat. "In that case, you could always move in with Zoe. She has a nice two-bedroom apartment with nothing in that second room but an old treadmill she doesn't use." He tosses the suggestion so nonchalantly that I'm not sure he recognizes the depth of what he's offering.

"Are you serious? Because I have to be honest, my sense of humor is really limited right now. And if this is just some sick way of making fun—"

"Darcy," he says, cutting me off. "I know I'm not always the most sensitive person in the room, but I would never minimize what you're going through. I do know a little of what it feels like to be homeless."

I nod, feeling bad that I assumed the worse. It's a well-known fact that Bryson moved in with Cameron our senior year of high school to get away from his stepdad. The details are vague, and Cam has never shared the *why*, not even with me, but I do know that event has shaped Bryson's life. At least I assume as much, since that's when the black wardrobe started.

He stands, and though Bryson moves with an air of easy living, I can't seem to shake the idea that he's upset. "I'll ask her if you're interested."

Of course I'm interested, but the stars would have to align and my luck hasn't exactly been leprechaun status lately. "You're welcome to try, but I doubt she'd even consider it. Zoe and I have never really bonded." Even though Zoe is six years younger and we only interacted in youth group one year, it was a very painful year. I'm work boots and no makeup. She's gel polish and perfume. To say we clashed is an understatement.

"You leave my little sister to me." His eyes grow serious, and I'm mesmerized by the intensity that consumes them in a split second. "If you want this, I'll make it happen. Or . . ." And then his demeanor shifts just as quickly back to the apathetic, couldn't-give-a-flip attitude I've come to expect. "You can move in with Cam and plan the next ten years of your life. It's your call."

My call. My decision. What a change from the compressing black hole I've been falling through for a week now.

I hesitate for a second because I know this choice is opening a world of uncertainty, especially with someone like Zoe, but I also know that moving in with Cameron is not something I'm ready to do. It's too big a risk when his friendship is the only absolute in my life. "Call her and ask," I finally answer. "If she says no, then I'm no worse off than I am now."

His mouth turns up into a barely perceivable smile. "Consider it done."

FOUR

As Mafia-like and convincing as Bryson's promise was to me, I'm still surprised when Zoe calls me the very next day to schedule a tour of the apartment. A feat that seemed way harder than it should be for a twenty-three-year-old, but as she put it, "My new marketing career keeps me so busy, it's impossible to swing any free time."

But after a ten-minute list of all she'd accomplished in her first year out of college, and then another five minutes of fumbling through a myriad of scheduling conflicts, we finally settled on noon Thursday.

My first thought when I pull through the gates of her apartment complex is that I misread the directions. My second thought is that Zoe's marketing job must be paying better than average.

Bryson's toss off about a spare room did not prepare me for the opulence that is to be my new home. Rock balconies with dormers jut out from slate-gray buildings, giving them a very high-end Craftsman feel. The bottom floor apartments have garages, while others have reserved carports, not that it's necessary. There's a ton of area parking, and with the security gate, I doubt this place gets too many unintended guests. Not like my old apartment, which had a tight twenty-car parking lot that often filled to the point I had to park along the street.

I follow the curve of the drive, scoping out all the amenities a place like this would offer. Chairs and large beige umbrellas dot the decking around a huge serpentine pool, the water clear and glistening in the sun. No one is utilizing the area, which I find surprising considering it is full-blown summer in Texas. It makes me wonder what type of residents live here. Probably ones like Zoe, who implied she had little time for such frivolous activities.

Building 7 is easy to find. It's right next to the pool, clubhouse, dog park, and fitness center. Zoe lives on the second floor, apartment 723. I park the car, ease from the driver's side, and force myself to take the stairs versus explore the complex. For a year now, I've eliminated all luxuries from my life, a way to prepare my mind and heart for living in a Central American country. Now I'm so overwhelmed by them that I totally understand why other nations think all Americans are rich.

I pause at the top of the landing. Each side of the long walkway has a small personal alcove and fancy wood door with etched silver numbers. I walk forward, looking to the left and right for Zoe's. Hers is halfway down, left-hand side. There's a stunning summer wreath on the door, a welcome mat in cursive, and two potted plants to greet me. Another reminder of how different Zoe and I are from each other. My idea of decorating is making sure there's no residual pet hair on the furniture. Although now that my dog-grooming days are over, or hopefully so, maybe it's time to collect some nicer things.

I ring the doorbell and remind myself that no matter how

difficult Zoe is, living with her is only temporary and by far the best option on my pathetic list.

She opens the door with her phone crushed between her ear and shoulder. "Yes, and I'll take care of it first thing tomorrow morning." She waves me in with a perfectly polished hand adorned with two silver rings and rushes back to an open laptop on her kitchen counter. "Two hundred. Not a problem."

Left alone by the door, I take a second to assess my new surroundings, which could only be described as modern. No, ultramodern. Everything is white. The leather couches, the lacquered furniture, the area rug, even the wood flooring has a whitewashed finish. What isn't white is furry, mirrored, or dangling with crystals. And worse, nothing looks even the slightest bit used.

"Sorry about that," Zoe says from behind me. "I swear that office would shut down if I took a day off." She comes to my side and claps her hands together. "Well, this is it. Two bedrooms, two baths, thirteen hundred square feet. We have a balcony that overlooks the pool just through those French doors, and the area is super safe. Want to see the spare room?" She smiles, and though it's hardly genuine, it makes her entire face glow.

Zoe as a preteen was pretty, but Zoe the adult is the kind of beautiful that turns heads in a crowded room. Her hair is long, blond, and full of trendy waves. She has Bryson's eyes, only bigger. Same color, though, and with it that same combination of complexity and intrigue. Her skin is lighter than his, giving her that delicate porcelain appearance. Her nose slopes slightly, and her mouth has a bow shape that makes her more old Hollywood glamour than the average pretty girl. If any person could fit the décor in this space, it's her. Whereas I'm more like that old piece of antique furniture your aunt gives you that's too much of an heirloom to throw away so you stick it in the corner where no one can see it.

"Yes, that would be great. Thanks," I say and follow her to a little hall.

"My bedroom suite is at the end. Your bathroom is here." She pauses by a door in the hall, leans in, and flips on the light. "Sorry it's not private, but no one really comes over except my boyfriend, and he'll use mine."

I peek in. It's simple. Two sinks, a shower and toilet. Plenty of storage, not that I need it. My makeup routine is mascara and lip gloss, and that's only if I'm meeting friends somewhere. "This will work just fine. Thank you."

She turns off the light and walks two more steps before opening another door, this time on the right side. "Here you go."

The room is medium-sized, probably a hundred and fifty square feet. Not bad for a second bedroom. There's a four-paned window that lets in a lot of light and a chandelier-type ceiling fan dripping with more silver crystals. The treadmill Bryson was referring to is still against the back wall, along with a set of small dumbbells.

"This is really perfect, Zoe. You sure you don't mind me putting you out like this?"

"Not at all. I haven't used this room in ages. The treadmill was my mom's genius idea," she snorts sarcastically. "But come on. What's the point of working out if you can't go to the gym in cute leggings and pick up boys?"

"No idea," I say, even though I've never worn fitness leggings or tried to pick up boys.

"But that's Mom. She's always trying to . . . and I quote, make me stronger." She rolls her eyes. "Talk about compensating. Anyway . . ." She checks her watch. "I need to head

37

back. I'll get the spare key for you." Then she's gone in a flash of perfume.

A whirling sickness grows in my lower belly. This wasn't what my life was supposed to look like this summer. I was supposed to be sharing a room with another missionary teacher, not bunking with Bryson's half sister. I look at the raised ceiling and wonder again what I did wrong to deserve such disappointment. "Where are you? Why did you do this to me?" I ask under my breath.

I've been a Christian my whole life and never have I wavered or doubted. Until now. First my family is destroyed and now my future, too. I swallow down the hurt and blink away the sorrow so I can return to the kitchen with at least a little dignity intact.

Zoe's waiting by the counter, laptop packed up in a bag slung over her arm. She holds out a single key for me. "Here you go. I'm not home much, so move in whenever you need to."

"Thank you." I stare at the key as it passes from her hand to mine and realize in our lightning-fast tour she never once addressed logistics. "Bryson didn't mention rent or utilities." I'd already calculated what my max might be and hope her answer doesn't exceed it. My plan is to live off the savings I've recovered from the trip until I can figure out what I want to do with my life. "How much do I owe you?"

"Nothing." She waves her hand again like it's the silliest question in the world. "Just don't mess with my things or try and steal my boyfriend and we'll be good."

"Zoe, I need to give you something. My being here is a complete inconvenience to you. Not to mention, I could be totally psycho. You've hardly asked me any questions."

She opens the door and passes the threshold, examining

me the way I've been examining her all day. "It took a lot for my brother to call. If he's willing to do this for you, then I'm pretty certain you're not the next Single White Female stalker." She closes the door, then pops it back open. "Make yourself at home, roomie."

The door clicks shut and I'm left alone, still dissecting Zoe's words. She said *willing to do this.* As in something in the future. What exactly did Bryson agree to, and why in the world would he even bother? It's completely out of character for him.

I push aside the questions and tell myself it doesn't matter. Every time I begin to think Bryson still has that sweet little boy inside, I'm painfully reminded he doesn't. If he did, he wouldn't have fired his best friend, and he certainly wouldn't have dumped Alison.

Lost in the silence, I take a moment to peruse the apartment alone. The fridge is empty minus three salad kits and some kind of bottled fruit and vegetable drink. What a shock it's going to be when I stuff my ice cream, Dr Pepper, and lunch meat next to whatever paleo diet thing she must have going.

The kitchen drawers are all pristine and organized, every single one. I keep going, checking the living room and bathroom for some kind of proof that my new roommate isn't completely OCD.

I meander to the laundry room, though it's bigger than any laundry room I've ever had. My old apartment's consisted of a stackable washer/dryer combo with a flimsy accordion door. This one has side-by-side appliances and a folding counter. Underneath, there's a deep two-foot drawer I can't help but open. To my delight, it's stuffed to the top with junk. I don't know why this makes Zoe feel more human, but it does. I move aside the hammer and screwdriver, lift the duct tape, and freeze when I spot an old faded journal I immediately recognize. It's identical to one I have at the bottom of one of the boxes taped up in my storage unit. Grace Community gave them to all incoming seventh graders when we joined the youth group, and I'm pretty sure the tradition continues to this day.

I gingerly lift it from the drawer, having no intention of invading her privacy, but the pull of something so concrete and familiar in my life is too tempting to resist. Most kids look back on adolescence and hate that period in their life, but not me. I miss it. I miss the youth group and how our family would intentionally make Sunday a rest day. We'd play games or watch movies. Even after my brother left and it was just me, Sunday nights were still my favorite.

Unlike mine, the leather on Zoe's journal is worn and well used. I think mine might have had two pages filled out before I realized that writing down my feelings was not exactly part of my personality code. I press the book to my chest, memories of good times and laughter filling my heart. A tear falls, then another. Not for my trip this time but for the greater loss that I still haven't quite accepted.

Mom and I still do Sunday night dinners, every week without fail, but they're painful now. A shadow of what it was intended to be.

I move to tuck the journal back in its hiding place when a page slips from the cover and floats to the tile floor. Black words stand out on crisp white paper, scratched and messy, like someone didn't just want to get the words out but wanted to hurt the pristine sheet in the process.

"Forever invisible. Forever forgotten. Forever unseen."

Horrified that I've stumbled upon something so intimate,

I snatch it from the floor, slide it back in the journal, and return everything where it was before my invasion. I don't know when Zoe wrote those words or even if she did, but they certainly don't match the self-assured, time-deficient businesswoman who gave me a tour just ten minutes ago.

I push the drawer shut and return to the kitchen. The last thing I need is to press my nose into someone else's pain. Especially when I'm still trying to cure mine.

FIVE

When I was little, my fourth grade Sunday school teacher told us that God puts people in our lives for a reason. She had us make links out of construction paper and bond them to each other with Elmer's glue until we ran out of paper. Rows and rows of purple, blue, and red weaved between chairs and table legs to give us a visual on how God's kingdom is uniquely tied together. I clearly remember picking up one section and telling Cameron that he and I were linked by forces beyond the universe, so he really didn't have a choice but to be my best friend. Somehow I knew, even back then, he would be in my life through every storm.

"Well, that's the last box. You ready to go?" Cameron stands next to the driver's door of his brother's truck, watching me. He called in reinforcements this morning. The entire Lee clan, including his brother-in-law, came out to move my couches to the storage unit, sort through the mess for my bedroom set, then haul it right back to my apartment to load the last of the boxes. And to top it off, his sister and cousin stayed behind to clean my entire place while I was en route.

I'd scheduled three hours for this nightmare, and it took

less than two. They offered to meet me at Zoe's for the unloading, but it just felt like too much imposition.

"Please tell your family again how much I appreciate their help. Especially your mom for taking Piper for me today." This move is traumatic enough. Adding a spastic Maltipoo, running up and down the steps in a frenzy, would have done me in.

"I think you sufficiently thanked them with the massive amount of breakfast burritos you provided."

"I hope so." My throat swells as I take one last glimpse of my apartment. Now that the task is finished, I have nothing left to distract me from the cold reality sinking in.

Cam puts his arm around my shoulder for the first time all day. While he's come through as he always does, he hasn't been happy about my choice not to move in with him. "They wanted to be here for you," he says as if he can sense my growing sorrow. "You're part of our family. You know that, right?"

I swallow back rising tears and lay my head on his shoulder. The term *family* doesn't mean what it used to, at least not to me. Not one member of mine was here, and I doubt any of them care that today is the hardest day I've had since getting that miserable call two weeks ago. I've lived in this building seven years, nearly a quarter of my life, and I was supposed to leave in victory, not in defeat.

"Anything you want to do, remember? We're going to turn in your keys and consider it freedom." His pep talk comes with another gesture that's been missing all morning. His smile.

"Can I assume this means you're not mad at me anymore?"

"I was never mad at you." Cam squeezes my arm before dropping his hand. I shouldn't have said anything. His voice has returned to the blank monotone it's been all morning. "It's Bryson I'm not so pleased with."

"Don't get all moody again." I push his torso, but he hardly moves. "I'm the one who complained about my options. Bryson was just being helpful."

An annoyed hiss escapes through Cameron's teeth. "I wish he'd minded his own business like he usually does."

I return his jab with a steely glare.

"What? I'm bummed, okay? You and I have barely seen each other in months, and now, when we finally get this opportunity to hang out daily, you turn it down. I just can't figure out why."

Sadly, I can't explain why, only that I knew it wasn't right for us. "It wasn't just you, remember, it was also moving in with Brian and Darrel. Not to mention the fact that we'd be sharing that closet you call a bedroom. You'd be miserable, Cam, and sick of me in two days."

"I'd never get sick of you."

His voice turns more serious than I'm comfortable with, so I reach out and tickle his side. "Fine, then I'd be sick of you in two days. I can only comment on a new song so many times."

He swings his arm around my neck and pulls me in for a knuckle rub. "You drive me crazy, you know that?"

I push him off, laughing. "That's my job." I pinch his cheeks. "To keep you humble. Goodness knows, no one else does."

My attempt at easing the tension works, and we each head to our vehicles. My little single-cab Chevy truck is packed tight with boxes, while Cam's brother's F-250 is hauling my bedroom set. I chuckle a little when I think of the contrast. Distressed oak furniture against Zoe's wonderland of white.

Oh my, what a pairing this is going to be.

~🙰

The drive to Zoe's apartment takes fifteen minutes through traffic and at least twenty stop signs. Gone are the days when Cam and I could pop over to each other's place in less than five minutes. A thirty-minute round trip is going to take some more planning, and by his annoyance this morning, I imagine will include a lot more complaining.

He slams his driver's door the same time I step out of my truck. "This is fancy." He glances up and then around the complex. "And far away."

"I know. But hey, they have a pool." My attempt at optimism falls on deaf ears.

"It's not too late to change your mind. We're still loaded."

I don't bother answering, especially since I know it's not a real suggestion, and walk toward the stairwell.

Bryson's midnight-black truck is waiting on the far end of the building with a dolly in the back. It's the same one he's had since our junior year when his stepdad bought it brand-new off the lot, and I imagine he'll drive that machine until the day it dies. Paint's chipping on the fenders, the engine's been rebuilt, and the passenger seat has a tear in the leather. When he added a lift kit about five years ago and a rumbling muffler, Cam and I joked that if there was ever a vehicle that mirrored its owner in appearance and personality, it would certainly be Bryson's black beast.

I look at the stairs and then at the two trucks. "What should we start with? My furniture or boxes?"

"Furniture." Cameron pulls down the tailgate and hops into the back. "And don't think I'm not racking up hundreds of you-owe-me points, because there should be a law against stairs on each end."

"Dude, are you seriously complaining already?" Bryson calls out.

I look up and catch him descending from the landing. He's in all black again. Joggers instead of jeans this time, and his T-shirt has the sleeves cut off. A tattooed ring of barbwire encircles his left arm. It's faded some since high school but still gives that *I'm untouchable* vibe.

"Already?" Cam retorts. "Where have you been for the last two hours?"

"Fixing my hair," he says with far too much arrogance. Cam ignores him and starts unlatching the tie-downs. Bryson's expression changes when he finishes his descent and stands in front of me. "How are you feeling this morning? I know today can't be easy."

I hesitate. "No, it's not." This isn't the Bryson I'm used to engaging with. His voice holds too much concern, and his eyes keep watching me as if he can somehow see all the upheaval swirling inside. "But that's life, right? No need to complain about what you can't change."

"I don't know. There's something to be said for verbal processing."

"Really?" My voice is half surprise, half teasing. Never in our history has Bryson been one to talk about anything, let alone his feelings. "And how would you know?"

He smirks. "I read it in a magazine somewhere."

We stand there for a brief second, both seemingly unsure of what else to say. Already this conversation is well out of the norm for us.

Bryson clears his throat. "Well, we better get to work. Rehearsal starts at three."

Yes, rehearsal. The one thing Bryson lives and dies by. And I guess I can't totally blame him. Bryson wears many hats in the band: lead singer, manager, and bookkeeper. He's also the only band member to go in full time. Jay, Harrison, and Cam all still keep part-time jobs. I guess in the grand scheme of things, he has the most to lose if Black Carousel doesn't reach its full potential.

Bryson jogs to his black beast and lifts the dolly out of his tailgate while Cam pulls at the bed frame until it's hanging over the edge of the truck. "Do you know where all of this is going?" He wipes his wet brow with the bottom of his T-shirt, and I know he's completely miserable out here.

"Yeah. I've already taken measurements and have a layout in my head."

"There really wasn't any hesitation, was there?" He sets his hands on his hips and sighs. "Why didn't you just tell me you didn't want to move in? We could have figured out something better than Zoe's apartment all the way across town."

"Cameron."

"Forget it." He turns away and pulls the metal slat out farther. "It is what it is."

And I know my best friend well enough to back off and let him stew. Which he does in monumental fashion.

The next hour is proof that heavy furniture, summer heat, and a flight of stairs are a recipe for drama. Bryson and Cameron argue about everything. Which way to go through the door, how to hold the mattress going up the steps, what blasted music to listen to. Ugh. I was half tempted to send them both home and do all the heavy lifting myself.

Thankfully, when one only has a bedroom to furnish, unloading doesn't take long.

"Last box," Cam says and drops it on my bare mattress.

He's soaked in sweat, as is Bryson, who disappeared into his sister's bathroom a few minutes ago.

"Want me to make some lemonade?" I offer tentatively. The most I've gotten out of him are grunts and one-word answers since our tiff outside, so I'm surprised when he attempts a smile.

"Thanks, but I need to get Caleb's truck back to him." He starts to run his fingers through his hair, then thinks better of it. "And obviously shower before rehearsal."

"Okay, I'll walk you out."

We walk in unison to the front door, but each step feels like acid on my feet. This awkwardness isn't us. We don't fight. We hardly ever argue.

"Hey, Cam," I call out when he crosses the threshold. "Maybe after practice we could go get ice cream?"

This time the smile comes with dimples, so I know it's genuine. "Haven't you eaten enough ice cream to dry out every dairy cow in the metroplex?"

Relief spreads through my whirling stomach as I fake outrage. "You cope in your way, I'll cope in mine. And Rocky Road is not just ice cream; it's heaven's perfect treat."

He cinches his eyebrows. "It's marshmallows and chocolate."

I spread my arms and wait for more fodder because he pretty much just validated my point.

He must realize it, too. "Fine. You win. I'll call when we're finished."

"Sounds good."

I shut the door, relieved he's no longer angry, but also relieved he's gone. Despite all the reasons I love Cam, and there are many, his ability to make every situation about him is not one of them.

I move through the stark apartment, wishing Zoe would allow some color in the room besides metallic gray. It's making my skin itch and aggravating all the frustrations I've kept buried for the past hour.

The balcony is the quickest escape I can find. The doors swing open effortlessly, the sheer curtains billowing as if they enjoy the oppressive heat from outside. I don't care that they remain open or that I'm releasing a room full of air conditioning. I just want to close my eyes and go back in time to warn my younger, naïve self to abandon all her worthless dreams.

"Cam take off?"

I turn around, my mood still sour. "Yeah, just a couple minutes ago."

"Good. He was getting on my nerves." Bryson leans against the doorframe, freshly showered. His hair has that towel-dried look and is far wavier than he usually wears it. He's changed his shirt, as well. "Do you want me to show you around the complex? They have a pretty cool dog park."

I shake my head because what I really want right now is to be alone in my misery. "I've seen it."

He pauses like he's not sure if he should stay or leave.

I give him the out we're both looking for. "Well, thanks for your help. I'm going to unpack and get settled."

He runs a hand through his already-messy hair and sighs. "I know you said you didn't want to talk, but I'm here if you need to. This is a lot of change in a short period of time."

"Yeah, well, I'm good at change," I lie.

His eyebrows peak. "Since when?"

"Since now, okay?"

"Are you sure, because from where I stand, you look ready to implode. In fact, a lesser person would already be to the moon with the amount of pent-up tension you have rolling around in there."

Words, dry as chalk, lie on my tongue. He doesn't know what he's asking. The enormity of what's lodged in my chest, crawling up into my throat. Hurt, frustration, anger, sadness, fear, and the list goes on. If I dare to let one shred of what I'm feeling escape, it will be a flood of unending chaos. I swallow, forcing calm into my voice. "While I appreciate this whole attempt at counseling, I'm fine."

"You are?"

"Yes."

He steps closer. "Then why do you look one breath away from crying?"

"Stop it," I growl, because he's right. I *am* one second away from bursting into tears and I refuse to do that in front of him. "Saying yes to this apartment was not an open invitation into my life. You helped me, and I genuinely appreciate it, but you and I are much better off sticking to what you do best—mindless banter and zero expectations."

His head rears back as if I've slapped him. "Where is all this hostility coming from?"

"Where do you think? Or did you not notice the absence of two people who should absolutely be here. Except they aren't here, or even speaking to us . . . because of you." My thoughts whirl while my biting words slice across the space between us. "You have this ability to cut people out of your life when you're done with them, and I really don't feel like being the next person on your list who thinks for one second you might care."

Hurt flashes, and then just as quickly, the cold, unfeeling hardness I'm used to seeing from Bryson returns. "First off." His voice lowers, the tone now matching mine in both curtness and accusation. "I didn't cut Mason out. I told him from the beginning he wasn't permanent. His choosing not to hear me or strive to get better is his fault. And second off, Alison and my relationship was complicated in ways I can't explain to you. But don't think for a second I didn't care for her."

A tight silence follows while a balmy breeze dances across the balcony. He studies me, his eyes as dark and deep as a raging sea. I look away, unable and unwilling to battle with him on the subject.

"You know what? Forget it. There's no point in even trying to explain when you've already played judge, juror, and condemner without my participation." He retreats into the apartment and walks right back out onto the balcony seconds later, a disgusted smirk twisting his lips. "A housewarming gift." He tosses me a small red package that looks like a five-year-old wrapped it. "Feel free to chuck it into the trash."

This time when he storms away, all that follows is the slamming of the front door.

Regret comes an instant later. I hold the little box, knowing I should go after him and apologize. Sure, those were all thoughts I'd had for months now, but I didn't have to attack him with them simply because I was feeling shaken.

I slowly tear open the wrapping and lift the box lid. Inside is a new pendant for Piper's collar. It has her name and Zoe's address engraved in a plastic pink bone. I squeeze the gift in my hand and dash toward the door, but by the time I make it to the stairwell, his truck is already squealing out of the parking lot. Guilt and shame make their dive in the cesspool of my emotional baggage, ripping at my chest all the way down.

My mom used to say that hurting people hurt people. Unfortunately, that statement is very, very true.

SIX

I'm still feeling like gum on the bottom of my shoe when Cam calls three hours later. And by the sound of his tone and general aggravation, I have a feeling he needs the ice cream as much as I do.

We agree to meet at Marcie's Parlor, a local ice cream spot halfway between his apartment and Zoe's. The inside tables are all packed, and the line is at least six deep.

I pull out a white metal chair from one of the tables outside and drop my phone on the tabletop as I sit. There's a striped canvas awning over the seating area and entry door, which blocks the worst of the sun, but it's still hot and sticky. I don't mind. In fact, the heat is about all I have left to hold on to when I look at where I was supposed to be.

My phone buzzes against the iron slats, obnoxiously pulling me from my introspection. It's my mom, and since this is call number three in the past hour, my conscience forces me to answer it.

"Hey, what's up?" I stretch out my legs and try to settle comfortably in the hard chair.

"Oh good, you're available. I was all ready to leave a voicemail." Her voice sounds giddy, almost breathy in its excitement. "Did today go well?"

I'm surprised that she remembered, especially considering we spent approximately five minutes on my move and the rest of Sunday night dinner talking about her "*amazing date*" with Michael. *Gag*.

"It went fine. I'm all moved in." Turns out unpacking one small bedroom only kills about an hour and a half of time. I'm going to need a new hobby, or maybe I should consider getting a job after all.

"That's wonderful, hun," she gushes with far greater a reaction than my response warranted. "So, you'll be at dinner tomorrow night?"

Ah . . . now it makes sense. Sunday night dinner is Mom's leash around my neck. Her way to stick it to Dad that he may have gotten the good TV in the divorce, but she got their only daughter.

Cam's car turns the corner and parks three spaces down from where I'm sitting. I wave and then refocus on my mom.

"I haven't missed one yet, have I?" My answer is dry, but I swear we have this conversation on repeat.

"I know. I know. I just wanted to confirm because this one is special."

My heart flutters, and that little girl in me who still hopes and dreams for her parents' reconciliation wrestles awake. "Why?"

"Well, sweetheart . . ." She pauses, and I can tell she's trying to choose her words carefully. "I invited Michael."

The flutters stop and drop like a sinking weight into the pit of my stomach. Cam must see it on my face when he walks up because he sits down next to me without saying a word.

"Now, I know you've made it clear you don't want to meet

any of the men I date, and I respect that, but Michael is different." Her voice takes on a dreamy quality. "This time is different."

I cover the mouthpiece with my hand, and whisper to Cameron, "Can you go with me to dinner tomorrow?"

He shrugs, then nods his head.

"Darcy, are you still there?"

"I'm here." I sigh. "I'm not sure what you want me to say."

"Just say you'll come and give him a chance."

A chance at what? To be my new daddy? To show me how life as I know it is now over?

"Yeah, Mom, I'll try. I'd like to bring Cam, though, if that's okay?"

She chuckles, and I seriously want to throw my cellphone across the parking lot. "Of course. He's practically my son-in-law anyway."

I ignore her comment, just as I have for ten years now. "Okay, well, I'll see you tomorrow, then."

"Thank you, Darcy. This means so much to me."

"I know, Mom. I'll talk to you later."

I hang up, stunned with disbelief, trying to find my voice. Sunday night dinner is sacred. It's family only, always has been. My parents didn't even let Dexter's wife come until they were engaged. "Mom's bringing Michael to Sunday night dinner."

"Oh, that's different."

And this is why I love Cameron. One sentence and he knows exactly why I'm upset.

"She's never introduced me to any of them before. Not intentionally, at least." There was the one time when I happened to be at her house when a guy showed up, but I left without so much as a hello. "And then, bam, she drops him

54

on me like it's no big deal, like we've always invited strangers to family night dinner. She didn't even hesitate when I asked if you could come. Not that I wanted her to, but still, she's *never* let you before."

"She must really like him."

I stick out my tongue like I swallowed something sour, but that's exactly how those words taste. "They've known each other a week," I argue. "And now I'm required to make nice with this guy like he's not some intruder in my life? My parents have only been divorced for a few months. How can she suddenly be so okay? I can't even walk into that house without wanting to choke."

"Have you told her any of this?"

"No, of course not. She still seems too fragile." I close my eyes and try to get the rising sickness in my stomach to settle. "I was supposed to be gone when all this went down." I look at Cam, those relentless tears finding their way back to my eyes. "Do you have any idea how many times that promise kept me going when the fundraising got so miserable?" I swallow back a sob. "I was supposed to be gone."

"I know you were." Cameron leans forward, slides his hand across the table, and squeezes mine.

I cling to him, the steadiest person in my life. The one who's never let me down, who's been my rock and support through the worst seven months of my life.

We sit a few more minutes in silence while he holds my hand. I think of Bryson's comment about my pent-up tension and realize he's right. Somehow I'm going to have to find an outlet for all this emotion.

"I don't want to think about this anymore. I need something positive to talk about." I release Cam's hand, giving him the freedom to stretch and go back to a more comfortable position in his chair. "How did rehearsal go?"

Cam snorts. "That is not the right question if you're looking for positive."

"Why? I thought you said Jay and Harrison finally picked up the song?"

"They did. It was Bryson who couldn't keep a beat or concentrate on anything, for that matter." Cam runs his hand through his hair, then pats it back down so it's not sticking straight up in the air. "I didn't think Bry was seeing anyone, but maybe he is. The guy only gets this way when there's a girl involved."

My pulse quickens, but I convince myself our argument couldn't possibly be the cause. Bryson doesn't care about anyone's opinion of him, especially not mine. "What do you mean?"

"Well, do you remember meeting Trina?"

I roll through memories until I land on her. Bryson had brought her to dinner with all of us a few years ago. Alison had hated her, of course, because Trina was—as most of his girlfriends are—extremely beautiful. But I remember thinking she was also surprisingly intelligent and very kind-hearted. "Yeah. She was probably the highest-quality girlfriend he's ever introduced us to."

"Exactly. And days after that dinner, he went into meltdown mode. Just like this. He broke up with her a week later."

"I remember. Though I never understood why."

"Same reason he bailed on Alison the first week we were on tour. The minute Bryson starts to feel trapped, he implodes. My guess is he needs to hurry up and break it off with whomever it is this time. Especially since we have a gig in two weeks and we kind of need our lead singer to sound better than a bloated fish." He slaps his palms on his shorts and stands. "I'm dying out here. Can we go inside? You did promise me ice cream after all."

He comes around the table, takes my hand, and pulls me until I'm folded in his arms and he's hugging me with the force of a bear. "Sorry I was a jerk this morning. I have all this stuff going on in my head right now and I let it spill over into our world."

Relief unwinds the tension in my shoulders. "It's okay."

"It's not okay, and I'm going to try hard to be more understanding through this transition." He pulls back but keeps his hands around my upper arms. "It's you and me. Always."

My throat turns scratchy. "Even if it means horribly uncomfortable dinners with my mom and her new boyfriend?"

He slides hair from my cheek and smiles. "Even then."

"Thank you. You're the best friend a girl could ask for."

"Yeah," he sighs, like it's a hardship, and pulls on the door to the ice cream shop. "I know."

~

After ten minutes of waiting in the driveway for Cam on Sunday night, I'm ready to take back all my comments about him being a great best friend.

> **Me**
> Where are you??? Been waiting forever.

> **Cam**
> Sorry. Practice is going long. Still struggling.
> Can you manage without me for a little while?

> **Me**
> Are you serious?

He sends me a prayer emoji. I send back the red-faced, ready-to-explode one.

Cam
I'll be 20 minutes tops.

But Cameron's promises are worthless when they're spun around music. An hour is a minute in that world, so I know, even when I send an *OK* in response, that I'm stuck navigating the bulk of tonight all on my own.

I begrudgingly exit my car and scowl at Michael's Escalade in the driveway. My mom has a two-car garage, and he could have parked to the right or left to give me space to pull in beside him, but no. He parked right in the middle, so I'm left parking along the curb like a guest.

The air is hot and sticky outside and it seems to settle against my lungs, choking me, or maybe it's just the dread I can't seem to shake no matter how many pep talks I've given myself today. I knock on the door and wait instead of walking in. This house doesn't feel like my own anymore, tonight more than ever.

Mom opens the door, still laughing until she spots me on the other side of the threshold. "Hey, sweetie. You didn't have to knock."

"I wasn't sure . . ." I trail off because this already feels miserably awkward.

Her expression softens. "You don't have to be so nervous. Just be yourself and he'll love you."

I clamp my lips together and attempt to smile. I couldn't give a flip whether Michael likes me or not. As far as I'm concerned, I'm here because I was raised to respect my mother and father, even when I completely disagree with their choices. No other reason.

"Cameron still coming?"

"Yeah. He's at practice and running late."

"Okay, good. I have enough chicken for an army." She closes the door behind me, and the smell of garlic and butter fills my nostrils.

I look at my mom, incredulous, and my heart squeezes to a cold knot. "You made scampi?" Chicken scampi was my father's favorite dish. The one she would cook for him on every birthday and special occasion.

"Yes. Is that okay? I thought you loved that meal."

"I do, but . . ." How can she be so oblivious? "Never mind. Scampi is great."

"Okay, whew." Mom's chest deflates with way too much relief. She's nervous, too. "Michael is really important to me. I really want you to like him."

"I know. And I'm going to try, Mom. For you."

"That's all I'm asking for." She wraps an arm around my stiffened shoulder and guides me into the dining room. "Michael, this is my daughter, Darcy."

The man in question turns and offers me a smile as broad as his build. "Darcy, so nice to meet you." He takes one stride forward, which would be two for most men, and stretches out his hand. "Your mom has told me so much about you."

"Likewise" is all I can say as he crushes my poor fingers in his own.

The man is Goliath. So much so he has to duck under the chandelier to walk over to me. He also has streaks of gray running through his sandy-blond hair and is wearing jeans that haven't been in style in ten years and a button-up plaid shirt.

Mom wraps her arm around his elbow and smiles up . . . way up at him. "Michael is a dog lover, too," she croons at him, even though I'm the one she's addressing. "He has two boxers that are the sweetest things."

"And hyper," he adds with the same adoring tenor. "I bet you could give me some tips."

"Definitely. Darcy trains dogs for a living. Right, hun?" She smiles brightly in my direction.

I shrug one shoulder. "Not really. Or at least I haven't in a very long time." Sure, my certification is in dog training and it's always been a passion of mine, but I've spent the last two years grooming overprivileged pups to raise money, so to label me one feels like a lie. "I'm currently unemployed." If Mom's trying to impress him, she's going to do it without me.

Mom's brow furrows the way it used to when I was misbehaving as a kid. "Don't sell yourself short, honey." She turns back to Michael and shoots him the exact opposite expression. "Darcy is extremely talented with animals. She's always had a gift, even as a child."

"Thanks," I say in little less than a grumble.

A pulsing silence rears up between us. An inevitable lull in the conversation taking root.

I fiddle with the hem of my shorts. This is so much harder than I thought it would be. If Dad were here, he'd crack a joke or tell a story in a way that would make everyone feel like they'd known him forever. Michael just stands there, lanky and bony and far less interesting than the man my mother loved for over thirty years. Is this one more way to stick it to my father? Pick someone who's the complete opposite?

Michael clears his throat. "Your mom told me you, um, had a mission trip fall through recently. I imagine that was very difficult." He actually sounds like he cares. I guess he's in impress mode, as well. "Any chance of a different location?"

"No. I've retired from missionary work." I walk along the now-empty walls in the room. There used to be a family photo in the spot above our gas fireplace. They'd had it professionally done to look like a painting. We were all dressed in blue. Dad and Dexter in a shirt and tie. Mom and I in stiff dresses. We smiled, posed, argued, then smiled some more. Finally, the photographer gave up and told us to take a break. He secretly got us when we weren't paying attention. Dad had made some comment about burning his shirt, and both us kids cheered and said we wanted to do the same. The photo was of all of us laughing. And my favorite part was that Dad wasn't looking at the camera or even at us kids. He was staring lovingly at my mom.

A buzzer shrills from the kitchen, and we both turn toward the lady of the house, who quickly apologizes. "I'll be right back. Just a few more minutes and dinner will be ready. Darcy?" Her eyes turn pleading because, let's face it, I'm not exactly winning at the small talk right now. "Can you keep Michael company for me?"

"Yes, ma'am," I say automatically.

She hesitates, but finally the buzzer wins and she leaves the two of us to awkwardly stare at each other.

Mom always wanted an open floor plan. One that allowed her to participate in conversation from the kitchen, but when house renovations began, it came down to a five-figure kitchen expansion or a three-thousand-dollar man cave. Unfortunately, frugality won, which is why Michael and I are stuck here in painful silence.

"So . . ." He draws the word out like he's trying to come up with anything we could possibly talk about. "I have a daughter close to your age. She lives in Ohio now with her husband." Michael sits in the chair he vacated earlier and takes a sip of his water.

"That's nice," I say as politely as I can and lean up against the bare wall. Sitting feels too much like acceptance at this point.

"I keep waiting for that call with news of a grandbaby, but it hasn't happened yet." He clears his throat again, checks behind him to see if Mom is ever coming back, then turns around to smile uncomfortably at me. "What about you? Any plans for a family?"

"Right now, I'd settle for my own apartment. Kids are way off."

He nods. "Yeah, my daughter says the same. Career and all that."

"Yep." *Oh, my word, this is agony.*

He must feel it, too, because he gets up from the table with far too much nervous energy. "Well, I should probably see what's taking your mom so long."

Yes, because it's been all of two minutes. Then again, it feels like a lifetime already.

"Good idea."

And then he's gone like the Road Runner in a Bugs Bunny cartoon.

I pull out my phone and text in hyperspeed.

> **Me**
> I've changed my mind. You are definitely not the best friend a girl could ask for.

> **Cam:**
> It can't be that bad.

> **Me:**
> It is that bad! Like pouring buckets of hot-molten-lava-on-my-skin kind of bad.

Cam:
10 more minutes.

Me:
Cameron Joseph Lee. If you do not get over here right now, I'll call Cassie and tell her that you were the one who told your parents about her secret boyfriend in high school.

Cam:
You wouldn't dare.

Cam's baby sister was grounded for three months and missed her junior prom because he ratted her out. She may be twenty-four now, but she'd still kill him.

Me:
Try me.

Cam:
Fine. Leaving now.

And for the first time all night, I feel a little bit of relief.

SEVEN

It turns out that the internet is a fabulous way to waste time. In merely two days, I've planned my dream vacation, which totals close to a year's wages, played every solitaire game possible including the really boring ones, and watched a dozen old episodes of *Dog Whisperer* on YouTube.

Maybe taking the summer off from life wasn't the best idea I've ever had. If I don't find something to do, and soon, I'm going to officially die of boredom.

The options, few that they are, filter through my mind. Cameron's dad offered me a data-entry position at his company once. Knowing him, the offer would still be open. I picture myself getting dressed up, chatting mindlessly with co-workers twenty years my senior, and sitting in front of a computer all day, then immediately scratch that one off the list of possibilities.

Which pretty much leaves me with Laurette. She's called twice and offered me my old job back. I suppose I could say yes. Go back to what I know and do well and forget that I ever had plans to be more. I close my eyes and groan at the thought. It wasn't that I hated it at Pampered Pups, I didn't all the time, but it was never meant to be forever. And returning now feels like an enormous step backwards.

Piper hops up onto Zoe's stiff leather couch, then turns and turns hoping to find a comfortable spot. Eventually, she learns the sad truth that things are not always what they appear and hops off, disappointed.

"Yep, I know. They look comfortable, but they aren't." I readjust my position, trying to keep my right leg from going numb. "Don't worry, I understand if comfort trumps companionship."

Piper trots to her doggie bed in the corner and settles with a tiny chew toy. She, not unlike myself, is still trying to find her place in the new apartment. Zoe tolerates us both, but I can't say there's been any love connection on either side.

I return to my endless clicking, my lids getting heavier and heavier.

"Zoe, let's go!"

I jolt awake the minute Bryson comes barreling through the front door, obviously on a mission to find his baby sister.

"Come on. I'm already late. That idiot mechanic made me wait forty-five minutes just to tell me the stupid part wouldn't be in till Friday."

Piper, the vicious thing she is, pathetically growls from her corner but makes no move to defend her territory.

Bryson pauses, stares at my little dog, who's wearing her adorable pink tag, and then finally turns to see me on the couch.

I wave, unsure which one of us is more surprised to see the other.

"Oh." His brows pull together in a scowl. "I'm sorry. I should have knocked."

"It's fine. You belong here more than I do."

"All the same, I'll keep my distance, at least for the next couple of months." Any question about how we left things is fully answered with that one statement. He and I may never have been besties, but we've also never had such immense discomfort between us either. He's still upset from the other day, and I can't really blame him. I want to apologize, need to apologize, yet doing so with a guy like Bryson is new territory for me and I don't quite know how to begin.

"Zoe's not here," I say instead.

"Great." He pulls his phone from his back pocket and dials while walking toward the kitchen. "Where are you? You said one o'clock. It's one-ten." His shoulders tense as he turns his back to me. "What do you mean you can't get away. I just talked to you thirty minutes ago." Another long, furious pause. "Yeah, I know, which is why I had the guy drop me off here. If you couldn't do it, you should have just said so. I promised Charlie I'd be there before two, and now I'm stranded. . . . No, I can't just get an Uber. He lives twenty minutes outside of town!" He shoves his free hand through his hair. "Well, that's just lovely. Thanks. Nice to know I can always count on you." He presses his phone hard enough to know his last sentence was dripping with frustration and sarcasm.

I watch silently as he grips the counter, takes two deep breaths, and then shoves off. The refrigerator door gets his next dose of annoyance. He tugs it open, pulls out an armload of Zoe's fancy organic bergamot juice drinks, and slams the door shut.

I can tell what he's about to do even before he turns the first bottle upside down over the sink. "Those are fifteen dollars a bottle."

He smiles sardonically at me from across the bar counter-top. "I know."

I carefully set my laptop down next to me and unfold my legs. "Well, considering I'll probably get blamed for drinking those, could you maybe stop at just one?" I walk to the other side of the bar and slide between the two stools. "Or leave her a note exonerating me?"

His eyes narrow, more laced in humor, though, than bitter-ness. "I don't know. Sounds like two birds, one stone."

Yep. He's still mad at me.

"Or you could let me give you the ride you obviously need, and we can call it even?" I bite the corner of my lip and raise my brows, hopeful an apology will be that simple. With Cam, it usually is, but Bryson is a much more complicated person. At least to me.

He turns the bottle upright and puts the cap back on, even though it's empty. "Sure you want to do that? My evilness may just rub off on you."

"I never said you were evil."

"No, that's right, what you said was far less insulting. What was I again? Oh yeah, a self-serving narcissist who drops people the minute they're no longer useful."

Ouch. Okay, I was pretty rough on him the other day.

"You're right. I was out of line. I'm sorry."

He crosses his arms and studies me. "Sorry because you didn't mean it?"

I could lie, but that's not really my style. "Sorry because I was cruel with how I said it, and you're right, I didn't give you an opportunity to give your perspective."

"No, you did not." He glances at his phone to check the time. "But lucky for you, I'm in a bind, so you have a twenty-minute drive to apologize."

"So now you're doing me a favor?"

"Groveling is acceptable, too." He grins, and despite the fact that it's Bryson and I know I should be wary, I can't help but grin back. He's devilishly charming when he tries to be, which isn't very often. "Are you driving or am I?"

Since I have no idea where I'm going, I grab my keys from the hook by the door and toss them to him. "Consider this my apology. And for the record, I don't grovel."

If I didn't feel completely sure that Bryson was harmless and not a deranged serial killer, I'd be starting to worry. We've been in the truck twelve minutes and are now halfway between this-is-where-you-bury-the-body and yes-there-are-places-in-America-with-no-cellphone-service.

"Wishing you had asked more questions?"

"Something like that." I create a sunshade with my hand and try to find any traces of human existence in the acres and acres of farmland. "Where are we going anyway?"

"A little community called Griffith. I have a friend who lives out here, and he's had a rough go of it lately. He's got a big decision to make, and I didn't want him to have to do it alone." His answer surprises me, and he must sense as much because his jaw ripples with tension. "Wow, you really do think I'm a horrible person."

"I don't think you're horrible. Your explanation just took me off guard for a second."

"Which part? That I actually have a friend, or that I'm going to help him?"

I stare down at my fingers because I don't know what else to say. In some ways, yes, I've always seen Bryson as the black sheep in our little group. If someone was insensitive or hurtful, it was him. If someone got in trouble, it was him. If someone was the first to take a risk or rebel, it was him. Always.

"Listen, it's obvious that you have some pent-up resentment over Alison and Mason, so let's just get it all out in the open now." He glances at me and then back to the road. "What do you want to know?"

Once again, I'm taken aback—not by his bluntness, that's common with him. More by his openness. Bryson's the kind of guy you hang out with for twenty years without actually ever knowing him.

"Okay . . ." I pause, taking the time to compose a reasoned answer free of yesterday's accusation. "Alison was in love with you. I knew that. Everyone knew that, and I know deep down you knew it, too."

"I did."

"Then why date her? Why risk your friendship that way?"

"Because I was selfish." He studies the road, his hands squeezing and twisting the steering wheel. "We had just gotten the final dates for the tour, had gigs lined up for months. It was a rush, the biggest thing I'd ever accomplished, and I didn't want to do it alone." He shifts uncomfortably in his seat, clearly hesitant to share the rest with me. But true to his offer, he continues, and I find my respect for him growing. "I knew within a few days that I'd made a mistake, but I thought maybe if I just tried harder, it could work. But then . . ." He trails off like he can't bring himself to say everything he was feeling during that time. "I wanted to love her the way she loved me. I just didn't. And I knew the longer I pretended, the worse it would be, so I ended things. And now she hates me, and so do you, I guess, but I still know I made the right call."

He waits for my response like he needs me to exonerate

him or something. And maybe on the Alison thing I can do that, but I'm not sure I'll ever fully trust him. At least not the hardened version he's become.

"I don't hate you, Bryson. I just don't like seeing the people I care about get hurt."

"I don't like seeing them get hurt either." He stares at me, his eyes restless. "If you're wondering if I regret it, the answer is yes."

And really, what else can I ask for? He made a mistake and he's owning it.

"Do you regret firing Mason?"

Bryson pulls in a deep, slow breath, and I search for the same remorse he had with Alison, but it isn't there. "No, I don't. He wasn't good enough."

"But he started the band with you."

"No. I started the band. Mason was simply the first addition."

"And that doesn't deserve some measure of loyalty?"

"He got loyalty," he returns sharply, his voice turning indignant. "For five years I let him play, despite being completely stagnant."

"You could have warned him."

"Trust me, I did. Multiple times." His jaw twitches. "When Black Carousel came into being, we were equally average. But I killed myself to get better, worked two jobs to pay for lessons, sunk every extra penny I had into better equipment, and Mason, he just stayed the same. I told him year after year that he had to commit all the way, but either he didn't care enough or he just didn't have the talent. Personally, I think it was a little of both. And I wasn't going to sit back and let his inadequacy destroy my future, especially when Cameron was ripe and ready to take his place."

The cab falls into an uncomfortable silence, neither of us speaking; there's just the sound of cool air pumping from the air-conditioning vents and the rumble of my old V8 engine.

"Mason's leaving was inevitable," he finally says with complete surety. "He wasn't good enough. And like it or not, you know it's true."

As much as I want to argue, I can't because Bryson's right. I'd witnessed the difference myself. Cameron had begged me to come out and watch his first performance, so I pulled a hundred dollars out of my precious savings, drove two hours to a popular college bar in Waco, and watched Cameron step onstage for the first time as an official Black Carousel band member. They killed it that night. It wasn't just a great performance; they'd blown the roof off.

"Thanks for explaining. You didn't have to, but I'm glad you did."

"So we're good?"

"Not quite," I say with an air of jest so he knows I'm kidding. "I have more questions."

"That wasn't enough?" He groans. "What is it with women and their need to make men suffer?"

"How am I making you suffer?"

"I'm trapped in this truck, sharing feelings and regrets. You may as well be pulling out my fingernails."

I can't help but chuckle. "It's the last one, I promise."

"Fine. Let's get it over with."

"Okay." I rub my hands together just to make him nervous. "Why did you go out of your way to help me? I know convincing Zoe couldn't have been easy."

He snorts like I have no idea exactly how hard. "I helped you, Darcy, because contrary to what others in this truck may believe, I do consider us friends."

"We are friends." And I mean it, probably more than I have since we were kids. "And thank you. The dog tag was a really thoughtful gesture."

"You're welcome." His expression softens when he glances from the road to me again. "I wanted you to feel at home, even if it is just temporary."

"Well, I do. Sort of. Zoe's a bit of a puzzle, but she's not there much so it's kind of like living alone."

"Better than an apartment with three guys and a mattress?"

I laugh at the absurdity that I even considered moving in with Cam as an option. "Yes, much better."

"Good." Bryson slows, and I spot the first house I've seen for miles.

"Is this it?"

"Yep."

"Wow, it's . . . beautiful." The words come out in a loud whisper as we ease down the drive flanked by small oak trees on each side like a tunnel welcoming us home. "What a change from all the flat farmland."

"Yeah. It's a gem for sure. There's over sixty cedar trees on this property and two large tanks."

"Tanks?"

Bryson smirks at my ignorance. "You'd probably call them ponds. Tank is terminology we use for a livestock watering hole."

"Oh, okay."

The trees clear, offering a full view of all the buildings on the property. The main house, though quaint, is a beautiful one-story brick structure with the Texas star etched into the porch overhang.

Bryson follows the road to the right and parks between the detached garage and a massive tractor parked on the side. He stares out the windshield, his eyes clouded in thought. "You should have seen this place a couple years ago before Charlie's wife got sick. Sue Ann was a master gardener, and there would always be some kind of seasonal flower to welcome you in."

I don't miss the use of the word *was* or the sadness in Bryson's voice.

He cuts the engine and twists in his seat to face me. "Not to sound inhospitable, but you should probably stay in the truck or hang outside. It's been a pretty terrible year for Charlie, and he's not the best version of himself right now."

"I'll hang outside. It will be a nice change from my pity cocoon." I hear a faint sound of barking in the distance. "Does he have dogs?"

"Five of them. Each worse than the other." Bryson rubs his neck as if just asking about them brings a new measure of stress. "When Sue Ann adopted them, she thought she was heading toward remission."

"What happened?"

"She spent a year on chemo, and the tumors shrank miraculously to the point that her doctors felt they could get the rest through surgery. She never woke up." His voice catches. "That was three months ago. Since then, Charlie's barely been able to care for himself, let alone five unruly animals."

Hearing his grief lace through every word squeezes the air from my chest. "I'm so sorry, Bryson, I can't imagine."

"That's life," he says curtly. "Something always pops up to punch you in the face. I just hate that I was on tour when it happened. Charlie shouldn't have been alone. Not after everything . . ." The ache of what he doesn't say swells in my throat, but I remain silent as he reaches for the door. "Ready?"

It's more than just a question. It's the endcap on his sharing of feelings. I shouldn't feel so disappointed. Bryson's given me more today than he ever has before. If anything, I should be grateful we finally aired our grievances. Now we can go back to what we've always been.

I grip the door handle and pull. "Yeah. I'm ready."

EIGHT

As soon as we exit the truck, the barking turns from faint to obnoxiously loud. The noise seems to be coming from two sources, each located around back and out of my line of sight. Based on tone and depth, I'm guessing they're both large breeds, and one is not happy at all to hear strangers descending.

"Here." Bryson tosses me a small bottle of bug spray. "I only got the tractor to about half the property last week, so some spots are still pretty high."

He mows too?

I carefully spray my shins and tennis shoes. "How did you and Charlie meet?"

"At Grace Community, actually. After things blew up with my stepdad, Mr. Lee thought it would be a good idea for me to talk to someone. It wasn't really my thing, but I was crashing at his house, so I couldn't exactly say no."

I chuckle because Cameron's dad is a lot like him. Persistent. "You probably wouldn't have been able to say no even if you weren't crashing there."

"True." He takes the bug spray from my outstretched hand and tosses it back into the tractor. "Lucky for me, Charlie was way cooler than some therapist. We mostly just hung out and worked on the land together. This place was my refuge for many years." He pauses and sets his hands on his hips. "Now it's my turn to be there for him."

"I'm sure he appreciates it."

"I doubt it," he snorts. "But I'm the only one as stubborn and bullheaded as he is, so he's stuck with me. For better or worse." Bryson unlatches a small wood gate and holds it open for me. "Last chance to take shelter in the truck."

"Nah. I want to meet his dogs."

"You are an odd woman."

"I know." I step through the gate and start the trek down the brick pathway. "But it's part of my charm." I glance back to see if he agrees, and he must because he's smiling, a rare thing for Bryson, and I feel pretty good that I've managed to provoke one several times today.

The path takes us around the house and into a giant backyard with a canopy of oak trees. An old barn stands just thirty feet away next to a huge windmill so preserved and picturesque, it makes the entire farm feel like an old western backdrop. Remnants of carefully tilled gardens sit on different corners, though each now is more filled with weeds than vegetables or flowers. "There's too much beauty to take in at once," I say in awe. "Every time I turn my head, I see something new."

Bryson nods, but it's sad, and I decide not to gawk anymore. This place now hurts to come to. That much is written all over his face.

We continue toward the dog kennels. There are three of them all spaced a good ten feet apart. Each one is made of hog fencing and large enough to be comfortable, although they seem more like temporary housing than permanent.

Two of the dogs are visible. The first, a massive yellow Lab mix whose frenzied gait lends more to excitement than fear. He rushes to the gate, jumps against the fence, and spastically barks. Then he runs in a quick circle around the pen again.

"Did Sue Ann plan on keeping them?" I ask loudly enough to be heard over the other dog's manic barking, which has only increased in severity. It surprises me, especially since I can now clearly make out his breed. It's a blue Great Dane, and from his size and markings, he's very likely pure.

"No. She would adopt them, try and rehabilitate the bad behavior, and then find permanent homes." He points to the kennel on the right. "That's Louie. She only got him a week before the surgery, and he's either barking or hiding. It goes on for hours."

I turn toward his cage, and Louie backs away, hair straight up on his neck. The initial warning type of bark transitions into a panicked shrill. He's terrified. More than terrified; he's convinced I'm here to hurt him. Charlie's wife was more than just a dog lover. I haven't seen dog behavior this extreme since volunteering for the animal rescue society. "Poor thing. He must be exhausted."

Bryson huffs. "Poor Charlie. He has to listen to it twenty-four hours a day." He points to the middle kennel. "That's Sam. She's been here four months. Super sweet, but she's in rough shape physically. When Sue Ann got her, she had some kind of skin disorder and her hair was falling out in patches. It's cured now and a lot of the hair has grown back, but Sue Ann died before she could properly groom her."

I look for Sam, but she must be hiding in her doghouse. I don't blame her. Louie's barking is already starting to give me a headache. "And the excited one over here?" I point to the Lab, who has not stopped running since we walked up.

"That's Bentley. He's a nightmare. Try to feed him and he jumps all over you. Try to pet him and he gnaws at your hand. He's knocked Charlie off his feet twice. I bought those continual feeding and watering stations so he wouldn't have to come out here every day. It's helped a little."

I hear the weariness in his voice, and a newfound admiration settles in. "You're a really good guy, Bryson."

He smirks. "I'll try not to be offended by the surprise in your voice. Then again, considering how we started the day, this is progress."

I huff and push his arm until he teeters. "You're going to punish me forever for my outburst, aren't you?"

"Nah. I just like teasing you."

I roll my eyes, but I have to admit, it's nice to be treated like a normal human again. Between my parents' divorce and my fundraising efforts, the last several months have been the hardest, most stressful ones in my life. And unfortunately, that's not a combination that lends to being any fun. In fact, I can count on one hand the number of times I've truly laughed in months. "You said five, right? Where are the other two?"

"Inside. One is so depressed she hardly gets up to do her business, and the other is so aggressive she has to be crated. Thankfully, she's a terrier so she doesn't cause much damage."

"What is Charlie going to do with them?"

Bryson shrugs. "I don't know, but that's what he called me here to talk about. Sue Ann loved these dogs, and he wants to honor her. But he can't sustain the upkeep. It's too much." He takes a breath like he's been avoiding what he has to do and now has no choice but to face it. "Well, I better get inside. You good?"

"Yeah. I'll be fine."

"It might be a while." His grimace implies apology, but I don't need one. It feels good to be outside after so many days cooped up.

"Take as much time as you need. I'll be busy exploring."

"You sure?"

"Yes. Go." I push him toward the house and finally he acquiesces and disappears through the back door.

I head toward the middle cage, still curious about the dog that has yet to make a sound. Louie darts back to his doghouse and hides, though the barking never stops. "It's okay, big guy. I'm not going to bother you." Louie doesn't care. He still feels the need to yell at me.

I squat down in front of the middle gate as a bushy nose peeks out from the doghouse. "Hey, Sam, can you come see me?"

A head follows, then the body of a golden retriever mix.

"Oh my, you are a mess." Hair is completely matted on the underbelly, with patches missing from both front legs and on the neck. She takes a hesitant step forward and quickly lifts her leg, moving in a more three-legged hop. Bryson didn't mention any injury.

There's no lock on the gate, and while this probably isn't recommended for a novice, I know enough about dogs to take some risks. I carefully unhook the hinge and slide inside the kennel with her. She only makes it a couple of feet before giving up and waiting in a sit position with her paw raised.

I approach carefully. Bryson said she was sweet, but you never know how a dog is going to react to a stranger. "Hey, girl. Is your paw hurt?" I keep my voice smooth and careful, showing her I'm no threat. She whimpers and tries to walk again, only to quit after two agonizing steps.

"Don't worry. I'll come to you." I get within arm's length and her mangled tail wags excitedly.

Kneeling, I begin at her neck and start checking her fur and skin for any residual damage. There's still some healing spots and scar tissue, but no new sores.

Her response is immediate and heartbreaking. She howls and pushes her nose into my neck like a big doggy hug.

"There, there, sweet girl. It's all going to be okay."

A great grooming, along with some tender loving care, and she'd be a wonderful pet for anyone.

I pick up her front right paw, and she whimpers, tugging slightly. Inside a massive amount of fur, three sharp burs are nestled into her foot. The pads are swollen and raw where she's tried to bite at the pain. And based on the amount of hair around each bur, they've been in there for a while. "Poor Sammy girl. No wonder it hurts to walk." I attempt to pull at the first one and quickly pull my hand back. "Ouch." Two dots of blood form on my index finger.

Thankfully, I'm the type who likes to stay prepared.

Running as quickly as I can while not completely freaking Louie out, I make the trek back to the passenger side door of my truck. In the glove compartment is a first-aid kit, along with one of Piper's many dog brushes. I grab them both and my Leatherman and head back to Sam, who hasn't moved from her spot.

"Okay, now this will hurt a little but not nearly as much as keeping those wretched things in there." I turn her paw over and she yelps, high-pitched and pathetic. Her back legs press into the ground while she attempts to jerk her injured leg from my grip. I readjust my hold and slowly begin clipping at the hair until I can see how deep the burs have settled. Two are surface, but one is pretty severe.

I set down her paw, and Sam begins licking and biting at the spot while I search through my first-aid kit for any kind of ointment. The best I can find is some petroleum jelly. It's not ideal, but as long as I get it off and she doesn't swallow any, it should be fine. I squeeze the tube slightly and carefully massage it into her swollen pad. It seems to lessen the pain some because her chest relaxes and she stops gnawing at my hand. I flip open the pliers on my tool and tug at the first bur. It comes out quickly and easily but also exposes the infection that's begun around her foot.

The second bur takes a little more finesse yet also comes out smoothly. The last bur is implanted in her foot, and the skin is so red and raw that I feel it will be too painful to simply try to pull it out. I hold her paw with one hand and search my kit with the other. There's some antibiotic cream with a numbing agent in it. Again, not ideal, but leaving this thing in there isn't an option either.

Careful with every motion, I take the process excruciatingly slow, alternating between easing out the bur and rubbing the cream into each newly exposed piece of flesh. Sam whines at first, but as the pain increases, her barks and growls are nearly as loud as Louie's. I firm up my grip on her foot, even though she's actively fighting me now. "We're almost done, I promise."

It feels like hours have passed when the bur finally comes completely free of the skin, grabbing on to overgrown fur as I pull. I cut away more hair until victory is achieved.

"We did it." I sigh, exhaustion coating the words. Sweat trickles down my forehead and through my shirt. My knees and thighs ache from planting them into the ground, but the sacrifice was worth it. "Can you walk for me?" I stand and pull a little on her collar.

She takes a tentative step, feels the relief, and hobbles forward. She still has a limp, but with a few days of cleaning and treatment, she should be good as gold.

We walk over to her water station. After removing the three-gallon jug, I dip her foot inside the bowl to wash away any dirt still lodged in her paw. She licks at my hand while I'm cleaning, letting me know she's not super comfortable with what's happening.

"Almost done, sweet girl, I promise." I use my T-shirt to wipe her paw dry and inspect the pads again. I don't have a wrap, so I opt not to put more antibiotic cream on her foot today. "I'll come see you tomorrow and get you completely squared away." I scratch her bushy neck, and she plants a sloppy wet kiss on my cheek. Yeah, Sam is definitely a best friend waiting to happen.

I spend the rest of the time in her kennel pulling at weeds and shaking out the mat in her doghouse. She follows me everywhere despite her obvious soreness. The devil bur plant is growing along the outside of her cage and is way too vicious to uproot with bare hands. It's also too thick to cut with any of the tools on my Leatherman. The barn I noticed earlier has a hose attached on the outside. I'm guessing that's where Charlie keeps his tools and dog supplies.

Sam whimpers when I exit the gate, her water station jug in hand.

"Don't worry. I'm just going to spray this out and get you some fresh water." And maybe find some garden shears and gloves to take down the plant.

I'm halfway done with refilling the water when Bryson emerges from the back of the house. It's only then that I check the time and realize it's been nearly an hour since he went inside. It's also then I realize this is the first time in weeks I haven't counted the seconds hoping the day would end soon. In fact, nothing, not even my umpteen pints of ice cream, has made me feel as invigorated and satisfied as this last hour has.

"I came to check on you," A flash of surprise brightens his face and he laughs. "And it's a good thing I did." He eyes me from my sweaty red face, down my wet T-shirt, to the scratched skin on my knees. "What on earth have you been doing out here?"

I toss the running hose where it won't soak my tennis shoes and walk over to turn off the spicket. "Sam had burs in her foot. I cleaned them out, but we need to get rid of the bur weeds along the edge of her cage." I wipe another round of sweat from my forehead and rest my hands on my hips.

Bryson stares at me, mouth open, eyes wide. "She let you touch her?"

"Yeah. She's super sweet, just like you said."

"I know she is, but she's never let me touch her." He glances over at Sam, who's waiting patiently at the gate for me. "I tried last week and she nipped at my hand."

"Weird. She came right to me. Maybe I remind her of Sue Ann."

"Maybe." He stares at her again, and this time I sense a regret that wasn't there before. It bothers me, sending a jolt of protectiveness I can't ignore.

"What did Charlie decide?" I ask, even though the pit in my stomach tells me I won't like the answer.

"He's going to surrender them to animal services tomorrow."

"What? No! I thought he couldn't part with them. I thought they reminded him of Sue Ann."

"They do." He turns sharply, his tone laced with stress and

defeat, "But what other choice does he have? They aren't adoptable in this state, and he's doing more harm to them and to himself by keeping them."

Adrenaline pulses through my limbs, conviction and passion I haven't felt in months filling my chest. "I'll do it."

"Darcy."

"No, really. I can do it." I step closer, my voice coming close to a plea. "I'm a certified trainer, and yeah, I'm a little rusty, but I know how to read animals. It's one of the few things I'm really very good at."

He jams his hands through his hair and latches them behind his head. "It was an agonizing decision, but Charlie finally made it. I can't go back in there and tell him not to do it."

"He's grieving, Bryson. And I know the death of a dream is not even in the same stratosphere as the death of a wife, but you don't think rationally when you're in the midst of trauma like he is. Let me take care of them and work with them. And afterwards, if he still wants to get rid of them, then at least they have a fighting chance to be adopted."

He's wavering; I can feel it. "How are you even going to have the time to do this?"

"Are you kidding me? All I have is time. So much in fact that I'm haunted by it. Please. If not for them, then for me." I look out at Sam, hopefully trusting me to return, and feel more certain than ever that this is the path to healing my still-broken heart. "I need some kind of purpose in my life, Bryson." The words choke me, and I take hold of his hand and squeeze it to my chest. "Will you please just ask?"

"Fine," he growls, and I leap into his arms in a thank-you hug that nearly knocks us both to the ground.

Strong arms latch around my waist, keeping us securely

planted. I expect him to release me as soon as we're steady again, but he doesn't. Instead, his grip pulls me closer and his breath teases the skin on my neck.

Electricity that feels completely different from the earlier adrenaline tingles down my spine and into my fingertips. I back away, embarrassed not only by my boldness but also my reaction to his touch, and put some distance between us.

His eyes lock with mine, and it's a look I can't define because I've never felt such intensity from one stare. It touches deep in my bones, makes every inch on my skin flush with confusing heat.

"Thank you," I whisper.

He jerks his gaze away, first to the ground and then toward Charlie's house. "I'll be right back." Without looking at me again, he heads to the back door, his strides long and deliberate.

I busy myself with finishing the task at hand, needing some kind of distraction before he returns. There's a scooper as well as a pair of shears in the barn. I take the water jug and flip it over into Sam's station, then return for the tools.

Bryson's gone another fifteen minutes, and I'm grateful. It gives me time to rationalize. Time to convince myself that whatever strange feeling that hug provoked, it was directly related to my overwhelming need to help these five animals. Nothing more.

When he finally appears again, Sam's kennel is clean and free from plant hazards. I meet Bryson at the gate, trying my best to read his body language. It's impossible.

"Well?"

Bryson sighs like I've lost my mind, and excitement simmers beneath my skin. "He'll give you until the end of July. Not a day longer."

"Yes!" I leap but am careful not to touch him this time.

"There's a caveat. He wants them all adopted in that time-line. He has some of Sue Ann's contacts and mentioned different adoption dog fairs that happen on the weekends. And he wants to see progress. Meaning he expects there to be fewer dogs here over time. If not, he's going to reconsider."

I nod, willing to agree to anything at this point. "No problem. A little TLC and I could have Sam placed this weekend."

"Are you sure, Darcy?" His eyes hold a warning I don't miss. "This isn't the kind of thing you can change your mind about."

"Have you ever known me to quit something?"

He shakes his head. "No."

"I won't let you down. I promise." The word burrows inside, takes root, becomes more than simply a promise, but a surety beyond any explanation. I was meant to save these dogs. Every single one of them.

fter Bryson delivered the good news, he took me inside to meet the other two dogs and Charlie, who said approximately two words to me before disappearing into his bedroom.

Bryson apologized for him, but I know it's not personal. After all, it wasn't that long ago that I refused to open the door for my best friend or answer phone calls. There's a bit of security in isolation, like if you can pretend the world doesn't exist, you won't have to face your present reality.

I scribble another note on the page in front of me, using Zoe's coffee table as my new workspace. I have my plan all laid out for each dog. The easiest one is Sam. I spoke to Sue Ann's contact at the rescue foundation today and got their adoption-fair schedule, which basically runs every Saturday during the summer. They primarily stay within Ellis and Tarrant Counties so none of the fairs are too far away.

Ms. Elledge put me down on their list and then went into great detail about what an amazing woman Sue Ann was and how much they miss both her and Charlie. She's also going to see if she can find any additional history on the dogs Sue Ann adopted so I know exactly what I'm dealing with.

Done with four of the five plans, I tear a new page out of my notebook and move on to Louie. He's the one who stumps me the most. He's not aggressive, yet I wouldn't put it past him to lash out in fear. He hides the minute you come too close to his cage yet barks until his throat gets too hoarse to continue. In the two hours we were there, Louie only stayed quiet for the fifteen minutes I was inside the house. Getting him to trust me enough to even begin making progress is going to be the real challenge, especially in six weeks' time.

"Knock knock."

"Hey!" I wave Cameron in from the couch and bite my pen. Louie will definitely have to be the last one placed. He'll need to see me care for him safely for a while.

"No Zoe tonight?" Cameron shuts the door behind him. He brought his guitar and our ongoing list of summer movie rentals.

"Nope." I set down my notebook and shift over to give him room.

The minute Cam sits, Piper is up in his lap giving him a slew of kisses. She adores him, even though he mostly tolerates her. "How's life with a roommate? Things going okay between the two of you?"

"Yeah. She's hardly ever here, so we pretty much do our own thing. It feels a lot like living alone, actually."

"I guess that's better than catfights and hair pulling, which was a real possibility. This is Zoe we're talking about."

I chuckle. "She's not that bad. I mean, what little I've interacted with her doesn't seem that bad."

"I'll take your word for it," he says dryly as he sets Piper on the floor. Normally, she'd hop right back up, but she seems to have gotten her fill of affection and trots back to her doggie bed in the corner. "So what's all this?" He picks up one of my pages, studies it like it's illegible, and sets it back on the coffee table.

"I'm finalizing my strategy for Charlie's dogs."

His perplexed expression tells me my answer did nothing to explain.

"Charlie's a friend of Bryson's, which is crazy because he's seventy years old. Oh, your dad knows him, by the way. Bryson said he connected them after he moved in with you guys." I shuffle my papers into a pile. "Anyway, we went out to his farm today, and Charlie has these five incredible dogs that he was going to surrender to animal control, which we all know means they'll be euthanized. Especially these dogs. They're all in really bad shape." I take a breath as my story comes out more like a run-on sentence. "I don't know what happened: I just found myself volunteering to get them adopted. Well, begging was more like it, because Charlie's mind was made up, but somehow Bryson convinced him to let me find them homes." I fall back on the couch. "Pretty insane, huh?"

"Very insane." Cameron stares at me, and I can't tell if he's still confused or just trying to filter through all the data. "I had no idea Bryson had friends, especially ones who are senior adults."

"I know, right! But I'm excited. This feels . . . good. And nothing else has."

"That's great, Darcy." He squeezes my thigh in his usual supportive manner. "I'm glad you have something to keep you busy. Your TV and internet habits were getting a bit concerning." He winks at me, and I push his arm away, fighting a smile. He pushes me back, and luckily we've grown up a little since high school so it stops there. "Exactly how did all this come about? I mean, I've never known you and Bryson to hang out before."

"It's kind of crazy, actually." I cross my legs in a pretzel and tell him the entire story from the moment Bryson stormed into Zoe's apartment until the last twenty minutes when he had me drive home so I could get a feel of the area. Cameron listens without a word, his fingers periodically picking at the guitar strings. Music is so ingrained in him that half the time he doesn't even realize he's playing.

"Now I have a month and a half to place these dogs, and from what I saw today, it's going to take a miracle to pull it off." I look down at my stack of notes and feel the enormity of failure. "I can't explain it, but I can't *not* do this. They need me, and after all the disappointment lately, it feels really good to be needed."

He pauses, somehow bothered by that last comment. "Of course you're needed. I wouldn't have made it through this past year without you. I mean, it's great that you have the dogs to focus on and not all the disappointment, but don't think for a second that they're the only ones who value you being here." There's too much desperation in his voice not to catch my attention, and it's the first time I really notice the stress in his forehead and the darkness under his eyes.

"Cam, is everything okay?"

"It's fine." He shakes his head. "I already promised myself I wasn't going to unload all my problems on you again."

"You're not unloading. We're friends. That's what we do. Goodness knows, you have a lot of *I-owe-you*s piled up from my one million phone calls during the divorce." I squeeze his hand. "Talk to me."

"Honestly, I don't even know exactly what it is." He sets down his guitar and glances around Zoe's immaculate apart-ment. "I feel like I'm running on a treadmill, or worse, moving backwards." He stands, his movements agitated. "When I left the praise band, I made myself a promise. I was going all in, no excuses, no limits. And if we didn't get signed by my thirtieth birthday, then I would be done, with no regrets because I knew I'd laid it all on the line. Darcy, these next eight months with Black Carousel are it for me. If we're not signed by March, I'm done. I won't spend the rest of my life chasing a fantasy." He blows out a shaky breath. "Before, when you were leaving, it all made perfect sense. You'd pursue your dream; I'd pursue mine. But now that you stayed, I need you to know there is an end date to my obsession. I want a family one day. I want a wife and kids. I promise you; I won't feel this unsatisfied for the rest of my life."

"I know you won't." I stand and walk to his side. His shoulders slump. Spent. Weariness all that's left in his expression. My heart tugs in my chest. He's sacrificed everything for this shot. To watch it slip through his fingers would be devastating. "But more importantly, I know it's going to happen, Cam. All of your dreams. The music, the stage, the screaming fans, your name as a headliner. It's all going to work out."

He shakes his head as if to ward off any more unrealized promises. "I'm not so sure anymore. I feel like I'm watching my life slip through my fingers. You included. Which I know sounds ridiculous since you're here and we're us, but I can't help but have this sense that I'm going to lose you."

"That's absurd. We've been best friends our entire life. Nothing is going to change that. I won't let it."

An anguished smile pulls at his lips. "Sorry, it's been a tough week. Bryson won't even discuss another tour, and rehearsals have been horribly inconsistent. Plus, we both know I'm not at my best when things feel uncertain."

"Hey, if you need something to take your mind off things,

you could always help me with the dogs." It's a rhetorical offer. We both know that while Cam respects my love for furry beasts, he does not share in the joy.

"As appealing as that sounds . . . between work and rehearsal, I'm lucky to even get a night like this." He rolls his shoulders like he's trying to pull himself out of the mood he's in and sits down, his guitar immediately finding its way into his lap. "At least one good thing has come from all this turmoil; I have another new song."

I try not to cringe. "Good for you. That's four now, huh?"

"Six, and they just keep pouring out of me. You'll really like the one I wrote yesterday."

That I seriously doubt. I haven't liked any of the songs Cameron's played for me lately.

"I'm going to go make some popcorn. Wanna pull up the next movie? They're all in my watch list."

"Yeah, sure." He grabs the remote to access my online video library while I make my way to the kitchen.

I feel bad for avoiding the song conversation, especially when music is usually a great tool to pull him out of his head. Ten minutes of playing and singing, even though I'm pretty much the worst singer in the world, and we end up laughing away all our problems.

But music, like so many other things these days, no longer has its healing powers. Cameron's songs have grown increasingly dark, and the last one was so heavy, I wanted to mourn for the innocence he used to have.

A man bleeding never stands
On his knees he begs, watching them all, knowing,
     waiting
Who will see, who will fight, who will break?

I shake away the words that have haunted me since hearing them and focus on the popping sound coming from the microwave. In twenty-nine years, I've never felt uncomfortable around my best friend. But lately, I don't know. It's like we're both treading water, desperately fighting for breath, and neither of us has the strength to pull the other to shore.

The popping slows to that critical point, and I quickly open the door to avoid burning.

"Go ahead and make two," Cam calls from the living room. "I'm starving." He smiles at me from across the room, and it eases some of my fear that he's right and we are slipping away from each other.

We've both suffered great defeats this year. And I'm living proof that, good or bad, it changes a person. We just have to find our new normal, together, now that all the dust has settled.

I dump the first batch in a large bowl and start the microwave again. "Wanna order some pizza, too?"

Cam jumps from the couch. "Darlin', you read my mind!"

I chuckle at his impression of a Southern belle as the rest of my concern melts away. We'll get through this. We have to.

TEN

By Friday, Sam's coat has been completely transformed. It's taken hours of work, but I was able to salvage eighty percent of her fur. She seems to instinctively know she looks good even without the benefit of a mirror. She's strutting around with her head held high. And it hasn't escaped my notice that Bentley has been pacing much more often along the fence that runs parallel to hers.

I set down his food bowl. "Sorry, old boy, but she's way out of your league."

Bentley takes his usual running leap and tries to knock me to the ground. I grab his collar, force him down despite his hundred-pound girth.

"No," I say forcefully, annoyed that I now have mud smeared on my shirt. "We do not jump." This guy is going to need some serious one-on-one leash training. I've tried several tactics this week and none of them has been successful. "Just you wait, mister. As soon as Sam finds a home, you and I are going to start bonding. And my definition of what that looks like is very different from yours."

His tongue hangs from his mouth, his slobber coming out in streams as he tries to lunge at my face again.

Exhausted and ready for a shower, I give up on his bad manners for today and ease out of the kennel.

It's time to go inside, though it's that final task I dread the most. Charlie spends most of his day in the recliner, aimlessly staring at the TV. He's acknowledged me once, but only to tell me I need to get that blasted dog to stop barking. I told him I was working on it, though truthfully, Louie has only gotten worse. He used to stop barking when I went inside the house. Now it continues until . . . well, I don't know when because it never stops the entire time I'm at the farm.

I knock on the back door as a warning and slowly open it. The rooms are dark as usual, and I can hear the hum of a news channel in the background. Penny and Macey are the two indoor dogs. Penny is a purebred Jack Russell terrier, while Macey is a hodgepodge with so many different markings, I've only been able to narrow the breeds down to Red Heeler, pit bull, and possibly some Ridgeback in there as well. Ironically, it's Penny who's had to be crated because she viciously attacks Macey every time she's let out of her cage. From what I've been told, despite having a fifty-pound advantage, Macey simply cowers and takes the beating.

"Charlie?" I call out carefully. "It's Darcy. I'm going to feed and exercise the dogs real quick, okay?" I hear a grunt coming from the living room, which is my signal to go ahead but also to mind my own business.

Macey's dog bed is in the living room with Charlie, and I swear she moves as little as he does. It's like they're both steeped in the same depression, even though they stay on opposite ends of the room.

I follow my daily path through the kitchen first, no longer noticing its beauty like I did the first day—high ceilings, a huge wood-topped island that has to be eight feet long. The cabinets are a distressed white, while the countertops are black granite. Despite being an old farmhouse, the interior is elegant and welcoming. Or at least I see how it could have been that way at one time. The dining room is similarly special with a long, distressed farm table and buffet. At one point, I imagine there were people filling each chair. It makes me sad for Charlie all over again. Surely, he also sees the ghosts of what once was here.

Neither Macey nor Charlie acknowledges me when I step into the living room, not that I had much expectation otherwise. Macey hates it when I come because I force her to get up, walk at least two loops around the barn, and do her business. She, like Charlie, would rather sit here and waste away until they share Sue Ann's fate.

I clip the leash to Macey's collar and get her to reluctantly stand. "Um, Charlie, I just wanted to let you know that I'll be taking Sam to the dog fair tomorrow morning. Just in case . . ." I let my words trail off, unsure if I should finish advising him to say goodbye.

Charlie lifts his hand and rubs it over his face like he's waking up from a long dream. His untamed white beard reaches the collar of the same red robe he wore yesterday. "I saw her last night. She looks real good."

I wait to see if there's more, but there isn't. His hand falls back to his side, his head transfixed on the bright TV screen. I tug on Macey's leash, and she slowly moves along the hardwood floor.

It wasn't a real conversation by any means, but today definitely feels a little like progress. In my world right now, that's a lot to celebrate.

It's five-thirty by the time I get back to the apartment, and I'm gross enough to want to douse myself in hydrogen peroxide. My shirt is covered with hair, my boots caked with a layer of thick, black Texas mud.

The private alcove has become my transition space. I unlace my shoes, shake out my shirt, and brush as much dirt off my jeans as possible. When I feel sure I won't trail filth inside Zoe's apartment, I pull out my keys and opt to leave the boots until I can get back out here and clean them.

I slide in my key, surprised to find that I didn't need it at all. Not only is the door unlocked, but Zoe is sitting on the couch, legs curled in front of her, a book in her hands. She looks cute enough to be in a TV commercial, even with her hair pulled into a messy bun. More shocking is that Piper is snuggled next to her while Zoe mindlessly scratches her back.

I close the door, and both of them jerk up and turn to look at me.

"Oh, hey." She sets her book in her lap and smiles. "I made dinner if you're hungry?"

I should probably not look so surprised, but not only has Zoe been a relative phantom in this place, but I've seen no evidence that cooking has ever occurred here.

"Um, yeah. Famished." It's only then that my Benedict Arnold of a dog hops off the couch and comes to greet me, though barely long enough to count. She hasn't been super thrilled with the smells I've been bringing home with me. It was the same when I worked for Pampered Pups. My dog barely spoke to me until I showered. "I just need to change real quick." I walk carefully to the laundry room and shed the rest of my soiled clothes. I've learned to keep at least two spare outfits in here lately so I'm not streaking across the living room in my undergarments. I slide on a fresh

T-shirt and a pair of athletic shorts and head back to the front room. "Sorry. I was way too disgusting to get anywhere near food."

I continue into the kitchen to find a plate already waiting with a warming lid on top. After washing my hands, I carefully remove the plastic cover and see a visual masterpiece that could be photographed in a food magazine. On a bed of rice lie thinly cut strips of meat in a teepee formation, cooked perfectly medium, and layered on top of that are four asparagus spears. I look over the bar at Zoe. "This is really impressive. I didn't know you cooked."

She sets her book on the coffee table and eases off the couch. "It's a hobby I picked up a couple years ago. I tend to do it more often when I'm alone and bored." Her tone reveals hurt, like being alone isn't necessarily her idea. "Nate's doing boys' night tonight, which basically means he's going to show up here at two in the morning completely hammered." She rolls her eyes, but I get the impression that despite her annoyance, she doesn't plan to turn him away. "What do you have going on tonight?"

"A long shower and a very early bedtime." When she gives me a horror-filled expression, I add, "I have to be up at six tomorrow morning."

She slides onto a barstool and sets her elbows up on the counter. "On a Saturday, why?"

"I have to pick up Sam for the dog fair, and unfortunately, Charlie's farm and the park we're setting up at are in opposite directions. Plus, I want to make sure I have time to groom her again before people start coming."

"Makes sense. Those adoption fairs are kind of like a farmers' market but for dogs, right? People weave between station after station and pick out the best-looking option?" She glances at my untouched plate. "You should eat that before it gets cold."

"I don't know if it's that impersonal. I mean, most people who come to these things are looking for a lifelong companion." I scoop up a forkful and put it in my mouth after making my point. The rice is a little dry, and the meat could use more salt, but overall I'd say Zoe definitely has a future as a chef.

"So, the appearance doesn't matter at all?"

I sense I'm being baited yet answer honestly. "No, it matters. That's why I've spent all week painstakingly brushing out Sam's coat. She'll definitely stand out tomorrow."

"And what about you? Do you have a come-check-out-my-dog outfit picked out?"

I set down my fork, even though I want to keep eating. "It really doesn't matter what I wear."

Zoe's perfectly plucked eyebrow soars to the ceiling. "I beg to differ. You aren't just selling . . . her name is Sam, right?"

I nod, though I don't care for her terminology.

"I thought so." She pauses as if trying to remember exactly where she left off. "You're not just selling Sam, the product. You're selling a feeling. A promise of fun, comfort, companionship. They're going to judge both of you for that feeling."

"Sam isn't a product. And I'm not 'selling' anything." I return to my plate and finish off the last of the meat medallions.

"Well, technically, you're asking the adoptive family to pay for food, vet bills, and grooming for the next ten-plus years. That's a big financial commitment."

I hadn't ever looked at it that way.

"So . . ." She claps her hands together, and I have a sinking suspicion I've somehow solved her boredom problem. "This is what we're going to do. Tonight we are going to find you the perfect outfit for tomorrow. Then I'm going to show you how to add a little volume and curl to that hair of yours so you won't have to pull it up into a ponytail."

Maybe Cam was right about the catfights after all. "I appreciate the offer, Zoe, but I can dress myself."

Determination sparks in her eyes. "So you're willing to risk Sam's future on your pride? Because here's what half those people are going to see when they come up to you. A beautiful dog being held by a girl who looks frumpy, tired, and depressed. But then next to you is this sharp-looking guy with trendy jeans, a crisp, clean button-up, and an adorable dog who makes him look like a magazine model. Which one would you want to be?"

I'm too stunned to speak. Too offended to even know how to answer her question. "I don't look frumpy and depressed." Okay, I'll admit I've been a little lazy with the hair brushing lately, and half my stuff is buried in storage so my clothing choices have been pretty limited, but I'm not *that* far from where I used to be.

"Have you looked in the mirror once since you've moved in with me?" When I don't answer, she continues, "You're an incredibly striking girl. You always have been. I sort of hated you for it growing up. But lately, your outside"—she motions with her hand up and down—"looks like a walking ad for Prozac."

I bite my lip and look down at my plate, suddenly wishing I hadn't eaten that last bite. It's rolling in my stomach now, along with a sudden shot of anxiety. It never occurred to me that I was wearing my feelings so blatantly.

"You've been through trauma, Darcy, I get that. Trust me. But at some point, you're going to have to pick up the pieces and move forward." Zoe must sense that she's hit a nerve because her tone softens a little. "A bit of physical updating might just be the spark you need."

I think of Sam and how her confidence soared with each tangle we freed. How brush after brush was healing to her brokenness. It's wild how our life can be reflected through an animal. "You really think it will help Sam's chances if I—" I can hardly get the words to come out of my mouth—"dress up a little?"

"Without a doubt." Zoe's victory smile is wide and excited. "Trust me, this is what I do for a living. When we're done, you're going to be so irresistible that not only is Sam getting adopted within the first hour, but I bet you'll have at least two date offers, as well."

"Random dates with strangers is the last thing I want." That is reserved solely for my mom, although the Michael guy is still around, which I find a bit unnerving. "But I will concede that my current wardrobe is lacking."

"Lacking? Darcy, those jeans you wore the other day were the same ones you wore to youth camp when I was a seventh grader."

"How do you know?"

"Because you sat on a blue highlighter, and it stained the denim right below your left back pocket. That blue stain is still there, next to the fraying pocket that is only halfway attached to your pants."

Oh my word. She's right. And maybe it's the end of a long week or just the fact that I'm standing in Zoe's kitchen, getting a lecture about clothing, but I suddenly find myself laughing.

The disease catches on and Zoe joins in. Even Piper responds with a melody of barks.

When we finally ease to a stop, Zoe jumps off the barstool

and pulls her wallet from her purse. "Now go shower. We have a lot to do in a very short amount of time." She slides a gold plastic card from one of the credit card slots and waves it in the air. "And don't worry. If there's one thing I'm an expert at, it's retail therapy."

ELEVEN

*J*ames McKnight Park in Mansfield is a beautiful treed area with lots of walking trails and baseball fields. It was a bit chaotic when we first showed up, mostly because I hadn't ever done one of these before. It took me fifteen minutes to find my point of contact, all while navigating a lawn chair strapped to my back, a rolling cooler in my left hand, and a very curious dog in my right. Keeping Sam close by my side and away from a tidal wave of unruly foster dogs was a feat in itself.

However, once I was sufficiently schooled on the paperwork and adoption criteria, the lady in charge showed me my reserved area and scurried off to help the next novice. By eight, everyone was settled, and by nine, the radio station along with six bounce houses were set up and ready for action.

Sam and I are near the half-mile marker and well shaded from the summer sun. It's not the prime location, since most of the families haven't left the play area, but it's not Siberia either. And since I've chosen optimism today, I'm going to appreciate the fact that my location will cut out being bombarded by curious onlookers who have no interest in adopting a pet.

I squat down and run a brush once more through Sam's silky fur. I added fish oil to her diet this week, and it's already having a huge impact on her coloring and skin quality. When satisfied she looks as beautiful as possible, I stand and tug at the denim skirt Zoe talked me into buying.

Overall, the outfit isn't too impractical, though the skirt is on the edge. Luckily it reaches to my knees, so I can still bend without showing unmentionables. The top is a lightweight button-up that ties at the waist. It's simple, fur-resistant, and actually really comfortable. The shoes were a bit of an argument, but we settled on slip-on Vans in a dark gray. They aren't the well-worn, comfy tennis shoes I bought last year, but far better than the two-inch open-toe sandals she suggested.

Surprisingly, the night was kind of entertaining, even though shopping is at the bottom of my fun list. In some ways, Zoe reminds me of Bryson, and in others, she's the polar opposite. They share the same charisma, especially when passionate about a topic, but Zoe has a layer of insecurity I've never seen in Bryson. Then again, the guy's been on his own since he was seventeen, and I seriously doubt he's ever once used his daddy's credit card.

Zoe, on the other hand, is a spending machine. Shoes, a leather purse, a pair of sunglasses that cost more than my entire outfit. When I mentioned the growing tab, she laughed it off, saying, "Daddy likes paying for my things. It makes him feel like we're bonding." I didn't say a word, but I imagine there are mountains of self-help books written specifically on the dangers of that kind of daddy-daughter relationship. Then again, my own relationship with my father is therapist worthy right now, so who am I to judge.

Sam and I wait as another ten minutes drag by without any guests, and Sam chooses to lie down on the grass and stretch out. I'm close to wanting to do the same when I spot a tall guy dressed in all black walking toward us. I know in a millisecond it's Bryson. Who else wears combat boots in June?

He looks my direction, squints, then glances back down at the paper in his hand. Then he spins around and seems to count the spaces leading up to mine again. This time I wave, and even though he has to see me, I swear the man hesitates before coming closer.

Sam jumps to her feet, tail wagging.

"Sorry, girl. This one isn't in the market for a new puppy." In fact, Bryson isn't in the market for much more than a hit record, so I have no idea why he's here.

"Wow," he says the minute we're within earshot of each other. "You two look like you belong on the cover of *American Canine*." His gaze trails from the top of my head down to my no-show socks. "How is there not a line in front of you?"

I shrug off his compliment but can't help the way his words cause my stomach to dip. "You know what they say about location. And the magazine-cover thing is Zoe's doing." I pick up a wavy lock of hair. "Down to the blisters I now have from her curling wand."

"Tell me you didn't fall for the 'you need to sell the product' line."

I open my mouth and close it again. "How did you . . . ?"

"She gave me the same pitch last week."

I cross my arms. "Did she call you a walking advertisement for Prozac?"

A smile plays behind his eyes. "Not that I remember, but then again, I block out half of what Zoe says." He squats down in front of Sam and scratches the thick fur on her neck.

"Her hair feels like silk. Charlie was right. You've worked a miracle with her."

Warmth fills my arms at his praise. "Charlie said that?"

He glances up at me. "He did. He also gave me the address and told me to get out here and help you."

Now I know he's lying. "Nice try. What did he really say?"

"Something I probably shouldn't repeat since it wasn't PG. Turns out you were right. Giving up the dogs in theory sounded good, but he's hurting especially bad today." Bryson stands back up. "I figured if I could tell him a little about the family that adopted her, it might ease the sting a little."

"That's if I can get a family over here to meet her."

"You will. Just let the excitement of the bounce houses wear off a little." He scoots next to me in the shade, and I can hear his relief as the air cools at least ten degrees. His shirt is tight and likely Dri-Fit, but it's still black, and in the Texas sun, that's enough to roast a person.

"So, what did Zoe want to change about your style?"

He turns his head to look at me. "She thinks the all-black thing has run its course and that we should update our image now that Cameron's in the band and we actually have a real shot at making it."

It's funny how Zoe's honesty feels a lot less biting when not directed at me. "She has a point."

He sighs like he knows I'm right. "It's a tough thing to re-shape your identity, no matter how important the reason. I guess I haven't felt ready to do it."

"I understand. My entire adult life I've been known as the missionary girl. I'm still struggling with what I am now that it's gone."

"Well, to the five dogs on Charlie's property, you're a savior. Not bad for an identity, at least for a little while."

Our gazes meet and my cheeks flush from the sincerity in them. "Thanks."

He clears his throat as if embarrassed and glances back to the crowd. "Hey, don't look now, but I spot a single dad with two kids coming your way."

"Really?" I follow his gaze, and sure enough, the trio is approaching, the older of the boys pulling on his frazzled dad's arm, fighting to get him to hurry. The younger one clings to the dad like a draping monkey, disheveling both his polo shirt and pressed khaki shorts. "Okay, Sam, this is it." I tug her collar and she sits, her back straight, her hair billowing out around her. I turn back to Bryson, but he's backed away almost to the edge of my assigned square. I wave at him to come forward, but he shakes his head. I guess I understand. He's pretty intimidating in his current attire.

The eager boy releases his dad's hand when they get within a few feet of us and comes rushing over, only to halt a few inches from Sam's nose. His hair is a tight buzz cut, and his matching Reebok shirt and shorts combo looks just slightly too small. I wonder if that's why Bryson assumed the guy was single or if it was the sheer exhaustion and panic written all over the poor man's face.

"Can I pet him?" the boy says in an excited squeal.

"Joshua," his dad scolds, walking as fast as he can while lugging a smaller boy on his hip. "What did I say about running up to dogs like that? You can scare them."

I squat down so I'm eye level with the little boy. "Your dad's right. You have to be really cautious with new animals." I scratch Sam's head. "Luckily, Sam here loves to be petted, although you should know she's a girl, not a boy."

The kid carefully touches her fur. "Isn't Sam a boy's name?"

"It's short for Samantha, I think."

"Hi, Sam, I'm Joshua, but my friends call me Josh, so my name is shorter, too. I think you and I are going to be great friends."

Sam must agree. Her tail wags to a spastic degree and she inches as close to him as I'll allow before starting a lick fest on the boy's throat.

Joshua laughs and laughs, going from hesitant touches to full-on hugging. "Can I have her, Dad? Pleaaasseee. She's the best dog ever."

Yeah, that poor guy is going home with this dog for sure.

Dad sets down the boy on his hip, who seems old enough to walk by himself, and presses two fingers to each temple. "Let's look around some more first. You may find one you like better."

I'm thinking not. Sam and Josh are now rolling in the grass together.

"I'm Darcy," I offer with an outstretched hand.

Dad shakes it, his eyes darting between me and Bryson in the corner.

"Sam really is a great dog. I've been working on leash obedience, and she's picked up on my cues really quickly. I'll be happy to show you some techniques if you're interested."

"Looks like I am whether I want to be or not," he grumbles. Joshua is now getting thoroughly soaked by Sam's tongue and loving every second of dousing. "How intense is the upkeep and shedding?"

Smart dad.

"I won't lie, you will need to brush her daily and add fish oil to her diet. But a little each day will prevent a great deal of long-term problems. You may want to get her professionally groomed each quarter just to thin out the hair and help with shedding, but we've found that kids who take responsibility for a pet at that age are more likely to apply that work ethic in other areas of their lives." I finish my speech with a tug on Sam's leash, and she hesitantly returns to my side.

Dad checks on his younger boy again and sees he's inched closer and closer to Bryson. The kid's nearly identical to his brother minus the four-inch height differential. Same buzz cut, matching outfit, similar inquisitive nature. "Jacob, come back here," the man calls out.

"That's my friend Bryson. He's only scary on the outside." I smile reassuringly and head-motion for Bryson to come join us. "We can keep an eye on Jacob if you want to see how Sam does on a leash with Joshua."

Behind us is an open field that would be a perfectly safe place for the two of them to practice.

Joshua pulls on his father's shorts. "Please, Dad. Come on. You promised."

Dad looks at his kid, then at Sam, who is rocking some seriously potent puppy eyes, and caves. "You're sure you don't mind?"

"Not at all."

He turns to Jacob, who's eye level with a squatting Bryson.

It takes me aback for a second, seeing him in such a parental position. Especially since he's now pulling out a small metal thing from his pocket and bringing it to his mouth. A beat later, harmonica music fills the void, and the little one laughs and claps and begs to try to play it for himself.

Dad returns his attention to me. "Okay, we'll just be a few minutes."

"No problem." I hand Sam's leash over to Dad. "Two tugs mean she needs to stay next to you on your left. One tug means to sit. If you give her slack, she knows she's free to explore, so only give her what you're comfortable with."

Joshua unsuccessfully attempts to pull the leash from his dad's grip. "Stop," his dad says firmly. "I'll let you try when there are less distractions around us."

I watch them leave, proud of how carefully Sam is behaving. People don't give dogs enough credit. I have no doubt that she feels the weight of this moment nearly as much as I do. I return my gaze to Bryson—who's wiping down the harmonica with one of my antibacterial wipes—and move closer to the duo.

"Okay, little guy, blow out and suck in."

Jacob carefully holds the instrument to his mouth and attempts to make sound come out of it. Nothing happens. Bryson adjusts the boy's hands and where the metal is placed against his lips. Two more attempts later, an ear-piercing shriek comes from the other end.

Bryson doesn't flinch like I do but continues to instruct and encourage the little boy. By the time his dad returns with Joshua on leash duty, Jacob can sustain a shaky sound for almost five seconds.

"Well, how did she do?" I ask the father-son duo, both of whom are smiling now.

"We're going to adopt her," Joshua says firmly. "Dad said so."

I wait for the decision-maker to concur, and he nods. I can't tell if he's totally on board at this point, but I can see that Sam's already charmed him a little.

The next fifteen minutes are spent filling out paperwork and giving a list of suggestions on upkeep and food. I give Sam one more big hug. "I knew you'd find a great family," I whisper in her ear. She nudges me with her head, and I have to blow out a shaky breath to avoid a barrage of tears.

Slowly, I stand and hand over the leash, forcing myself to let go.

"We'll take good care of her," their dad promises, and his compassionate words only make it that much harder to remain composed.

"Bye, Darcy!" Joshua yells, waving as he skips beside his new best friend. Dad holds the leash in one hand and Jacob's hand in the other, though I doubt the little boy has any intention of running off. He clutches the harmonica to his chest as if it's his most prized possession.

Bryson comes to stand next to me, and while he doesn't make any attempt to touch me, I still feel as if his proximity is an intentional offer of support. It breaks the little bit of control I have left as tears leak from the corners of my eyes.

"This is so stupid," I say, angrily swiping at my lashes. "I'm happy for her. It's what I wanted."

"I know." He sighs as if he hurts for what I'm going through. "Doesn't mean it's not hard letting go, even when it's the best thing."

I wipe the remaining moisture off my face. "You were really good with Jacob, by the way."

He shrugs. "I like kids."

"You do?" How is it that I learn something new about him every time we talk?

"Yeah. It's why I got my teaching certification." His brow lifts when I stare at him like my head just exploded. I think maybe it did. "I substitute a lot at the elementary school by my house."

"Don't you have to have a degree to do that?" Last I knew, Bryson made no attempt to go to college.

"Yes," he says in a tone that's more amused than offended. "And as of four years ago, I fall into that category."

My mind reels from this newest revelation. Bryson . . . teaching little kids. "What grade?"

"All of them. K through sixth. Wherever they need me."

"Wow. All this time I thought you were doing the band thing full-time."

Bryson snorts. "I'd be out on the streets if I relied on Black Carousel to pay my bills. Maybe one day we'll get there, but certainly not by booking a gig every few weeks."

I think back to how effortlessly Bryson engaged with Jacob. "Is that how you knew he would take so quickly to the harmonica?"

"Nah. That insight was unfortunately learned though the nuances of life." He averts his eyes, looking out at the bustling scene of gleeful children. "Music is a voice for the voiceless. Jacob said his mom went away, and I figured if his brother was getting a dog, why not give him something, as well."

"Divorce sucks," I say with a measure of heat.

"Yes, it does."

We stand there quietly for a few minutes, me contemplating how that one word has affected my adult life. Bryson contemplating . . . well, I don't know what. The two of us aren't close enough to surmise each other's thoughts. Although, for some reason, that fact bugs me today.

"I guess I should pack up." I look around the small area and realize there's really very little left to bring home. I sent the cooler full of dog food, toys, and grooming supplies with Sam's new family, so all that remains is my unopened folding chair.

Bryson leans down and swipes the small bag from the ground. "I'll walk you to your truck."

We move in tandem down the walking trail while I resist every urge to stop and cuddle with all the adorable animals.

"When did you realize you wanted to be a dog trainer?" he asks when we get through the thick of the chaos.

"College. Before that, I thought I wanted to be a veterinarian."

"Yes. That's right." Bryson laughs. "Remember when we'd play Treasure Island on the playground? You were always on the ship pretending to operate on sick parrots."

"And you were the pirate thief who was out to steal all the gold."

"Only because Cam would never let me play the hero," he grumbles.

"Gosh, that feels like forever ago." Memories come flooding back. "How many times did you walk the plank that summer?"

"At least a hundred."

Our laughter trails to silence as we reach the parking lot. My truck is two rows in and down to the very left.

I stop when we reach my driver's door. "Sometimes I wish I could wake up and do it all over again."

"Do what over again? Your childhood?" Bryson heaves the lawn chair over the side of the bed and lays it down.

"Maybe. I guess part of me wishes I'd made different choices."

"Like what?" He crosses his arms and leans his hip against the truck, his full attention narrowed on me.

I don't know why, but his question makes me squirm a little. Bryson is an intense person by nature, but there's something unnerving about his focusing on every word I say. Or maybe it's just that I've never shared something so personal with him before. Well, with anyone really, except maybe Cameron.

"I wish I hadn't spent so much time following all the rules. I wish I'd lived freer, like you."

He rears back as if slightly horrified by my comment. "You wish you had my life?"

"Not exactly your life. But in some ways, yes. I mean, when we were kids, you made being the thief look fun. And even now, you do what you want, when you want to. No apologies." I fall back against the truck and play with a piece of my hair. "I spent so long doing the 'right' things, making all the 'right' choices, and yet here I am: my parents' marriage imploded, my mission trip canceled, my apartment gone in a blink. I mean, what is the point of working and straining to hear God's will when in the end I'm just as lost as if I'd never tried in the first place?" I stare down at my shoes and kick at the gravel. Two steps forward, one step back. "Wouldn't it be easier if I just didn't care at all?"

"There's a lot of subtext with that question. Are you asking me if being a rebel worked in my favor, or are you mad that you couldn't bribe God with your good behavior?"

"I don't know what I'm asking or even what I'm saying." I kick the gravel some more. Watch as the dust rises and disappears into the air. "I just feel like a fool for playing by the rules my entire life with nothing to show for it. Maybe it's time to break out, do whatever I want to do, and stop waiting for some audible voice to make my decisions for me. Just look where I've ended up—confused and disappointed."

Bryson quietly digests my words, and the longer he doesn't say anything, the antsier I become.

"What are you thinking?" I finally demand.

"Honestly?"

"Yeah. I wouldn't have asked if I didn't want your opinion."

"Okay then. I think it's a slippery slope that you're on, and if you're not careful, you may end up doing something you regret." He walks over and opens my truck door for me. "You

114

want to know what it's like to be a rebel? Well, Darcy, I truly hope you never have to find out."

I stare into his eyes and see there is so much he's not telling me. "That's not really an answer to my question."

"It's the best I've got." He jerks his head toward the door, a nonverbal command to get in the truck.

I comply even though I don't want to, which is my ongoing problem. Doing what I'm told, following orders. Well, maybe after this, I just won't do that anymore.

"I'll tell Charlie what a great kid Joshua is. You should feel proud of what you did here today."

My annoyance with Bryson's stubbornness fades slightly. "Thanks for coming. Sorry I unloaded on you."

"Don't worry about it." He smirks, and I'm thrown by how my stomach flips at the way it makes his eyes crinkle on the sides. "Next time we play Treasure Island, I'll save the parrots and you can be the thief."

"Promise?"

He doesn't answer but instead shuts my door and backs away with a small wave. I guess some things about Bryson will never change. There will always be that impenetrable layer of self-preservation. To hope for otherwise would only make me a bigger fool than I already am.

TWELVE

The minute I walk in my apartment, I'm struck with another first for the century. Zoe is sitting on the couch, wearing a faded, oversized, wrinkled T-shirt and crying into a ball of tissues. And not only is her hair not styled to salon perfection, it doesn't look as if she bothered to brush it at all.

I quietly shut the door behind me. "Zoe, are you okay?"

She blows into her tissue and wipes at her fire-red nose. "Nate broke up with me." And then she starts crying again. "I knew something was up when he didn't come by last night, but I had no idea he wasn't happy." She drops her hands into her lap. "I did everything to make him happy. We went to the restaurants he preferred; I even watched his stupid sporting games." She grabs a new set of tissues and presses them to her eyes. "What is wrong with me?"

"Nothing," I quickly say, moving toward her. "Nate's an idiot." I don't exactly have a lot of experience in girl drama since our group was mostly guys, but I remember a very similar scene when Bryson broke up with Alison. And like then, my job as a friend is to list all the ways she is way better off without the scumbag, or whatever choice term she's using. Of

116

course, the Bryson who was Alison's ex-boyfriend is nothing like the Bryson I saw today.

"He's not an idiot. He was perfect for me. Successful, funny, cool. I should have tried harder to be what he wanted. I shouldn't have worked so much."

Zoe's obvious rose-colored glasses shake me out of the confusion that's haunted me since Bryson shut me away in my truck. Figuring out Bryson can come later. Right now, his poor sister needs a healthy dose of reality.

"No, Zoe, the perfect guy won't want you to be any different from who you are. The perfect guy will appreciate how generous and hardworking you are. And he won't be threatened by all your success."

"What success? I'm just a stupid assistant." She blows her nose. "Not even an assistant. An assistant to the assistant," she wails. "Everything I told you was a lie. Or wishful thinking, I guess. I don't get to make marketing decisions. I go for coffee runs and pick up ads from printers all over town. Nobody takes me seriously. Some even call me Workplace Barbie when they don't think I can hear them."

I press my lips together to avoid laughing.

"See, even you think that's all I am."

And now the guilt slides in, because that was exactly how I'd stereotyped her in my head. "I admit I may have thought that when we first interacted, but I don't anymore. And if they would take two seconds to talk to you and get past their own insecurities, they'd see how great you are, too."

Zoe shakes her head miserably. "It's been a year. I'm never going to change their minds."

"Then stop trying to. You're beautiful and blond. That doesn't make you stupid or give them the right to make you feel less for it. We can't spend our whole lives worrying about how some random person perceives us."

"I guess you're right. I mean, being called Barbie isn't the worst insult in the world. She is famous after all." Zoe sniffles and then seems to notice what I'm wearing for the first time. "You look really cute, by the way."

I chuckle because that's the first thing she's said that actually sounds like Zoe. "See, someone did listen to you, and look what you accomplished. Sam got adopted by the very first family that walked by our section."

"Really? You're not just saying that to make me feel better?"

"Nope. Your plan totally worked. Even Bryson said we looked like we could grace the cover of a canine magazine."

"Well, of course Bryson said that, he's had—" She stops herself abruptly. "I need chocolate. Nate had a thing about me eating sweets. He was all stressed out that I'd get fat."

Wow. This guy was a real winner. "Zoe, from everything you've described, I'd say Nate is lucky you gave him the time of day to begin with."

"He is lucky, isn't he?" She scoots her tissue into a big pile. "You should have seen his last girlfriend. Her teeth were like fangs, and she reeked of cheap perfume. I'm the hottest girl he's ever going to get."

Not really what I meant, but . . . baby steps. "You're far more than just a pretty face, Zoe. You cook, you're excellent at makeovers, and you've managed to charm Piper, and she's a very good judge of character."

At the mention of her name, Piper pokes her head up from underneath the mound of Kleenex. Zoe picks her up and nuzzles her with her nose. "Piper is pretty awesome."

Yes, and she unfortunately has way too much experience with tissues and tears.

"What do you say we order a slew of junk food and watch hours of cheesy romantic comedies?" I offer.

"I'd say heck yeah!" She sits and lifts her chin like there might actually be hope for the evening. "You know, I wasn't sure what to expect when Bryson asked me to let you move in, but I have to say, it's nothing like I anticipated. I mean, look at us. We're polar opposites."

"Agreed."

"Yet somehow, in just five minutes, you made me feel better than my mom has in twenty-three years." She picks up a book from the end table and shows it to me. "This was her idea of a pep talk."

I study the cover. The title *Take Control* runs from corner to corner in bright red. "Is this for work?"

"No. That might actually have been helpful. This gem is the fourth in a series of books she's given me on self-assurance, which is totally hypocritical coming from her, since she cares so much about what others think that she waxes her legs, even in winter. And who is she kidding about taking control? My dad controls her like a puppeteer." Zoe tosses the book onto the floor, a physical representation of her disgust for the subject. "I swore I'd never become her and that's exactly what I let Nate do."

I don't say a word. There's no need to when Zoe's seeing the truth likely for the very first time.

She shakes her head. "This probably seems really immature to you."

"It doesn't, actually. We all go through a time when we question who we are or where we're going. You're lucky you see it at twenty-three. If I had at your age, I wouldn't be crashing in your second bedroom, trying to figure out where it all went wrong."

"Well then, it sounds like junk food is exactly what we both need tonight." She stands, empowered. "You are going to rock your next dog-adoption fair, just like you did this one. And I'm going to rule my next relationship. Girl power." She offers me a fist bump I have no ability to ignore and return the gesture. "Oh, and before I forget, I have something for you." She eases around the coffee table and waves at me to follow her.

Zoe's bedroom wasn't part of the original tour, nor has she invited me into the space before now. The room's a mess, which is nice to see considering she keeps the rest of the apartment immaculate. Clothes hide half of the floor; her sheets and comforter are thrown to the side as if she intentionally left them disheveled. I take one step over the threshold, hoping this is what Zoe wanted. I hear her riffling through her walk-in closet but hesitate to enter her bathroom to get there.

Instead, I take advantage of the invitation and fully examine the space. There's a half-full water bottle on the nightstand next to the journal I found buried in the laundry room drawer. Any question as to whether or not those words I read were hers has been answered.

"Zoe?" I call and step closer to her bathroom.

"One sec. I'm almost done." Her voice is muffled but clear enough to stop me from following it.

I lean against the doorframe, noticing the artwork on her walls. They aren't pictures but letters artistically painted in different sizes and directions. The word is hard to make out at first, but soon I follow the pattern: *Forgive.*

Tears are drawn as droplets from the last *e* and fill the bottom of the frame with a pool of dark water. Five other art pieces cover her walls. I step closer to the next one, determined to find the hidden word in that one, as well.

"Okay, this should be it."

I jump back as Zoe emerges from her bathroom with an armload of clothes.

"What's all this?"

"Yours." She continues through her room and back into the hallway. "I paid attention when we went shopping, and you and I are practically the same size."

I have no choice but to follow her again since her destination is becoming apparent: my bedroom. "Zoe, I have clothes. You don't need to give me half your wardrobe."

She snorts. "Girl, this is not half. This is one tiny corner, and it's all stuff I'll never wear again." When she finally makes it to my bedroom, the pile is transported from her arms to the center of my bed. "It's mostly jeans, a few sundresses, and shirts that are casual without being dumpy. Basically, I stuck to your carefree style and simply elevated it a little."

"Zoe . . ."

She spins around and crosses her arms. "Look, if you wanted the clothes in your storage unit, you would have gotten them by now. But you haven't. And maybe you will, and maybe you won't, but in the meantime, you can have options."

I massage my temples, my head suddenly throbbing. Zoe isn't completely out of line. I haven't wanted to go into that storage unit, though it has nothing to do with hating my wardrobe and everything to do with hating how it represents my failure.

"Girl power, remember? Part of that is helping each other feel better. You need to stop hiding behind fraying clothes that are a decade old." When I don't say anything, her arms drop and her voice becomes a plea. "Just promise me you'll try them on. I only picked ones I thought would look really good on your body type."

I chuckle because there's no use arguing with her. Call Zoe what you will, but she certainly does make life a lot more interesting. "Fine. I'll wear the new clothes . . . when practical," I clarify. "If . . . you promise me you'll never change who you are for a guy again. That means no weird vegetable diets because some jerk is superficial enough to worry about your dress size." The more I think about Nate, the angrier I get. "Stay true to you. That's my bargain."

Zoe swallows, and I can tell she's fighting back tears. I expect her to argue or at a minimum defend her choices. Instead, she walks over and hugs me, tightly and with purpose.

I'm affectionate by nature, my whole family is, but I get a sense that neither Zoe nor Bryson had that luxury while growing up. This hug feels too wrapped in need to be something commonly received.

"It's all going to be okay," I say, rubbing her back the way my mom used to rub mine when I was little. "I know it doesn't feel like it, but it's all going to be okay."

They're the same words I've been telling myself for weeks now. Maybe one day I'll believe them, too.

THIRTEEN

Zoe's already gone when I wake up on Sunday morning. So are the awful vegetable drinks, which means she's hopefully sticking to our bargain. I found a six-pack of them in the trash when I poured my second cup of coffee.

Normally, I'd be getting ready at this time, eagerly anticipating morning worship at the church I grew up in, but something in me refuses to go today. Maybe my inner rebel is coming out after all.

Besides, I need to get out to Charlie's and start working with the other dogs. Sam was a win, but an easy one. The others are going to take far more time and discipline. Starting with Bentley. If I don't get his jumping under control, there's no way I can place him in a home with children. And this dog, more than any other, needs lots and lots of playtime.

The drive to Charlie's has become routine now, so much so that I no longer need Bryson's hand-drawn directions or the barely there bar on my phone. I don't even have to slam on my brakes anymore to make the turn into Charlie's sharp driveway, which is a good thing since I practically fishtailed the first time I took this route without Bryson's help.

Louie's barking penetrates through the windows the minute I cut the engine. The edge of fear in his bark means more to me now that I know his history. Ms. Elledge was able to find information on both Penny and Louie, but not the others. Penny's story is one I've heard too many times to count. A family bought a breed of dog they didn't do the research on and was later surprised to learn that dog behaved as nature intended. After crating and neglecting Penny for a year, they tried to surrender her to a no-kill shelter. By then, her temperament had become so fierce, the shelter declined and she ended up at the local pound. Sue Ann kept her number on file with the front desk for just such an occasion and picked Penny up the next day.

Louie is an entirely different story and especially heartbreaking. Ms. Elledge thinks he's two years old, but they don't know for sure. The first family who found him said he'd been dumped in the country and showed up on their property searching for food and water. She wrote that she suspected he was repeatedly abused prior to the dump. His fur was patchy, his paws were split, and he walked with a limp. The first family was scared of him, but their neighbor knew Great Danes were gentle giants and found him a home versus calling Animal Control. Unfortunately, that home had no training for Louie's erratic behavior. So for six months he'd been sent to one place after another, until a friend of a friend called Sue Ann for help. At that point, Louie had been in seven different homes, and despite knowing she was going into surgery, Sue Ann didn't have the heart to refuse him a stable environment.

It's weird. I never knew Charlie's wife, and yet I feel her loss every time I step foot onto this property.

Louie's barking is joined by Bentley's when I emerge from around the house. Bentley seems especially agitated today, but

I imagine it's because Sam is no longer next door. "Sorry, buddy, but I promise she found a great place to live, just like you will." I stop at his kennel and he leaps forward, his paws punishing the posts that are already bent. He waits for me to pet him, but I refuse. "Down," I say forcefully. He doesn't get down. Instead, he barks in my face, a way to prove he's still the alpha.

I leave him there and start getting the food bowls ready. I do Louie's first; mostly because I'm one to get the hard stuff out of the way. As he has since I took over his care, Louie darts to the side of his doghouse the minute I touch the latch on his gate. The space is only a few feet wide and butts up to the back corner, but the tight fit seems to give him an extra measure of security.

"Now, how are we going to get to know each other if you keep yelling at me?" I ask him in my most calm and tender voice. His bark gets more severe, but I expected as much.

Like Bentley, Louie's food and water are in gravity-controlled feeders. They should require filling at least every three days, but Louie barely eats enough to stay alive, so once again they don't need any filling. My stomach curls at the thought of him starving himself. Abused, abandoned, passed off again and again. Of course this poor dog is traumatized. Who wouldn't be?

"Alright, Louie, we're going to try something new today." This exercise isn't a cure, by any means, but it will show him I'm not a threat. And while I know in my heart he's not either, I prop the gate open just in case I need a quick escape.

Ever so slowly, I lower myself to the ground in a position my mom used to call crisscross applesauce. The barking escalates and he's added a growl in there, as well. An extra warning for me to stay away. "It's okay. I'm just going to sit right here. You and I have to learn to trust each other."

The barking continues with a quicker cadence. I can tell he's getting tired, so I just sit there and wait, taking the opportunity to examine him fully.

Louie's blue markings are nearly perfect, except for a white patch at his toes. His light-gray fur is thinner than I'd like to see, and his protruding rib cage confirms his poor eating. His elbows are marred with scar tissue, which is common for Danes but excessive on him. He likely spent many months on concrete without any bed. His head is nicely shaped, square with a thick jaw. Even with the continual barking, I can tell his jowls are huge.

"Something tells me you're a big slobberer, huh?" We used to get a lot of Great Danes in our salon, not for a grooming but to clip their nails and clean out their ears. Louie's head is bigger than any I've seen, and his size is pretty exceptional, too, especially since he won't stop growing for another few months. "I bet you're already thirty-four inches at the shoulder. What do you think?" I pause to see if he'll react in any way, but he continues to yelp, his voice growing hoarser.

"I'm not leaving until you calm down, so if I were you, I'd save all that energy for tomorrow, because we're going to be doing this exercise until you stop barking at me."

This close, the noise echoes in my head like a clanging gong, but I push through, knowing this dog has suffered far worse than I am in these seven minutes.

Louie finally drops his hindquarters in a tense seated position.

"Now, that's not so bad. Just stop shouting and I'll let you be all by yourself."

Another excruciating five minutes pass until finally there's a short pause between each bark. He slides his front paws forward and eventually drops to his elbows, his stomach flat on the ground. The pauses get longer and longer, and then finally Louie lays his head between his front paws and only lifts it to bark three more times before going silent. His torso is manically constricting in and out, so I know he's still agitated, but at least he can sense he's not in immediate danger.

I continue to sit, relishing the stillness. My back aches and my tailbone has gone numb, but it's all worth it. Louie is staring at me, examining me the same way I did him earlier. Louie's eyes are an especially vivid blue, and his ears, though clipped, were likely not trained as long as they should have been. The tip of the right one flops over periodically, giving him a much less intimidating profile.

"You're quite the beauty. It probably saved your life. People tend to keep the pretty pets."

He sighs like he agrees with me, and I can't help but smile. I know I can help him. I know it so clearly that it makes my stomach twist and my heart rate spike. Me and dogs; I don't know why God gave us a bond, but He did.

"Okay, buddy, I'm going to get up now. Nice and easy." I move my legs first and freeze when he growls. I give him a few seconds to calm again before pushing myself to my feet along the fence. Louie stands, too, and soon the barking starts back up.

I temper my frustration as I close his gate and force myself to focus on the small victory. He didn't bark for two minutes with me inside his kennel. It's minor, but it's something.

Bentley runs along his cage as I pass by him again, eagerly awaiting his turn. "I'll get to you, but I need to take care of the other two first." Plus, it's good for him to wait. He wants to be in charge, and there's no way I can properly direct his behavior if I let him win.

I do my usual courtesy knock and let myself in the back door. "Charlie, I'm here to feed the dogs."

The routine grunt doesn't come. Instead, a much younger, much more familiar voice answers. "Go right ahead."

Bryson's here? I glance out the window looking for his truck, but there's only a small Toyota Corolla in the driveway.

I quickly take care of Penny, who tries to nip at my hand while I unlatch her cage. She's unruly today as if she, too, can sense that another change has taken place. Turns out that Sam didn't just calm my anxiety but all theirs, as well.

After two running laps around the barn and a near catastrophe when Penny's leash slipped out of my grip and she hightailed it for Bentley's kennel, I get her back in her crate and vow to bring some toys with me next time. The only time Penny isn't snapping at something is when she has some loud and squishy object in her mouth. Go figure.

I wash my dirt-stained fingers in the kitchen sink and grab a paper towel from the holder. I dry my hands, wipe my face, and try to figure out why I suddenly feel butterflies in my stomach. Maybe it's Bryson's presence, or maybe it's just the idea of seeing Charlie now that Sam is gone. Yeah. I'm going with the Charlie theory. The other is too confusing to consider.

Both men are on the couch, hunched over and watching a small laptop. I pause when the voice I've listened to every Sunday for the past six years echoes from the speakers. Pastor Thomas.

Quietly, I move around the living room until I'm standing behind them, watching the same thing they are—a livestream video of today's worship service.

Guilt gnaws at my chest. Unlike Charlie, who's still in the throes of grief, I really have no excuse to skip except my own stubbornness.

Bryson turns around and acknowledges my presence with a small lift of his chin. It brings another wave of guilt because I can see the question in his expression. Why am I here when I should be there? Even worse, he knows the answer because I practically spelled out my rebellion in the parking lot yesterday.

I slip back around the couch and ignore how Bryson's gaze follows me across the room.

Macey's tail wags when I clip a leash onto her collar. She's peppier today, and I wonder if it's the result of Bryson being here, or maybe it's simply that Charlie is dressed in real clothes and not the robe and sweats he's been wearing all week.

I tug on her collar and guide her out of the room and into the backyard. Pastor Thomas is preaching on obedience this morning, and right now that's the last thing I want to hear.

FOURTEEN

By the time the back door screeches open and Bryson emerges from the house, I'm so frustrated with Bentley that I nearly scream.

"How's it going out here?"

"Terrible." As if he feels the need to show him what I mean, Bentley lunges toward Bryson, nearly pulling my arm out of its socket. "I can't get him to listen to me because he's too busy trying to go after all the things he's not able to chase while in the kennel." I get my footing, and now Bentley is the one who's running and running with no forward progress. "I need a smaller yard. One without trees and squirrels running everywhere." Bryson chuckles at my misery, and I throw him a hot glare I usually reserve for my brother. "It's not funny."

"I'm sorry," he says, pressing his lips together to stop the ongoing smile. "It's just rare to see you so frazzled. Especially with an animal in your grip."

"Bentley is no ordinary animal. He's a tank. A stubborn, bullheaded, will-not-listen-to-anything tank." I look down at my boots, which are covered with Bentley's muddy paw prints. Failure, once again. "I don't know, Bryson, maybe I was too confident. Maybe I can't—"

"There's no second-guessing now. You made a promise. To Charlie and to these dogs."

I look up at him, relieved he doesn't give me an out, but feel no less defeated. "Then what am I supposed to do? I can't train him here."

"We'll go to my place. Small backyard. No trees. And if he ruins something, it's no big deal because half my stuff needs an upgrade anyways."

I consider the offer. It could work, and at this point I'm willing to try anything. "Any idea how we're going to get this beast to stay in the back of my truck?"

"Let me look. Sue Ann had plenty of supplies. I'm just not exactly sure where she put them." He darts into the barn while I continue to wrestle with Bentley's leash. Minutes later, Bryson returns carrying a large metal crate that will easily hold a massive yellow Lab.

"And you said you never play the hero," I tease, following him.

"No, I said Cam never *let* me play the hero." He slides the crate into the bed of my truck and opens the latch on the crate's small door. "Two very different things."

I guide an eager Bentley over to the tailgate, and it takes no prodding for him to leap up into the cage. He's obviously done this sort of thing before and enjoyed it. I give him a treat all the same when he lies down and lock the crate up so there's no chance of his flying out the back.

"Why did you always let him win?" I'm curious because I've never considered Cam to be dominant, especially with Bryson.

"I don't know. I guess some things are worth the fight and others aren't." He pauses and rests his elbow on the truck. "Back then, there was so much turmoil at home. I didn't want any on the playground. And besides . . ." He pushes off and studies me with that superior smirk I'm starting to think is more defensive than arrogant. "Every good story needs a villain, and I'm an expert at playing one."

Guilt returns again but for a very different reason. I judged Zoe without truly knowing or understanding her. Every day I'm learning I've done the same thing with her brother . . . for years now. "If you say so." I toss my keys to Bryson and hop into the passenger seat. Maybe it's time to fix both of those mistakes.

~

The headway Bentley makes in Bryson's backyard is staggering. In only an hour, I managed to get him to sit, stay, and even take a pig ear without mauling me.

Now I get to bask in the glory of my progress while Bentley gnaws vapidly at his treat in the corner of the yard.

The screen door opens, and Bentley looks up once but then quickly returns to his mission.

"I thought you might be thirsty." Bryson holds two large glasses of iced tea, and I eagerly accept the gift.

"I am. Thank you."

He leans lazily against one of the overhang posts and watches the now-calm canine. "Wow. I don't think I've ever seen him not moving."

"Food is a very good motivator."

"True." He holds his sweating glass to his chest and leans his head against the post, his eyes closing. "It's nice out here today." It's so rare to see Bryson still that I can't help but watch him more than anything in the yard. The black is still there, covering his torso and legs, and today more than ever it feels like a shield instead of a part of him. Bryson's always had a quiet strength about him, but lately it's the hidden things I see more. The loneliness, the self-deprecation, and that same quiet need his sister has that he never expresses.

"I heard you playing inside. Is that a new song?"

His eyes open as if he's forgotten I'm out here with him. "Yeah. No lyrics yet, but I can't seem to get the melody out of my head."

"I liked it." And I really did. It was soft and gentle, unlike anything I've heard him play before. "I think Bentley did, too. He seemed to behave a little better when the music was going."

"Nice to know." Bryson shifts so his back is against the post, and his eyes are now focused on me. "It's always a good sign when a dog doesn't feel the need to howl in agony at one of my songs."

"Play him Cameron's new one. I'm sure the reaction would be very different." Bryson tenses the moment the last word leaves my lips, and I want to kick myself. They aren't just Cam's songs, they're Black Carousel's now, too. "Sorry. I didn't mean to be insulting."

"Yes, you did," he says plainly. "Though I can't understand why. I think it's the most honest thing he's ever written."

I shake my head, the lyrics coming back with horrible clarity. "Nothing in that song reminds me of Cameron."

"Then maybe you don't know him as well as you think you do."

I stare up at Bryson. His head is blocking the sun, leaving his features shadowed. It bugs me. I can't read the sudden shift in his tone or his expression. "I know him. Maybe not this new version that's popped up since you guys got back from touring. But the real Cameron, I know."

Bryson sits, not on the swing next to me like before but

in the chair farthest away. He was like that in the truck, too. Distant, though more emotionally than physically. "Ever notice how no matter what we're talking about, Cam seems to slip into the conversation?"

I open my mouth to protest, then close it because he's right. "I guess he's always been the link between us, even though we've known each other for nearly as long."

Bryson sets down his drink and puts his elbows on his knees. "Let's try for the next ten minutes to talk about something that doesn't include your best friend."

"Okay." Though even as I agree, I feel my head swimming with confusion. Everything in my life is linked to Cam in one way or another. Everything except . . . "Zoe and Nate broke up yesterday."

"Nate?" He tilts his head like I'm confusing him. "I thought she was dating Sean or John or something like that."

"Nope. Nate. And why, I couldn't tell you because everything she described was disgusting."

"Sounds like every boyfriend she's ever had." He shakes his head. "My sister is notorious for picking losers. Then again, she has my stepdad for a father, so it makes sense." The spark of anger in his tone is hard to miss.

"Yeah, she mentioned her dad . . ." I hesitate because I'm not sure if our conversation was supposed to be confidential or not. Then again, Bryson lived it, so I wouldn't really be telling him something he doesn't already know. "She said he could be controlling."

"That's the understatement of the century," he grunts. "But money is money, and both my mom and Zoe let him rule with it. He pays for that apartment, you know, and her car and everything else she could possibly desire. I keep hoping at some point she'll wise up and get out from under his fist."

His voice rises with his conviction and lowers again when he looks at me. "Why is it that our parents can have such a profound effect on us even now?"

"If I knew the answer to that, I wouldn't be hiding out here, trying to kill enough time to avoid Sunday night dinner with my mom and her new boyfriend."

"You don't like him?"

"I don't just not like him." I look down at my fingers. "I hate him. Or maybe I hate the idea of him, I don't know. The two are impossible to separate right now." The same indignation I've been struggling with all day rears its ugly head again. "For months I've been the dutiful daughter, walking on eggshells, holding in all the things I wanted to say because my mom was too broken to hear them. And now, when I'm the one who needs support and guidance, all she wants to do is talk about her new love interest, who, by the way, is nothing like my dad." I tug my phone viciously from my pocket and hold up the screen. "Three texts in the last fifteen minutes. *Michael's grilling. What kind of steak do you want? Can you pick up A1 on your way over?*" I shove it back in my pocket. "She just assumes I'll go. Because that's what I've always done. Well, you know what? I'm sick and tired of doing what people expect me to do." My arms cross in staunch determination. "I'm not going. Not tonight, and maybe not ever again."

Bryson listens, not moving or saying a word, just like he did yesterday. And like then, I want to rip out his voice box and demand a response.

"If that's all you have to say, maybe we should go back to talking about Cameron." I don't mean to sound resentful when the words come out, but part of me is. Bryson keeps opening this door of honesty in me, and once I say all the horrible things I'm feeling, I can no longer deny they exist.

His brows pinch together. "Why does my quietness bother you so much?"

"Because I can't read you. I don't know if you're judging me, or if you agree with me, or if you understand at all."

"I understand. A little too much." He bolts up and returns to the spot by the post, as if all the things running through his head are forcing him to move. "I just feel inadequate to offer you any kind of advice, except to say don't do what I did when I was faced with the same crossroads."

"What did you do?"

"I cut them off."

"Completely?" As much as my mom frustrates me, I couldn't imagine not talking to her.

"Yep."

My heart squeezes for the boy I know still exists under all that armor. "Why?"

He crosses his arms against his chest. "How much has Cam told you about why I moved in with him our senior year?"

"Nothing really. It was a simple, 'Hey, by the way, Bryson lives here now,' and that was it."

Bryson chuckles. "You sound just like him."

"I've had a lot of practice." And once again my best friend springs up between us. Maybe it's becoming both of our defense mechanisms. Well, not today. "Why did you move out?"

"I didn't move out. He kicked me out." Bryson pauses, his eyes meeting mine. A vulnerability, totally out of character for him, leaks through his stare. It whittles into my chest, makes me want to leap from my spot on the swing and erase all the pain he's gone through. "We never got along. Ever. I hated him from the first day I met him, and that opinion did not change over time. The only thing that did change was my size and my attitude, and once I couldn't be physically bullied, he moved on to controlling me through other means—money." His fist closes and opens again. "It worked for a while, especially when he showed up with that incredible truck on my seventeenth birthday."

I remember that weekend. Bryson drove up to the church like he owned the universe, and to most in our group, he did. I was the only one who refused to gush over something so insignificant, especially when it only seemed to rot away at his character. "What happened?"

"Not one particular thing." He shrugs. "It was more an awakening to the fact that I, too, had been bought off by this man I despised. This man who would shake hands with people at church and act like he was so strong in his faith. He'd hug my mom like she was his soulmate when people were around and then belittled everything she did at home. Insulting her. Mocking her. He was a fraud, our life a smoke screen dictated by what he wanted the world to think of us. And my playing the obedient stepson was all part of the image." Bryson tugs at the back of his neck. "It took four months of my calling him out on all his crap before he snapped.

"It was a random school night. Nothing special. He was badgering me about rinsing out my cereal bowl, and I made some snide comment about how it must be nice to have his wife bought and paid for so he didn't have to lift a finger. Just a stupid teenage comment that was really more insulting to my mom than to him, but it was the last straw. He exploded. Then I exploded. And just when I thought the guy was going to bury his fist into my face, he turned away and stormed out of the room." He pauses, and I'm sure he's picturing the moment in full color. I can see it in the set of his shoulders, in the way his stance has moved into a defensive position. "I thought we were done, but then he came rushing back through the living room with my guitar in his hand. He threw it on the lawn, along with everything he knew mattered to me at the time. He said if I couldn't respect him and his rules, then I could figure out how to live without them." Bryson's jaw clenches. "I had ten dollars in my wallet and a quarter tank of gas. He knew it, too. He wanted to see me beg him to stay." His eyes get dark, the anger pushing through. "To this day, I've never stepped foot into that house again. I picked up my things, loaded the truck, and never looked back."

Nausea rolls in my stomach. I knew the relationship between Bryson and his stepdad was strained, but this is way beyond normal conflict. I think back to Bryson's music, to the songs I've never understood or appreciated till now, because even though that event took place over a decade ago, his lyrics prove that rejected seventeen-year-old kid still haunts the man he's become.

He starts to speak again, to correlate the story to my situation, but I can't register anything about that now. I'm too busy standing, too busy closing the gap between us, until my arms are wrapped around him in a hug I know he needs as much as his sister did.

I press my check to his chest and squeeze, though he's made no effort to respond besides turning to stone next to me.

"What are you doing?" There's a hint of fear in his voice that makes me even more determined to shatter the wall he lives behind.

"Hugging you."

"Why?"

"Because that story breaks my heart. And I think it broke yours, too."

He tries to wrestle free. "It was twelve years ago. I've recovered."

I squeeze tighter. "Well, I haven't, and right now I need to be held, even if you don't."

My last words seem to break the remaining resistance. Bryson's hands slide to my waist and then land around my back. The surrender is immediate. I feel it in his muscles, his chest, even in the way he sighs like he's lost whatever fight he has left. For three blissful seconds, we stay there, holding each other in an innocent bond of friendship. And then, like it did the last time we dared to touch, a spark eliminates all chance of platonic denial.

Only this time, instead of letting go, Bryson's body takes the lead, his legs brushing against mine, his arms tightening like a ratchet moving me closer to him.

My nerve endings flare as awareness takes over every inch. His nose nuzzling my hair, his breath caressing my neck, his heartbeat matching mine in unfamiliar cadence.

"Do you feel better?" he whispers, his words offering me a way out while his body pulls me closer.

I should say yes and let go, but I don't want to. I want to inhale the scent of him, to wonder what his touch feels like on bare skin, to lift my head and feel our lips—

Two sharp paws slam into my hip, carrying the full force of a giant Lab. Gravity takes over as momentum pushes us sideways, forcing separation as we scramble not to fall. Bryson's successful. Me, not so much. My elbow bangs against an unsuspecting chair as my knee scrapes along the hard concrete. Bryson's last-minute attempt to catch me breaks the worst of the impact but doesn't stop the stinging pain of broken skin.

"No jump!" I growl, trying to find my footing despite the obnoxious animal standing over me.

Slobber rolls down Bentley's tongue and lands on my forearm. He's smiling at me like he did me a favor, and maybe he did. Ten more seconds and who knows how much of a fool I might have made of myself. "Stupid dog," I say, half laughing as I use his collar to pull myself to my feet.

"You okay?" Bryson's not laughing. In fact, he looks ready to strangle the poor dog at my side.

"I'm fine. More annoyed than hurt." I rub at the scratches that are peppered with red droplets of blood. Minor injury considering I was completely upended. "Sorry. I about took you with me." I drop my arm and force a casual smile. "Thanks for, um, appeasing me. And for your advice. I think I will go to dinner tonight."

He watches me carefully as if he knows I've just minimized this moment between us. If it bothers him, I can't tell. He already has a smirk in place. "That's the shortest-lived rebellion I've ever witnessed."

"Who says it's over?" Bentley pushes his wet nose against my thigh, and I instinctively reach down and scratch at his neck. "Maybe I'm just pressing pause for a juicy piece of steak." I smile up at Bryson, ignoring the way my pulse still races or the way I catch just a hint of disappointment in his eyes.

"You did say food was a good motivator to behave."

Before I can agree, Bentley barks twice as if to concur and demand his prize. I squat down and rub his head affectionately. "Nice try, ol' boy, but you and I still have a lot of work to do."

FIFTEEN

It's not the steak that brings me here, as I claimed. It's not even Bryson's story or his obvious regrets about severing ties with his mom, though those did have an impact. No, I'm here because it's not easy to break a twenty-nine-year habit of surrendering to expectations.

I mash on the doorbell and wait for my mom's call to come in. It never comes. Instead, the door opens and I'm greeted by a man who has no business answering my childhood front door.

"Darcy, hey, perfect timing! I was just asking your mom how you like your steak cooked, and she was guessing medium-well." Michael's wearing a long black apron that says *Barbecue King* and holding an unopened Coke bottle he very likely just pulled from the fridge. My dad's fridge. My dad's grill, too.

"Medium," I say, though I'm still reeling from Michael opening the door as if he's the new man of the house.

"Great. I will make a note for the future." He says future like it's a foregone conclusion, and immediately my nerves bristle. I thought I could do this again, but now I'm not so

141

sure. Having Cameron as the buffer last week made a bigger difference than I realized. I wait for him to move so I can enter the house. Instead, he glances over my head and waves. "Hey, Mrs. Snyder. How's Henry doing?"

I turn around and gape as my notoriously grumpy neighbor, the very one who used to chase me and my brother from her yard with a broomstick, beams at the man in the doorway.

"So much better, Michael. Thank you for coming over so quickly."

Michael moves past me and down the driveway. "Anytime." He gives her a quick side hug. "And you tell him to stay off that ladder from now on. I'm just a few feet away, okay?"

A few feet? I nearly choke on the words. How much time is Michael spending here?

I leave the two of them to their lovefest and walk inside the house like a detective. A pair of reading glasses I don't recognize sit on the end table by Dad's recliner, along with a book my mom would never read. I consider going into Mom's room but realize I really don't want to know how serious they've gotten.

"Mom?" I call with a shaky voice as I check the kitchen and laundry room. I open the back door and find her on a lounge chair, sporting a very revealing swimsuit she would have never let me wear while growing up. Her hair is piled on her head, shades cover her eyes, and AirPods fill her ears.

"Mom." I practically have to shout before she finally reacts, sitting up with a jolt.

She gently pulls the white earbud out of her left ear. "Oh, hey, honey. Did you get the A1 sauce?"

I show her the bottle, still having no idea how to stomach Michael's new comfort level in my childhood home. Random dates were one thing, but this . . . this feels much too permanent.

Mom swings her legs over the chair so she's sitting. "You look upset, honey. Is something wrong?"

Before I find the courage to answer with the truth, the back door opens and closes.

"Well now, that was quite a blessing." Michael emerges holding a cookie sheet with three seasoned chunks of raw meat. "I was telling Mrs. Snyder about Dexter's recommendation on the ski resort in Utah. Her daughter lives up there and knows the owners. She promised to get us a family discount." He turns to me. "We're taking Dexter's family skiing this fall. You should join us."

My mouth literally hangs open. "You've been talking to my brother?"

Michael misreads my tone and chuckles like I'm somehow happy with the news. "Yeah, he gave me the third degree until we realized we have all the same hobbies."

"It was quite funny." My mom carefully makes her way over to Michael's side, and for some reason it feels like a choice. Him instead of me. "Dexter calls now more than he ever has. I think he likes Michael more than he likes me."

"Not possible," Michael adds in a sickeningly sweet tone.

Mom smiles up at him and rubs his back with her hand. "Do you need any help?"

"Not at all, beautiful. You relax and let me do the hard labor." He leans down and kisses her right in front of me, and it's the final break to my control.

I suddenly don't care that Bryson hasn't talked to his mom in twelve years. In fact, right now I welcome the idea. I look between my mom and her new boyfriend and feel complete clarity. No matter how nice he tries to be, or how many gourmet dishes he tries to make me, there is one thing he will never be able to do. He will never be able to replace my dad.

"I'm sorry, but I have to go," I say and set down the A1 bottle on the closest flat surface. I'm back in the house seconds later and halfway through the living room when I feel my mom's hand around my arm.

"Darcy, what is going on? Why are you leaving?"

I turn around, and gone are the shades covering her now very concerned eyes. "Sunday nights are supposed to be for family, Mom. *Family*. That's why I come every week. Not so I can play nice with your new boyfriend."

"But I thought you liked Michael."

I close my eyes because I have no idea how to express what I'm feeling, especially to her. "Aren't you the tiniest bit concerned about how fast this is moving? He's here every time I call; he's cooking, answering the door, making vacation plans with Dexter. He's rooted himself in your life, and you hardly know him."

"I know him better than I ever knew your father," she says unapologetically. "He's kind, considerate, and has never cheated."

Her words are a slap across the face, and I look away because it suddenly hurts to breathe.

A gentle touch lands on both of my arms. "Darcy, you have to let go of this fantasy that your dad is ever coming back. He's not, nor do I want him to. We don't love each other anymore."

"Do you love me?" The question catches in my throat.

"You know the answer to that."

Maybe I do, but it doesn't lessen the spear in my heart. I feel lost and alone, as if no one understands or cares how much it still hurts that Dad is gone. The family I'd known and counted on my entire life no longer exists.

"Come back outside. Spend some time with him, try having a real conversation, and then maybe you'll see why—"

"This isn't about Michael!" I yell for the first time since my parents sat me down and told me the news. "You're happy and I'm glad you are, but I'm not, okay? I'm not happy seeing another man sit in Daddy's chair or cook on his grill. It hurts me, every single time. And maybe I'm the one who's wrong here. Maybe I need to do the growing up, but I don't know how to do that. All I know is that I need my mom and dad, and I don't recognize either of you right now." Mom drops her hand, and I back away, hating that I'm hurting her but also knowing it's the only option for me right now. "I need time. Time to figure out how to cope with this new reality. And I can't do that while you're acting as if everything is rainbows and butterflies. I'm sorry, Mom, but I just can't."

"I knew you were angry with your father. I guess I didn't want to see that you were angry with me, too." Tears snag on her eyelashes.

I shake my head. "Mom . . . I'm angry at everything right now." It's the most honest I can be, and it's enough for her to nod and let me leave, even though I know she doesn't want to.

On the edge of completely breaking down, I flee from the house that's no longer mine and run to my old faithful truck, slamming the driver's door as hard as I can. The steering wheel gets my next dose of fury. I punch it, once, twice, four times until my knuckles burn from the contact.

The pain doesn't help.

I set my forehead on the steering wheel as those cursed tears that never stop flow down my cheeks once again. How,

145

after twenty-nine years of life, am I in this place? What did I do to deserve this for my life? I've been good. Kind to people. I prayed, went to church, went out of my way to make people feel loved and welcome. "I did everything right," I cry out.

Once again, no answers are given. No explanations or comfort.

Instead, a new feeling creeps in, though to call it a feeling is a stretch. It's more like a void, a numbness that seeps into my limbs, climbing into the chambers of my heart.

Emptiness replaces the anger and the hurt, and somehow, the nothing feels a whole lot better.

SIXTEEN

The next five days are an exercise in avoidance. Me avoiding my mom's cautious, are-you-ready-to-talk-yet texts, and Bryson apparently avoiding me, though I'm not sure why.

He's been cordial enough, still allowing me to use his backyard for Bentley's training. But the first day I came back, he hung outside for five minutes, hardly looked me in the eye, and then bolted. The second time, he simply texted that he'd left the gate open for me.

It's probably a good thing. My growing desire for his friendship is more than unnerving. I've longed to talk to him about my mom and what went down at dinner. I want his advice and maybe even help understanding how I suddenly feel nothing toward either of my parents. Crazier yet is that I haven't shared any of what happened with Cameron. Not that I've seen him much either. In fact, this past week has felt more isolating than any to date.

Maybe that's why I all but begged Cameron to call his brother to let me come over to socialize Bentley. Caleb has two American bulldogs who are the biggest babies in the world. They're indestructible, friendly, and the perfect test to see if Bentley can be placed in a family with other dogs.

I park along the curb and exit my poor truck, which has logged tons of miles these past couple of weeks. "Not too much longer, ol' girl," I say, patting her metal side. Each day is a ticking clock looming over my head, but if all goes well tonight, Bentley might actually be ready for the dog fair in the morning. He's already made more strides than I ever thought possible.

He barks excitedly as I unlatch the crate and clip the leash to his collar.

"Okay, come on out."

In pure Bentley fashion, he leaps from the cage, off the back of the truck, and lands gracefully on his feet. He tries to tug when he sees the grass, but I quickly remind him who's in charge now. Reluctantly he submits, and we walk in tandem to Caleb's front door.

I ring the doorbell and wait. A few seconds later, Cameron's brother answers, sporting the same dimples as the rest of the Lee clan. It's the only real similarity to my best friend, though. Caleb favors his mom in both build and facial features, whereas Cam is the spitting image of his dad and arguably the much more attractive brother. Not that Caleb isn't cute; all the Lees won the gene lottery. Caleb is just shorter, his skin and hair paler, and he's always been a self-professed nerd. A title he wears proudly in both style and personality.

"Hey, Darcy. Cam's running a little late. Come in." He moves aside to let us enter, but I shake my head.

"I think it's better if we introduce the dogs outside. I'll go through the gate, let Bentley get settled, then maybe we could do one at a time?"

He shrugs. "Whatever works is fine with me. I'll meet you

out back." He shuts the door, and I marvel at another very different trait from his brother. Caleb is as easy-tempered as they come. He never gets mad; I've never even heard him raise his voice. Cam, on the other hand, is an emotional roller coaster most of the time—the tortured artist to an infinite measure. Maybe that's why Caleb and Cam have always had a sort of love/hate relationship. Or maybe it's just a brother thing.

I reach over the fence and unlatch the wooden gate. Bentley tugs, barely containing his eagerness, but again I pull him back and force him to wait. As much as he's grown in the past several days, I still wish I had more time with him. Whoever decides to adopt him should strongly consider investing in more obedience training.

As soon as I have the gate securely shut behind us, I free Bentley of his leash. Caleb appears seconds later and examines the dog with a smirk.

"Lots of energy, that one," he says.

I join him on the porch. "You have no idea."

We stand side by side and watch as Bentley races through the backyard, sniffing and marking every available vertical post.

"Cam told me you're training dogs again. Any chance I can get you to work with my two fireballs?"

"No way." I laugh at the thought. "Those dogs are far too spoiled to change." I give him a sideways glance. "Plus, their owner is a complete pushover who will unravel all my good work."

"Yeah. It's true. I admit it."

Kelly, Caleb's wife, sneaks out the patio door, barely holding back her eager pets. "Jasper and Jupiter are ready to play. Is it safe yet?" She's blond like her husband and petite enough to shop in the juniors' section.

I give her a hug and shake my head at the two wet noses pressed against the glass. They may be spoiled rotten, but they sure are cute. And since Kelly and Caleb have yet to have kids, these two are unquestionably their surrogate children.

"Let's try Jasper first," I advise. "She's female, so it may go better." All the dogs are fixed, but the alpha thing is still alive and well, even when neutered.

We work together to hold back Jupiter while freeing Jasper, and after the poor guy howls his objections, Kelly goes back inside to keep him company, which doesn't surprise me. She's also one of the kindest, most selfless women I've ever met. But those are the type of people the Lees attract. Every one of Cam's in-laws are solid, faith-filled, and eager to serve. It's a high standard that's been set and probably the reason Cameron has never introduced any of his girlfriends to his family.

I carefully guide Jasper to Bentley and supervise while they sniff each other. Within seconds, they're prancing and playing together. Ironically, it's Jasper who won't stop jumping and mauling at Bentley's neck playfully. He even glances at me to help, and I intervene.

"See, now you know how it feels, don't you?" I tug Jasper off and get her to calm down before releasing her again. This time, she's much less spastic.

A few minutes later, we let Jupiter come out and play. He does a lot more sniffing, but in the end, the three of them settle into a nice rhythm together. In fact, it goes so well, I feel comfortable leaving them to play while I join Caleb on their outdoor sectional.

"Well, did that go how you expected?" he asks when I sit.

"Better, actually." I continue to watch the three dogs run back and forth along the fence. "He seems to improve when

I take him off the farm." I think of Bryson's backyard and im-mediately my mind catapults to our afternoon together and the rare moment of vulnerability he shared with me. "Hey, can I ask you a question?"

"Sure." Caleb twists so we can face each other easier.

"You were living at home when your family took Bryson in, right?"

He nods. "I wasn't around much, but yeah." Caleb spent his first two years at college living at home to save money. "Why?"

"What was he like when he got there? Cam's never talked about it."

Caleb raises an eyebrow. "Probably for a reason. It was a pretty bad situation."

"Bryson told me about his stepdad kicking him out."

Maybe it's the confirmation that Bryson already told me what transpired, but Caleb seems to take those words as per-mission to open up. "It was more than just being kicked out. Bryson lived out of his truck for a week before Dad learned about his situation and called his parents. His stepdad actu-ally had the gall to tell Dad that Bryson was old enough to fig-ure it out. The poor guy was dehydrated and starving by the time he showed up here."

My stomach turns inside out. "A week? Why did Bryson wait so long to tell someone?"

"Because that boy is more stubborn than a mule. He prob-ably would have stayed living out of his truck indefinitely if Dad hadn't threatened to call the cops."

Disbelief rocks more of my preconceived notions. "All this time, I thought it was Cam who initiated the rescue."

Caleb shakes his head. "Nope. It was Dad. Cam agreed, of course, but you know how he is about sharing his stuff. You'd think the guy was an only child." Caleb cocks his head to the side, studying me. "Why the sudden interest?"

"I don't know," I say, still reeling from the knowledge that Bryson spent a week cold and alone. "I've spent some time with him these past couple of weeks, and I'm starting to realize he's not who I thought he was."

Caleb's expression morphs into that of a protective older brother. His reaction makes sense. I am practically his little sister. "Be careful, Darcy. The guy's not known for being gentle when it comes to breaking hearts."

My cheeks burn. "It's not like that between us. He's been a good friend, that's all. Especially lately."

The furrow in Caleb's brow tells me he doesn't believe a word I'm saying. "I really hope so because I've seen his patterns. And chances are, his 'friendship' has some kind of string attached."

I'm struck with a sudden need to defend Bryson. To somehow verbalize what I've seen in the man he's become. But before I can form an argument, Caleb rushes on.

"Trust me on this, Darcy. There's always a motive with him, and it's usually ninety percent self-serving. He manipulated Cam into quitting the praise band, and he'll manipulate you, too—it's what he does."

"You're not giving him enough credit."

"And I have no doubt you're giving him too much." His voice turns sad. "Bryson lost something in himself a long time ago. Just listen to his music. It's not for show. The blackness . . . it's part of who he is now."

A year ago, even a month ago, I would have agreed. But no one can love as deeply as I've seen him love Charlie and be empty. I know this firsthand, because right now I don't love anything . . . not even myself. But Caleb can be unyielding in his expectations. He doesn't understand brokenness, so he has no capacity to see that I've become more like Bryson than the person he grew up knowing. So instead of arguing a futile point, I fight for a smile that will dismiss his worries. "I appreciate the concern, Caleb, I really do, but it's unnecessary. I've known Bryson a long time. There are no blinders here."

"Nobody really knows Bryson. He makes sure of it." With that warning, Caleb leans forward, his eyes growing intently serious. "Some scars don't heal, Darcy. They just pass from that person to the next one he decides to damage. And in this case, there's more than just you to consider. I don't want to see either one of you get hurt."

"Who's getting hurt?"

I twist behind me to see Cam and Kelly approach with fresh glasses in their hands.

"No one, hopefully," Caleb says before I can answer. "What took you so long?"

"Rock 'n' roll, what else." Cam plays an air guitar, and Caleb rolls his eyes. The two of them argue less now that they don't live together, but Cam still likes to poke at his brother's calm-and-collected shell.

"Darcy, are you staying for dinner?" Kelly asks, joining her husband.

"Of course she is," Cam answers, plopping down next to me. "Aren't you?"

I check the dogs, who are doing just fine. "Sure, if it's not an imposition."

"Please. You're family." Cam pats my leg, and once again I notice the admonishment in Caleb's expression. Now I wish I'd never opened my big mouth. Older brothers. They're the same no matter what family they come from.

"How'd practice go?" I ask, though the answer is obvious in Cameron's good mood.

"Outstanding. We're so ready for tomorrow." He stops as if he just considered a horrible thought. "You're coming, right?" He twists toward his brother and sister-in-law. "Y'all too. We play at nine o'clock."

"Sorry, kiddo. I'm halfway to dreamland by then. Besides, you know I hate the bar scene."

"You've never even been in one." Cameron scowls. "And don't call me kiddo. I'm only two years younger than you are."

"In age, yes." Caleb stands, not needing to say any more because it's true. He's been married five years and has had the same steady, full-time job for twice that long. Cam, well, he still lives like a college student. "I think our fur babies are good." He takes his wife's hand and pulls her up. "Want some help with dinner?"

"Well now, that is an offer I won't turn down." She smiles sweetly at the two of us. "We'll call you when it's ready."

Cameron sulks until they disappear. "I hate it when he gets all judgmental like that. Not everyone has the same dream to be old and retired at forty."

"I'm sure he didn't mean to insult you. Caleb's all about order and routine and comfort. You're a risk taker and a dreamer. He has no idea how to relate to you."

Cam stretches his arm around the back of the couch. "You've managed to do it."

"That's because I'm awesome," I say, hoping it will get his good mood back. I much prefer Cameron when he's happy.

"True." He smiles and I'm relieved it worked. "You look good, by the way." He studies the clothes Zoe gave me. "Are those new?"

"Sort of." I don't bother to explain. "And thank you. I've been trying not to wear my depression like a coat."

"Well, it's working. Maybe this is a turning point for both of us." He lifts his glass in a toast, and I *clink* mine to his.

"Maybe." Except I'm currently not speaking to my mom or my dad, and Caleb thinks I'm crushing on Bryson, which I certainly am not. But yeah, I guess this is still an improvement over ice-cream slobber and stale breath.

"Oh, before I forget . . . I have a flyer for you." Cameron jumps off the couch, his eagerness as explosive as his movements. "Our photographer was incredible. Bryson was spot-on in his vision for us." He disappears into his brother's house, leaving me nothing to do except watch three frolicking animals and digest the information Caleb gave me. Bryson had been homeless a week. Seven days living out of his truck, acting toward the rest of the world like everything was normal. No wonder he cut those people out of his life. How they could do that to a kid is beyond my comprehension.

I turn around to check for Cam, irritated by the way my fingers itch to text Bryson and just talk with him. To try to understand why he's spent so much of his life pushing everyone away when he already has so few people in his world who truly care.

The back door opens, and Cam finally returns, tossing a handful of peanuts into his mouth while he walks. A brightly colored paper is gingerly held in his other hand.

"Is that the flyer?"

"Yep." He sits and offers me the smooth page with the headliner in the middle, Black Carousel on the top left, and a smaller duet on the top right. Below the band names are three times listed. "The updated picture turned out great." I run my thumb along the faces of Black Carousel. Bryson stands in front, dressed in his signature black T-shirt and jeans, accented by his black leather jacket. His hair is a mane of rebellious waves, his arms crossed and tense. My chest constricts when I study his face. Maybe because it feels like a contradiction that his expression can be so strikingly handsome and yet so hardened by life. What was he thinking about when the camera flashed? His stepfather? The night he was kicked out? Our moment in the backyard?

Flutters assault my stomach and I force my gaze to wander left, where Cameron stands in the photo, holding a violin by his side. The distraction works and the flutters dissipate one by one. I study this new rock-star version of my best friend. He's also in black jeans, but I'm grateful to see his shirt is a patterned button-up of dark and light grays. He's giving a slight grin, which shows just a hint of his left dimple, and though his type of handsome is totally different, Cameron definitely will get lots of female admiration from this shot. Jay and Harrison aren't nearly as attractive as this picture makes them out to be. Jay's blond hair is spiked high, and his wrists are adorned with multiple bracelets. Harrison holds drumsticks as usual. Tattoos cover most of his arms, and his head is shaved bald. Both guys are older than our group by five years, and I'm pretty sure Bryson found them through an ad. They've never hung out with us, besides the occasional post-performance drink.

I fold the flyer and put it in my back pocket. "It feels weird not to see Mason on here."

"I can't believe that's the only thing you noticed." Cameron stands and paces near the edge of the patio, defensiveness laced through every word.

"It wasn't the only thing I noticed. You all look amazing.

I just…" The backpedaling isn't working so I give up. "I'm sorry, Cam. I wasn't trying to make you feel bad."

"I know you weren't. It's my own guilt I'm dealing with." He sits back down and squeezes my knee, perhaps perceiving the harshness in his tone. "Our gig this weekend. It's big. Huge. Potentially life changing. And Mason won't be there."

"You miss him." I understand the feeling. I miss every part of our old life.

He sets his elbows on his knees and folds his hands together. "Yeah, I do. We had plans, you know? Dreams, and I feel like maybe I stole his."

I set my hand on his, my voice as reassuring as I can possibly make it. "Mason's tough. Knowing him, he's already moved on to his next big adventure." I think of my conversation with Bryson and his reason for firing their old friend. "Honestly, I don't think Mason ever understood or loved music the way you do. He liked being in the band because it was fun, and he got to be with his buddies, but he never took it seriously."

"I know. That's the only thing that makes me feel any better." Cam glances toward the sky. "I just feel this constant rumbling inside of me. Sometimes it fuels me and I'm good with the sacrifices I'm making. They feel worth it. Other times, all I can feel is the void of every person I've lost in the process. And worse, I don't know if God's preparing me for greatness or if I'm being punished. At this point, they feel exactly the same."

"You're not being punished for pursuing your dream," I say with absolute certainty. "Change is inevitable. And there's no way God gave you the talent He did just to see it fizzle away."

Cameron's entire body deflates, the tension leaking away. "Thanks. I needed to hear that."

157

"You're welcome. Besides, if anyone deserves to be punished right now . . . it's me." He looks my way, confusion making his eyebrows vee. "I yelled at my mom and made her cry."

The line creases deeper. "Whoa, back up. When did all this happen?"

"Sunday. Michael was at dinner again, and they were kissing and making plans." I shiver. "It just all came out, everything I've been stuffing down."

"Why didn't you tell me?" Cameron's voice hitches like he can't believe I didn't lead with that fact.

"Because I'm embarrassed that I don't feel bad about it. I feel justified." The truth is, I resent my dad for leaving, but even more, I resent my mom for never giving me a chance to mourn. She made me her friend, her rock, her confidante when I needed to be her daughter. "She's tried to call me, but I can't talk to her right now. I'm too . . . numb, and I worry I'll make it worse."

"I'm sorry, Darcy." He squeezes my shoulder affectionately. "What can I do?"

That's just it. There's nothing he can do. Nothing anyone can do. I take a deep breath and smile. "You can go back to being happy Cam. The one who bounced in here all high on music and potential fame."

"You got it." He winks at me, and I love that he knows when not to push. "Okay." He slaps his hands together. "It's time to start the negotiations."

"What negotiations?"

"The ones you're going to make me go through in order to get you to stay and watch part of Firesight's performance."

When I start to shake my head, his voice turns more urgent. "Darcy, this band we're opening for is legit. They won't be playing the bar scene for long, and if things go as I hope tomorrow night, this opening gig may very well extend into the future." His lips morph into a kiddish pout. "Please? I really want your opinion."

"You look like you're five when you do that."

He fights a smile. "So, is it working?" His pout gets more extreme, and I can't help but chuckle.

"No," I lie.

"Not even a little?"

I push his face away. "Fine, I'll stay for two songs and two songs only . . . on one condition."

"Our friendship is conditional now?"

"Apparently."

"What is it?"

"Just a teeny tiny small favor."

He scowls. "Last time I did you a favor, I ended up hauling furniture up and down stairs for three hours."

"It's nothing that hard," I assure him. "I need some help with Bentley tomorrow morning." Somehow, I know without asking that Bryson will not be dropping in this time. "I just need you to carry my stuff so I can focus on keeping Bentley from running toward everything that moves. You won't have to stay. I'm good once we get settled."

"What time are we talking?"

I hesitate to answer. "Eight-ish?"

He groans and slouches down in the couch. "Why are all your favors early on a Saturday morning?"

"Because I'm awesome."

"That answer doesn't work in this context."

I catch the dogs starting to fight over one of Jasper's toys and stand to intervene. "That answer works in any context."

He watches while I put space between the agitated animals

and confiscate the offending piece of plastic. "Are you going to miss him?"

"Bentley?"

He nods.

"A little." As big of a pain in the butt as he is, I do admire his gumption. If Bentley were human, no way would he have spent the last twenty-nine years trying to say and do everything right. I scratch his favorite spot behind his ear and consider Bryson's comment about trying to bribe God with my good behavior. Obviously it's not working, so what's the point? If my life is going to feel like punishment anyway, I might as well have a good reason why.

SEVENTEEN

Turns out that Zoe is not just good at retail therapy and makeovers, but she's also a NASCAR driver in three-inch heels. We're twenty minutes late leaving the apartment, which, yeah, is mostly my fault because I didn't get home from the dog fair until seven. But it was Zoe who insisted I shower and primp versus my usual throw-my-hair-in-a-ponytail routine.

Unlike my experience with Sam, this dog fair was a nail biter. Bentley got lots of attention, but he also made a lot of mistakes. Knocked down two little girls and made them cry, barked, tugged at the leash whenever another animal crossed our path, and got so excited once that he peed on a poor guy's shoe. By six, I was ready to pack it up and call the day a wash, but then a miracle arrived in cowboy boots and Wrangler jeans. An old rancher—not too much younger than Charlie—took one look at Bentley, asked how fast he could run, then signed the paperwork. "I'm looking for a cow dog with lots of spunk," he said. I warned him of Bentley's bad habits, but the guy assured me this wasn't his first unruly animal and, to my utter shock, had Bentley securely at his hip when he walked away.

I feel a little guilty that there were no tears during our goodbye. As much as I loved the stubborn ol' boy, I can't say I'm not relieved that he's gone.

"You'll never guess who called me last night," Zoe says, zooming into the right lane only to zig back into the left one after passing a car easily going sixty-five—the current speed limit, I might add. "Nate. Can you believe that? He's all apologetic, like I don't know he just got dumped by the girl he dumped me for."

I grip the dash to keep from being thrown into the door. "What did you say?"

"I said, 'Too bad, sucker, I've moved on.'" She grins at me, and I nearly yell at her to watch the road. "Liam is so much better than Nate. He's cuter, smarter, and I've had a crush on him for *months*." She slows when both lanes are blocked. "Anyway, he's supposed to be meeting me here tonight and"—she winks at me—"he has a friend."

"No thanks."

"You don't have to date the guy. Just keep him occupied so he doesn't feel like a third wheel." She gives me a sideways glance. "Who knows, you might just have a good time for once."

"You say that like I'm incapable of having fun."

"Aren't you?"

I scowl and don't bother to answer her question. There was a time before I made the decision to go overseas that it would have been easy to refute her implication. But now, I can't say. It's like a line has been drawn between the before and after, and everything before feels blurry. Resentment boils as I try to remember any time in the last year that hasn't felt burdensome and come up short.

"You know what, Zoe, you're right. Tonight, I'm not going

to think. I'm just going to do whatever feels . . ." I stop there because I don't know what I want to feel. Happy maybe? But that seems like a leap. Mostly, I just want to feel something else entirely. Something that isn't sadness or anger or depression or even this new overwhelming numbness. I want to be free of it all, even if it's just for a night. "Let's just say it'll be a new me."

Zoe hoots like a sorority girl on spring break. "It's about time!"

~

There's already a line to get in when we finally make it to the bar, and parking is nonexistent. Zoe circles the block once, then pulls into a hotel valet drive.

I eye the sign on their podium. "Parking is twenty-seven dollars a night."

"So," she says flippantly and checks her makeup one more time before the valet opens her door. "It's not like I'm paying for it."

She hands off her keys, and we walk the two blocks to the venue entrance.

"Where are all these people coming from?" I ask when we join the line. Black Carousel has never had this kind of following.

"It's Firesight that's drawing the crowd. Why do you think I'm here?"

"For your brother?"

"Hardly. Bryson hates me coming to these things. In his mind I'm forever sixteen."

We make it to the front, show our IDs, and pay the cover fee to get in.

I hear Bryson introduce himself and the band, pocket the

loose cash, then hurry inside. The treads of my Vans stick as I walk across the smooth floor, and I'm immediately grateful I won the shoe battle. If I'd worn the ones Zoe suggested, the only thing I'd get out of tonight would be a sprained ankle. It's bad enough that I caved on the sundress she insisted I wear.

As soon as we enter the crowded room, the vibration of Harrison's drums beat against my chest. They've started with their most popular song and by far the loudest and edgiest in the set. It's not my favorite, but the crowd seems to love it. Several girls are already lining the foot of the stage, their arms in the air and their hips swaying. I stare at them a little too long before Zoe nudges me.

"Jealous?" she asks in my ear.

"No." The idea is ludicrous. "The guys can do whatever they want."

"Even Cameron?"

"Especially Cam." I look for any space that isn't packed with people and come up short. The room is smaller than expected, the stage barely ten feet from the massive bar at the center. Zoe pushes me that direction. The stools encircling the counter are all full, but there are pockets of space we can squeeze into. Zoe takes the lead and somehow manages not only to find us a corner but also to snag two stools.

"What do you want?" she asks, her credit card in hand.

"I don't know. I don't usually drink."

She turns back to the waiting bartender. "Two lemon drops. One of them easy on the alcohol." He takes her card, and she tells him to keep it open.

I lean my back on the bar in a spot no larger than twelve inches and watch my best friend hypnotize the room. He's electric tonight, his violin firing out sounds as if he were in competition with the devil. Bryson is equally thrilling, his charisma and dark sensuality making the crowd scream for more. I watch him closely, study each line in his brow, examine the way his lips form each word, then focus on his eyes, barely visible through half-closed eyelids. For a moment, I think maybe he sees me, too, only to scold myself for being so ridiculous. There's easily two hundred people here, and between the lights and the crowd, I'm lucky if I'm barely another face among many.

"Here." Zoe nudges my arm and offers me a glass that looks like a funnel of lemonade. The edge is coated in sugar, and a thin slice of lemon is hooked on the side.

"It looks more like artwork than alcohol."

"It also tastes like candy," she says, sipping on her own drink—the one that did not go light on the alcohol. When I hesitate, she scoots her stool closer so we can hear each other over the booming music. "Come on, Darcy. You said you were going to have fun tonight. You're at a bar. This is what you do."

Despite being nearly thirty, I've never really explored the bar scene like most of my friends did in college. Truth be told, I spent more time hanging out with Cameron on the weekends than ever taking the time to fit in with the girls on my floor. Maybe that's why I fast-tracked my general studies degree and came back home to pursue a certification in dog training. How crazy that years later, I'm here, having a drink with Bryson's little sister, watching Cameron sing about darkness and fear and sticking it to the man, whoever that is. I feel fairly certain our younger selves would not approve.

But instead of letting the guilt win, I bring my lemon cocktail to my lips and tell my annoying conscience that my younger self never envisioned being purposeless and a failure before thirty. She was also naïve and sheltered and believed in people and commitment. She hadn't experienced the disappointment this year has brought, and she has no right to judge me or Cameron for our chosen coping mechanisms.

"To no rules," I whisper to myself and take my first sip. Cold tartness fills my mouth, along with the sweet sugar. My eyes widen in surprise. It's not just good, it's really good.

"Like it?" It's a rhetorical question since I'm already taking another drink, this one much larger.

"Yeah. It's surprisingly yummy."

"Can't go wrong with a lemon drop." Zoe lifts the edge of her glass to her mouth and takes a drink, smooth and quick, as if she's done it a thousand times.

We both refocus on the band. They've moved on to a second song, one Bryson wrote his senior year of high school. Back then he'd perform it acoustically, just him, a microphone, and a guitar. Now there's two electric solos, a bridge that showcases Bryson and Cameron's harmony skills, and a tempo twice as fast as the original.

I've heard Black Carousel perform this song at least three times, yet the words hit me differently tonight. They aren't just a run of angry lyrics but a weaving of scar tissue that has yet to heal. Bryson leans into the microphone, belts out the climactic note that soars an octave higher than a man should be able to reach. The crowd explodes in cheers while my heart aches with indescribable compassion. Bryson's voice is roughened by agony and pain, and he's stuck in it. Just like I am.

The song ends, and Bryson flips his sweat-soaked hair back. He grins at the girls by his feet. Leans down and touches a line of fingers. Cameron sets down his violin and picks up his Fender. I can tell by the color in his cheeks and the joy in his eyes that he's loving every minute onstage. Music is his first and only love, and he's reveling in it.

"Cameron looks hot tonight. I don't remember him being so sexy." Zoe's voice turns smoky, and I nearly fall off my stool. "I bet he's a good kisser." She turns to me and bites her bottom lip. "He is, isn't he?"

"I have no idea," I say with horrified laughter. "Cam and I don't . . . We're just friends. Only friends."

She eyes me skeptically. "You mean you've never . . . in all this time . . . explored more?"

"No. Never." Well, unless you count one teeny tiny experiment when we were twelve, which I don't. And based on Zoe's tone, I'm sure she's not referring to an innocent peck on the lips by two kids. "Really. Totally platonic."

"Hmm. Interesting."

I don't like her tone or the way she's studying my face. "What's interesting?"

"Nothing." But there is unquestionably something. Zoe may use her stunning looks and silky blond hair to appear needy and brainless, but the girl is far more calculating than anyone gives her credit for. She raises her drink, finishing it off while I still have half of mine. She lifts her finger until she catches the bartender's eye, then twists back around. "It's funny, you know, how people surprise you."

I take another sip, unsure where this is going. "What do you mean?"

"I mean, you surprised me." She takes her second drink, and I don't miss how the bartender's fingers linger on the glass just a little longer than necessary. Zoe certainly can charm anyone. She smiles coyly and settles back into her stool. "I always thought you were this holier-than-thou, judgmental, stuck-up . . . well, you know. But now I actually think you're pretty cool."

I'm too shocked to do anything but chuckle. "Gosh. Tell me how you really feel."

"Sorry. Lemon drops bring out the honesty in me. It's the only drawback to this drink." She gulps down more, apparently not too concerned about it.

"If you felt that way, why did you let me live with you?"

"Bryson made me an offer I couldn't refuse." Her voice shifts, and just around the edges there's hurt. Not the kind of hurt I saw after the breakup with Nate, but a deeper kind. The kind that shapes futures and decisions and self-esteem.

"What did he offer?"

She hesitates as if she knows, even two truth-serum drinks later, that some secrets should not be revealed. Instead, she focuses on her brother. "I was just a little girl when he left. I came down from my room when I heard all the shouting and saw Bryson standing outside, his guitar and clothes at his feet. It's the only time in my life I've ever seen him look . . . afraid." She closes her eyes and breathes in the music. "It's hard to love two men who hate each other, but I do."

Her words sink down into my chest, much like the song they've shifted to onstage. This one's softer, not quite a ballad, but definitely more swaying than head banging. The houselights come up a little, making the room's vibe feel less like a concert and more intimate. My eyes trail back to Bryson, the heat in my checks doubling. His voice is so fluid, not silky like Cam's, but more like a dark espresso, layered with that hint of bitterness to make it special.

He shakes his hair from his face, and this time when he looks up, I know he sees me. Either that, or the guy has an incredible ability to make a girl feel as if she's the only person in the room. His eyes stay laser-focused on mine, his words raising goose bumps up and down my arms and legs. The lyrics are all about need. Needing peace, needing purpose, needing something you aren't allowed to have. His gaze shifts then, and now the first two rows get his attention.

I'm left gutted and, more than ever, I have to know what Zoe meant earlier. I touch her arm, my voice a plea. "Please, Zoe. If you consider me a friend at all, I need you to tell me what he offered."

She sighs like she knows she's going to regret telling me. "He agreed to come to Thanksgiving this year."

My mouth opens, the shock reverberating through my chest. "Why would he do that?"

"Why do you think?" She shakes her head. "Darcy. My brother gave up twelve years of silence . . . for you."

My face freezes, yet somehow I find a way to speak. "I don't understand."

"Please tell me you're not that naïve." She pauses, studies me. "Oh my gosh. You *are* that naïve." Zoe spots someone in the crowd and sits up straighter. "Word of advice. It's time to start paying attention . . . to both of them." She waves and then pats down her hair. "Liam's here. Remember, you promised to keep Tony occupied."

EIGHTEEN

The minute Liam joins us at the bar, Zoe snaps into full flirtation mode. I never saw her interact with Nate, so I'm not sure if this behavior is typical for her, but I'm quickly learning why none of Zoe's relationships stick. The girl she's portraying is nothing like the person I know she is.

Even worse, I'm stuck entertaining Liam's talkative friend when I really just want to listen and try to make sense of the confusion in my head.

Tony leans in and shouts over the music, "They're good, aren't they?" He's the collared-shirt type with playful brown eyes and light hair styled just enough to look unintentional. Not nearly as striking as Liam, who's arguably prettier than Zoe, if that is possible.

"Yeah, they are. They're friends of mine." I glance at my roommate, who hasn't taken her eyes off Liam since he walked up. "The lead singer is Zoe's older brother."

"Really?" He surveys the stage, then turns back to me. "Cool. Maybe you can introduce me to them after their set." In truth, Tony isn't a bad guy. Just, I don't know, simple and a little too free with the hand grazes. I guess that's the drawback to having an extraordinary best friend. My standards have always been ridiculously high. Thankfully, I've had two more lemon-drop cocktails in the span of our conversation, and a warm sensation has replaced all the earlier shock waves. Well, most of them anyway.

Tony continues to talk, asking me where I'm from and what my hobbies are. He volunteers that he lives and works in downtown Dallas, running some kind of computer program for AT&T.

"What about you, Darcy? What keeps you busy during the week?"

I swallow the final drops from my glass, disappointed it's empty. "Dogs," I say simply.

He chuckles and takes the glass from my hand to set it on the counter. "And what does that entail?"

I turn toward him, accepting my fate that I'm stuck keeping Tony occupied. "I train them. Right now, I'm working with a group of foster dogs in hopes they can find permanent homes."

He inches in, his finger sliding down my forearm for not the first time. I subtly pull away, wondering when he's going to finally get the hint. "Wow. I never would have pictured you as an outdoorsy type. You're so tiny and feminine."

It's a good thing I don't have a drink because I know I would have spit it out on him. I place my hand on my mouth, holding in a burst of laughter. "Um, thanks." And now I understand why Zoe pretends. This environment isn't where you go looking for a long-lasting relationship. It's all about the persona you want to project. "The best things often come in little packages." Why not throw some clichés in there? He's not really interested in getting to know me anyway.

"True." Tony's smile grows bigger than it has all night. "How about another drink?"

I hesitate, but I guess something in my face says yes because Tony's already on his way back to the bartender. Part of me is relieved. It gives me a chance to properly dissect Zoe's words.

"For you," she had said, like some great love affair came and went, and I was too blind to participate. Which is ridiculous because, despite what implications Zoe made about my not paying attention, I know one thing for certain. Bryson has never not gone after something he wanted. It's part of what makes him, him. Not to mention that he's had multiple chances to make a move, and the only thing he's done lately is avoid me.

And now I'm frustrated with myself for letting Zoe detonate a bomb of self-doubt. The girl is an emotional wreck, and this wouldn't be the first time she's lied to me in order to maintain her image. If Bryson did agree to go to Thanksgiving, then I'm sure his reasons were way deeper than just me.

Black Carousel's seventh song ends with two drumbeats and a flash of stage lights.

"Thank you, Dallas! You've been fantastic tonight," Bryson yells into the microphone, every muscle in his arm flexing as he extends the microphone to let the crowd respond. And respond they do, cheering and screaming for one more song. Bryson pulls the microphone back, his adrenaline obviously racing through him and into the crowd. "Take it away, Lee!"

When his last name is called, Cameron moves the strings on his electric guitar like they're running from the law. It's overwhelming, the sound and energy he releases. I feel it, the crowd feels it, and I know Bryson and the band feel it, because when they come in on the beat, it's like witnessing magic in the making.

The noise becomes deafening until suddenly I feel lost in it all. The atmosphere, the crowd, the sheer perfection that is their performance tonight. The vibration rocks my bones, and I want to dance and jump as ridiculously as the girls down by the stage. Byson and Cam come together, backs touching as their guitars belt out a duet that could rival the greatest of classic rock icons. They turn, sing into the same microphone, their voices blending, Cam's high and smooth, Bryson's deep and edgy. They work as one, a rhythm only possible when two people know each other like they do. And even though their relationship is complex, you can't fake the kind of bonding that happens when two people share a childhood of laughter and now an adulthood of mutual dreams.

My heart fills with an impossible emotion for these two guys I've known forever. Though my future has died, their futures are just beginning, and it feels surprisingly euphoric to get to witness the birth.

Two hard beats of Harrison's drums and the lights onstage go black.

Tony appears like an apparition, and I'm surprisingly grateful when I see the shiny yellow drink coming my way. My throat is dry, and my heart is pounding like someone just scared me from the bushes. I take a gulp and then another one. The second one burns though, so I quickly stop my guzzling.

"Zoe and Liam took off," he says with a suggestive grin. "She wanted me to tell you thanks and that she owes you one. Whatever that means."

My eyes dart to the corner, where she and Liam have been sitting all night, and confirm Tony's words. She knew I was planning to ride home with Cameron, but still, she could have at least said goodbye. "She wasn't planning to drive, was she?"

"Nah. Liam's got her. He hasn't had a drink all night."

I consider the information and hope Liam is as good a guy as Zoe thinks he is. At least she knows him and isn't going home with a complete stranger.

"So, I was thinking . . ." Tony slides his arm around my waist, and I realize he's expecting the same result from our little encounter. I guess the warnings I heard my whole life about not letting guys buy me drinks are true. His touch has shifted from careful to aggressive. "My place isn't far from here, if you want to check it out. We have this private roof terrace on our building where you can see all the lights in Dallas."

"I'm sure it's lovely." Not that I have any intention of finding out. "But I need to go meet up with my friends." I try to move away from him, but his grip tightens.

An uncomfortable eeriness settles over me as I realize Tony isn't as nice a guy as I originally thought. Zoe was right about my naïveté. I'm not used to guys hitting on me in bars, nor am I skilled on how to get away from them once the moment becomes uncomfortable. "Really, I'm sure they're already wondering where I am." I somehow untangle from his hold, finally able to back up enough to make my pulse stop pounding in my ears. "It was nice to meet you," I lie, taking one more step back, only this time I collide with a hard body, one that not only doesn't move but seems to shift in closer. I jerk my head and freeze when I realize it's Bryson next to me, his eyes cold enough to commit a felony. Suddenly his arm is around my shoulder in an act of possession so overt that even I can't miss it, especially since he pulls me in so tight I nearly drop the drink in my hand.

Tony's surprise is no less obvious than my own, though he doesn't share my relief. "Oh, hey, man. You're with the band, right?" He takes a step away from us, and I can't blame the guy. Bryson is pulsing with bottled energy, the high from the stage visible in his flushed cheeks and wild eyes. Tony clears his throat. "You guys were really good."

Bryson doesn't say a word. Not one word. He just stares at Tony with me clamped to his side. A horrible tension fills the space between us, and I would feel bad for the guy if I didn't want him to disappear.

"Bryson, this is Tony. He works for AT&T." I have no idea why that's the one fact that flew from my mind, but it is.

Bryson looks down at me, and I see his mouth twitch in a barely-there smile. It fades the minute he looks back at Tony, and again he doesn't say a single word.

By now, my new admirer is at least four feet from the two of us and slowly backing away. "Darcy, it was a pleasure. Maybe I'll see you arou—"

"No, you won't." Bryson's words cut the air like a chainsaw, and Tony must feel the residual sting because he turns away without a goodbye.

Bryson's arm falls away. "You okay? You looked scared."

"I think cornered was more like it. I was probably overreacting." I swallow, trying my best to act unaffected. It's harder than it should be, mostly because my head suddenly feels like it's full of air and being tossed by the wind. I blink my eyes and try to shake away the odd sensation. That seems to work a little. "I'm sure Tony is harmless. His friend works with your sister." The same sister who told me Bryson broke twelve years of silence for me. The same one who said I wasn't paying attention. I stare at the way his damp shirt hangs over every muscle in his chest. Well, I'm certainly paying attention now.

Bryson snorts. "Trust me, the way he was looking at you was definitely not harmless. Guys like that make me sick. They know who to prey on. And you, Darcy, are an easy target."

"I am not."

"Really? Did he buy this for you?" He takes the glass from my hand, sniffs it, then takes a sip. Immediately his eyes widen and he coughs as if it went down the wrong pipe. "Please tell me you were smart enough not to drink this."

And now I'm offended. "I'm not a teenager, and I'm not driving." I steal back my glass. "And I don't need your permission to have a lemon drop . . . or four for that matter."

His eyes narrow, and I understand a little why Zoe might not have liked me when growing up. There's no fun in being judged. "Since when do you drink?"

"Since I decided I'm done playing by all the rules."

"And you think a stiff martini is going to solve all your problems?" His voice grows rougher. "I got news for you, it won't."

"And yet here you stand, the picture of mutiny, and every one of your dreams is about to come true." And now the anger is back, alive and well. "Why does everyone expect so much more from me?"

"Because you're better than this."

"Obviously, I'm not."

Before he can respond, a girl comes stumbling forward, her arms draping over the very chest I had admired before his words turned cutting. "Hey, you guys were amazing. Can I get your autograph?" She unbuttons her shirt down to the end of a long cleavage line and offers Bryson a sharpie.

He smiles sensually at her but writes his name on the inside of her wrist instead. "Thanks for coming." His arm finds its way around my shoulders again, and I realize this time he's not doing it for my benefit but his own.

She takes the hint and leaves, though I quickly realize she's not the only one who's noticed Bryson is now in the audience.

"Where's Zoe?" He eyes the group moving toward us. "We need to get backstage."

"She left with a guy from work."

"Of course she did." Bryson mashes his lips together and glances at the half-finished drink in my hand. "Who would have thought that she'd be the one influencing you." And then with lightning-fast speed, he snatches the glass from my fingers and sets it on the bar. "Let's go."

His grip securely around my wrist, Bryson pushes us through the crowd until we're in front of a closed black door blocked by a beefy bouncer in a tight black T-shirt.

"She's with me." Bryson waves his pass and opens the door without a pause. Beefy guy smiles, and I don't like the once-over I get or the way he lifts his chin at Bryson as if it's a secret high five.

"Is taking random girls backstage something you do often?"

Bryson stops and turns to look at me, his eyes dancing as if he can see the jealousy slithering up inside. "Are you calling yourself random?"

"No."

He steps closer, his voice dipping with arrogance. "Then why are you worried?"

"I'm not."

Bryson smirks but doesn't call me out on my lie. Instead, he leads me through the dark corridor until Cam and the rest of the band appear, each exuding the same buzzing high that's been springing from Bryson since he stepped offstage.

"Well, look at you, sexy mama." Jay whistles, turning everyone's head, including Cameron's. "Bare legs, flushed cheeks. Just my kind of fangirl."

"Save it, Casanova. She's way too smart for your golden tongue," Cameron says, pushing him aside affectionately. He eyes me with confusion. "Where'd you appear from? I was just about to come find you."

"Bryson got me backstage."

He lifts his chin toward his bandmate. "Thanks for looking out for my girl."

"Anytime." Bryson's voice is flat, and I don't miss the way he turns around right when Cam envelops me in a hug so tight I can hardly breathe.

"Did you feel it?" He nuzzles his nose into my neck and inhales like he's only just begun breathing again.

"I felt it." I may not be an expert in music like Cam, but I know when I've seen something supernatural. "You guys were perfect."

Cam swings me into the air. It lasts only a second, which is a good thing because he's come dangerously close to wearing regurgitated lemon on his shirt. When the room settles, I look for Bryson, but he's gone.

"I knew tonight was our shot. After all the sacrifices, the wasted time . . . it's finally going to happen." When he releases me, his eyes are blurry, and I'm suddenly hit with a trunkful of emotion I can't seem to control.

"I'm so happy for you, Cameron. Really."

Footsteps fall behind us, and we shift out of the way as three guys in leather huddle by the stage entrance. They each seem to have a pre-performance ritual. One's bouncing on his toes, another is cracking his neck, while the third is moving his mouth like he's going through the alphabet.

The neck cracker spots Cam when he's on crack number six and pauses. "Are you the guitarist who just did that solo up there?"

Cam stiffens beside me. "I am."

"Incredible sound, man. If you have some time after, we should hit some chords together."

My poor friend falls speechless. I subtly elbow him in the side.

"Yeah, maybe," he answers as if it's even in question.

The guy knows it, too. "And feel free to bring your girl-friend. It'll be a bunch of us."

"Thanks."

And since Cam spent most of the morning giving me this band's credentials, including their brand-new deal with Island Records, I know he just possibly got the "break" he's been waiting for.

We both remain completely still as the headliner the crowd is begging for fans out onstage. The lights go up, drums pump a beat through the air, and Cam looks at me in complete shock. "Did that just happen?"

I can't breathe. "Yes, that just happened."

He comes at me even more high on life than earlier. I give him the stiff arm, unwilling and truthfully unable to be spun around again.

"No spinning, please," I beg. "My head is already swirly from all the excitement."

"So you'll stay and hang out with us?"

I pat his hopeful cheek and shake my head. "Not a chance. I promised you two songs. That's it. Besides, do you really want to be worrying about me having a good time?"

He shrugs, disappointed, but we both know I'm right to decline.

We stand together and watch the manifestation of Cameron's dream. "That's us in six months," he whispers next to me, his envy strong enough to taste.

My stomach tumbles at the surety in his voice. As much as I've cheered him on, supported his dream, and encouraged him when his faith started to falter, this is honestly the first time I truly believe he's right.

NINETEEN

When my obligatory two songs are over, I head out the backstage door and realize a little too late that it's the wrong exit. Instead of the beefy security guard and a roomful of half-inebriated people, there's a parking lot with ten reserved signs and a gate.

"Darcy?"

I look up just as Bryson closes the back of Jay's van. "Bryson . . . hey."

"What are you doing out here?"

"I think I may have underestimated the power of lemons." I walk toward him, feeling a sway in my step that hasn't been there before. "How'd you end up with loading duty tonight?"

"I volunteered."

"Why?" Cam hates loading and unloading the equipment. In fact, sometimes I wonder if part of his desire to make it big comes from the idea that he'll have roadies to do all the heavy lifting for him.

"Because I'm tired and ready to go home. If I wait for them, I'll be here all night."

"Yeah, makes sense." I nod, but the act seems to teeter my already questionable equilibrium.

"Whoa." He cups my arm, keeping me steady. "Okay, Cinderella, the clock has definitely hit midnight for you."

"I know. I'm trying to get home," I slur, mashing my screen again. "But I can't get the stupid app to come up."

Bryson takes the phone from my hand. "Come on, you lush. I'll drive you." He guides me to the passenger side of his truck and helps me get inside.

I lean my head back against the headrest and try to close my eyes. Bad decision. The truck goes into a spinning carnival ride until I force my lids open again.

Bryson slams his door shut and turns to look at me with both amusement and a little pity in his eyes. "Where's Cameron?"

"He's watching Firemight or whatever their name is."

"And he just let you leave by yourself?"

"Nah. He offered to walk me out, but I assured him I was good." My head feels heavy and flops to the side. "He didn't know about the lemon drops. Though I don't think he'd be quite as rude about it as you were." I attempt to poke his arm but miss twice.

"I wouldn't be so sure of that."

I open my mouth to argue when different words fall out. "You've been avoiding me. Why?"

He sighs and slides his key into the ignition. "Let's just call it self-preservation and leave it at that." His answer doesn't make sense to me, but that could also be because my head is squishy.

I close my eyes again, thankful there's less spinning now. "Well . . . I missed seeing you. Just so you know."

Bryson's truck rumbles to a start, and it feels like only seconds pass before I hear him ordering cheeseburgers from a drive-thru.

I sit up in the seat and look around at my surroundings. We're in Midlothian. Only a few miles from Zoe's apartment.

"Did I fall asleep?"

"Yep, and you sleep like the dead. I had to check your pulse twice." Bryson eases the truck forward and pays the attendant.

The smell of grease and French fries drifts through the truck window, and my stomach immediately growls in response. "You are now my favorite person in the world. That smells like heaven."

He snickers at me and reaches for the large paper bag the cashier is holding. "That's because you're drunk."

"I am not."

"Oh yes, you most definitely are. But this will help." He hands me the greasy treasure, and I immediately go for the nearest bag of fries.

"Oh my goodness. These taste soooo good." I shove another handful into my mouth. "Why have I never eaten here before?"

Bryson rolls up his window and puts the truck in drive. He's laughing at me, and I should be offended but I'm not. In fact, I feel like giggling myself.

"That AT&T guy tried to get me to go to his apartment," I say, unfolding the paper surrounding the most beautiful cheeseburger I've ever seen.

"I'm sure he did."

I ingest two delicious bites and wipe my mouth. "It's weird. I've never had a guy come on that strong before."

"Sure you have."

"No, really." I shake my head, grateful the worst of the

dizziness is gone. "I think it's the sundress. Tony said I looked tiny and feminine." Again the giggles come. "Imagine what he'd think if he saw the real me."

Bryson glances at me, then back to the road. "He'd think the same thing we all do. That you're just as gorgeous without all the frills as you are with them."

"Ah, that's sweet." I take another bite of my cheeseburger and wonder why his compliment makes me want to start crying.

"If I were a betting man, I'd say the only reason men aren't beating down your door is the fact that Cam stays permanently attached to your side. The two of you are pretty oblivious to the rest of the world."

"Please, Cam could get a master's degree in flirting. I swear he's had more girlfriends than I've had haircuts."

Bryson snorts out a laugh like I've said the most ridiculous thing tonight. "Name one that wasn't an exercise in passing time."

"I can name five."

He turns and raises his brows, waiting for me to continue.

"Okay, there's Cindy."

"Nope. She crushed on him for five months, so he gave her a few pity dates just to get her off his back."

"Fine. Lydia." I wait, knowing he won't have a rebuttal for that one. Lydia is Cameron's longest relationship to date.

"Boredom. She was there and available. Cam never had any real feelings for her."

"You're changing the rules. I said girlfriends, not soul-mates."

"And I said ones who weren't smoke screens." Bryson pulls the truck in front of our apartment and shoves the gear into park. "Try again."

I narrow my eyes at him, even though he's smirking. "Alright. January."

That wipes the grin right off his face. "Doesn't count."

"How so?"

"Because January was smokin' hot, and Cameron was blinded by it."

"You're just saying that because you hated her."

"I didn't hate her. I just didn't trust her. When you grow up in a family like mine, you get very good at spotting frauds."

"All the same, Cam's feelings for her—or at least the 'her' he thought she was—were very real. And I feel certain that if she hadn't lied, the two of them would still be together." I crumple the bag in my hand, my stomach now full and my smile nice and smug. "Now admit it. I win."

But Bryson doesn't continue our banter the way I expect him to. Instead, his expression turns hard, a deep line creasing his brow. "And that never bothered you? Seeing them together?"

My skin suddenly feels itchy. "No. Cam was happy. That's all that matters."

He shakes his head like I'm missing the point and shoves open his car door. "Let's get you inside."

The giddiness I felt for the last ten minutes falls to a pit in my stomach. I ease from the car, exhaustion and sadness wrapping me up like a blanket. Still, I trudge up the stairs and try not to feel completely humiliated by the fact Bryson has to help keep me steady.

He unlocks the door, and immediately Piper leaps at our feet, barking madly. I lean down and pick her up. My throat burns as I nuzzle her soft fur. At least she is too loyal to know what a colossal screw-up I am right now.

"I'll take her out for you," he offers.

I reluctantly hand her over and use the wall to stabilize my walk into the bedroom. Bryson was right. Slamming back martinis all night has accomplished nothing. I'm still here, stuck in this apartment, my professional life a complete disaster. My parents are still divorced, and my mom is probably sleeping next to Michael right now.

The bed whines when I drop down onto the mattress, my shoulders slumped, my arms hanging lifeless between my legs. And then the tears come. One at a time, rolling down my cheeks and onto the floor.

I feel Bryson settle next to me but can't seem to look at him. "I didn't set out to drink this much."

"No one ever does."

"I just thought if I tried something new and forbidden, then I wouldn't feel so cheated."

"How'd that work out for you?" I know he's trying to lighten the mood, but I can't seem to pull myself from the sorrow.

"I've spent my whole existence in this bubble with everything mapped out in perfect order. My parents sheltered me too much, and now that it's all gone, I feel like the ground won't stop moving."

Bryson's palm touches my back, moves up toward my shoulders, and squeezes. "They didn't shelter you; they shielded you, and that's not a bad thing. Boundaries are there for a reason. When I have kids, I'll do the same exact thing."

I chuckle through my sobs. "I thought you were never getting married."

"I'm being hypothetical." He studies my tear-soaked face, and compassion fills his normally stormy eyes. "You'll find your way through this." His voice shifts, its softness and layers of empathy reminding me that he isn't saying anything he hasn't already experienced himself.

"Thank you." My hand slides across the comforter and touches his. He startles at the contact but doesn't move. "For listening. And for taking care of me." I inch closer, my fingers trailing over his knuckles to the inside of his wrist.

"Darcy." His voice is full of a warning I don't want to hear right now. My hand trails up his forearm, the muscles underneath tensing with each lingering stroke.

I lift my gaze from his intoxicating skin and stare into the same eyes that captivated me when onstage. They blaze, a molten steel, and his gaze holds me like fire. My fingers continue their forbidden exploration. They're at his bicep now, my nails pushing against the hem of his tight sleeve. I scoot closer, the heat of his body surrounding me, filling this room, filling my head. He swallows and his breath comes out in quick hot waves. I glide my other hand closer until it lands lightly on his thigh.

If Bryson was tense before, he's now a solid rock of frustrated energy. He pulls his arm away first, then stands. "Time for bed."

"I don't want to go to bed." I want to go back to doing exactly what I was just doing.

"Maybe not. But I'm not interested in being another one of your experiments tonight."

Bitterness rises in my throat but there's no fighting the edge in his voice or the violent way he tosses aside the multiple shams that sit against the headboard. He folds back the sheets and waits, expectantly. I begrudgingly crawl over, kicking off my shoes in the process. He tucks me inside, sundress and all, and then walks out of my room without a word.

A hive of bees swarm in my chest and I nearly throw off the covers to follow him when he suddenly appears back in the doorway with a glass of water and a bottle of aspirin in his hands.

"Drink lots of fluids when you wake up and take two of these." He kneels so our faces are level, and slowly his tight, stubborn mouth relaxes. "Don't stay in this place too long, Darcy. You have so much more in you than this rebellion."

My insides jumble as though everything has been kicked and shaken. Strangely, he looks exactly how I feel. "Why did you do it?" I slide my hand through his, lace our fingers together. "Why did you make sure I lived here?"

He pauses as if trying to figure it out himself. "You needed options."

"No. If it were just that, you wouldn't have agreed to spend Thanksgiving with your family."

I can tell from his expression that he's surprised I know the truth. His shoulders are square, and his jaw holds the edge of a man busted. He sighs. "I did it because I'm selfish."

My voice feels weak. "How is that selfish?"

He detangles his hand and gently brushes a wisp of hair from my cheek. "The fact that you don't know the answer to that is exactly why I have no business being here right now." He stands, his body language suddenly cold and guarded. "Sweet dreams, Darcy. If we're lucky, you won't remember any of this in the morning." He then reaches his hand under my lampshade, and the room goes dark.

TWENTY

I made it out to the farm this morning, though how, I don't know. Throughout the entire drive, the sun scorched my eyes while my head pounded in a painful rhythm that mimicked the knocking of my aging truck engine. Twice, I had to fight the urge to pull my truck over to the side of the road and regurgitate the lemon drops that would undoubtedly taste worse coming up.

Bryson said if I was lucky, I wouldn't remember anything.

Well, I'm not lucky. I remember every humiliating moment from the last twenty-four hours, including the way I practically ripped his shirt off.

I grip the steering wheel, unable to move until the nausea subsides, and let my head rest against the warm leather. How did my life get so screwed up? I was going to be a missionary a month ago, and now I'm the girl who's not only skipped church more than I've gone but can't even find the words to pray. Or maybe I just don't want to pray. Because even though the initial trauma has subsided and my miserable attempt at rebellion has failed, I still feel this gut-wrenching anger I can't seem to get past. And worse, it all seems to be directed at the very entity I would normally go to for peace and comfort.

Sweat beads on my neck until I'm forced to move. My old truck has decent enough air conditioning when it's moving at a constant rate of speed, but not so much when it's simply idling in a driveway.

I push open the door and take my first shaky step onto the gravel. The sound is eerily quiet, and the nausea is immediately replaced by anxiety. Louie isn't barking. A phenomenon that has never occurred since the first day I met him.

Adrenaline takes over and I rush faster than I've moved all morning to the back of the house, only to find the dog in question is not only okay but standing in the middle of his kennel as if waiting for me.

"Now, aren't you full of surprises." Or maybe even Louie can sense that I'm teetering close to the breaking point.

I slide open the lock and take two careful steps inside, expecting at any second for him to scurry back to the corner and begin barking. He doesn't. Instead, he comes closer.

While Louie's erratic behavior has improved some in the past couple of weeks, never before has he gotten this close to me. I glance at Bentley's empty kennel on the left and wonder if his absence might be the very thing Louie needed to begin to trust.

I take two careful steps forward, watching the skittish Great Dane for any signs of distress. Normally I wouldn't let a dog I'm training set the tone, but I'm sensing Louie needs to be the one to take that first step in deciding if I'm really going to be his person or not.

With my arms at my sides, palms out, I wait. "Go ahead. Check me out. I can tell you want to."

He takes one step forward, then slides back and barks twice.

I don't move. "It's okay. Come on."

He tilts his head and watches me with those sad blue eyes. I can tell he wants to believe better times are coming; he's just too jaded to know what to look forward to.

"I understand, you know. My life hasn't exactly gone the way I planned it either." Though saying it out loud doesn't make me feel any better. "But you and I, we're overcomers. At least that's what I keep telling myself."

As if he understands my words, he tries again, making it within a foot of me before jumping back and barking so erratically one would think I'd lashed out.

"Now, how scary can I be? You outweigh me by at least thirty pounds," I say as soothingly as I can and wiggle my fingers a little. "And in case you haven't noticed, I'm not exactly in tip-top shape this morning."

My voice calms him, and this time he gets close enough that I feel his cold, wet nose on my palm. His ears perk up. I can tell he smells the dog treats I always bring with me.

He sniffs with purpose now, first against my hand, then his snout presses into my pocket. A bark comes, sudden and loud, and it's so unexpected I jump, which of course sends him flying back to the corner.

"I'm sorry. I'm sorry. You scared me." I reach into my pocket and pull one of the treats free. Kneeling on one knee, I extend my hand to him. To take the meaty morsel, he'll have to come closer, will have to believe I'm safe enough to touch my fingers again.

He does the inching forward, jumping back thing two more times before he's close enough to take the peace offering. His large wet nose brushes against my knuckle, and then his tongue gently swipes the treat from my fingers. I don't make him sit, don't give him any commands at all. This isn't about obedience; it's about trust. Trusting me to provide for him, trusting me not to harm him, trusting me inside his broken heart.

"That's a good boy, Louie."

When he's done swallowing, he comes back to my hand, sniffs my palm for more, and this time I'm ready when he barks at me.

"Sorry, that one was a freebie, but barking demands is not how we are going to communicate." I stand and reach into my pocket. Louie dances in front of me in a mix of fear and excitement. He barks again, this time with an agitated tone. "Oh, I know you want this treat, but you're not going to get it that way. I need you to sit."

He stares at me, obviously confused. He doesn't know the command, and unfortunately he won't let me close enough to show him, but I have a feeling the big guy is smart enough to figure it out.

"Can you sit?" I move closer and raise the treat up.

His head naturally follows, and the momentum causes his backside to dip. Not all the way to the ground but close enough.

"Very good." I give him the treat and feel the scrape of his teeth on my skin. We'll have to work on that, too.

He watches curiously as I refresh his food and water. I wonder if he can see my renewed strength or if he even understands how much this one victory has nourished my hurting soul.

When I'm done with all the housekeeping, I pull one more treat from my pocket. "Want to make it three for three today?"

He comes forward, only hopping back once.

"Sit," I say and hold the treat up high. This time when his head rises, his hindquarters go all the way to the ground. "Good boy!"

He takes the treat from my hand a third time, and as much as I want to reach out and touch his silky fur, I know it's too soon for contact. Today was a huge step forward. And considering how my luck has been going lately, I better stop while I'm ahead. "See you later, buddy. I need to get inside and take care of the other two. Penny's probably bashing against her cage by now."

I lock Louie's gate and head toward Charlie's back door. I'm two hours later than usual, which make me feel a double measure of guilt. I know Charlie handles the inside dogs when they need to go out, but I'd established a morning routine with them over the past couple of weeks that shouldn't have been broken. Not when Penny's my next training case and she's so far from ready.

I knock on the door, poke my head in, and right when I'm about to call out my usual I'm-walking-into-your-house greeting, I see Charlie standing in front of the stove, cooking eggs and bacon.

Awkwardness and shock cement me in place. "Oh, I'm sorry."

Charlie turns enough to glance at me and then back to his sizzling meat. "Don't be. Come inside."

I step through the doorway and gently close it behind me. "I'll grab Penny and get out of your way."

"No need. I just took her out a little while ago." He pulls the pan from the burner and turns the knob. "Have you eaten yet?"

My stomach growls at the invitation, and I wonder if the food will make me feel better or worse. Going off the cheeseburger last night, I'm hoping for better. "No, I haven't. I'm running a little behind this morning, on everything . . . it seems."

Charlie turns around and leans against the counter. "Bryson told me you may not make it by today. Something about a rough night?" His voice is teasing, but I'm mortified.

"I, um . . ." I have no response.

Charlie may have chuckled, but I can't tell since his beard is so shaggy it covers his lips. "Don't look so stricken. You're not the first person to overindulge in this room."

"I just can't believe he called you." I guess it's true that one bad night can erase a lifetime of responsibility.

"I wouldn't recommend feeding him to the wolves just yet. He didn't say why it was rough, but I've experienced enough hangovers to spot the signs. You look like you've been run over by a semi."

"I feel like I've been run over by one." There's really no point in downplaying the situation when he already knows what happened.

"Well, I have the cure. Grab a couple plates out of the cabinet and we'll get some food in that stomach."

I wash my hands and do as he asks, holding out the plates to Charlie so he can fill them up with eggs, bacon, and two slices of toast. He gestures to the small kitchen table in the corner, and I set both heaping plates down carefully. In minutes we have forks, orange juice, and uncomfortable silence as Charlie says a quick prayer for our food.

The silence continues as I take my first bite of scrambled eggs. "This is really good, thank you."

"You're welcome. I figured I owed you an apology for my continual grumpiness. Nothing says sorry like a plateful of food."

I smile around my bacon. "There's no need to apologize."

"You're a sweet kid for saying so, but I'm long past due telling you how much I appreciate what you've done for the dogs

. . . and for me." His voice goes soft, the grief still audible in every syllable. "Sue Ann would have really liked you."

"I would have liked her, too." Charlie goes back to his silent eating, but I sense there's more he wants to say. I swallow a crispy piece of bacon and hope I'm not crossing an invisible line. "How did you two meet?"

He glances at me, surprised by the question, but then I see it. The relief that follows. He just got permission to talk freely about the person he loves most in this world. "She was a cashier at Tractor Supply, and I went in every week. At that time, I was at the bottom of the barrel you could say. Partying, drinking, hating life and myself. But when I'd see her and her gorgeous, optimistic smile, it would get me through days of self-loathing. Eventually I learned her schedule, and then after two months I got up the nerve to ask her out." He stares off as if reliving the memory. "She said she'd go if I could last one whole month without a drink."

"I take it you succeeded."

He nods. "That day was the last time alcohol touched my lips. She pulled me out of all of it. Helped me find the Lord and all the pieces of myself I'd lost." He stares at the plate in front of him. "It's always tempting to find answers in a bottle, but they don't exist there."

My heart squeezes as shame presses in from his words. I fell into the same trap, only worse because my motivation wasn't grief or addiction. Mine was so much more selfish. I set aside my personal convictions just to prove a point that didn't need to be proven. And look what I have to show for it now—regret and embarrassment. "Is the drinking still a struggle for you?" I ask, mostly because I want to make sure my behavior and the aftermath of it didn't cause Charlie any harm.

He looks at me, his eyes full of sadness. "No. I wouldn't dishonor Sue Ann that way." Relief from his words eases away a little of the guilt. "But I haven't exactly been coping well." He shakes his head. "Turns out answers don't exist in front of a TV screen either, though I've certainly tried to find them the last few months."

"When my mission trip got canceled, I watched TV for eighteen hours straight. In Spanish."

That gets a chuckle out of him, and I'm surprised by how much it warms my chest to see him smile. "Bryson says I need to start returning to my old activities. I know she'd tell me the same thing."

"What were they?"

"Sue Ann and I were pretty active in the community center in town. She liked to dance, and they'd have instructors come once a month."

"That sounds like fun."

"Yeah, it was." He looks at his plate, sorrow crashing down again. "We'd also do archery together and take Macey for long walks each day. Archery stopped when the treatments started, but Sue Ann never missed her daily walks. Even on the worst days, when my poor wife could barely get around, there was something therapeutic about the click of the leash. Sometimes we'd only get as far as the driveway, but it helped her all the same."

I look toward the living room and catch a glimpse of Macey curled in her usual spot. She's getting thinner and thinner.

Charlie must notice where my attention has gone. "You're worried about her, aren't you?"

"I think it's odd that she didn't come over when bacon is on the menu."

"Yeah. I can't seem to get her to do much but lie there these days." He sets his fork down and sighs. "It's probably my fault. Macey was Sue Ann's baby. That dog went with her everywhere. To the store, the post office. She even tried to come with us to the hospital when Sue Ann had her treatments."

"Macey lost a lot when Sue Ann died. Sounds like she's grieving, too."

"We're quite a pair, aren't we?"

I finish off the food, amazed by how much better it makes me feel. "You could maybe take her when you resume some of your activities. Was there something she especially loved to do?"

Charlie leans back in his chair and contemplates my question. "Our neighbor has a dog about her size. They'd play together a lot. But, um, I wasn't the nicest to her when she tried to bring me food after the funeral." He scratches his long, shaggy hair. "But I suppose we could start there."

"I think Macey would really like that. And if you're looking to impress, you could always shave a little before going. Might help the apology if you didn't look like the Unabomber."

Charlie's eyes narrow, but there's a hint of amusement in them. I can almost picture the person he might have been before this tragedy. The guy who mentored an angry young boy. A guy who undoubtedly was instrumental in helping Bryson turn into the man he's become.

I stand and pick up both our plates, unsure if I should suggest the other thing that would help Macey's depression. I decide it's worth it. If Macey continues this way, I shudder to think of the consequences. "There's something else that might help her, but it may be difficult for you." I rinse the dishes and put them in the dishwasher. Charlie hasn't moved or said another word, so I have no idea if I should continue. I don't want to push too hard, not when he's finally getting up and getting dressed.

He stands and brings our empty glasses over. "Can't imagine anything more difficult than what I've already experienced."

I press my lips together to suppress the sudden desire to cry for his broken heart. "Well, if you're willing, I think Macey would greatly benefit from a piece of Sue Ann's clothing. An old shirt of hers, maybe? Something you could part with?"

Charlie grips the edge of the counter as if I've asked for the world. Maybe I have.

"It's just an idea. You don't have to."

"No. It's okay." He leaves the kitchen, and while he's gone, I busy myself in cleaning up the remnants of breakfast. When he still hasn't returned, I check on Penny's food and find my way into the living room, where Macey is curled tight into a ball.

I pet her soft fur. "I know you're sad, sweet girl, but I need you to try to eat, okay?"

"She likes popcorn."

I startle at Charlie's abrupt entrance but work to keep things light. "Butter or kettle corn?"

"Butter. Just like Sue Ann." He comes closer and hands me a dirt-stained white T-shirt. "I haven't been inside her closet since she died. I thought it might kill me to do so, but it was nice. The room still smells like her."

I take the material gently, knowing exactly what a sacrifice it is for him to offer it. "Thank you." Carefully, I press the cotton to Macey's nose. Immediately she jolts to a seated position, her head rearing up. She whines and nudges the shirt with her snout. I lay it at her feet and stand.

She presses her face against the soft cotton, then barks and rolls on top of it like an old companion. I look over at Charlie. His eyes glisten and it shreds a piece of my heart. I open my mouth to offer some kind of comfort or maybe just to thank him again for being so continuously unselfish. But I don't get the chance. Charlie's door is already closing, hiding him once again from the pressing grief that will never fully go away.

TWENTY-ONE

I once read that reliving positive memories from childhood can bring a small measure of peace to those struggling with anxiety, even years later. Tonight, I'm really hoping that theory is true.

I'm in the playground at Grace Community. The old one behind the gym. The one they long ago quit using when the new children's building was built.

What used to be a 1960s hallway with low ceilings and a constant mildew smell is now a 20,000-square-foot, two-story children's wonderland. One that's filled every Sunday. But I miss the days when I knew all the faces that passed me in the halls. I miss my dad making my brother and me sit with them instead of our friends. But most of all, I miss feeling safe like I always did when I came to this building. Cameron says I'm the worst when it comes to change. That people like me keep the world from progressing. Maybe he's right. Change has never been a friend of mine.

Even when I'm the one forcing it.

My phone reads 5:45 p.m., and Sunday night dinner starts at 6:00. This will be the first one I've ever intentionally missed, except for a handful while I was away at college. But even then I'd make it as often as I could. Never have I been in town and not gone. Never.

Each minute drags on like an hour: 5:47 . . . 5:48. If it could just get past the six o'clock mark, then maybe this wrenching in my gut would finally go away.

I set my phone facedown in my lap and continue my rhythmic swinging, racking my brain for any kind of distraction. Cam is working until eight tonight, and I've already exhausted all my other time wasters. The only things left are the two things I'm avoiding: apologizing to Bryson and answering my mom's umpteenth text today.

I kick at the dirt, my stomach taking a somersaulted leap at the thought of dialing Bryson's number. Then again, time is only going to make the humiliation worse, so I may as well do it now and put the final nail in the coffin marked "rebellion."

My thumb slides across the glass, and I take one stabilizing breath before pressing his number.

"Hey." The answer is short and more direct than I expect.

"Hey, I um . . ." I scramble to find any common ground that doesn't include the night before. "I wanted to talk to you about Charlie."

"Really?" His voice dips like he knows I'm stalling.

"Yeah. He made some progress today. I just thought you should know so you could go by there tomorrow. Make sure he actually gets out of the house like he said he might."

"I will, thanks." He's quiet for a second. "Is that all?"

"Yes . . . I mean, no." I squeeze my eyes shut, the embarrassment of the night before coming back in full color. "I'm sorry . . . about last night."

He sighs into the phone. "It's really okay." His voice is different now. As if he needed to know that I knew I'd treated him poorly. It's ironic. A few weeks ago, I accused Bryson of using people and yet I'm the one who did that very thing to him. "How are you feeling?"

"Better. And you should know that my little drinking experiment is over. I will be shelving the lemon drops for an indefinite period of time."

He chuckles. "Good."

I press my toes into the ground and push the swing backward.

"Darcy, you okay?"

"Yeah, just thinking, I guess."

"About?"

"Life, family, Sunday night dinners, or in my case, skipping Sunday night dinners since my last one did not go so well."

He's quiet, and I wonder again why all my secrets seem to spill out to him. "Could that be part of the reason you went a little heavy-handed last night?"

I shouldn't be surprised anymore by this new profound version of him, but I still am. "Probably."

The line goes silent, but it doesn't feel awkward or tense. It feels like he's giving me time to reason through my feelings. And maybe that's why I want to share them. Why even though I made the excuse that Cam was working, the truth is that he has never once not taken my call when I needed him, so it was never about availability. I didn't want Cam tonight. I wanted Bryson.

"Do you want to hear something ridiculous?" I ask, twisting the swing until the chains cross, then uncross.

"Sure."

"I've been sitting in front of Grace Community for an hour now. Just sitting here in that old playground where we'd tag each other and run around until our parents made us pack it up and go home." I bite my lip and feel a sting in my throat.

"My life is so screwed up right now that I've come to a point where the only thing I recognize anymore is an old swing set and our youth building." I shake away the looming sadness and think back to all the days and nights I'd spent here. "Do you ever miss high school?"

That gets a snort. "No."

"Really? I do sometimes."

I hear a dinging sound and then a car door slamming. "What is there to miss? On top of not having any control over our lives, we had to deal with acne and insecurity and school-work."

"True, but we also had youth group every Wednesday night to connect with friends and feel empowered about our future."

"I think you have a selective memory. If I recall, you hated high school even more than I did."

"I guess. Maybe I just miss feeling a part of something." I look at the structure in front of me. Inside is a full-sized basketball court, several Bible study classrooms, and an entire section of the building set aside for junior high and high schoolers. And thankfully, other than a new paint job to match the worship center, the building has stayed relatively untouched. "After all this time, this place still makes me feel safe. I'd love to go hang out in the Shop just one more time." The Shop was our nickname for the youth room back when I was in school.

"They have foosball and a pool table in there now. A stage, too, with a seventy-inch screen and about a thousand digital movies and games."

"What? We so got the shaft when we were kids." The best thing we had back then was a slanted Ping-Pong table and an old Xbox. A rumbling engine echoes through the air. "Oh, hold on. I think someone's coming." I stand from the swing and watch as Bryson's unmistakable black beast turns the corner.

He parks the truck and emerges, still holding the cell-phone up to his ear. "I thought you might want some company on your trip down memory lane."

I end the call and take a shaky step toward the fence that separates us. Images of last night fill my mind. His strong arms holding me steady up the stairs, my fingers sliding over his skin, the way his body heat rose with every inch I explored. "You got here fast," I squeak out, mortified by my own thoughts.

"I was in the neighborhood. Wanna go inside?" His lips tilt up into an endearing smile. It's sexy and daring and adorable all at the same time.

"I don't think breaking and entering a church is the best way to prove I'm back on the straight and narrow."

"It's not breaking and entering when you have a key."

I look at him through suspicious eyes, knowing there has to be some kind of catch. "How do you have a key?"

"Are you kidding me? I'm beloved around here."

I snort out a laugh. Our youth pastor couldn't stand Bryson or the obnoxious chip on his shoulder. The feeling was mutual, and Bryson quit coming here the minute we graduated. I assumed he quit church altogether until I saw him watching the service online with Charlie. "Seriously, where did you get the key?"

"Mr. Berny gave it to me. Though he'd probably deny it if you asked him." Mr. Berny has been the church's custodian for almost twenty years now. "The night my stepdad kicked me out, I drove straight here. I figured if I had to sleep in my car, at least it would be somewhere I knew was well lit." He leads me between two of the buildings and down a hidden sidewalk. "Mr. Berny tapped on my window at five-thirty the next morning. He took one look at all my things stuffed in the back and told me to get up and use the bathrooms before anyone got here. I later found this key in my duffel bag." Bryson pulls silver metal from his back pocket. "For a week, I'd wait until all the staff went home, then let myself in to shower and crash on one of the Shop couches."

I feel relieved to know Bryson didn't spend a week in his truck, though it pierces my heart to imagine him sneaking inside the building just to use the bathroom.

He slides the key into the lock and pushes the door open. "Voilà!"

"You're telling me that they haven't changed the locks on this building in over a decade?"

"Nope. Only the security code." He mashes four buttons on the keypad by the door. "But I have friends in important places, so I know that, too."

Bryson closes the door behind us and turns on the lights down the hall and into the old youth room.

I walk ahead of him, eager, terrified, excited, and enter the room that consumed most of my teenage years. They've painted it all black. The walls, the floors, the stage. A collage of old records covers an entire wall, giving it a retro vibe I admittedly kind of like.

Bryson settles next to me and rests his forearm on the doorframe. "It's pretty cool, huh?"

"Of course *you'd* like it. It's your signature color."

He grins and slides into the room. "You're just jealous that a generation half my age wants to be like me." He winks, smug and arrogant, and darn if it doesn't make me swoon just a little. He tosses the foosball into the air and catches it. "You up for a game?"

"Heck yeah. But a warning . . . I can be ruthless."

"Can you?"

"Yep. Cam found this old game store in college. They'd let you pay a cover and then play board games, pool, and foosball all night long." I take a spot on the other side of the table. "You have no idea how many free dinners I got that month."

Bryson's smile falters. "Only a month, huh?"

"Yeah. Cam's the worst at strategy and doesn't have the best attention span, so his desire to keep getting beat waned pretty fast." I drop the ball through the serve feed and quickly try to match Bryson's movements. "We later found this coffee shop that had open-mic nights. That became our go-to." I move my goalie a half inch too far to the right, and the ball rushes past into the goal. "Dang it." I look up and see Bryson smirking at me.

"You said the wager is dinner, right?"

"Not if you keep slamming in goals." I slide the ball in again, determined to talk less this time and pay more attention. I focus and spin, move, spin again, and barely get past his goalie for a score. "Yes!" I hop up and down, fully embracing my inner teen.

"You willing to wager dinner now?" There's challenge in his eyes, and I instinctively know it's about more than this simple game. Yet at the same time I find myself wanting to play along. Really just wanting to do anything that feels as good as I always seem to feel lately when Bryson's around.

"Now . . . you're on."

We go back and forth, each taking turns scoring on the other, until Bryson makes a play that challenges all rules of physics and scores.

"No way!" I scream, staring at the winning point sitting in my goal. "That was an impossible shot."

He lifts both arms above his head in victory. "The impossible is what I do."

I pick up the ball and throw it softly at his chest.

"Ouch." He rubs playfully at the spot. "Talk about a sore loser."

"Oh please. I didn't throw it that hard." I lean over and pick up the ball from the floor. "So what's next? Pool? Ping-Pong? You have to give me a chance to redeem myself."

"I think we need some music first." Bryson's mood has changed, much like mine has in the last twenty minutes. He's energetic, funny, and a version of himself I didn't even know existed. "What are you in the mood for?" He connects his Bluetooth to the sound system receiver and scrolls through his playlists. "I have just about every genre you could possibly want."

I glance at the stage, where an acoustic guitar sits ready for just this moment. "Why don't you play that song you've been working on? The one Bentley liked so much."

Insecurity is an odd look for Bryson, but it's etched all over his face with that request. As if I'm not just asking him to play a song, but inviting myself into his life, his hurts, and past that shield of armor he's carried so proudly since we were kids.

"I still don't have any lyrics."

"So? It's beautiful, even without all that."

He hesitates, then concedes, though his gait around the sound booth looks more like a man about to face a firing squad, not play for an eager fan.

I pull a chair close and watch as Bryson slides the guitar strap over his torso and sits on one of the stage stools. He checks the tuning and, when satisfied, begins his first strum.

Strings fill the room, enveloping me with the rich sound. He changes chords, speeds up, then slows again, all while humming in that dark, silky voice of his. Then he moves to a new part, one he hadn't written the last time I heard him play, and my heart seizes at the agony of the sound. It's not angry like so many of his other songs. It's pain, real and authentic. It's a place one only finds after the rage is gone.

He hits the side of the guitar, then strums, creating a tempo that's unique and hypnotic. And then it settles back into rich, lengthy chords. If peace were a song, this last part is what it would sound like. He slows as it ends, pulling me along, tearing away any defenses I may have left. And then the room goes silent.

Bryson runs a hand through his hair and smiles tentatively at me.

"That was . . . incredible." More than incredible. It's a completely new sound for him. "Have you written more like this one?"

He shrugs. "Ballads don't make rock stars."

I think back to the night before. The energy and spark and sheer violence that came pouring off that stage and know he's right. Still, it seems like a waste that his song may never be heard by anyone but me.

"What's it feel like?"

He sets the guitar back in its stand. "What do you mean?"

"To be onstage. To have the whole crowd screaming at you like they did."

"Want me to show you?" He stands and waves for me to come forward.

I glance around the room, confused. "How can you show me without people?"

"Come here and you'll see." There's that spark in his voice

208

again. That edge between daring me to step out of my comfort zone and a certainty that I won't.

I hop up onstage, more for myself than to prove something to him. "Okay. I'm here."

He smirks and gently clasps my arms, turning me until we both face the empty chairs throughout the room. My breath catches when I feel him press into my back. "Close your eyes."

I do as he says, trying to steel my rising pulse. Music begins playing around me, pouring from every hidden speaker, quietly at first and then louder, until I'm sure he's turned his phone all the way up. "Let everything else out of your head and feel the music."

Maybe it's the darkness my closed lids have created or the way his chest vibrates against my back, but Bryson suddenly turns into that captivating man onstage. Confident, demanding, and so incredibly hypnotic that I can barely breathe.

"Let the chords dance over your skin." The tip of his nose brushes against the side of my cheek. Intentional, unintentional, I don't know, but I melt into his body, our shared heat penetrating through the thin material of my shorts. His fingers skim my skin, and it's such a sensational tickling that I begin to wonder if it's the music making my body hum or just the tender way his body has melded into mine, like he wants to experience every sensation I'm feeling.

"Feed off the drums, the beat slamming against your chest." Bryson angles his head, his mouth so close to my earlobe that his lips graze the sensitive skin as he speaks. Pleasing goose bumps form along my neck as his breath dances against the surface. "Now picture the crowd. Imagine that pulse of energy that soars from them to us and fills the air with power so intoxicating, it drives out exhaustion, hunger,

209

thirst, whatever, and makes you just want to play until your fingers bleed."

I suddenly feel the same way about Bryson's breath on my skin. I want more contact. Want his arms to wrap around me and his lips to graze my jawline.

And then he stops talking but doesn't let go. I breathe in when he does, out at the same time. I don't know how long we stay there, it can only be seconds, but I feel as if we're journeying to an alternate universe where Bryson and I together might actually make sense.

He backs away, and my body suddenly turns cold.

I spin around, feeling like I've somersaulted into a world I've never seen in real color. "Wow."

"I know. It's addicting . . ." He glances at the floor and back up again, this time with a smile that's soft enough to send an army of tingles down my spine. "It's like an escape from every part of the world, including my own head."

"Well, you're lucky. I've spent the last month trying to find something that can get me that kind of escape, and being inside the Shop tonight is the first time I've even come close."

"Why do you think that is?"

I fiddle with the microphone cord. "Because it reminds me of life before the divorce. Before my dad abandoned our family. Before my mom started dating. All of that." My voice thickens with the anger that always seems to come when I think of my father and the bomb he detonated in my life. "That probably sounds really dumb coming from someone my age."

"Not at all. I have a place just like that. On the hard weeks, I go out there more often than I care to admit." He glances at the walls, the ceiling, and the couch that looks very similar to the one we had when we were in high school, and then back at me. "It makes sense that Grace Community would bring you peace. You always did fit here."

He says it like he didn't, and I guess I can see why he would feel that way. Bryson has a way about him that makes you want to know the deepest parts and yet feel certain he'll never share them with you. It makes it easier not to try. I know. I didn't bother for most of our lives, but that's not the case anymore. "Is your place nearby?"

"Somewhat. Why?"

I shrug. "I don't have anywhere to be right now, and if you don't either, I thought maybe you could take me there."

Hesitation comes again, along with the same insecurity he showed when I asked him to play for me. "It's nothing special."

I doubt that. If it wasn't important, he wouldn't look so afraid. "If you're willing to show me, I'd really like to go."

He comes closer, but there's restraint in his movement. A stiffness in his stride. A holding back. "Why?"

"Because it's important to you, which makes it important to me." I glance down at his hand. The same one I held the night before. I look back up at him and wait to see if he'll open up or if he'll bolt like he did the last time we shared a moment of intimacy.

Of course, last time I was drunk, and he was being a gentleman. This time I'm one-hundred-percent sober.

"You should know something about me." His eyes burn into mine and I see a hundred questions behind them. "I don't easily let people in."

"Tell me something I don't already know." I smirk, trying to clear the heaviness that's fallen between us.

Bryson will have none of it. "I'm serious here." He rakes back his hair, hesitating. I know with that small movement he's struggling to give me what I'm asking. "I'm an all-or-nothing guy, Darcy. I can't exist on the surface. I'm not programmed that way."

"I understand."

"Do you? Because if we take this step. If *I* take this step with you, everything's going to change. There are some doors that don't close again once they're opened."

My heart does the same fluttering it seems to do more and more when in Bryson's presence. Heat creeps up my neck and flushes my face. I don't know what he's asking of me, but I know I want to say yes, especially if behind that door is the man I'm only just starting to really see.

TWENTY-TWO

When Bryson admitted to having a special place, I was certain it would be something related to music. Never would I have guessed that it would be a baseball complex.

Bryson parks his truck, and I pull in right next to him and cut the engine. The parking lot that can easily hold two hundred cars is empty, and the sun is beginning its slow descent to the horizon. I exit my truck and wait for Bryson to meet me on the sidewalk. He seems rooted in place, and I wonder if maybe I asked too much of him this time.

Finally, his door creaks open and his leg appears. He's obviously in no rush to start this tour, as it takes three times the normal length to completely emerge from the vehicle.

"You play baseball?"

He shifts on his feet, glancing down for a moment. "I did . . . a long time ago."

We walk side by side up the long sidewalk separating two different baseball fields. A concession shack waits at the end, its window covered in wood and locked tight. There are remnants of an active Saturday in and around the trash cans, but not a soul lingers now. It would feel eerie if not for Bryson

213

next to me, and I find myself inching closer as we get deeper into the heart of the complex.

He still hasn't said anything, and I don't know if I'm supposed to fill the silence or let him think. The whole experience seems to be new for both of us.

"This is it," he says when we reach the farthest field. It's smaller than the others, the bases closer. He walks through the nearest dugout and onto the field, me close behind. "I played here when I was six." He takes a deep breath, inhaling the air around us. "Even now, the smell of the clay dirt and that touch of hot breeze on my neck brings me back to that spring." He glances my way and smiles. "It's the last time in my life that I remember feeling completely secure."

I picture him as a little boy in tiny cleats and a baseball cap, his dark curly hair poking out under the brim. "What position did you play?"

"Dirt digger." He laughs out of nowhere and grabs my hand. "Come on, I'll show you."

I have to jog to keep up with him, until we're standing on the right side of the field where the dirt gives way to a big stretch of grass that, upon closer inspection, is mostly weeds and the kind of stickers that will cling to your socks and never let go.

"This is what I'd do, every game." He squats down and runs his fingers through the hardened red soil.

"What happened if a ball came your way?"

"It never did. Kids from all over the field would descend on the ball like ants on a jelly bean. There wasn't any point in trying to be one of the many." He stands and slaps his hands together to brush off the dirt. "Honestly, I thought the game was pretty boring."

"If you didn't like playing, why is this your favorite place?"

"Same reason you like to sit in the playground at Grace Community. The field reminds me of before. Before my step-dad came around, before I was old enough to realize I was never going to have a father." He stares off toward the dugout and words fade into silence. I see the struggle, his search for the apathy he's always painted on his face. It's beyond his grasp now. "I had the best coach." His voice turns soft, nostalgic. "Coach Tucker, but we all called him Tuck."

I step closer and gently touch his back. "Tell me about him."

A tortured smile pulls at his lips. "He was kind and chubby. I remember because my mom has always been super thin, and when he'd pick me up, it'd feel completely different, like being held by pillows." He turns and my hand falls away. "He was in love with my mom, poor guy."

"She didn't love him back?"

He shakes his head. "Nope, but that didn't keep her from leading him on. She liked being adored, and he certainly adored her and me." His voice catches, and the same anger that flows through each of his songs wraps around every word. "Until Charlie, he was the only example of a father I'd ever known, and she shattered his heart."

"What happened?"

"She met my stepdad." He pauses, a deep breath filling his chest, his nostrils flaring. "And because she didn't want to ruin their budding relationship by having me tag along, she kept me a secret and used Tuck as a fill-in babysitter whenever she'd have a date. Only she didn't call it a date. Mom told Tuck she'd decided to go back to school, so he was very understanding whenever she needed to study."

I flinch at the cruelty. "That's terrible."

"She's a shrewd woman, my mom. And now that I know

215

my stepdad like I do, she was probably right to keep me a secret. He would never have willingly raised another man's child." I hear the disgust in his voice and feel equally sickened. "Meanwhile, Tuck and I got closer and closer. He even brought me to pick out the ring. We both thought we were one yes away from being a family."

I cross my arms against my chest, my heart squeezing as if it can already feel the heartbreak that's coming in this story.

"He asked her to marry him on a Friday night. By Sunday, Tuck was out of our lives and I was meeting the man who stole my mom away. A man who only stuck around because Mom was already pregnant with Zoe." Bryson sighs. "I guess in some ways, the two of us never had a chance. From the very beginning, we both resented the other's existence." His voice catches, and the pain in it makes me want to wrap my arms around him and kiss away all the hurts he's ever suffered.

But I tried that once, and his stiff rejection made it clear he didn't want my comfort or pity, at least not in that way. I think of the foosball game and how cathartic it was to detach from the sorrow, even if just for a few minutes. Maybe that's exactly what he needs right now.

"You know what I liked to do as a kid?" I step backward until I'm out of the dirt and on the grassy area. I find a spot somewhat free of pokey weeds and plop down like a toddler. "On summer days, I'd pick a comfy spot, spread out my arms, and use the clouds to tell a story." Slowly I lie back, ignoring the sharpness underneath me or the way my ponytail snags on the tiny plants. "See, there's a knight holding his sword high above his head."

I hear the crunch of Bryson's steps and then feel the heat of his body as he lies next to mine. I resist turning to look at him, too afraid of what the closeness might do to my already elevated nerves.

I point to the spot in the sky where the pink clouds form a blob with a long streak. "Do you see it?"

He chuckles. "Not even a little."

"What? It's right there." I point again, and this time he takes my hand and laces our fingers together. It feels important, like our worlds are uniting in this moment. I ignore the surge of adrenaline and continue. "And look, there is his castle." He pulls until I'm forced on my side, facing him. "You don't like this game?" I ask, my voice shaky.

"I didn't bring you out here so we could pretend to be kids again." He leans up on his elbow, his other hand still entangled in mine. "I brought you out here because I thought you wanted what I do . . . for us to finally be honest with each other."

"Okay . . ." I search his eyes, my voice as unsteady as my heart suddenly feels. "You go first."

"I find your confidence staggering." He releases my fingers, but only to reach out and pick two stickers out of my hair. "The way you go through life is so genuine. From your effortless ponytails to your casual clothes to the crazy things you do without a thought to who's watching. It's why last night bothered me so much. It was the first time you didn't feel like you." His hand falls slowly and lands on the soft skin inside my wrist. "I spent my entire life suffocating under the image my mom and stepdad had for our family. It didn't matter what was true, only what people saw." His touch continues down to my palm. "But with you, I never have to wonder what's real and what's not."

He pauses, and I know it's my turn to reciprocate, to give him back the honesty he just gave me.

"I truly admire the man you've become."

His brow creases. "You do?"

"Yeah. You've overcome so much. Even your story tonight. It wasn't laced with grief like you're still living in it." I search his eyes and know he's done the impossible. "It didn't make sense before, but I see it now. Your willingness to go to Thanksgiving, your song, even your advice to me the other day. You've forgiven them."

"Well, it's more a work in progress."

"I understand. Every time I think of my dad or pull up his contact on my phone or ignore his weekly attempts at reconciliation, all I feel is this gut-piercing rage that refuses to go away." He opens his mouth, but I quickly beat him to it. "Nope. I don't want to talk about him. Not right now." I inch closer. "I just wanted you to know that I recognize the battle you've faced, and even more, how you're winning."

His eyes darken the way they always seem to when emotion hits him. "Sue Ann's death was the turning point. That's when everything spun upside down, and all the stuff that seemed so important at the time became insignificant. Suddenly, relationships mattered, and the people I'd all but let go of became a pressing thorn of regret in my side."

I nod in understanding. "Grief can certainly make you question everything."

"And sometimes it's exactly what you need to finally go after what you've always wanted."

I think of the band and how hard Bryson worked to get Cameron to join. "Black Carousel," I say, disappointed for some reason.

"No, Darcy. For the first time in years, I couldn't care less about what happens to the band." His fingers blaze a trail up my arm, his eyes never leaving mine. "But I care a great deal about what happens to you." There's a pause as if he's deciding how honest he wants to be. "When you told me you were moving in with Cam, it made me so nauseous, I thought I might lose it, right there on the swing next to you. I tracked Zoe down that night and refused to leave until she said yes. I wasn't kidding when I said I was selfish, Darcy. I didn't want you living with another man. Even one you claim is only a friend."

My heart slams against my chest, the air between us crackling as if lightning were about to strike us both for daring to say these things out loud. "In the spirit of honesty . . . I *was* jealous last night when that girl came up to you, and then again when I thought about you bringing groupies backstage."

He grins, slow and sexy. "You have no reason to ever feel jealous."

I lick my lips since they've suddenly gone completely dry. "Why's that?"

His hand moves across my shoulder and cradles my head, his fingers burying deep into my mess of a ponytail. "Because . . . when I was nine years old, I met the most beautiful girl I'd ever seen in my life." He closes the last of the space between us, his breath a whisper against my cheek. "And twenty years later, I'm still completely mesmerized by her."

His touch is gentle at first, a soft brush of lips against mine. The type of kiss you give when unsure if the other person wants the same thing.

I don't let him wonder for long, responding with my own pressure, deeper and more demanding. Sparks sizzle in the air, and my pulse races as each inch between us becomes an inferno of emotion and desire.

He eases his body over mine, slow and gentle, his hand and forearm taking the full brunt of the ground. I knot my fingers in his hair, pull him closer until I'm trapped beneath his weight, my skin so charged with want that I finally understand why every romantic kiss in a movie comes with music and fireworks.

The kiss slows, Bryson taking us back to the original pace. His long, artistic fingers caress my temple as the space between us grows and grows until he hovers over me, waiting for a response.

My breath is suddenly trapped in my chest. What do you say after kissing a guy you've known for twenty years? That was great, thank you?

He studies me, his eyes traveling over every inch of my face, his gaze apprehensive.

I wiggle free until I can sit up, my throat closing around my sudden uncertainty.

Bryson notices the retreat, his mouth growing tighter as I put more space between us. "Are you okay?"

"Yeah." But even I'm not convinced it's true, especially since my legs feel wobbly as I stand. I check my pockets. My phone is missing, and my car key has almost freed itself from my pocket. I shove it down and look over the ground for my lime-green phone case.

"It's right here."

I spin around, my breath matching the erratic feelings I can't seem to compartmentalize. "Oh, thanks." But as I go to reach for the device, Bryson pulls it back and forces eye contact instead.

"What's going on in your head?"

I shouldn't be surprised by his directness. He's been exactly that since the moment he sat next to me on the swing and upended my personal life. I take the phone, my mind tumbling, and slide it in my pocket. "I'm nervous, I guess."

"Why?"

"Because I don't have any experience with this type of thing. And you're . . . well, you're you."

Silence vibrates between us as hurt spreads across his brow.

"And you're you," he says slowly, carefully. "The girl who's always been off-limits, the girl who never once noticed me until your life fell apart." The tremble of fear in his voice slays me. He reaches up and caresses my cheek. "That doesn't exactly leave me with a lot of security either."

I don't move. I'm not sure I'm even breathing. Zoe had been right. I'd missed everything. "I never knew you felt this way."

"Like I said, I don't let people in very easily."

I stare into his beautiful, waiting eyes, the enormity of his admission pressing against my chest. "I would never hurt you."

"I know you wouldn't on purpose." He presses his forehead into my neck, runs a trail of delightful kisses to my ear. "Which is why I'm willing to risk being vulnerable, if you are."

I sigh, closing my eyes, lost in the wonderful sensations he's creating. "Oh . . . I'm definitely willing."

"I'm very happy to hear that," he whispers, moving to the underside of my jaw.

I giggle at the way it tickles and pull away. "Easy, tiger. Too much of that and we'll be back on the ground."

Creases deepen around his eyes. "You don't hear me complaining."

"Well, my stomach might pretty soon." I back away, unable to stop the perpetual smile on my face. "Last I checked, there was a dinner wager."

He swings his arm around my shoulder and pulls me tight

against his side, leaning down to kiss me one more time before we start our trek back to the cars. "Yes, and if I recall, you lost, which means I get to pick the place."

I pause, realizing I have no idea what Bryson's favorite restaurant is or even what type of food he likes. The thought warms my insides even more than his kiss did. It's nice that there are still some mysteries there. Ones I'm truly looking forward to discovering.

TWENTY-THREE

*I*n all the years I've known Bryson, I've never once seen him be affectionate, not even with his girlfriends. Yet in the past five days we've spent together, he hasn't gone one minute without holding my hand or finding some way for the two of us to be touching.

Even now, while I'm wet with perspiration, trying to get Penny to listen, his fingers graze the tips of my pulled-back hair.

"What is the point of this again?" he asks, his hand sliding lazily across my back.

We're both standing outside of Bentley's old kennel, watching Penny trot around with a tennis ball in her mouth.

I sigh, frustrated, not with him but with Penny's stubbornness. "She needs a job. Something that makes her feel useful so that we can redirect her aggressive energy into something positive."

"I think she'd rather just chew on the ball." He leans his forearms on the top of the kennel, the wire bowing slightly under the weight. His tattoo peeks out when his shirtsleeve rides up, and without thinking I drag my fingertips across his skin.

"Why did you get this?"

"To tick off my stepfather."

I push his sleeve until it stays tightly around his shoulder. "I'm serious."

"So am I." He grunts a laugh, his hazel eyes teasing me. "And if you keep touching me like that, I'm going to have to break your 'no making out in front of Charlie' rule."

I glance toward the house and confirm he's not around. "Why won't you tell me what it means?"

His muscles tense, which is how I know he's not being totally honest. Bryson's tells have become clearer since that first day on the swing together. When he's angry or upset, he distances physically and uses sarcasm or arrogant comments to force even more separation. But when it's deeper, when he's hurt or threatened, his entire body locks up. It's as if he creates a cocoon around himself to protect from oncoming blows.

"It's okay if you don't want to talk about it."

"It's hard to admit weakness." His struggle for words cuts a hole through me. He lifts his arm and stares at the ring of barbwire that has no beginning or end. "I got it a month after he gave me my truck. A reminder that I sold out. That like my mom and sister, I let him own me."

"I thought you loved that truck."

"I hate that truck and everything it represents."

"Then why keep it all this time?" And not just keep it. In just the short time we've been close, I've seen how much energy and money he's poured into it, just to ensure it stays running.

"Because it's also the last thing I have that connects me to them." He stares off toward the driveway, where the truck in question sits. "How's that for screwed up?"

I scoot closer and softly press my lips to his marked skin. "You're not screwed up." I don't have the words to tell him how strong I think he is, or how much I love seeing the tenderness of the sweet little boy I knew peek through the hardened shell he's formed.

Bryson reaches out and touches my hand. His fingers slowly slide up my arm to my neck and his thumb traces a slow, lazy circle over my collarbone. Then it's an invasion of my personal space, every part of him connecting to every part of me. Hot embers burn in my chest. I inhale the scent of him, one I'm starting to crave more and more.

"You're so beautiful." His lips brush against my eyelids, his voice tender.

"I'm a sweaty mess." I duck my chin, wondering when this feeling of light-headedness that he seems to bring out in me will go away.

"You're beautiful," he says more emphatically this time. "You always have been, but lately it's gut-wrenching how much I want to be near you."

He bends over and his lips meet mine, soft, loving, and I shiver beneath their touch.

"You're trembling." A crease deepens between his brows. "Did I admit too much?"

"No." I gently finger the hair at his temples, reassuring him. "I'm just trying to reconcile who you are with who I've always known you to be. You're so different. Or, I don't know, maybe you're not and I'm just finally seeing who you always have been."

"I'm no saint, if that's what you're implying." He grins mischievously, and my knees turn to water. "But I am happy, Darcy. For maybe the first time in my entire life, I feel completely . . . content. That alone will change a person."

A growl comes from our feet, and I reluctantly look away from Bryson to see what Penny is complaining about. The ball she'd been gnawing on is a completely mangled mess at her feet.

I untangle my arms from his embrace and stare at the shredded green material on the ground. "If you think I'm just going to get you another one to destroy, you're delusional."

Bryson scowls at the stubborn terrier. "I think you're the one who's delusional. That dog is never going to listen to you. She's too far gone."

"Don't be a hater." I throw him a glare that makes him laugh instead of cower. "Penny's smart. She'll learn."

"If you say so. I for one am going back inside where it's air conditioned." He slides his hands around my cheeks and kisses me deeply before letting go. "Join me when you're done beating your head against the wall." He winks when I push him away, my grin practically schoolgirl silly. He walks backward, never taking his eyes off me, until finally he reaches the steps and disappears through Charlie's door.

I watch the empty space, longer than I should, before turning back to my task. Any residual giddiness fades the minute I see Penny lying down with a new ball in her mouth. "Okay, it's time to get serious." I unlatch the gate and join the little dog inside the kennel. "No more fooling around."

Immediately she growls, a warning that I better not try to take her toy away. Not to worry, I need her to *want* to do this. Forcing her is only going to spark more aggravation. Mimicking what I want her to do, I jog to the shallow barrel on the far side of the kennel, pick up one of the tennis balls, and jog back to the gate to drop it into the empty identical barrel. I hold up the treat. "Now it's your turn."

She drops the ball in her mouth, eager to get a bite, but I

pull it back. "Nope, come get the ball first." Once again, I jog toward the full barrel, this time with Penny at my heels. No surprise, she's got this part down. It's the letting go she's not so good at.

"Good girl." I give her a small reward and point to the waiting pile of tennis balls.

She grabs one in her mouth and we both jog back to the barrel. Like before, Penny runs around the metal pot but refuses to drop the ball inside.

I motion for her again, wave the treat, and coax her forward. Nothing. In fact, I think she's laughing at me. "Ugh!" I growl up at the sky and lace my hands behind my neck.

Penny's fur rises on her neck, and I know I need to calm down before I do more damage than good.

"Tell you what, let's take a break, and you can chew all you want." I pick up the end of her leash and tie it to the fence. The spaces between slats are small, but if she really wanted to escape, she could easily push herself between them.

I lock the gate behind me and head to the water hose. It's ninety-five and climbing, and I want nothing more than to douse myself with a bucketful of water. For now, though, I'll settle for a good hands-and-face washing.

A bark stops me mid-step. I turn toward the only dog capable of making that kind of noise. Louie's out of his doghouse and standing by the gate, staring at me.

"Well, look who finally decided to make an appearance." I glance at Charlie's house and then back to Louie. Makes sense that he waited until we were alone to appear. It's not that he doesn't like Bryson, but he certainly doesn't share my same level of trust.

I abandon my trek to the hose and let myself into Louie's cage. "You smell those treats, don't you?"

He dances around and then eagerly sits the second I fasten his gate. "Wow. Look at you, Mr. Smarty-Pants." I reward him with a chunky morsel, only having to remind him once to take it gently from my hands.

He finishes chewing and sits again, closer this time.

"You're going to have to do more than sit for a second one." I carefully reach out and wait to see if he pulls away. He remains still, his ears relaxed, so I inch close enough that my fingers graze the soft skin on his snout. "Good boy," I whisper, careful that nothing I do is jarring in any way. I run my hand along his head and down the back to his neck.

Louie whimpers and leans his head into my hand like my touch is the most remarkable feeling in the world. My throat aches as I move closer, using my other hand to scratch behind his ear and down to the white patch of hair on his chest.

His back paw moves like Thumper, matching my scratches. "Oh, you like that spot, don't you?" My voice is caught between a laugh and a cry.

I squat in front of him, and Louie pushes my head with his nose, a fight for dominance, as well as his own try at reciprocating the affection. I lift my chin, keeping my head higher than his, all while eagerly scratching down his side.

My back pocket belts out a song that makes Louie freeze and look around as if he's missed something.

"Easy, boy," I say, standing upright again. "It's just my phone." I pull out the device and sigh at the name on my screen. Cam's calling me again. It's the third time today, but it felt weird to answer it earlier when Bryson was standing over my shoulder. Louie sniffs the metal, the continuing vibration making him bark emphatically. "Hey," I half say, half laugh into the phone.

"Well, it's about time. I was beginning to think you were abducted."

Louie pushes his nose into my stomach, obviously wanting more scratches. I oblige with my free hand.

"Sorry. I've been busy this week with Penny."

"I think you love those dogs more than me."

"Well, they do obey . . . sort of. And believe it or not, I'm currently petting one not-so-freaked-out Great Dane."

"Louie let you touch him?"

"Yep. First time ever."

Cam's voice hitches. "See, now we have two reasons to celebrate."

"What's the other one?"

"Have you not listened to any of my voicemails?"

"No. I'm sorry." I sigh, guilt rolling in for some reason. The last five days have been such a beautiful cocoon of Bryson that I haven't even thought of Cameron.

"We got a second gig with Firesight, and this time their label is coming to watch and consider us for their new tour." His giddiness is palpable. "If we impress, we'll be opening for them in twenty cities across the U.S."

"Cam, that's . . ." I don't know what to say. I'm beyond happy for him, but it also means a second tour. One even longer than the last one. "How did all this happen so fast?" I glance at Charlie's house, the real question filtering through my mind. *Why didn't Bryson tell me?*

"You remember their guitarist, Jax, the one who commented on my solo? Well, we met up after their set and played till three in the morning, just messing around. Darcy, he's the first person I've ever met who sees the music the way I do. Oh, and his girlfriend is amazing. You'll love her, and she's thrilled there's another girl around. Promise me you'll come hang with us next time. The whole band is really down to earth."

I listen silently, methodically petting Louie's head. "Sounds like you two hit it off."

"More than that. Jax wants us, and he's convinced this tour, with our combined talent, will make us both household names. I told him we were in, but you know how that goes. Promises mean nothing in the music industry. Plus, Bryson has been so weird about the band lately. Refusing to set up another tour and turning down two gigs just because they were a couple of hours away. Honestly, I half expected him to say no." His clipped tone highlights his frustration but the edge fades quickly. "By some miracle, it all worked out. Just like Jax promised. The contract for the opening set was signed this morning. Which means you and I are going to dress up and splurge on a swanky steak restaurant in Dallas."

"Are we?" I work to sound as excited as he is. "And when exactly is this outing supposed to happen?"

"Tonight. I'll pick you up at seven." He sighs like he's still in shock. "It's so surreal. I'm three weeks away from all my dreams coming true."

"I'm really happy for you, Cameron."

"For us, Darcy. I wouldn't be here without you." His voice turns soft. "I'd all but given up. And I would have if you hadn't been there cheering me on, reminding me why I'm sacrificing so much. You're my rock."

"You're mine too."

He's quiet for a second. "I hope so. More than ever, I feel like we need to take advantage of this time. Like something big is about to happen."

"Sounds like it already has."

"Yeah, I guess you're right." He laughs like a man who won the lottery and doesn't quite believe it. "So, seven?"

"Seven. I'll see you then." We say our goodbyes, and I slide my phone back in my pocket, my mind in a daze.

Three weeks. And then what?

Insecurity flares where it's never been before. Bryson admitted to dating Alison because he was going on tour and didn't want to be alone. And yeah, he regretted it, but that doesn't mean he's not prone to making the same mistake again.

I immediately shake off thoughts of my former friend. Bryson isn't the same man he used to be. He's proven that fact over and over again.

But even as I work to calm the growing unrest, Caleb's warning comes back with haunting clarity.

"Nobody really knows Bryson. He makes sure of it."

~

I slam my foot against the concrete step to knock the dirt off, Penny squirming in my arms. I'm mad, and not just at the twenty failed minutes of training I attempted after Cam's phone call. I'm mad because Bryson willingly chose to keep a monumental secret from me. And while it's only been five days and this relationship thing is new to both of us, I can't help but see multiple red flags, especially after watching what secrets and lies did to a thirty-five-year marriage.

When did he find out? That's the biggest question on my mind. I mean, come on, contracts had been signed. This wasn't like a missed email.

When my shoes are no longer caked in clay, I push through the door and try to calm down. Penny's already agitated, and my bottled-up emotion isn't helping. I set her on the floor and wrap the leash twice around my hand to keep her close.

Bryson's head pops up when I enter the kitchen. "You

done?" He's sitting at the island bar, reading something on his phone. Probably research on all the cities they'll visit while on tour.

"Yeah. We're definitely done."

"Good. We're just about to walk Macey to the neighbor's. Charlie's changing now."

Penny gives one warning growl before shooting toward the island, where Macey sits next to Bryson's stool.

My hand jerks forward, but the leash snaps taut just in time to stop the assault. I grit my teeth to keep from screaming. "No," I say firmly and roll the material tighter around my hand, the stitching pressing into my skin. Penny slides backward instead of forward, hopping on her back two feet.

The empty stool next to Bryson topples over as Macey tries to escape, creating more aggravation and chaos. I glance at Bryson, who's watching Penny with the same contempt I've seen on Charlie's face multiple times. "Can you help, please?" I say with more accusation than is fair. "Take her into the living room or something?"

His eyes pierce mine, obviously catching the bite in my tone, but instead of coming back with any defense, Bryson gets up and pushes his stool out of the way to get to her. When she refuses to move, he squats down and heaves her fifty-plus pounds in his arms. "It's ridiculous a dog this size is scared of that rat," he grunts and hauls the terrified dog out of the room.

I lean down and pick up Penny, who still has yet to quit growling and barking. "What am I going to do with you?" One on one, she's actually not bad. Stubborn but certainly not crazy. But the minute another dog enters the mix, she becomes a poster child for neurotic behavior. "People don't really like to adopt dogs that attack. Just FYI."

Penny pokes my cheek with her tiny nose and licks my face.

I take her inside the laundry room and wrestle her back into her crate. She hates this thing now, and the more time we spend outside, the harder she fights when I put her back. "I know, girl. I want to let you out, too, but I can't if you don't get your aggression under control." She continues her manic barking until I shut the door, and then slowly it fades into acceptance.

"I don't trust that dog," Bryson says when he returns to the kitchen. "You okay now?"

"I'm fine." I slide onto the stool and rub my face, exhaustion and the crash of my earlier emotions settling like a blanket over my good mood. "I just need more patience and time."

"The fair is tomorrow." He takes the seat next to me and hesitates a second before squeezing my tense shoulders with his hand. I guess he's learned my tells, as well. He seems to sense my frustration. "Surely you're not thinking of taking her."

"I was, until just now." I rub my temples. There are only a few more fairs left this summer, and I really need to take advantage of every one. "I guess waiting one more week won't kill the timeline."

"No, it will not." He leans into me and kisses my shoulder. "Plus, that frees you up to spend the entire day with me."

I know his statement should make me feel warm inside, but it only reminds me that three weeks from now, he could be leaving. Not could . . . *will* be leaving. Firesight's manager is going to see exactly what all of us did last weekend: Bryson and Cameron are magic together.

"Hey." He leans his elbow on the counter, turning himself until I'm forced to look into his eyes. "What am I missing?"

"Nothing." I should just ask him, straight out, but talking about the possible tour is not something I plan to do in the middle of Charlie's kitchen, especially when I still have no idea exactly what I'm feeling.

Charlie emerges from his room, and it's a transformation I'm completely unprepared for. He's dressed in thin khakis and a blue collared shirt. His hair is still long but tamed and styled, and his beard is four inches shorter.

I leap from my stool, grateful for a distraction. "Wow! I wouldn't have recognized you."

His cheeks redden. "I figured it was time for some grooming."

"You look great. And check it out, Bryson, blue." I glance at him over my shoulder and force myself to smile. He's still watching me with far too much concern. "You've heard of it, right? It's a color that isn't black."

Bryson comes behind me, wraps his arms around my waist, and sets his chin on my shoulder. "I'll wear blue if you really want me to," he whispers, and all my negative thoughts begin to unravel. No one could be this good at pretending, could they? Then again, my parents hid their fractures for years, and I blissfully went through life never noticing the ground beneath me was near collapse.

I try again to relax or at least appear that way. "Don't tease me, Katsaros. I will hold you to that."

Charlie shakes his head at our open display of affection, but I see a hint of a smile appear. He turns and whistles, the sound cutting the air as if it came from a toy. Macey comes running at a speed I didn't know she possessed, slipping twice on the hardwood floor. "Well, lookie here. It still works, even after all this time." He squats down, and she showers him with kisses.

I shift my focus from the swirling questions in my head to the pair in front of me. At least one thing in my life makes total sense. This job. And even though I'm skipping the fair tomorrow, I still get a win. Because whether he knows it yet or not, Charlie just became the proud, permanent owner of an adorable, ridiculously skittish mutt.

TWENTY-FOUR

Charlie's closest neighbor lives nearly a quarter mile away and down a small country road that has become more gravel than asphalt. It's a beautiful walk, though, bathed in shade by large oak and cedar trees.

Macey tries to stop at nearly every tree, sniffing and digging as if this is the first time she's been out of captivity in months. I guess, in a way, she has been locked away. Charlie too. Grief can be a prison if left unattended without hope or progress.

We crest the final hill, and a row of fencing breaks to reveal a gorgeous two-story home painted white with bright green shutters.

Charlie must recognize my awestruck face. "Pretty amazing, isn't it?"

"I'll say. It's like a postcard."

"There's a ten-acre lake right over there." He points beyond the house, and I barely make out a patch of blue glistening in the sun. "Bryson can take you sometime. Best fishing for miles."

My stomach tumbles at the mention of his name. We've barely spoken the entire walk. "Sounds nice."

Charlie's body suddenly jerks forward, Macey nearly up-ending her owner in her quest to explore. I lunge to steady him the same time Bryson grabs at the leash.

"I'll take that," he says, unraveling the leather from Char-lie's wrinkled hand. "She's too excited to behave right now."

Charlie watches his pet with sorrowful yet optimistic eyes. This walk really has been a step toward healing. I can see it in both of their faces.

We reach the front door, quicker than any of us intend to, but Macey has set the pace for the last hundred feet.

"Well, here goes nothing," Charlie says and rings the door-bell. "Word of warning. Sheila's the type to tell you how it is, and I have a feeling she has a few choice words for me. Most of them deserved, I'm afraid."

The door opens to reveal a slim older lady with white hair and tight jeans. She pushes out the screen door. "Well now, look who finally came over to grovel."

Sheila and Charlie share a look that tells me everything is going to be okay between the two of them. Forgiveness is ex-pected between old friends, grace given without the need for apologies. It's the backbone of relationships. The very thing that sustains time and distance and, in this case, the death of someone they both loved dearly.

Charlie clears his throat. "I brought a peace offering." With that, Bryson eases his viselike grip on Macey's leash, and her tail is wagging so hard she practically wiggle-runs to Sheila. The older lady squats and meets the dog with equal excite-ment.

"There's my girl! I've missed you so much." She stands, her eyes glistening. "Well, come in. No need to stand here and let out all the A/C."

Charlie steps forward, and before he can make it past the

doorway, Sheila gives him a hug that nearly cracks my resolve not to cry. I think it does his, too, because he nods and
quickly moves inside, Macey at his heels.

Bryson comes over and wraps his arm around my shoulder,
the first real contact we've shared since leaving the house.
"What do you want to do?"

"I think we should give them some time."

He nods. "Hey, Sheila, you mind if I take Darcy out to the
lake for a while?"

"Not at all." She smiles warmly, and her perfect teeth are
either dentures or she has the best dentist in the world. "And
thanks for getting him over here. We've missed him." She
doesn't linger, which I like. Maybe it's a farmer/rancher thing,
but this no-nonsense, straightforward world is definitely
something I could enjoy for a long time.

"Ready?" Bryson's hand fills mine, his fingers sliding in between my own as he steps closer.

I nod and let him guide us down a path, first made of flat
stone, then as it passes through the final fence and turns into
caliche. With each step, the lake gets closer and seems to go
on without end. A wooden deck juts out at least ten feet into
the water. It looks new and sturdy, as if it's only been here a
few years.

He pauses when we reach the edge and turns so we're facing each other. "Now that we're alone again, want to tell me
what's upsetting you?"

"Nothing's—"

"Yes, it is," Bryson says, cutting me off. "You've been different with me since you came in the house earlier."

I watch the water as tiny ripples form from unseen
sources. "I've just got a lot on my mind right now."

"You're worried about Penny?"

"No, I mean, yes . . . a little, but that's not what's bothering me." I already know that Bryson isn't going to let me deflect, and truthfully I don't want to. I may not have a lot of experience with relationships, but I do know I don't want one where I can't be completely honest. I force myself to turn back to him, to watch his eyes when I admit what's had me in turmoil for the last thirty minutes. "I guess I'm trying to figure out why you didn't tell me about the concert and the tour."

He stiffens, which answers one of my questions. He was intentionally keeping it from me.

I swallow down the hurt. "I mean, it's an incredible opportunity. I would think you would be thrilled about the news."

"You talked to Cameron." A statement. Not a question. Bryson inhales deeply, the same way my mom did right before telling me she was ready to start dating. "Nothing's a guarantee, yet. There's still a lot of stars that need to align before anything definite is going to happen."

"You signed a contract, Bryson, and didn't say a word to me about it. That's concerning, especially considering your history with Alison." I let go of his hand and take my first step onto the treated wood. The deck creaks but doesn't move, so I take one more, then another, leaving Bryson at the shore. My stomach knots with each foot of distance I put between us. I don't want there to be tension, but I also can't help but wonder if I should have put more stock into Caleb's warnings.

When I reach the end of the deck, I sit and let my sneakered feet hang over the water. A shadow appears, and Bryson sits next to me, close enough that I consider scooting away to get some distance.

"You're right." He tugs on the back of his neck. "I should have told you. I'm sorry. I guess I didn't want anything to mess up what we've started."

"Unless . . . this was why we started in the first place. You did say the road gets lonely."

"Hey." He shifts to face me instead of the water and picks up my hand. "This isn't like before."

Maybe it is, maybe it isn't, but either way, I'm going to give him an out. Something Alison never did. "It's not too late, you know. We could stop this thing now and still retain some semblance of friendship."

He groans and stares at the cloudless sky. "This is my punishment. This is what I get for ever dating her."

I pull my feet up and sit crisscross to where our knees are touching. "I'm not trying to punish you."

"I know you're not, but for some reason you still doubt me."

I look down at my fingers because it's true. A part of me still expects Bryson to hurt me.

"Do you want to know why I broke up with Alison when I did?"

"You already told me. You didn't love her the way she loved you."

"Yeah, that's true, but I didn't tell you when I finally accepted that reality." He sets his hand on my knee, his fingertips rubbing the inside skin, oblivious to the fact that it's sending tingles up and down my leg. "It was our first performance with Cam at lead guitar, in Waco."

"I was there that night."

He grins as if I'm missing the point. "I know. Cam didn't say a word about you coming. He just kept looking out at the audience, agitated, until finally I guess he saw what he was looking for and settled. I had no idea it was you until I stepped up to the microphone and there you were, sitting front and center." He picks up my hand and kisses the inside of my wrist. "I knew you weren't there for me; you hadn't been to one concert of mine that Cam didn't drag you to, but still, I spent the entire night watching you and hoping you were watching me. Let me tell you, that's a pretty sickening feeling to have for a girl, especially one who's sitting next to your current girlfriend." He looks down, shame written in the slump of his shoulders. "That's when I knew I had to end things. Even I couldn't stomach looking myself in the mirror that night." He glances back up, the plea in his hazel eyes far too vulnerable to be lying. "Darcy, these feelings I have for you . . . they aren't new, and they aren't small." He leans in and presses his lips to my neck right at the edge of my T-shirt. "I've spent *years* wanting to kiss this very spot." Fire races down my arm as he scoots closer, his breath trailing to my ear. "You tuck your hair to one side when you're nervous. I used to watch your fingers run right along this line and have to get up from the table to keep from touching you."

I close my eyes, no longer aware of the lake or the deck or even the pressure of Bryson's confessed feelings. All I can feel is the pleasure of new beginnings. Dangerous beginnings. Beginnings that threaten the last bits of security I'm furiously clinging to.

"You're not a fill-in or a distraction. You're the one I could never have." His nose runs along my cheek, his breath tickling the skin. "And for the record, I am way too far gone to ever go back to how things used to be."

I can't argue. My skin burns with his touch. Burns in a way it shouldn't between friends.

His lips lightly brush against mine. "Do you need more convincing?"

Unable to stand his teasing any longer, I kiss him, hard and deep. Bryson immediately responds, gripping the back of my head, cradling my body until we somehow end up horizontal. I want to melt into the feel and taste and scent of him. My hands roam over his back, clawing at the hem of his shirt, eager to explore the muscles underneath.

Bryson immediately pulls back, his face flushed, his lids half closed the same way they are onstage. "We need to slow this down." He sits against the deck railing, his breath coming fast and labored, and runs his hands over his face.

I lie there, nearly as stunned as he is. I always knew I wanted passion in a relationship. I just never knew until now what that might actually feel like. I sit up on my elbows, my legs still stretched in front of me, and choke out a laugh. "Yeah, I'd say I'm thoroughly convinced."

He lowers his head, his elbows resting on his knees, and begins to laugh with me. It's a nice sound, light and inviting, a release of so many battered moments in our lives.

He stands and offers his hand. I grip it, the skin callused and warm, and let him pull me upright. He wraps his arms around me, clasping his hands together at my lower back. "What do you say to dinner at my place tonight? Believe it or not, I am good for more than dog wrangling and clandestine make-out sessions."

I duck my head into his shoulder, slightly mortified by how quickly I lost control. "I wish I could, but I promised dinner with Cam. We're celebrating your big break."

The tension comes slowly but seems to grow as he processes my words. "I haven't seen him since the concert." He backs up, and it forces me to look at him. Every muscle in his face is tight with restraint. "How'd he take the news of the two of us dating?"

I can tell by the way he asks that he already knows the answer. "I haven't exactly told him yet."

Bryson's jaw ripples with tension, and I hate how it reminds me of the face he makes whenever he talks about his mom. "Darcy, I'm pretty sure this secret trumps the concert one."

"It's not a secret. I'm just trying to be delicate."

"Why? It's not like you haven't dated before. Cam dealt with it then. He can deal with it now."

"I know, but it's different this time. He knows you. We all are interconnected. Plus . . ." I disentangle from his embrace, which only seems to add to his rigid posture. "Cam will worry about you hurting me." Just like his brother. They've both seen too many of Bryson's bad choices. "He's protective that way."

"No. He's territorial. He always has been when it comes to you. It's why everyone, including me, keeps waiting to see a shiny engagement ring on your finger."

His words hit a much too familiar nerve. "Stop it. He's my best friend. That's all."

"Then tell him." He crosses his arms in front of his chest, a mountain of challenge in his stance. "If I'm wrong, your *best friend* will be happy for you. If I'm right, then we need to have a very different conversation."

"You are wrong. And I will tell him. Just not tonight. Not when he's so happy." I step forward, feeling the need to apologize for some reason. "Please, Bryson. Cam's already lost so many people in his life this year, and true or not, he'll feel like he's losing me, too. He can't compartmentalize like you can. He feels everything, and I don't want to cause issues right when he needs to focus the most."

"Do you even realize how much energy you spend trying to keep Cam happy? If he worried about your happiness even a fraction as much, he would be thrilled you found someone

who cares for you as much as I do." He presses his lips together, a thing I'm learning he does when he has more to
say than he's willing to. "I'm not naïve, Darcy. I knew when
I leaped into this thing with you that Cam has been the
number-one guy in your life for years now. But I took the risk
because you somehow convinced me that your feelings for
him are platonic."

"And they are." I take Bryson's hands and enclose them
next to my chest. "He's our friend, not to mention a critical
part of Black Carousel's future." Bryson flinches at that
reminder. "I think it's only fair that we ease him into this
slowly."

"Fine. I'll let you set the timeline." He steps back, sighs,
and everything about his stance conveys impatience. "But I
want to make it one-hundred-percent clear that I'm uncomfortable." He doesn't say with what. Instead his expression
turns cold and scrutinizing, far too much like the man he
used to be. The hardened version. The one who's been hurt
and abandoned by every person he's ever cared about.

I want to believe it's just the secrets and the timing he
doesn't like, but a deeper part of me knows it's more. I lay my
head on his chest and hug him until he finally acquiesces and
hugs me back. I'll just have to do better at easing his doubts,
just as he did for me today. It's the only option I have. I've
given up so much this past year, and I won't, not for anyone,
give up my best friend, too.

TWENTY-FIVE

Cameron's promise of a swanky steakhouse in Dallas turns into piles of Mexican food on the patio of Trinity Groves, our new favorite dining spot right over the bridge to downtown. The Dallas skyline is gorgeous this time of night. It's right after dusk, and each building is coming alive with thousands of lights.

"I'm glad you changed your mind about the restaurant," I say around a bite of our shared fajitas. "This is much more us."

He leans back in his chair, his dimples forming as he watches me eat very indelicately. "Well, I decided paying rent was more important than impressing you."

"Please." I lightly kick his foot with mine. "You know I'm cheaper than you are."

He laces his hands behind his head. "Maybe so, but I still owe you a big juicy steak. In fact, you better cash it in soon, because once I'm filthy rich, I'm going to be way too important for anyone but my new celebrity friends."

"What?" I toss my balled-up napkin at his face. "Where is your loyalty?"

"I'm kidding." His grin turns warm, almost insecure. "Trust

245

me, there's no scenario where I see my future and you're not in it."

I swallow, oddly uncomfortable. "Good."

An awkward silence falls that has never been between us before. Cameron shifts in his seat, feeling it, too. Maybe he can sense a change is once again coming.

"Cam?" My heart pounds in my chest, a nervousness I didn't expect all but closing around my throat. "Can I ask you a question?" I hadn't planned to bring this up tonight, but the words suddenly spill out.

His brows form a vee. "Since when do you need that as a lead-in?"

"Well, it's kind of a personal one."

"So?"

I wring my hands in my lap. "How did you deal with your girlfriends when they would get jealous of the two of us?"

He stares at me and slowly settles back into his seat. "That's out of left field. Why do you want to know?"

I should have guessed he wouldn't take the question at face value. The downside of his knowing every one of my expressions. "Just curious."

He tilts his head. "Curious because . . . you're chronicling our life together? Or curious because you're seeing someone and he's not comfortable with our friendship?" There's an annoyance in his voice I recognize. It's the same one he gets every time I venture into the boyfriend conversation. He has yet to like any I've introduced him to.

"The second one."

He swallows like he didn't expect my answer to be yes. "Who's the lucky guy?"

"That's not important," I say, even though I know he would disagree.

Cam blows out a long exhale. "I knew you'd been distant this week. I guess it never crossed my mind you might have met someone."

"Sorry. We're kind of in that mushy want-to-spend-all-our-time-together stage."

"So, it's a new someone. When did you meet him? We've hung out every weekend except this past one." His eyes widen, and I can see his mind calculating time. "Was it at the concert?"

"He was there, yes. But that's not the point. The point is he has some concerns, and I don't know how to ease those."

"Concerns about me?"

I nod, wishing I had more practice with this type of thing.

Cameron's pause is long and heavy, as if he's still accepting my line of questioning. "Well . . . it's simple. It's not your job to ease his shortcomings or insecurities." Cameron leans his elbows on the table. "You tell him the same thing I've told every one of my girlfriends. Our friendship always comes first."

"That is not what you told January," I remind him. "In fact, I remember a serious heart-to-heart where you made it clear to me that we needed to, and I quote, '*back off and consider her feelings*.'"

He shoots me a scowl because he knows I'm right. "Fine. Maybe I was a little enticed by her. But . . . I would have told her that if she'd tried to make me choose. Lucky for me, she was too busy lying about her entire existence to bother with jealousy." His sarcasm makes us both chuckle and thankfully eases the tension in our conversation. Cameron reaches out and squeezes my hand. "January is proof of what we both know is true. People come in and out of our lives, but every time we land right back here—with you and me.

247

No new relationship is going to change that. Don't even let him try."

"You're right." I squeeze his hand back and think of all the times Cameron has been there supporting me, caring for me, walking me through all the hardest moments in my life. Bryson doesn't understand it because he's never known the purity of a friendship on this level.

Cameron flashes a grin that is pure mischief. "So, when do I get to meet him?"

My stomach flips at the question. It's inevitable that my two worlds will collide; I just have to find a way to minimize the impact. "When I feel sure that you're not going to be rude to him."

"I'm never rude to them."

"Please, you interrogated Adam for an hour."

His mouth opens in feigned outrage. "That's because he wouldn't stop undressing you with his eyes. Right in front of me, I might add. That guy was a jerk. You're lucky I had your back."

Okay, yeah. Probably not the best example. "Fine. I concede Adam was a dud."

He smirks, knowing he's winning our little battle. "Now, back to my question. When do I get to meet him?"

"Soon."

"Give me a date."

I hesitate, but then throw out an option that ensures the least amount of collateral damage. "The night of your concert. We'll all go out afterward and celebrate."

"That's three weeks away."

"So?"

"So, considering your usual patterns, he'll be out of the picture by then and I never would have met him." Both dimples appear, and his voice turns teasing. "We both know you don't exactly have the longest attention span when it comes to men. Except me, of course."

I narrow my eyes but have no ability to counter without giving more information than I'm ready to share. Never have I been as close to someone as I am to Bryson, and the fact that I'm this worried about making the three of us work is proof that I fully expect this thing with him to go long term. "Trust me. He'll be there."

"If you say so." Though nothing in his voice implies he believes me.

"I do." I settle back in my chair, relieved to have the conversation over with. It's probably for the best that Cameron doesn't think the relationship is serious. If he did, he'd push, and I'd cave and then we'd be forced to have a much more uncomfortable conversation. It's odd. I've never really cared if Cam liked the guys I dated or even if he approved, but that was often because I already knew they weren't right for me. Bryson's different. He sees me. The changed me. The one who woke up one day and discovered her life was a lie. He sees the one thing Cameron has yet to accept—I'm never going to be the person I once was.

"Hey . . ." Cameron waves a hand in front of my face. "Where'd you go?"

"Nowhere."

"You've been staring off into space for over a minute."

"Sorry." I go back to eating and try to push away all thoughts of Bryson. "Tell me more about Jax and the band. How did the whole tour thing even come up?"

"We were talking about a few places we'd both played, and then I mentioned how I want to venture into Oklahoma and Louisiana. Jax said I should be looking much bigger, and that was it." He chews on his fingernail, his voice far too lifeless for his usual favorite conversation.

"That's it?" My brow furrows. "Never have you ever talked about music in two sentences or less. And that was before you had the opportunity to play with another musical genius." Cameron suddenly can't meet my eyes. "What's going on?"

"Nothing."

"Try again. And this time don't chew on your nail while you're talking. It's a dead giveaway you're not telling me the truth."

"Okay, fine." He bites his lip, a complete departure from his usual confidence. "I didn't just bring you here to celebrate or hear about the next unfortunate guy in your life. There's something I've been wanting to talk to you about."

If my stomach weren't in knots, I'd smack him for the "unfortunate guy" comment. "Okay?"

"It's, um, well . . . it's about your dad."

I drop my tortilla onto the plate and try to ignore the rising nausea. "I take it back; you were right not to say anything."

"That's just it. I've been *not saying anything* for weeks now. And I can't keep quiet any longer."

"Cameron, whatever it is, I don't care. I don't want to know. And I certainly don't want to ruin the night by talking about him." I look toward the Dallas skyline, pain pouring into the places I thought I had shored up. My dad's apartment is only fifteen minutes from here, yet he may as well be a continent away. "He left me for a shiny new life. I tried to fight it and I lost."

"Darcy." Cam's voice is etched in compassion. "He left your mom. Not you."

"It's the same thing."

"No, it's not. Your dad messed up, yes, but I know for a

fact that he's tried to contact you several times with no response."

I scowl at my best friend. "And how would you know that?"

"Because he calls me to check on you. He says you haven't spoken to him since the divorce was final."

"He made his choice. There was nothing left to say. And I really don't appreciate your feeding him information."

Cameron snakes a hand through his hair, his expression suspiciously guilty. "It's not like that. Your dad wants to be a part of your life, even if it's just through me right now." He hesitates, probably weighing how angry I'm going to get. Finally he sighs, resigned. "He asked me to bring you to his birthday barbecue."

"Did he? And in what universe did he think I would agree to go?"

"Well . . . he wasn't exactly planning on me asking you. I'm kind of going rogue here." He scrunches his nose, realizing how bad those words sound out loud. "He thought if I could just get you there, even coerced, you might . . . talk to him."

Blood pumps in my ears. "You know, Cam, it's been years since you and I have really fought, but maybe we're due." Dad's backyard barbecues are legendary, down to the special rub he puts on the baby back ribs. A year ago, the party was at our house with fifty of my parents' closest friends, including the woman we later learned he was sleeping with.

"Obviously, I didn't agree with his method"—Cam's attempt at soothing my growing temper fails, especially when he adds—"but I do think you should consider going."

"Why?" I demand, my heart pounding with a ferocity I didn't know I possessed. "He's not the man I grew up with. This version is one I don't even recognize. So why should I sacrifice for him when every decision he's made this year has been one-hundred-percent selfish?"

"True, and I have no doubt he'll not be getting Father of the Year anytime soon. But . . . you miss him. And despite what he's done, he's still your dad, and it's his birthday."

I turn away, emotions bouncing so quickly between fury and heartbreak that my hands tremble. "It's like he doesn't even care what he's lost. He just goes on like nothing's changed—new home, new woman, same old party."

"The guy I speak to on the phone seems very aware of what he's lost."

The tears I've refused to cry for that man come tumbling over, and I can't respond for fear I might choke on anything I attempt to say.

Cam rushes around the table and slides in next to me. "I'm sorry I brought it up. Forget his stupid party. I always thought his ribs were overrated, anyway."

I chuckle despite my emotional turmoil, and Cam pulls me into his arms. They're warm and familiar, yet tonight I feel a twinge of unease that's never existed before. It's innocent, the hug, I know that, but I can't help but picture the hurt in Bryson's eyes when I admitted to keeping our new relationship a secret.

I pull away. "My dad's a jerk, yes, but his ribs are excellent, and you know it."

"Yeah okay, they are." His smile is wrapped in pity when he wipes away my fallen tears. "I hate that I made you cry. I just couldn't keep it a secret any longer. It was killing me."

I look down, suddenly guilty and uncomfortable. Here he is apologizing and I'm doing the exact same thing—protecting him with a secret. "It's okay, Cam. I understand why you did it."

When he sees I'm not mad at him, he returns to his seat across the table. "What do you want me to tell him?"

I realize then what a terrible position my dad has put him in. It's unfair. Cameron already shoulders all my burdens. He shouldn't have to shoulder my dad's, as well. "Tell him to stop calling you." Cameron is opening his mouth to protest when I continue, "If I want to talk to him, I will be the one to initiate it. I'm really sorry he involved you."

"Can't fault the guy for trying." Cameron shrugs and winks at me from across the table. "If I lost you, you'd better believe I'd fight to get you back."

My body warms, his words reinforcing my need to be careful with his feelings. Cameron's my person. Now and always. "I know. I'd fight for you, too."

TWENTY-SIX

I knock on Bryson's door, a detour I hadn't planned on this morning, but since he hadn't returned any of the texts I sent after Cameron dropped me off last night, I figured he might need some reassurance. I know I do, anyway.

The door swings in, and I'm struck by the physical reaction I have to seeing him wearing a tank top and gym shorts. My gaze trails over the lean muscle and olive skin he rarely shows. His hair is disheveled, and his face all but screams his sleep was as restless as mine last night.

He leans his forearm against the doorframe and looks down at me, his smirk far too reminiscent of the arrogant rock star he used to pretend to be. "How was your date?"

"It wasn't a date."

"Got news, Darcy. When a guy picks you up and takes you out to dinner . . . it's a date."

"Not when the guy is my best friend."

"A designation you and I still do not agree on."

"Are we really back to that? What can I do to make you believe me?"

He shoves a hand through his hair. "Rewrite history, I guess."

"Well, I can't exactly do that." I stubbornly cross my arms and look up at him with the same challenging stare he's giving me. It doesn't work. Bryson remains a brick barrier, refusing to let me pass. I redistribute my weight from my left foot to my right, suddenly nervous. "Are you really not going to let me in?"

He must sense my growing insecurity because he presses his back against the door to give me passing room.

I step forward, my insides tumbling. He told me he was uncomfortable, but he never said going to dinner with Cam was a deal breaker. "I texted you when I got home. You never responded."

"That's because it came in at midnight. About two hours later than I thought it would." There's a chill I'm not used to from him, which makes the hair on my arms stand up. He shuts the door but doesn't move any closer to me. It feels bigger than a physical rejection; it feels like we're breaking up.

I swallow, trying to keep my voice steady. "Well, if you had answered my text, I would have informed you that I told Cameron last night I was seeing someone, and you were wrong. He didn't get upset at all."

"Really? And did that someone have a name?" I bite my lip, my nonresponse answering his question. He shakes his head. "Yeah, I thought so."

I lift my arms and let them drop back to my sides, completely out of options. "What do you want me to do?"

His eyes meet mine, sharp and angry. "I want you to tell him. Not hint. Not leaving out details. I want you to tell him it's me. And that we're serious about each other."

"I will. I promise you, I will . . . when it feels right."

He grunts a laugh completely devoid of humor. "It's never going to feel right. That's the problem." No matter how much Bryson's softer side comes out when we're together, there's always that hint of darkness hovering right near the surface. He must sense it, too, because he rolls his shoulders, a motion I've often seen him do when he's trying to relax. "Do you have any idea how hard this is for me?" He rubs his forehead like it suddenly hurts. "I've watched Cameron pine for you for years. I've had a front row seat to the long, lingering stares. Been the recipient of the passive-aggressive warnings to back off. And it's not just from high school. It's now. It's all the time. It's him calling you 'his girl' and hugging you like he needs you in order to breathe. And despite how much you try to justify those behaviors, I'm here to tell you . . . they're not normal. I've had many friends who were girls, but there were lines, boundaries. Always. You and Cameron have no lines."

"Then we'll draw some, okay?" I clutch the front of his shirt, lifting up on my toes to kiss the stubble on his jaw. "I just need a little more time. That's all I'm asking for. Let Black Carousel get through this concert and then we'll tell him together."

"Time is not going to change the outcome." He sighs and the misery in his eyes cuts through me. "If you don't want this, if you have any hesitation at all, I need you to tell me now."

"I want this." He turns his face away, and I cup his cheeks to bring his eyes back to mine. "Hey, I want this. But you're asking me to do really difficult things. And I'm willing to do them for you, but you have to give a little, too."

He finally crushes me against his wonderfully hard chest. "How am I supposed to argue when you look at me like that?" he growls into my hair. Suddenly, my back is pressed against the door, his forearms creating a cage around me. "Tell me I'm not fooling myself." His face, his lips are inches from mine and all I can feel is Bryson, his eyes strained, his voice dark and smooth and hypnotic. "Tell me anything that will make me forget the last twelve hours of wondering."

Anticipation roars inside me, but he doesn't come closer, doesn't lean down or close his eyes or even tease me with the tickle of his breath. I press my palms to the wood to keep them from touching every inch of his beautiful skin. It's the contrast that makes my stomach whirl when he stares at me this way. Soft and hard. Angry and broken. Scared and sure. I've never met anyone so complicated in my life, nor have I ever wanted to understand someone more.

"I missed you." I bite my lip, feeling just as foolish as he admitted to feeling. "More than what's normal. More than I've ever missed anyone. More than I know how to express without terrifying both of us."

If words could calm a storm, those seem to do it. His entire body collapses into me. Bryson slides his hand down the door until it cradles my head. The pad of his thumb glides gently against my cheek. "I . . . missed you, too." He leans closer, his breath hot against my closed eyelids, then moves downward until finally he gives me what I've been waiting for. The contact, the reassurance, the same glorious shock waves that always seem to come when he kisses me.

The jerk knows it, too. He's all but cocky when he finally grins down at me. "So, is it safe to assume you're free today?" The question feels like a test, and luckily it's one I can easily pass.

"Yes. And I already ran by the farm this morning, so gold star for me."

He pushes off the door, allowing us both to breathe a little. "It's only nine o'clock. What time did you get there?"

"Six-thirty. Thankfully, Charlie was already up."

"After getting home at midnight?" Concern deepens his brow. "Did you sleep at all?"

"Not really."

"How come?"

"Just stuff with my dad." I shrug because that's all I really want to say on the subject.

"What stuff?"

"It's nothing."

"If it were nothing, you wouldn't have lost sleep over it." He takes my hand and kisses the inside of my wrist, intimate and comfortable. Two things I always seem to feel with him. "Darcy... openness has to go both ways."

I have no ability to deny his request, even though I know talking will do nothing but add to the hurt. Ever since Cameron mentioned the stupid event, an unexpected yearning has swelled in me. Memories I had all but buried have tumbled loose and with them the pain I've worked so hard not to feel. "Dad wants me to go to his birthday barbecue. It's the same one he's hosted every single year of my life."

"When is it?"

"Not for a couple more weeks, but time won't change how I feel. He isn't the man I knew and loved. He's just this person now who wrecked my family."

"Tell me what happened." He fiddles with my fingertips, that rare flash of insecurity popping through. "I don't have experience with divorce, but I certainly understand growing up in a dysfunctional environment."

I smile at his attempt to empathize. "That's just it. My home wasn't dysfunctional. I had a wonderful childhood.

The kind where I would lie in bed and thank God for parents
like mine. The kind people saw and wanted to have." My
throat tightens, and I pull my hand away, needing to pace and
breathe. "Do you know they didn't tell us until after Christmas even though they'd filed months before?"

Bryson shakes his head, quiet. His silence used to bother
me, but now it's one of my favorite things about him. He listens without passing judgment, without lecturing or trying to
convince me I'm wrong for feeling how I do.

"Dexter came down with his family for the holiday weekend, and it was smiles and hugs, even the required thank-you
kiss when they gave each other their gifts. Dad got Mom a
gold watch, and she got him Cowboys tickets." The words
choke in the back of my throat. "They even talked as if they
would go together." I slump down on the couch, my hands
shaking. "They waited until the night before Dexter was set
to leave to finally tell us the truth. His family was tucked in
bed, and I was saying my goodbyes when Mom politely asked
me to come into the living room. They sat us down, took each
other's hand, and told us they were getting a divorce."

Bryson sits next to me but doesn't take my hand. I'm grateful. I want nothing between us to remind me of that horrible
night.

"I couldn't breathe. I just sat there thinking this is a joke.
A sick, twisted joke that was in terrible taste. But then Dad
started crying, and Mom walked away and shut herself in the
bedroom. And all I could think about was that stupid gold
watch and the printed-out football tickets." A fierce ache
grips my heart as I stare at him, this wonderful new man who
truly cares, and admit the biggest shame in my life. "Bryson,
your parents aren't the only ones who pretended life was perfect. If Christmas was any indication, mine had been lying

to us for a very long time. Long enough that my mom firmly believes she knows Michael—a man who's been in her life a mere month—better than she ever knew my father. And now I'm stuck with the reality that my entire childhood, the basis of my beliefs and my choices, was all an illusion. I didn't just lose my dad and my mom that night; I lost every wonderful memory I had. They're tainted now because I can't distinguish between what was real and what wasn't." I glance down at my feet. "I've never even heard them fight. Not once. And now I resent them for it . . . I resent them for not fighting."

I feel the cushions give and Bryson's warm arms around me.

"Come here." He pulls me close, attempting to heal my pain with affection and care. I love the smell of him and the feel of safety his touch brings, but I don't feel better. I don't feel less angry or less bitter or less betrayed. In fact, if anything, I feel trapped. I want to run. To move and go until I exhaust myself of all the emotion clamoring to explode.

My head jerks up. "That's it. That's what she needs."

I scramble to my feet, leaving my confused boyfriend on the couch. "What who needs? Your mom?"

"No, Penny. She needs to run. She needs to exhaust herself, and then maybe I can finally start to socialize her a little. If she's worn out, she won't have the energy to fight me so hard." I jump and clap my hands together. "We need to go to a hardware store."

He stands and scratches his head like he still can't keep up. "A hardware store?"

"Yes, for supplies. Now go change." I push him toward his room. "I'm going to make a list."

"Darcy . . ." He halts the movement, and I'm nowhere strong enough to budge him. "I don't think immersing yourself in a new project is what you need right now. I'm here to listen, to help you get through this."

"I know you are, and . . ." I lift on my toes and kiss him with all the thanks I can show. "I appreciate it so much, but I want to do this. Now. Today. I don't want to spend another moment crying over my parents. I feel like that's all I've done for the past seven months."

He hesitates but then obeys, leaving me to rustle through his kitchen drawers to find something to write with. The rescue facility I volunteered at had an obstacle course with tubes and stairs and long bridges. I wouldn't be able to make anything that elaborate, but for a little dog like Penny, I could certainly figure out enough to keep her challenged during our training sessions.

I draw, turn the page sideways, and draw some more. The task works, and for a brief ten minutes, I gloriously forget about my dad calling Cameron. I forget that tomorrow is yet another Sunday night dinner I'll be missing. And I forget watching my mom throw a very expensive gold watch straight into the trash.

TWENTY-SEVEN

*O*kay, bring her out slowly," I call to Bryson, who's standing with Macey just on the other side of Charlie's back door.

It's been a week of nonstop obstacle training with Penny. She has the course down to perfection, weaving in and out like a circus animal, but the purpose behind the course has yet to be realized. Today we spent an hour running, twice as long as we have in the past. We're both exhausted, and hopefully spent enough that Penny will actually choose to be civil to her housemate.

The screen opens slowly, Macey eager to take the steps until she sees Penny by my side. I can't really blame her for the tentativeness. Penny's attacked her every time we've tried to socialize them.

"Come on, girl," Bryson coaches, and they descend together.

I keep Penny close by my leg. She sees the other dog but hasn't reacted yet, which is no small thing. Last time, I brought Penny forward and allowed her to be the pursuer—a monumental mistake. This time, I'm letting Macey approach.

Bryson watches me for guidance, and I nod for him to

keep going. They get to the grass, and Penny surprisingly remains silent at my feet.

"Good girl," I coo and give her a small reward that she gobbles down.

Macey's tongue hangs from her mouth, her breathing intensifying. She's nervous, poor thing.

"Keep coming, nice and slow."

Bryson does, but as soon as he crosses the four-foot-away mark, Penny stands and growls.

"No," I say. She glances at me, by now recognizing my authority. I reward her silence with another treat and motion for Bryson to continue.

Three feet . . . two feet . . .

Penny lunges, almost as if she's calculated exactly how much slack she had in the leash.

Bryson immediately pulls Macey back to safety, only Penny is now beside herself, pulling and barking and twisting to get away from me.

"Take Macey around front." I groan, feeling utterly defeated. "I'll put Penny up."

Bryson's expression is sympathetic, and I appreciate the fact that he doesn't say I told you so. No doubt he's thinking it.

Nothing I try seems to work with this dog. She hates all other animals. She even terrorizes the squirrels who happen past her. "We're running out of time, Penny. You have to get better." I can't stand thinking of the alternative, but I may be forced to.

Charlie loves Macey, and his tolerance for Penny's aggression is getting shorter by the day. Even Louie has started cowering when she's around. It's like her anger is spilling into every corner of her life, and the only option she's giving us is to fight back or give in. Lucky for her, I'm a fighter.

I wrestle her back into her cage, a task that's becoming as much of a battle as the socializing is, and then walk Macey around for a few minutes. She doesn't need much time from me anymore. Charlie takes her everywhere, and both seem to improve with each outing.

After we finish our walk, Macey trots to her dog bed and plops down. I watch her with satisfaction. At least I've had three victories here. It feels good to remember that when the other two are making me question my ability and resolve.

Bryson wraps his arms around my waist. "I have a surprise for you," he says, setting his chin on my shoulder. "Something that should help with your frustration."

"Yeah?" I perk up. "What is it?"

"You'll see." He pulls me by the hand, and I happily follow along.

Charlie's UTV is parked outside waiting for us. I didn't even notice him leave to go get it. "So the surprise is close?"

"Yep, just down the hill." Bryson walks me to the passenger side of the vehicle just like he does when we're out on a date together. It's sweet and gentlemanly and so odd coming from him.

"Why are you so good to me?"

His brow furrows. "Should I not be?"

"No, I mean, yes, you should be. I just . . ." I don't finish because his mood always seems to dip when I bring up the past. He wants to forget it, move on, but our past is always attached. It follows us even when we've outgrown it. "Never mind. Thank you." I give him a quick peck on the lips and hop into the seat. The Gator has thankfully been parked in the shade, so the vinyl is only slightly hot.

I watch as he jogs to the driver's side, still wondering when this fairy tale with him is going to end. It's not fair; I know this, but it's one of the drawbacks of knowing him for so long. I remember his past relationships. I remember how he treated his girlfriends in public and even had insight, mostly through Alison, on how he treated them in private. Bryson wasn't a bad guy. He didn't cheat or yell or anything like that. He was just always a little . . . cold.

He weaves us around the barn and down the hill to where Charlie, along with five archery targets, waits. Each one is a different distance away from a long wooden shooting table, which must be the starting point.

"I get to shoot!" I squeal, too excited to hide my elation. I'd been hinting for weeks that I wanted to see the famed archery range, but Charlie had dismissed it, saying the area was run-down and overgrown.

I take in the freshly cut grass and new golden pieces of wood holding up each target. I can see this job was not a quick or easy one. "When did you have time to do this?"

"I didn't." He parks several yards back from where Charlie stands and leans his forearms on the steering wheel. "Charlie did it all. I had no idea until he asked me to help him distance out the targets yesterday. I guess he's been coming out here early in the morning and working."

I run a hand along my boyfriend's back, knowing how relieved he is to see the Charlie he grew up with returning. "This place holds a lot of memories for you, doesn't it?"

He nods, and I can tell by his silence that not all of them are good. Bryson has slayed many demons on this range. I think maybe that's why he brought me here. To give me an opportunity to slay a few of mine.

"Okay, let's do this," I say, wanting to take away the new slump in his shoulders. "I'm ready to hit lots of bull's-eyes."

Bryson laughs. "You'll be lucky if you hit the target at all. It took me a month to even hit the outer ring."

I hop from the doorless vehicle and spin. "Well, I'm way better than you, so get ready to be embarrassed."

He laughs again. "Is that right?"

"Yes."

"You're positive."

"Absolutely."

He moves in, his breath tickling my forehead. "Enough to wager on it again?"

I shiver at the sexiness of his voice. He can turn it off and on so quickly, like a snake charmer who knows exactly which musical notes are the most hypnotic. I glance up through my eyelashes and give him my own dose of charm. Bryson isn't the only one who's learned what buttons to push and when. "What did you have in mind?"

He opens his mouth, but before the challenge can spill out, my pocket vibrates and Cameron's ringtone blares into the bubble around us, fizzling every ounce of electricity.

Bryson sucks in a deep breath. "How many times is that today?"

I mouth *sorry* and back away, pulling my phone free in the process. "What now?" I say into the receiver with a hint of both laughter and scolding in my voice. It's not uncommon for us to talk daily, or even multiple times a day, but ever since our dinner out, Cameron's been unquestionably clingier.

"Which shirt should I buy? I texted you some options."

"Um . . . did you forget who you were calling?" I'm only half kidding.

"No, I didn't forget, and I need your help. I've been to five different stores and nothing is right. Come on, Darcy, just give me your opinion. I have to look perfect for this concert."

266

"Okay, hold on." I put him on speaker and look through the multiple pictures he sent. Some even of him in the dressing room mirror. "They all look the same."

"What? No, they don't. Look again."

"I am looking, and they are practically the same shirt. Just pick one. You can't go wrong."

"But which is your favorite?"

I sigh, exasperated. I can hardly stand picking out my own clothes for the day, let alone his. My eyes wander to Bryson, who's standing next to Charlie and testing the string on one of the bows. His black shirt is wet where it clings to his back and fades right into the dark gym shorts he threw on. "Get the one with the least amount of black in it," I say automatically.

"Okay, yeah. Good call. I don't want to look like Bryson's twin."

I hear him shuffling clothes and then the scrape of a hanger. "Can I go now?"

"Oh, sorry, yes. Thanks."

I slide the phone back in my pocket and skip down to where two of my favorite men are standing. "So, which one of you is going to be my teacher?"

Charlie backs away. "Not me. I've seen how you girls shoot. Sue Ann nearly maimed me the first time."

"That's because they like to assume they're better than their instructor," Bryson inserts.

I scowl at my boyfriend, though it's layered in the same kidding jest he had when he said it. Bryson lifts the smallest bow from the table and walks it over. He's smiling enough that I almost think I'm going to come away from the interruption without a comment, until he leans down to whisper in my ear, "Five times, Darcy. Five times in two hours. I thought

267

you were going to draw some lines?" He isn't upset, more annoyed, which is his default each time Cam invades our time together.

"He's stressing over a stage outfit." I take the offered bow and tug slightly on the taut strings. "You should be glad that he cares so much."

"I'll be glad when he has his own girlfriend to call," he mumbles, watching how I'm handling the bow. "Not like that. You'll hurt yourself." Carefully taking the contraption from my hands, he settles behind me, his body flush against my back.

I feel a gentle nibble in the crease by my shoulder and pull away, giggling. "Hey! You're supposed to be teaching me, not trying to distract me."

"I can do both," he teases, and my cheeks flush with embarrassment.

"Stop. Charlie is standing right there." My scolding has no effect on the man whatsoever. He takes advantage of every opportunity to brush against my skin while he demonstrates how to shoot, and there are many, many chances for instruction because, as it turns out, I'm terrible at archery. Not just bad. The worst. My arrows not only don't make it to the target but they barely make it past my own feet.

The only saving grace is that Charlie thinks my lack of shooting skills is hilarious, and his laughter is so unexpected and welcome, I probably would have missed on purpose if I knew this would be the result.

Bryson, on the other hand, is a pro, and when he stands there, focused and confident, he's practically the picture of a Greek warrior annihilating the opposing side. I watch the way his muscles contract and release, the way his dark hair whips in the breeze, and the beautiful touch of sunlight on his tanned skin. My mouth goes dry and I'm hit with a twinge of insecurity. My feelings seem to multiply for him daily. And while I know he cares for me as much as he cares for anyone, I can't help but wonder if there's a limit to how far it goes.

Another shot slams directly into the bull's-eye, and I clap, long ago conceding my defeat. He glances behind and winks, waiting for my reaction. I fan myself and act starstruck, which he seems to love.

"One more, then it's your turn again." He pulls back, ready to take another shot, and blast it if my phone doesn't blare Cameron's song again. I was amused when he uploaded one of his singles as his own personal ringtone. Now it's a battle cry. Bryson's back goes rigid, and he misses the target for the first time all day.

I'm walking away with the phone pressed to my ear before he can give me what I'm sure is going to be a look of pure irritation. "You seriously have issues today," I say into the phone.

"I'm at the grocery store. What kind of pizza do you want for dinner—pepperoni or supreme?"

"Neither . . . I have plans tonight. I told you that."

"It's not fair. This is the first Saturday I've had off in weeks and you're off frolicking with your summer fling. Ditch him and come hang out with me."

I choose to ignore the fling comment. "I can't do that."

"Yes, you can. And besides, you owe me and I'm cashing in."

"How do I owe you?"

"I moved you in and out of two apartments, both with stairs. And I got up early on a Saturday to help you with Bentley, which, by the way, came with a glorious stain to my favorite pair of shorts." I hear the beep of the self-checkout. "I got you pepperoni."

"Cam . . ." I glance over at Bryson, who's in deep conversation with Charlie. "We'll hang out tomorrow. I promise."

"I work tomorrow and Monday. Seriously, Darcy, it's been a week. Tell him you need some time with your friends." His frustration has leaked past the banter, and I can tell he's getting upset with me.

"Fine. I'll agree to try, but I can't promise anything."

"Did I mention the world's most awkward Sunday night dinner you dragged me to?"

I sigh, beaten. "Okay . . . you win. I'll be there soon."

"Awesome! I got movie snacks, too."

I end the call and head back down the hill, dreading every step.

"All good?" Bryson asks, and his voice is relaxed like he's doing his best to sound casual about the entire thing.

I glance at Charlie and give a quick smile before taking Bryson's hand. "Can I talk to you for a second?"

He comes without hesitation, but I can feel his stress growing as we walk toward the UTV. I bite my lip, rehearsing the words in my head. If it weren't Cameron . . . if he weren't a guy, anyway, Bryson would understand. Friends always get a little uncomfortable when a new relationship shakes up the normal. I'd felt my own round of insecurity not too long ago myself when January had come into the picture.

We stop by the driver's side, and Bryson grips the vehicle's metal frame. "What's going on?"

I swallow. "I know we talked about grabbing dinner, but if it's okay, I really think I need to hang out with Cam tonight instead." I can feel the weight of Bryson's disbelief as he continues to stare at me wordlessly. "He's my best friend, and in two weeks you guys are leaving on tour and will be gone for months." He looks away from me and shakes his head. "I know you keep saying that nothing is for sure, but it could be. And if the three of us are ever going to find some kind of positive coexistence, Cam needs to know that I'm not abandoning him."

Bryson remains silent, maybe to see if I have more to say or maybe to digest what I've already given him. I kick the dirt at my feet and try to respect his need for quiet introspection. Finally, he turns back to me, his expression blank. "Is this another attempt to make Cam happy, or do you want to go over there and be with him?"

It's not a fair question; there are too many layers of context inside of it. I press my fingers to my temples and sigh. "I want my hanging out with Cameron to not be so complicated. That's what I want."

Bryson wraps a hand around the back of my head and gently kisses my forehead. "Have fun." And then he's gone, walking away with his hands in his pockets.

I watch him all the way to the shooting table, watch him pick up a bow, and watch as he once again hits the center of the target.

TWENTY-EIGHT

I'm restless. Restless and anxious, and my insides feel as if they've spent the last six days in a rotisserie oven. And maybe that's why I'm pulling into Bryson's driveway when I know the entire band will be here in an hour.

Despite Bryson's acceptance of my early departure last weekend, he was different the next day. Distant, guarded. It took two hours and the intentional act of putting my phone on silent the entire night to pull him out of his shell. But out of it he came, and if Bryson had lingering doubts about the two of us, he certainly hasn't shown any. It's as if time has become his enemy and he's determined to capitalize on every moment we have together.

I'm the one who can't seem to cope. There are too many things going on in my head. Too many decisions to be made and events to anticipate and parents to try to forget about. It's all pressing in on me, like my stay of execution is finished and I have to deal with all the turmoil right now, this very minute.

"Knock, knock," I call out, peeking around the corner into Bryson's living room.

"Hey, I wasn't expecting you to come by." Bryson smiles, soft and genuine, and lifts his guitar strap over his head.

"I hope it's okay that I didn't call first." I step inside the room that's already been transformed into the band's practice space.

"Of course it is. What's going on?"

"Nothing . . . I don't know." I take a breath, wishing for the umpteenth time that I didn't constantly feel as if I were getting off a roller coaster. "I guess I didn't want to go a day without seeing you."

He lays his guitar down carefully and comes to meet me in the middle of the room. "You guess, huh?"

Embarrassment singes my cheeks. "You know what I mean."

He chuckles and wraps his arms tight around me. "I do know what you mean. I kind of like seeing you, too."

I press my forehead against his chest to keep from turning into a melting pile of mush, but that's what it feels like lately whenever I'm around him.

"Full disclosure. Cameron's coming early to work on some harmonies." He kisses the top of my head and pulls back.

"Oh . . . okay." I'm disappointed. "I won't stay long, then."

A frown pulls at the corner of his mouth but he doesn't push the matter. I was hoping the elephant would disappear if I ignored it. Unfortunately, it's only gotten bigger. He backs up and squats down next to the microphone wiring, making whatever adjustments he needs to.

I follow him over and sit on the armrest of the couch he's pushed up against the wall. "I think I'm going to have to try something new with Penny today."

"And how many strategies will that make now?"

I scowl at the reminder of my continual failure with the

little dog. "Four, but the obstacle course wasn't a complete disaster. She does love it." Not enough to stop attacking Macey or stop lunging at Louie's cage, which was the whole point, but at least I can sort of justify the three hundred dollars it cost me.

"You know what I think?" He glances up at me from his hunched position. "I think deep down you know you need to cancel your spot tomorrow, and this is just one more attempt to stay in denial. Penny's not ready to be adopted. And in some ways, she's worse. She nearly took off my hand the other day when I put her back in her crate."

"I know." I rub my forehead, out of ideas. "But Charlie gave me until the end of July, which means I have only two more weeks to work with Louie, and he still only comes out of his doghouse when I'm alone. I don't have the energy to work on his fear when Penny's there attacking every moving thing."

"Charlie's in a much different place than he was before." Bryson slides the amp over and turns it at an angle. "He'll give you more time. You don't have to rush this."

"It's not just about Charlie." I groan. "It's everything. The estrangement with my mom, worrying about Cam and his reaction to the two of us, the tour that could very well mean you're leaving. And to top it off, Dad's stupid birthday party tomorrow is dangling over my head like a cartoon boulder. I just need something I can control right now. I *need* a victory."

Bryson stands, and I hate that he's watching me with a grin on his face. Hate even more that I think it's one of his sexiest expressions.

"Why is this funny to you?"

"It's not." He strolls over, his smile growing. "I just love how everything you're feeling rolled out in one breath." He pulls me up to standing. "One might even think you came over here because you needed to talk to someone . . . and yeah, the fact that I was your first choice makes me very happy." He nuzzles the skin by my ear, and wonderful tingles run down my spine.

I lace my hands around his neck. "What can I say, Katsaros? You've hooked me and now I'm no good without you."

He laughs into my hair. "Do you realize you only call me by my last name when you're feeling unsure of yourself?"

"I do not."

"Yes, you do." He kisses the top of my head with such tender sweetness I want to wilt. "But you don't have to be nervous with me. This transparency is what I've been waiting for . . . what I've wanted between us all along." He hooks his arm around my waist and pulls me forward with a jerk. "Now kiss me goodbye, because if you keep biting your lip like that, I can promise I'm not letting you go anywhere."

The contact comes just as furiously, my hands gripping his shirt in an effort to bring him closer and closer, all the way to my beating heart.

These are my favorite kind of kisses with him. The passionate ones. The ones that make me feel boneless and electric all at the same time.

The release is slow as neither of us wants to let go, but we know we have to.

"I'll come over after we're done," he whispers, his mouth still centimeters from mine. "And we'll figure it all out together."

For the first time in days, I feel a small measure of relief. "Okay. Thank you."

"You're welcome." He lifts his head, but instead of releasing me, he freezes.

"What?" But it only takes my following his line of sight to see the cause. Cameron is standing in the living room.

Our gazes meet and there's a condemning darkness in his eyes I've never seen before.

Ice fills my belly.

"Tell me I'm not seeing this." His eyes flick from me to Bryson, then back to me. "Tell me I'm hallucinating and he isn't the guy you've been dating." My best friend shoves both of his hands through his hair like his head is about to explode. "Tell me now, Darcy, that the lead singer of *my* band is not your summer fling."

Bryson's body locks up like a steel machine the minute those words dart across the room, but I don't have time to worry about misconceptions. "Cameron . . ."

His curse is loud as he storms away, the front door slamming with a force that makes the lampshades rattle.

I try to disentangle myself, but Bryson's grip only gets tighter. "Let him go. He'll cool down, and the three of us will finally have the conversation that should have happened a while ago."

"I can't let him leave like this. You saw how upset he was."

"He's not the only one upset here." Bryson's hold releases, though I can tell he doesn't want to. "Is that really what you told him? That this thing between us is just a fling?"

"No. He assumed that's what it was."

"And you didn't correct him?"

"Why does it matter?"

"Because it does."

My gaze shifts to the closed front door, every second a guarantee that Cameron will be gone before I ever get outside. "I have to go after him."

"Fine, then I'm going with you." Bryson moves to follow me, but I halt his motion with my palm to his chest.

"Please, stay here. Things are bad enough without him feeling like we're ganging up on him." Bryson stares at my hand, lingering for a long, scrutinizing moment before he finally steps back. I know I'm not being fair, but I'm also not going to participate in a three-way screaming match. Fair or not, Bryson's presence will only make this entire nightmare worse.

I rush to the door, ignoring the hurt and insecurity I'm leaving behind. Bryson is different from Cam. He's stronger. More mature. We can fix us later.

"Cameron . . . wait. I'm so sorry. I never wanted you to find out this way." I catch him just outside the front door, almost as if he was waiting for me to follow. "We were going to tell you."

He turns around, fuming. "When?"

I blink, taken back by the rage in his voice. I expected hurt and even a little anger, but not this. "After the concert. Just like I told you."

"Yeah, nice touch, by the way, with the whole 'trust me, he'll be there' line." His voice is filled with a disgust that's never been directed at me. "How could you do this to me? He's my bandmate, Darcy! He's tied to every one of my dreams."

"I didn't do it on purpose. It just sort of happened."

"Nothing just happens with him! It was premeditated from the first moment he saw you walk through this door." He throws his arms into the air. "Have you forgotten who you're dealing with here? It's Bryson! *Bryson*, Darcy. You know what he's capable of." Cameron walks across the lawn and then back again, his hard steps punctuating his growing anger. "What happens when he tires of you, huh? How am I sup-posed to get up onstage and pretend I don't hate him when

277

he breaks your heart?" He stops in front of me. "Because that's exactly what he's going to do!"

I stare at him, apology quickly turning to irritation. "He's different with me. He really cares—"

"Oh, bull." Cameron looks ready to vomit. "He's the same guy he's always been. He's using you, Darcy. And this is nothing more than one more way for him to prove that he can get whatever he wants."

"So what are you saying?" I ask through gritted teeth. "That I'm just some stupid girl who let him?"

He spreads his arms wide. "Apparently!"

The silence that falls between us is so heavy I feel like drowning under its weight. We both need to calm down. Both need to stop and talk about this rationally like we always do.

But Cameron is still incensed. His nostrils flare and his eyes narrow at the house he just stormed out of. "I knew something was up. He's been too cagey; his resentment obvious. I just didn't want to believe he'd try to push me out this close to us finally making it." He paces again, shaking his head, his hands drawn into fists. "January warned me. She nailed him in one interaction and told me he'd do this the minute I outshined him. The minute my influence superseded his, he'd find a way to get rid of me. I got us this contract." He slaps his hand against his chest. "I did, not him. And he couldn't handle it. He has to be the star . . . always." Cameron steps closer, his chest an imposing wall. His eyes glow like a beast. "Don't think for a second it's a coincidence you two got together after that concert. He knew I wouldn't leave without a fight. And this was his kill shot—you."

I stand there, stunned with disbelief, trying to find my voice.

"And what I can't understand. What my mind cannot wrap

around is the fact that you let him!" His hands tremble as he backs away. "What were you thinking? You watched what he did to Alison. You comforted her when she came home crying. Or did it not matter that in one thoughtless decision you put a knife in both of our backs?"

"Hey!" Anger and guilt punch through the strangle in my throat. "If you want to talk about you and me, then fine. But leave Alison out of it."

"I can't leave her out of it, and neither should you!" He viciously pulls his phone from his back pocket and tries to shove it in my hand. "Call her. Call her now and ask her what it was really like on tour with him. Ask her how cold he became the minute we left town. How he flinched at every touch and made excuses to get away from her. Ask her, because I'm sure there's more." When I refuse to take the device, he shoves it back in his jeans. "He knows how to play the part. How to suck you in and make you believe he's not completely broken. But he is, Darcy. He is. He's the kind of broken that brings a random girl to his bed the same night he sticks his devastated girlfriend on a bus home."

A chill seeps through my skin, and I cross my arms to ward off the shiver. "I don't believe you."

"Oh, it's true, every word." He steps forward, his tone ripe with sarcasm. "And unlike you, I don't make a practice of lying to the people I supposedly care about."

My eyes burn with misery. I hate every one of our words. Hate that this person in front of me feels like a stranger.

He studies me, the line of his jaw still tight with anger, but his brows pull together, plaintive, sympathetic. "What is going on with you? Because what I saw in there makes no sense. He is not the man you want. Not the man you've spent twenty-nine years waiting for. How could you, for any reason, settle for *him*?" He points to the closed front door, his voice rising once more. "A guy who is incapable of caring for anyone other than himself! A guy who will never be the kind of father and husband you need him to be, because he has no idea what love even looks like. Have you thought of any of that?"

Bile rises in my throat with each one of his cruel words. "Stop it."

"No, I won't stop it. Not until you see the truth." He grips my arms, and both our bodies shake under the intense surge of emotion. "Bryson is just like your father. In every way. He's selfish and cunning, and when he's done bleeding you dry, he'll walk away without a second thought."

"Let go of me," I cry, pushing him away. Angry tears blur my vision while my heart feels as if it might explode into a thousand pieces of shrapnel. "It isn't the same."

"It's exactly the same!" His voice lowers and comes at me like a blade. "Is that what this is, Darcy? Some sick Freudian transference? You couldn't get your father to stick around so you decide to find someone just like him to fill the void?"

The air freezes between us, his words dragging through me like a tangled line, ripping open all the wounds I thought I'd closed. "I can't believe you just said that to me." I push past him, but he grabs my arm and whirls me around.

"Somebody had to. Because I don't even know who you are anymore." His own furious tears pool in his eyes as we stand there, a churning fire between us.

I can't stand it. The pain is too great, the betrayal in his eyes too gut-wrenching to stomach. I jerk my arm from his grip and run to my old truck, the gears grinding as I peel out of the driveway.

The rules of the road make no impression on me. I blow

through stop signs, speed at a rate that would undoubtedly get me thrown in jail, and push my truck to its absolute limit before pulling into Charlie's driveway. The tears have long since dried until all that's left are Cameron's hateful words rolling through my head over and over again.

I slam my door and kick the tire. One, two, three more times until it physically hurts to kick it again. I set my hands on my hips, breathe in and out until I convince myself I'm calm enough to deal with the animals.

It's my job, after all, and isn't that what I've been preaching to Charlie for weeks? That Penny needs an outlet, that she needs to feel useful and important and not stuck in some cage she has absolutely no control over.

I storm through the yard, ignoring Louie even though he runs to the gate and wags his long tail spastically. "Not today," I mumble.

Charlie's gone and so is Macey, a very good thing right now.

Penny scratches incessantly at the crate when I open the laundry room door.

"I'm coming." I tear the leash from the wall, undo the latch, and click the metal to her collar before she can bolt away from me.

We do our usual walk around the barn, letting her do her business before the real work begins. With every step, I work to calm my nerves, work to silence the voice in my head that screams maybe Cameron is right. Maybe I did go for Bryson because he was different and dangerous. Maybe all of this is part of the swirling vortex that has become my pathetic life.

I tug Penny forward, irritated it's taking her so long today. Louie sees us coming and chases along the fence, agitated, just like he used to before, like he can sense the charged energy I'm emoting.

Penny growls and lunges for Louie, only I'm prepared for as much and drag her all the way to Bentley's old kennel, her paws digging in the dirt as she barks ferociously at the dog who's ten times heavier than she is.

"Get in there!" I yell and shove the fighting dog to the middle of the dirt floor before locking us both inside. "We're not doing this today, do you hear me?" The edge in my voice makes her retreat, and all the hair on her back rises in defense. "I'm sorry." I take a deep breath. "I'm calm, really."

But nothing feels calm anymore, especially not me.

Louie's barking turns erratic, and I take my eyes off Penny for one second to assure him I'm okay.

It's one second too long. The leash slips from my hand as Penny struggles through the kennel's hog squares and races free.

"No!" Blood pounds in my ears as I rush to the gate, my shaking fingers fumbling with the lock. "Open, please, please open!" Finally it does, and I make it to the yard at the same time Penny forces her way inside Louie's cage. I take off in a sprint as the horrific sound of two dogs battling for dominance assaults my ears.

Everything falls into movie-like slow motion. I can't get my feet to run fast enough. Can't reach the gate or stop the two dogs tangled on the ground, mouths open, biting, growling, hurting each other.

Fear and chaos claw from my gut to my windpipe. "Penny, no!" I scream. Her jaw is locked around the skin at Louie's neck. I'm paralyzed, helpless to stop the fight without putting myself at risk. "Louie, stop!" I scream louder, but it's useless.

He's left with no choice but to defend himself the way Macey never has.

An ear-piercing cry escapes Louie's mouth, and instinct trumps all sense. I rush between the dogs, forgoing all my training, and wrestle away paws and nails until I grab Penny in mid-attack.

Pain slices through my hand, but I don't stop until I have Penny against my chest and my uninjured palm clamped around her mouth so she can no longer hurt anyone.

Louie rushes inside his doghouse, whimpering. He lowers his head and licks at his paws. My body goes cold, my heart crushed by the reality that I did this. I never should have come here. Not like this.

"I'm so sorry," I say to the terrified Great Dane. "This is all my fault."

Still holding Penny tight to my chest, I free us from the kennel and rush to the back door. She's stopped fighting me now, which gives me a chance to check her over for damage. Blood soaks her sleek white fur, and panic rises until I ascertain that it's my blood, not hers, and that somehow Louie managed to defend himself without seriously hurting her, something he easily could have done if he wanted to.

I gently put her back in her cage and lock it up. It's the first time Penny doesn't fight me on it. For once, the crate feels like a safe place.

The floor trembles beneath my feet, the adrenaline drop so severe I reach for the wall as I slowly sink to the ground. Red handprints slide down the white paint, but it's all I can do to steady the drop. I work to breathe, the air catching in my throat like hot coals, burning my chest with every inhale. I scoot to the wall to find some sense of support. It helps. The tightness in my chest eases until once again I can exhale without pain.

Penny watches me through the slats in the door. Probably asking me the questions I keep asking myself. *Why did you come here? Why did you jeopardize so much?*

I lower my forehead to my knees, unable to answer either one.

TWENTY-NINE

The bleeding down my arm doesn't allow me to stay in my hunched position for long. Slowly, I rise to my feet, checking to ensure my balance is once again steady. My right hand screams out in pain as I spread it fully to examine the extent of the damage. The cut is in the soft tissue between my thumb and index finger, and it's deep enough that stitches are a real possibility.

I stumble to the kitchen sink, my body still fighting off the shock of earlier, and hold my hand under a rush of water. Burning fire scorches my skin at the contact, but I force it steady under the stream, all while pumping soap in my other hand.

Because my luck is just that terrible today, the back door opens right when I begin scrubbing the wound and long before I can clean up the trail of blood that extends from the door to the laundry room. Not to mention the permanently crimson-stained T-shirt I'm wearing that is supposed to be a butter yellow.

Charlie takes no time in assessing my state. He hurries toward me and grabs a handful of paper towels. "I'm calling Animal Control tomorrow."

"It wasn't her fault. I was upset and angry, and I should never have come out here."

"I don't care if you drop-kicked her to the moon. I will not keep a dog that bites in my house."

"She didn't bite me on purpose. She got loose and went after Louie. This happened when I was breaking up the fight."

"That doesn't change my mind."

"Well, it should!" I holler and immediately wish I hadn't. Charlie watches me like a handful of lit firecrackers. "Sorry." I hunch over the sink, my forearms bearing my body weight since my hand is still dangling in the stainless-steel bowl. "It's just that you and Macey, well, you deal with your grief by mourning quietly. Penny is different. She's angry at her circumstances, but deep down, it's still grief. Surely you can understand that."

He gently takes my hand and examines the wound, forcing me to stand back up. "I don't think it's deep enough for stitches, but you should still go get it seen."

"I had a tetanus shot this past year when I was getting ready for my trip. As long as I keep it dry and dosed with antibiotic cream, the cut will be fine. This isn't the first time I've been bitten by an animal." Though it is the first one I've felt responsible for. I watch him, my voice turning to a plea. "Please, Charlie, if you send her away because of my stupidity, I'll never forgive myself."

He presses his lips together and sighs. "Fine. But no fair tomorrow. I cannot in good conscience give that dog to someone else until I know this is an isolated incident." He sets my towel-wrapped hand on the counter. "Don't move. I'll be back with some bandages."

I hold my arm to my chest and lean my backside against the sink. Through the window I can hear Louie's barking, loud and steady, just like it used to be a month ago.

"Stupid, stupid," I moan, realizing for maybe the first time that it wasn't just Penny's progress that took a hit today but Louie's, as well.

Charlie returns with a first-aid kit in hand and finishes tending to the wound. From his silence and the scowl on his face, I know he's not happy with me or with his animals.

"I'm sorry," I say again, like it will make any difference.

"You said you were upset. What happened?"

"I really don't want to talk about it."

He glances up from his task, his eyes hard. "And I don't want to be bandaging up a dog bite right now. But here I am."

Since it's obvious I'm not going to get out of this conversation, I give him the quick version. "I got into a fight with my best friend, and he said some pretty horrible things."

He cuts the medical tape and presses the end to my skin, finishing the job. "This the same best friend who's also in Black Carousel?" When my eyes show my surprise, he continues, "Bryson's talked to me a little about the situation. He wanted my advice."

"And?"

"It sounds like it doesn't matter anymore."

I shake my head. "No, I guess it doesn't."

"So, what did he say?"

I drop my chin, a surge of anger coming back so fierce I want to scream. "Nothing I want to repeat."

Charlie crosses his arms, continuing to assess my body language like I'm feeding the story without saying a word. "I recognize this anger. Bryson had it for years before he finally dealt with the root issue."

I grind my teeth, too afraid that if I speak, it will only come out in curses and screams.

He squeezes my shoulder cautiously, like a father with an

estranged child. "It's a slippery slope, letting these feelings fester. Kind of like Penny over there, you end up taking your anger out on everyone else instead of dealing with the one person who caused it."

I think of my parents and know Charlie's right. I've avoided and coped and stayed away, but I haven't dealt with any of my feelings toward them. I swallow down the ache and push off the sink, refusing to look at the man who just pegged my issues to an alarmingly accurate degree. "I'm going to go check on Louie and make sure he's not hurt."

I'm almost to the door when Charlie responds. "This may not seem as bad as trying to drink away your problems, but, Darcy—" I look at him, and his eyes hold the wisdom that comes with seventy years of life—"burying the anger is just as dangerous."

~

It's dark by the time I pull into Bryson's driveway again, yet it's taken me this long to get all the raging emotions under control. I stayed with Louie until he stopped barking, a chore that took nearly thirty minutes. I spent another thirty petting him until finally he seemed docile and relaxed. Then I drove. Nowhere at first, but then I ended up on I-35 heading north toward Dallas.

My dad lives in a two-bedroom, fifteen-hundred-square-foot, ridiculously expensive apartment near Richardson. I've been there once . . . the day he took me for a tour of the area, spouting on and on about the benefits of not having to commute anymore. It was the same week my parents signed legal documents ending thirty-five years of marriage, and the last time I've spoken to him.

When his exit came, I took the turnaround and headed right back south.

Charlie was right about the anger festering. I'd been feeding an untamed monster for far too long. Stuffing it down until I hit the breaking point. And now, like with Penny, the aftermath is a mess for me to clean up.

I ease out of my truck, unsure what to expect to find. Bryson was mad before I left. Who knows what I'm walking into now? I close my eyes and knock on the door. I'd come here earlier because I wanted reassurance. Funny, I stand here now, feeling the exact same way.

No answer comes, but I know he's home. His truck is in the driveway, and I can hear music through the door. I turn the knob and enter, uninvited.

The living room is still set up for practice, even though Bryson is the only one here, sitting on a folding chair and strumming chords with focused aggravation. I know he hears me come in, but he doesn't move, doesn't even stop to acknowledge my presence.

I take a tentative step forward, unfamiliar with the tightness in my chest. I've seen Bryson this detached before, but never with me, even before we were, well, whatever we've been until today. "Hey."

His eyes lock onto mine and it seems there's no air in the universe. His stare reveals nothing; cold, calm, dead. Time stretches impossibly. And right when I finally find the courage to say more than a fumbling hello, he looks down at his fingers, strums a chord, and then mashes his hand against the strings to stop the vibration. "I guess I should have locked the door."

There's another chair close by. I pull it near his and sit down. Maybe if we're at the same level, he won't feel so far away. "You're angry."

"Oh, I passed angry a while ago. About the same time my girlfriend drove off without a word to me." He strums again, a clear indication he doesn't want to continue our conversation.

"I'm sorry. Everything got so heated, things were said . . ." I swallow down the sickness in my stomach. "You're right, though. I shouldn't have left that way."

He snorts in agreement but still doesn't stop picking at his guitar strings.

I reach out to touch his hand. A mistake. His physical rejection of my touch is as sharp as his verbal ones have been. I sigh, frustrated, and put my hand back in my lap. "I wish you'd at least look at me."

That gets his attention. His head jerks up, his stare icy. "You know what I wish? I wish for once you cared about my feelings as much as you do Cam's." He aggressively tugs off his guitar and stands. "I wish my walls were thicker than a sheet of paper so I wouldn't have had to listen to a complete annihilation of my character. But mostly I wish you had said one thing, just *one*, to defend me out there."

His words wash over me, and I feel sick with myself. Sick with the viciousness of Cameron's words—with how little I did to stand up for Bryson. "I didn't realize you heard us."

"Cameron wasn't exactly whispering, was he." He shoves agitated fingers through his hair. "Do you believe him?" When I don't answer immediately, he turns his back to me and stares out the dark window. "Of course you do. I was a fool to think it would ever be otherwise."

"So you didn't take a girl to your room that night?"

He spins back around, his jaw tight. I can almost see the explanation blazing in his eyes, but he holds back. "Would you trust my word over his if I said no?"

"I'd like to think I would."

"Funny. I'd like to think you would, too, but I don't." He works his jaw back and forth like he's having an argument with himself. Finally, he says, "Yes, I did take a girl to my room. She was an old friend from high school who happened to be in town. She stayed thirty minutes. We reminisced a little and then I hugged her goodbye. Any more details you need?"

I look down at my fingers, relief slamming into me.

"I'm not that guy, Darcy. I never have been. Something you of all people should know, considering what didn't happen in your room the night of the concert."

"I know you're not." And I did know, yet the doubt Cameron planted is still creeping up inside.

"Then why are you still looking at me like that?"

"Like what?"

"Like you did the day I moved you into Zoe's. Like I'm some kind of parasite out to destroy the people you love."

I hesitate, desperately wishing I could just trust Bryson's motives. Yet, even my father, the one man I thought to be above all reproach, found a way to lie to me. "The girl in your room wasn't Cameron's only accusation. Did you . . ." My throat is suddenly sand, and I realize I don't want him to tell me. My heart can't handle another crushing blow. And yet, not knowing is a fate I can't live with. "Did you use our relationship to try to get him to leave the band?"

He takes a step back as if my words are a shot and not a question. "You're really asking me that?"

"I have to." My voice is faint and weak, part of me recognizing I'm being completely unfair.

"No, you don't. You should have enough faith in me to answer it all by yourself." He stares at me for a long time, saying nothing, waiting to see if I'll take the question back. When I don't, he finally answers. "Darcy, if I wanted him out, he'd be out. End of story." He shakes his head, his breath hitching in disbelief. "I have spent the summer pouring my heart out to you, opening up about things I *never* talk about, all to show you who I am. He spends five minutes spewing pure hatred, and I'm the one in question here?" Bryson dips his chin, his eyes locked on the floor. "You know what? Forget it. I won't defend myself to you, not when I've given you no reason to doubt me."

"You're right. You haven't. I'm sorry," I say, lowering my head into my hands. "I've screwed everything up so bad today. You. Penny." I rub my temples, the throb from earlier coming in sharp, penetrating jabs.

"What happened to your hand?"

I jerk my head up and examine the bandage he's only now seeing. "It was an accident. She didn't mean to bite me."

"Wow, even a dog has more loyalty from you than I do."

"I'm sorry," I say again, completely at a loss as to how to break through this new layer of uncertainty between us. I've been spoiled. Up until now, he's given me everything I've asked for—honesty, trust, affection, forgiveness. Now he stands in front of me, a shell of who he was only hours ago. "Bryson." Finally he meets my eyes. "I'm sorry. I didn't mean to hurt you."

For one moment, there's a flash of the guy I was only beginning to get to know. "It doesn't matter anymore."

"Yes, it does." I rise from my chair and try again to get close to him. "Tell me what to say so I can fix this between us."

"You can't fix it." His voice holds more heartbreak than anger, though it's clear there's both. "Your words are meaningless when your actions continue to reaffirm a truth I haven't wanted to accept. I watched you two out there, and you don't get that kind of passion between two people unless they love each other."

"Of course we love each other. We've been best friends for nearly thirty years!"

"That wasn't the reaction of a worried best friend. If it were, I could live with it and even respect it. That was the reaction of a man who just had his heart ripped out." He throws his arms out and growls, "When are you going to open your eyes? He's been in love with you since he was eighteen years old. And not the surface kind. The deep, longing kind that has enabled him to stuff down his feelings year after year on the sheer hope that one day you will love him back."

Now I want to pull out my hair. "Why does it always come back to this? I've told you repeatedly that I don't have romantic feelings for Cam."

"Call it whatever you want to, but there's still something there. He's the first one you run to when you're upset. He finds his way into every single conversation we have. He's here between us, Darcy, and has been since we were kids." He laces his fingers on top of his head and presses his lips together. "I won't be Tuck. I'm not going to sit here in denial, holding my heart in my hands, until one day you finally wake up and realize what all of us already know."

"So that's it? One misunderstanding and we're over."

"This isn't a misunderstanding." His voice turns cold. "You walked out on me—twice. For him."

We stand there, eyes locked on each other, at a complete impasse. "This is how you do it." A sob rises up my throat. "You cut people out of your life and then turn around and make them feel like it's their fault."

"I didn't want this."

"Well, neither did I." I turn away, blinking, trying to make sense of what's happening.

"Darcy." He says it like I'm physically hurting him. "What else can I do?"

"Anything but this." I rush back, cradle his face and drag him closer, our foreheads touching, our breaths mingling. "I'm sorry," I whisper, and the apology throbs the air between us.

His arms circle around my waist, holding me tight as if every second spent in this embrace will erase time. "Okay," he finally says, and my heart leaps back into place. His hold loosens and he looks at me, tired creases at the corners of his eyes. "I'll once again deny every one of my instincts and try to move forward with us . . . on one condition." He pauses, and I know whatever he's about to say is non-negotiable. "I won't share your heart with another man. If you and I have any chance of making it, your friendship with him has to change."

My stomach crawls into my throat and I pull free of his embrace. "Change how?"

His lips tighten because we both know he means *end*, not change.

I shake my head, refusing to hear what he's demanding. "You're asking too much."

"Maybe I am. But that's where I stand."

A million thoughts collide in my mind. A thousand emotions, all of them hinging on the hope that if he would just listen to me, he'd see he doesn't have to do this. I work to calm my nerves, but my voice still comes out shaky. "Bryson, it doesn't have to be so black and white. We can find a middle ground. I'll do better. I'll put up clearer boundaries this time."

His eyes darken. "You asked what you could do to fix it; I'm telling you."

"No, you're giving me an ultimatum."

"I'm giving you a choice," he snaps back before taking a breath to calm down. "The same one I made when I got you Zoe's apartment and again when I kissed you, and I'll keep choosing you over and over again. Because it's *easy*. Because you mean more than Black Carousel ever has." Hurt leaks through his voice, and I know it's because I can't tell him the same thing.

"But I would never ask you to give them up for me."

A reply stills on his lips as if I punched the air from his argument, then he angrily runs his hands through his hair. "Darcy, there is no reality where the three of us happily coexist. He. Is. In. Love. With. You." Bryson's words come out in tight, emphatic clips. "This means every moment you spend together is driven by an ulterior motive. One I cannot live with as your boyfriend." He drops his hands and looks straight at me, his voice growing rough. "Just look at the damage he did in one moment. I thought we had crossed a threshold together. That we were moving forward into a new place of trust and openness and mutual respect. Now, just hours later, you've questioned my morals and my integrity, all because he told you to."

"Bryson, I admit I messed up. I doubted you and I shouldn't have, but my trust issues run deeper than just Cameron."

"Maybe so, but I can't forget the things he said or the obvious influence it has on your feelings for me. It will haunt me every time you're together, and that will ruin us." He sighs, his sadness contagious, and an ache falls over me. "Do you want to know the real reason why I didn't tell you about the tour? Because I never once thought we'd make it that far. I've known this entire time that Cameron was going to lose his mind when he found out we were together. I've just been waiting for the blowup."

"If that's true, then why did you let me think it would work? Why even agree to wait?"

"Because you weren't ready to let go of him, and I wasn't ready to let go of you." He reaches up, his knuckles tracing the line of my jaw. "I guess I hoped that if you had enough time, then maybe when we got to this point, you'd actually choose me." The air hangs heavy between us, and for a second I see that seventeen-year-old boy, bracing himself for rejection, all while hoping it doesn't come. And then just as quickly, the tenderness recedes from his eyes. The boy disappears, hardened and ready for the inevitable truth. I can't do what he's asking me to, and he knows it. "But that isn't what's going to happen, is it?"

"Bryson . . ." I feel crippled with loss, unable to say what I need to in order to stop this insanity.

"You don't have to explain. This one's on me. I knew better." His expression betrays no emotion except the glisten in his eyes, but it's enough to hollow me out. He walks to his door and pulls it open. "It's late. You should go home."

There will be no kisses goodbye, no promises of next-day phone calls, no teasing laughter. If I walk out that door, it's over. But if I don't, I'm making a promise I can't live with. Not yet. Maybe not ever.

THIRTY

Saturday comes like a baseball bat against the face. My hand throbs, my heart aches, and since I'm skipping the adoption fair, I now have no real excuse for missing my father's barbecue.

I struggle to sit up in bed, the bright sun shining through my windows. I should have bought curtains. Dark ones. Ones that would respect a person's need to wallow in misery.

Wet doggy kisses assault my face while little paws prance on my chest. I guess the lack of curtains isn't my only issue.

"You win, Piper. I'm getting up." I slide my legs over the mattress as Piper leaps off the bed, on the bed, and off again. "My goodness. Okay. I get it. You need to go outside."

She bolts to the front door the minute my bedroom door is cracked and barks excitedly.

"I'm coming. I'm coming." There's a pretty good chance I look like the Bride of Frankenstein this morning, but my neighbors will just have to deal with it.

I tie my robe around my waist, and just when I'm about to reach the door, Zoe comes barreling inside, nearly sending Piper across the room. Good thing my little dog is quick.

"Liam broke up with me," she says, dropping her overnight

bag onto the floor. Besides traces of her in the laundry room and kitchen, Zoe's been a ghost since the couple got together. "He said I was 'too young' for him. Please." She rolls her eyes. "He eats dinner at five o'clock, watches the news for exactly one hour, and says alcohol gives him a headache. I'm too young? The guy is practically geriatric at twenty-seven." She crosses her arms and studies me. "You look terrible, by the way."

"Thanks," I say dryly and return to my task before poor Piper has an accident on Zoe's wood floors.

Zoe jumps in front of me and unhooks the leash by the door. "I'll take her. You . . . go shower or something."

I cross my arms, annoyed. "I'm not that bad."

She raises her eyebrows but doesn't say another word before disappearing out the door, Piper right at her heels.

I drag my feet across the room, wanting nothing more than to crawl right back into bed. I go to the bathroom instead. A huge mistake. The mirror is as honest as my roommate. My hair is ratted, and there are still traces of my blood on the tips. Dark circles mar the underside of my eyes, proof of how little sleep I've gotten the past few days.

I've come full circle, with nothing but broken relationships to show for the journey.

My body suddenly feeling heavy, I ease myself onto the closed toilet lid. Elbows on my knees, face in my hands, I sit and wait for some kind of clarity. But there is none. No answers. No way forward. No promise of something better.

"Where have you been?" I whisper to the One I haven't spoken to in what feels like forever. "Why have you left me?"

I feel a pressing on my chest and a warmth around my body as if He were right here, holding me. Sobs burn in my throat, but I can't rein them back anymore. The flood comes, deep and heart-wrenching. And I let it. Let out all the tears I'd been holding on to long before Cameron shoved a knife into my chest or Bryson locked me out of his life. These tears fall for the first man I ever loved. The one I can't seem to find the strength to forgive.

~⁀

"Well now, that's much better," Zoe says when I emerge from my room forty-five minutes later. I've showered, dressed, even added some curl to my hair and a coat of mascara. I haven't seen my father in months, and as stupid as it sounds, I want him to be proud to look at me. "Where are you going all dressed up?"

"Actually, a better question is where are *we* going? I need some backup today."

Zoe's perfectly plucked eyebrows furrow. "My boyfriend just broke up with me. I'm entitled to a day of chocolate and really bad movies."

"Maybe, if this were an uncommon occurrence for you. But this is the second breakup since I've moved in, and let's be real here. The only thing you really like about Liam is how he looks."

"Yeah, I guess you're right." Zoe sighs and squeezes a pillow to her chest. "But I'm not agreeing to anything until I know what you have in mind. I've seen your definition of fun, and it's not normal."

Despite the heaviness of my terrible weekend so far, a smile finds its way to the surface. "It'll be fun. I promise. My dad is nothing if not entertaining." I walk to the refrigerator and grab the orange juice. "And worst case, you get a free lunch at a swanky apartment in Dallas."

"Will there be cute boys?"

"No, probably not." I set down the carton, annoyed. "We're not going to a bar, Zoe; it's a family barbecue. Believe it or not, life does exist outside of the male species."

"Gee, okay. I was just asking so I knew how to dress." She pops up from the couch. "Give me an hour."

"You have fifteen minutes!" I call down the hallway after her and again find myself wanting to chuckle. And cry. Or maybe do both.

I grab the leash and take Piper out one more time while I wait on my roommate. The weather is ideal today. Big puffy clouds in the sky, a slight breeze that shockingly doesn't feel like a blow dryer, and no humidity.

Piper sniffs along the edge of the grass, searching for that perfect spot. I wait, enjoying the serenity, until my phone buzzes in my pocket.

Immediately my mind goes to Cameron, and I'm shocked by the devastation I still feel. He hurt me on purpose. He wielded a power only someone that close has, lashing out and attacking every one of my insecurities.

The phone vibrates again. The second notice that I missed a text. I ease it from my shorts slowly, only to find the text is from my dad, letting me know how thrilled he is I decided to come and what parking lot to use.

Relief and disappointment hit in equal measure. Cam's silence puts us at a stalemate. Which also means I somehow hurt him to the same degree he hurt me. Though how, I still can't understand. Maybe I never will.

"Alright, chica, I'm ready," Zoe calls from the top of the stairs.

I tug on Piper's leash, and she comes quickly, beating me up the stairs without much effort. I grab my keys and the wallet that mostly stays locked in my truck and try not to talk myself out of today's adventure.

"So, if this is a family thing, why isn't Bryson going?" Zoe asks when we get strapped in.

I work to keep the surprise out of my tone while my stomach does a somersault that is less than pleasant. "Why would he?"

"Don't even try it. I know you two are dating. He's been eating all my food, and last week at lunch I started calling him the Joker because I couldn't get him to stop smiling."

I start the engine and try to ignore the nagging ache inside. She waits for me to confirm her theory, which I won't because it doesn't even matter anymore. I turn around, check the rear for any movement, then carefully back out of the parking lot.

"Breakups are the worst when you're around people in love. He's going to be absolutely impossible to deal with now." Her sigh is dramatic when she continues, obviously missing the fact that my silence means I have no interest in discussing this topic. "But I suppose his happiness is justified. He's had a thing for you since forever, even after you dissed him at homecoming."

Okay, that I can't ignore. "I didn't dis him at homecoming. Bryson didn't even go to our school."

"Duh. Which is why he had Mason put the rose in your locker for him. And let me tell you, that note was no easy undertaking either. He made me write it because his handwriting sucked so bad, and then he rejected my first four attempts."

"How do you even remember this? You were, what, ten or eleven?"

She shrugs. "It was right before Dad kicked him out. I remember everything from that time period."

I shift in my seat, my neck going tight. I don't want to think about that night or any of the other things Bryson confided in me over the last month. "I never got any rose, or a note, so I think you misunderstood."

"Trust me, I was a preteen. Bryson's love life was the only interesting thing going on." She kicks off her sandals and crosses her legs in the seat. "The rose was for you. And Mason put it in your locker. I read the text confirming it."

"Well, I never got it." I don't know why my words come out with such a bite, or why my skin suddenly feels itchy and uncomfortable. Maybe because Alison and Cameron were the only other people who knew my locker combination and neither of them ever said a word.

"Too bad. He had the whole thing planned out. Dinner, a rented limo, a rose cors—"

"We broke up, okay?" The truck's cab falls silent, and I squeeze the steering wheel. "So you can stop with whatever romantic notions you have going on in your head."

"You broke up?" The horror in her tone slices me. "Why?"

"A disagreement." My stomach rolls, and I wish I hadn't drunk the orange juice after all. It sits on the edge of my throat and makes my eyes burn. "One we couldn't get past."

She turns her head to look at me, and it's the first time I've ever seen judgment in her eyes. "And you lecture me on my relationship turnaround time?"

I click on the radio. I'm glad Zoe agreed to come along, but that doesn't mean we need to talk on the drive there.

THIRTY-ONE

As he usually does, Dad packs out the place with birthday guests. The parking lot was full, so we had to park a block down on the street. Zoe walks closely by me, carrying the card I picked up on the way. It's one of those generic dad ones, the kind that says happy birthday without saying anything positive about the relationship. Inside, there's a fifty-dollar Visa card. Another generic gift, and so different from the personalized grilling apron I custom ordered for him last year.

"You look nervous," she says, and I lower the fingernail I've been chewing on.

"My dad and I haven't really been on the best of terms lately."

To my surprise, her voice turns soft. "Did you use to be close?"

I swallow down the lump in my throat. "Very."

"Well, here's the thing with dads. No matter how frustrated they get, or how much we disappoint them, we're still their little girls." She chuckles as if she knows this from personal experience and hands me the card. "I'm sure everything will work out just fine between the two of you."

I study the woman who continually surprises me. "Thanks for coming, Zoe. I really needed you here."

"You know me, I'm always up for a party." She shrugs off the gratitude with a wink that looks so much like her brother's it takes me two steps to recover. "Which one is your dad?"

I scan the area in front of us. As usual, he's standing by the grill, the apron I gave him tied around his waist, a bottle of beer in one hand and tongs in the other. "Right there." I point, missing him so much it nearly trips me up.

"Oh my. He's a silver fox." She bumps my shoulder with hers. "I thought you said no cute boys."

"Gross, Zoe." I make a vomit motion that has her laughing out loud. It's a nice sound and much needed, since I do feel like throwing up, though for a completely different reason.

"I'm kidding. But he is handsome for an old guy. You look a lot like him."

"Yeah. People tell me that all the time." Not just that I look like him, but also that he's handsome and charming. The life of the party, my dad. Too bad that's the best thing he'll be remembered for now. The other stuff—loving husband, respected father, faithful man of God—will never again be part of his legacy.

He sees me a few seconds later and excitedly puts down the items in his hands. My feet want to plant themselves in the grass, or run away, back to my truck, back to the stupid bathroom where I made the reckless mistake of deciding to come here.

"Hey, sweetheart!" Fatherly arms wrap around me in a hug that tries way too hard to make up for lost time. "I'm so glad you made it." He releases his grip, looks me over like he hasn't seen me in years, and hugs me tight once again.

I work to get my arms to move, to make them lift and attempt to return the affection.

He finally lets go, and I don't miss the sheen in his eyes. "How was the drive?" He looks past me like he's waiting for someone else. "No Cameron today?"

I shake my head, emotion stirring in my belly. "Nope. No Cameron." It takes clearing my throat to make the sickness go away. "Happy birthday." I awkwardly hand him the card, which he takes much the same way.

"You didn't have to get me anything."

"I know." He looks down like he isn't sure if he should open it now or wait. I help him make the decision. "Dad, this is Zoe. My roommate."

Zoe and Dad do what two charmers always do when meeting someone new. They sparkle and laugh and make small talk look easy. When they're done, Dad puts his arm around my shoulder. "Well, come on. Let's get you young ladies some food."

It's funny how one's perspective changes over time. I've never noticed how short my dad is before. He's just always been my dad. But after meeting Michael, and then spending the last month next to Bryson's six-foot frame, I realize my dad must only be five-foot-eight, and that's probably generous.

A crowd stands around the picnic table littered with plates of food, and Zoe stealthily points at the two shirtless guys to her right. They're young, probably not much older than Zoe is. I study more faces and realize the trend isn't limited to the boys. This party is much more reminiscent of a college blowout than the usual crowd at my dad's birthday parties.

"Where are all your friends?" I ask my dad when I don't recognize a single person in the crowd.

His responding smile feels practiced. "They'll be by. You know these parties are come-and-go."

No, actually they're usually come and stay until Mom kicks everyone out.

He turns away from my confused stare and gathers two empty platters into his arms. "Go mingle. I just need to get these filled up again and then we'll catch up."

I look for the usual gifts, most of them jokes, but still piled there and wrapped every year. There's nothing. Only my lone card, which Dad set down on his folding chair. There isn't even a cake.

Moreover, the crowd that seemed so huge minutes ago has now dwindled. Some of them moved from the serving table to various picnic spots around the lawn. Others appear to have taken their plates back into the apartment building. A few of the guys throw a Frisbee, more joining them after disposing of their trash. Zoe and I stand and watch as they form into teams, neither of us interested in eating right now.

"Hey!" The cute one she noticed earlier comes jogging over. "We're starting a game of ultimate Frisbee." His eyes fall on my roommate's long, slender legs and trail up to her eyes. "Wanna join us?"

"How do you know my dad?" I ask, partly out of curiosity, and partly because I don't like how he's looking at Zoe, even if she doesn't seem to mind at all.

He shrugs like he doesn't really. "I think he's on the first floor by the elevators. That's where the flyer was, at least."

"Flyer?"

"Yeah. Said free food and beer. We all figured it was an apartment thing, until we came out and saw it was just one old dude. But hey, if he's buying, I'm drinking. So . . . you two playing?"

Zoe brightens. "Absolutely. Darcy?"

I'm still reeling from the flyer comment. "No, go ahead." They run off together, and it's only then that I see the real picture before me. The small, gated park is packed, but not with old friends who are here to celebrate another milestone in my father's life. It's packed with strangers, here only because they were promised a free lunch. I turn around and watch my dad with new eyes. He's all alone by the grill, clinging to a past life that no longer exists. I wonder if that's what Bryson sees when he looks at me. A person oblivious to the fact they're living in a memory.

I shove my hands into my pockets and walk back over to the pavilion, suddenly not so angry at the man in my line of sight.

"You decided not to play?" he asks when I sit on top of the picnic table.

"Nope. I figured I'd come keep you company for a while."

He lifts a rack of ribs onto a massive cutting board and gets to slicing it, the smell so familiar it almost feels like we've gone back in time. Dad at the grill. Me eagerly volunteering to be his sous chef.

I can tell I'm making him nervous. I guess that's understandable considering how we left things. Him trying to talk to me. Me slamming the car door shut and nearly running over his feet.

"How have you been?" My question is different from what I might have asked before. Filled with more pity and less accusation.

"Great. Just great." Again, he gives me the façade. A layer of lies that can't possibly be true. Not when his only friend at the party is me, and he basically had to coerce Cameron into convincing me to be here. "Business is booming. We're even considering opening another office in Austin."

Yeah, I guess maybe that would make things "great," especially when it's all he has now.

He glances at me, then back to his chopping task. "But I

want to hear about you. Cameron says your trip got canceled. I'm really sorry, sweetheart."

"It's water under the bridge now." And it is, especially in light of the fact that yesterday I lost my boyfriend and very likely permanently damaged my relationship with my best friend.

"I'm glad to hear it. We Malones are resilient people." He finishes his plating task and brings the platter to the now-abandoned picnic table. He actually looks around for something to do. Probably since this talk is as fun as listening to clawing on a chalkboard. After straightening all he can, he returns and sits down next to me. "This is a little weird, isn't it?" he finally admits.

"Yes. It is." I look down at my fingers and pick at a chipped nail.

"How's your, uh . . ." He clears his throat. "How's your mom doing?"

"She's the most resilient of us all, actually." I'm annoyed he's asking. Maybe that's why I give him back brutal honesty. "She met someone. His name is Michael and it's pretty serious, I think."

He presses his lips together, and I know it bothers him even though he says, "Good. I'm happy for her."

I shake my head, irritation rising in my throat. "Why did you do it?" He sighs, and I know he wishes I would go back to being that girl who worshiped him and never questioned his decisions. But that girl is gone, and the one she's become needs answers. "Was it just about the sex?"

"Darcy." His voice comes out in shocked indignation. "I will not discuss my personal life with you. It's wildly inappropriate."

"You didn't mind so much last year when your mistress sat down next to me, hoping to '*get to know me better.*'" His face turns a deep shade of red. Good. He should be ashamed. "Where is she, by the way?"

"Blair is no longer in the picture. And that's all I'm going to say on the subject."

"Fine. Then at least tell me why you didn't fight for Mom after the affair was over. Why did you give up?"

"Darcy . . ." Frustration colors every syllable, and he stands, his movements as agitated as his voice. "There are things you are simply too young to understand."

"No. You don't get to expect me to behave like an adult when it fits your and Mom's agenda and then turn around and treat me like a child when I dare to ask why." When he remains quiet and refuses to give me the answer I'm searching for, I look down at my fingers, tears threatening to come as fiercely as they did this morning. "Do you even regret blowing up our family?"

"Of course I have regrets." He presses my bowed head to his chest and kisses my hair like he used to when I was a child and scared of the dark. "I regret ignoring the little things until they became too big to handle. I regret that I made the problems worse instead of trying to solve them. I regret how much this has hurt both you and Dexter, even though he pretends like it doesn't matter. And yes, there are dark moments where I regret every step I took in losing your mom, just as I'm sure there are days she regrets every step she took in doing the same thing." His hand runs along the back of my hair, soothing me as only a father can. "But those are my regrets and my burdens. They are not yours to carry." He lifts my head, and the moisture in my eyes blurs his face. "Do you understand that?"

"It's not too late," I plead through my tears. "You two can still try to fix this. You can do all the things you didn't do before. Marriage counseling, or you can finally take that second honeymoon you always talked about."

"Sweetheart." He sighs again, and I know what he's going to say well before he says it. "Your mom and I are never getting back together. There's a point when the damage becomes irreparable, and we hit that milestone a long time ago. But I love you. And I really hope that one day we will find a way past all the hurt. Because I miss my little girl."

Overcome by emotion, I slide off the table and fall into the arms of my father. He holds me tight, just like he has every time I've been afraid or hurt or lonely. He's my dad, good or bad. I can't change his choices, but I can change mine.

I ease away and wipe my tears with the heel of my palm. "I'm still really disappointed in you."

He swallows and nods. "I know you are."

"But I'm willing to try and forgive you. Because hanging on to this bitterness isn't doing any of us any good." I squeeze his hand in mine and try not to cry again when I see my father's eyes fill.

"Thank you, sweetheart." He swallows again, working to get his emotions to settle. "We can start slow. Maybe a Sunday night once a month?"

I consider it for only a second before shaking my head no, and not just because Sunday nights are Mom's and she didn't do anything to deserve them getting snatched away. My answer is driven more by what my dad and I seem to be suffering from—an inability to let go.

"Why don't we try a Saturday night instead," I say when his chest deflates. "Maybe start some new traditions."

He blows out a long, relieved breath. "I'd like that very much."

THIRTY-TWO

Cameron's mom likes to scrapbook. She cuts out pictures, buys expensive, fancy stickers, and creates a chronicled record of each of her four children's journey through life. Cameron claimed to hate it as a kid, but he's fallen into the picture craze much like his mother. Only his snapshots and selfies aren't on 24x24 pages. Instead, they're kept in boxes, each one labeled by year and stuffed to the brim.

I have both collections sitting in front of me. His mom's beautiful book of memories she gave him last Christmas, and Cameron's 4x6 printouts that are as artistic as the amazing music he produces. I carefully turn page after page and marvel at the fact that even though I'm not in his family, my presence is captured on almost every single sheet. Cameron and me playing Sorry when we were only seven. Cameron and me at Hawaiian Falls Waterpark, soaked to the bone, our arms locked around each other's shoulders. Cameron and me in graduation gowns, both excited because we ended up choosing the same college.

I close the book and slide the picture boxes closer. There's less of me in here, but only because I quit letting him freely take my picture a long time ago. It's the rest of his life that's represented. Old bandmates, co-workers, past girlfriends.

I pick up the one of him and January. It used to be framed and sitting on his dresser. Now that frame holds a picture of Cameron onstage. The one I took at his first Black Carousel concert.

One by one, I take in the memories, too many to count, some good and some horrible, but ours nonetheless. Maybe that's why I'm here. Why I've been sitting on Cameron's bed for the past two hours, waiting for him to come home.

It's another hour before he does, and by the time I hear the front door open, I have a spread of every girlfriend he's ever had across his blue-and-white-checkered comforter.

Cameron barrels into his room, drops his violin case onto the desk, and kicks off his shoes. He doesn't see me yet, and I don't say a word until he goes to lift his shirt over his head.

"You may not want to do that."

He freezes, his stomach exposed, and then slowly he lowers his shirt back down. "How did you get in here?"

I shrug, only slightly surprised that his voice holds an edge of irritation. "You're not the only one with a spare key."

He backs up until he hits the desk, then crosses his arms. He's still mad. I guess that's fair. I still am as well.

I eye the violin case. "You guys had practice today?"

"I'm not quitting, and he hasn't fired me, so yeah, if he calls it, I'm there. We're professionals, Darcy. There's no law that says we have to be friends to put on a good show." He glances at the door as if strongly weighing whether to bolt or not, and then back at me. "Why are you here?"

"We promised to fight for each other. This is me fighting." I pick up a picture from my last fundraiser. Cameron and I are posed in a high ten because I'd just hit my funding goal. "My dad said that there's a point where the damage in a relationship becomes irreparable. I won't let that be us."

We begin a game of silence we've only played one other time, and it was over something so stupid I don't even remember what it was. Finally I cave, mostly because I came here to talk, or maybe to yell, but either way I came because I refuse to let one argument shake a lifetime together.

"You hurt me. The things you said about my dad were cruel and unfair." My voice is shaky, but I have to get that out.

"I know." He pauses. "And I'm sorry I said it the way I did. I was angry and confused."

I don't miss that he doesn't take back the words, only his harshness. His feelings weren't contrived from shock; they were real, and for some reason, that fact makes them all the more painful.

"You lied to me, and if I'd left my house even five minutes later, you'd probably still be lying to me." He stares down at his feet. "There's always been one absolute between the two of us; we tell each other the truth, even when it means hard conversations or disagreements."

I swallow down the guilt. "In my defense, I never actually lied. I told you I was seeing someone, just not who."

He jerks his head up. "That's a technicality and you know it." He moves again, getting close to the same spastic pacing he had outside of Bryson's front door. "I've been racking my brain for two days now, trying to understand why you didn't talk to me first, especially knowing the kind of impact it would have on the band. And then it hit me . . ." He looks at me and the hurt written on his face makes my stomach sink. "You already knew. That's what bothers me the most. You walked into that relationship fully knowing I wouldn't be okay with the two of you together, and you didn't care."

I have no counterattack because, deep down, it's true. It's why I left Bryson out of stories I'd tell. Why I put off telling Cam the truth, even though Bryson warned me that time wouldn't make a difference. "He's not the terrible person you think he is."

"I don't care if he's a saint, he's terrible *for you.* For any girl, for that matter, but especially for you."

"Is that why you got so mad? Because you were protecting me?"

"Yes . . . but it's more than that. He threatens *us*—what we have together. Bryson doesn't just exist in someone's life. He invades it. I mean, look what's happened. You've only been together a little while and he's already changing you."

I set down the picture I've been holding and pick up one of Cameron and Lydia. He wants to make this about Bryson's flaws, but I won't go there again. "Why haven't any of your relationships lasted?"

"Don't change the subject."

"I'm not. I actually think it's related to why you got so angry. Why this relationship—my first serious one—bothers you so much." My heartbeat grows when Cameron's face changes from frustration to the same tingling fear that's coursing through me.

"What are you asking me?" He takes a step closer, blowing out an unsteady breath as if he, too, can't stop the pounding of his heart.

We hold each other's gaze. One second. Two. It goes into three. He knows what I'm asking. He can see the trepidation all over my face.

Cameron takes another unsteady step forward. "Once we go here, Darcy, there's no going back." It's a warning that the territory we're stepping into is riddled with land mines.

"I don't think we have a choice," I squeak out, my voice catching in my throat. "Not after what happened." Either Bryson is right, and I've been naïve and blind, or he's wrong and our breakup was pointless. Regardless, I'm not leaving this room until I know exactly how Cameron feels.

Without another word, Cam sits on the edge of the bed and examines my handiwork. There are nine girls, all ranging from a few dates to serious long-term possibilities. And in every single case, Cameron was the one who ended things. He pushes the photos into a pile and drops them in one of the boxes I'd emptied. He then takes the pictures of us and lays them out in the same order and formation. "They didn't last because none of them was you." He looks at me then, the truth in his eyes a sledgehammer to all the denial I've clung to since high school when he first told me we were soulmates. "You weren't ready before, and I get it, we were only eighteen, and you had your dreams and I had mine."

I suck in a breath as years of innocent friendship are wiped away, replaced by the truth that between us the whole time, there's been this secret hovering on the fringe. "That was forever ago. Why haven't you said anything?"

"Honestly, I've been too big of a coward to chance a second rejection." He gingerly takes my hand. "I guess I've been waiting for you to feel what I do. And sometimes I think you do, and then other times it seems like you come up with excuses to put distance between us." He scoots closer to me. "But I've always known, no matter how long it took for you to be ready, that it was okay, because one thing has never changed in all these years. You've always come back to me."

I stand because Cameron is too close, and I need to move. To process all he just told me. He watches me from the bed, tentative. I know the look. It is practically the same one Bryson gave me when he asked me to choose. And even though Cameron doesn't say those words, I know I have to. And the choice is no longer between Cameron, my best friend, or Bryson, my boyfriend. Now it's a forever decision, because you don't just date your best friend. You marry him.

Cam rises from the bed, slowly, as if he knows that every step toward me will shatter who we are now.

I want to run, but I can't leave, not after being the one to insist we talk. I press my back into the wall, the one next to his dresser that has only about five feet of space before the corner.

He moves closer, never taking his eyes from mine. "Do you remember when we were twelve and we locked ourselves in the closet?"

I nod, panic rising in my chest, a trapped feeling I haven't had since I got an MRI my junior year closing in on me. We wanted to know what it would be like to kiss someone, and it just made sense that we'd practice on each other.

"You were my first kiss, and I've always been so grateful we had that," he says softly, delicately, his feet inching closer and closer. "I've thought of this moment so many times. Imagined it. Played it out in my head." He's right in front of me now, and I don't know whether to bolt or to let us try and see if I feel even an ounce of what I do when Bryson's near me.

Cam touches my cheek, and it feels different from before. Just as I imagine every look or touch or conversation between us will now be changed. His other hand goes to my waist, and my heart beats more frantically than I ever thought it could without going into cardiac arrest.

"Darcy," he whispers, "I've waited a lifetime to do this again." His head tilts and lowers.

I feel his breath, but it's not until he closes his eyes that I know I can't. I press both palms to his chest. "Don't."

He's so close, he could ignore me and I'd have no way to stop the contact. But true to the man I know he is, he pulls away, though it seems to be the most painful thing I've ever asked him to do.

"This isn't right. And it isn't fair, not to any of us." I take a deep breath, my pulse finally calming to a normal rhythm. "I need time to figure out what I'm feeling."

"You've had eleven years," he snaps, his mouth tight, his eyes bright blue with both desire and frustration.

Matching indignation roars inside me. "No. You've had eleven years. I've had about eleven seconds, so forgive me if I need a moment to catch up."

Cameron shoves his hands into his hair and turns his back to me. "What does he have that I don't?"

"That's not a fair question."

He spins back around. "Sure it is. You kiss him. You lie to me to be with him. You ignore all the warning signs of an inevitably damaged relationship. And now, when we finally have a shot at something mind-blowing together, you choose him. So, what is it that makes Bryson so irresistible? I truly want to know."

"I didn't choose him. I chose my best friend." I don't tell Cam about the ultimatum because he isn't stupid, and he can figure out what I'm getting at. "But now you're changing all of our history and asking me to promise more than I can. It's just too much, too fast." My lower lip quivers and tears burn my eyes. "I'm not good with change. You know that."

"I'm sorry." He comes forward, not as a pursuer this time but as the friend I've always known, and pulls me into his arms. "I shouldn't have pushed so hard. I didn't realize you had . . . ended things."

"He didn't exactly give me another option."

"They rarely ever do." Cameron chuckles, and his chest vibrates against mine. "I know this has been hard for you, so it feels wrong to be this happy, but I am. Bryson will move on; he always does. And you and I can go back to being *us*." He runs his hand down my back. "If being with you means I have wait a little longer, then I will. I'll wait for you forever."

But as I stand there, in the middle of his room, hugging the man I assumed would be a part of every important event in my life, I realize that making him wait indefinitely is crueler than saying goodbye. Because either way, whether it's Bryson or Cam or some other guy down the line making me choose, the truth is still vividly clear: I've been like my father, clinging to a memory that no longer exists. Cameron, my partner in crime, my childhood best friend, my safety net . . . is gone. And the real question looms over me like a phantom waiting to attack.

Can I love him any other way?

THIRTY-THREE

C ameron has never been good at waiting, so it was no surprise when his patience wore out only twelve hours after our conversation. Monday, he was respectful, only texting a couple of times to say how happy he was we made up. Tuesday, he called twice and left messages. Wednesday, it was five calls and two texts asking me to confirm I'm not dead. I sent him a thumbs-up emoji.

Needless to say, I wasn't surprised when the phone calls started early today, nine o'clock to be exact, right when I was pulling into the farm. But since today is supposed to be all about Louie, I left the device in my truck, feeling only slightly guilty.

"Do you think I'm a bad person for not wanting to talk to him?" I ask the massive Great Dane, who's currently snuggling with me on a picnic blanket. Louie stretched out is way longer than I am, easily seven feet from toe to nose. His front paws push against my shoulders, and I turn him on his back, exposing his big white stomach.

We're working on trust today, and putting him in vulnerable situations is the first step in showing him that I'm not going to hurt him.

"I know he's going to want an answer and I don't have one, so is it better to talk to him only to tell him I need more time, or just make him wait?" I rub the thin, sensitive skin on his torso, and Louie makes a loud *rawh rawh* sound. It's his way of talking to me. "Yeah. You're probably right. I already know what I'm going to say; I'm just avoiding the inevitable. But in my defense, Black Carousel plays tomorrow, and I'd never forgive myself if something I did ruined Cameron's performance."

Louie makes another noise, and I swear he calls me a scaredy-cat. His wet nose presses against mine. I move my face just in time to avoid a big lick of his tongue.

I push his giant head away. "That's sweet and all, but no licks on the face, okay?"

It's bad enough that I'm covered with Louie's tiny dog hair, slobber, and dirt on my clothes, and my ponytail is lopsided and loose. The last thing I need is dried saliva on my face.

I move to a kneeling position while fixing my wayward hair. "Up, Louie." He hops up, nearly knocking me over. I steady us both and pull his collar until he's in front of me. "Now sit."

Louie's backside hits the blanket and he's quickly rewarded with a treat. When he's done chewing, I pick up his left paw and carefully slide my fingers between each one of his pads. It's a very sensitive area for a dog and takes a great deal of trust to let me explore.

Louie leans down and licks my fingers. A reminder that he's a little nervous.

"It's okay. You're doing so good."

A car door slams, and Louie jerks his paw away, the hair standing up on his neck. I scramble to my feet and frown when Louie backs up and barks. He wants to go to his doghouse. Wants to retreat to what's safe versus facing the fear head on. "I guess I'm not the only one who's a scaredy-cat," I tease, holding his collar and trying to reassure him with long strokes down his back.

I watch the trail from the driveway to Charlie's back door, waiting to see who the intruder is, though part of me already suspects. My heart dances in my chest as I wait, anticipation as visible on me as it is on the dog to my left.

Bryson finally appears, and all the self-convincing I'd worked on for six days now disappears like powder in a storm. He doesn't look at me or for me, though I know he must have seen my truck here. Instead, he goes straight to the back door and swings it open. Charlie's waiting for him in the doorway, and Bryson obviously doesn't like what he's being told because he backs up and lets the screen slam shut. He turns, shoves his hands into his pockets, and finally makes the eye contact I've been waiting for. Though, once it comes, I question my desire for it. Bryson's eyes are dull, emotionless, and the black he wears today seems to strangle all other color from his face.

Louie sneaks forward, barks, and jumps back. He can sense our tension, which isn't good.

"Do you want to help me with a little experiment?" I call out, ignoring the way my stomach flips at the idea of his being closer. Bryson walks toward me, reluctantly, and Louie barks again. "Easy, boy. He's not going to hurt you."

Bryson pauses a few feet from us. "What did you have in mind?" His tone is flat, heartbreakingly absent of the tender affection his voice usually holds. I search his face for even a tiny hint of feeling but nothing's there but complete indifference.

Whereas I have to clamp my fingers not to reach out and touch him. "Louie is working on trust, and he's done great with Charlie and me, but it'd be nice to see how he responds to you."

Bryson eyes me suspiciously, and I can't help but smile. "Don't worry, he won't bite you. Just start slow. Maybe try to touch his head."

He reaches out while I encourage Louie the whole time. Both boys are hesitant and nervous, but as soon as Bryson makes contact, they both seem to exhale. Louie steps into the touch while Bryson's mouth twitches just slightly upward. "He seems to like it."

Louie leans his 160-pound body against me, nearly knocking me over. "Yes, he's very affectionate . . . and very heavy." I push him off, hopeful that maybe this exercise will do more than bond man and beast, but also maybe ease the discomfort between the two of us.

Bryson pulls his hand away and shoves it back in his pocket. "Looks like you've made a lot of progress."

"I have, and not just with Louie." I command the big guy to lie down, and he quickly does, stretching out again on our blanket. "Let me show you how well Penny's doing." I can tell Bryson doesn't really want to follow me, but he does anyway. "After our . . . um, incident, Charlie put chicken wire all around Bentley's old cage so there was no way she could get out during training. But then it hit me that I've spent all this time trying to fix the symptoms, all the while ignoring the root of her aggression. She hates the crate. It's a cage to her. A cage she is constantly stuck in." Our eyes meet for a brief second, and I quickly look away. "So we started putting her out here in the morning and leaving her until bedtime without any demands or training, and overnight she transformed." I stop at the fencing and lean my forearms on the metal. "Yesterday, she put the tennis balls in the bucket all on her own."

I watch as Penny trots along the wide space, toys all around for her to choose from. "All this time, she knew what she was supposed to do; she just wanted to do it on her terms."

Bryson slides in next to me, but it feels unnatural. Like every step he takes is carefully constructed to hide whatever he might really be thinking. "Does that mean Charlie's going to let her go to the adoption fair?"

I swallow down my rising emotion. "Yep, this weekend, finally. I just have to disclose the bite, and we both agreed she can't be placed in a home with other dogs." Bryson glances at my hand, and I roll it forward and backward. I'm down to just a small Band-Aid now. "Mostly healed."

"Good." There's a hard punctuation, like he's trying his best to end the conversation.

I ignore the effort. "Are you nervous about the concert tomorrow?"

"Nope. It's just one more stage and one more performance."

I wish that were all it was, but we both know it could very well be the last concert they play as an unsigned band. "And things have been . . . okay?"

Bryson turns and his gaze chills me. He's still angry, but I welcome it. It's the first real emotion he's shown since walking up to me.

I brace myself for whatever fiery remark he decides to throw, but Charlie appears before he gets the chance.

"Hey, Darcy, you ready for more lessons?" He winks at me like he has no idea Bryson and I broke up, which I know for a fact he does. "I can't in good conscience let you finish out the summer without hitting a target."

I glance at Bryson, who used Charlie's arrival to steadily ease away from me. He doesn't outright uninvite me, but his body language certainly wants to. "Maybe later. I still have some exercises I want to run Louie through."

"Yeah, that's probably a good call." Bryson rolls his shoulders, struggling to relax. I give him credit for trying. The old Bryson would have ignored me completely. This one is at least attempting civility.

Charlie passes by us in a hurry but stops when Louie stands, excited to see him. "Hey there, you crazy giant." He rubs Louie's face like they've been touching forever and not just for a few days now. "You want to walk with me to get the Gator?"

"I can get it," Bryson offers, his eagerness to get away from me more than apparent.

"Nah. You guys chat." Charlie's brows lift, and we both know it's more an order than a suggestion. "I'm going to get my workout in for today. Oh, and, Darcy, remind me to talk to you later about a phone call I got this morning."

"Okay? We can talk about it now."

"Nope, this is a sit-down kind of conversation." He pats his thigh. "Come on, Louie. Let's leave these two knuckleheads alone." They walk away, Charlie in old mud boots and a hunting vest, Louie leaping as they trot, because he's just now learning that there's more to life than hiding in a ten-by-ten-foot cage.

"Do you know anything about the phone call?"

"Nope." Bryson leans his back against Penny's kennel, annoyance written all over the set of his shoulders. He looks as though he's trapped here with me, and I hate that he might feel this way. Sure, we have some things to overcome, but that doesn't erase all we've shared together.

"I went to see my dad this past weekend," I throw out, desperate for something to break past his shell. "It was hard, really hard to see him, but I'm glad—"

"Don't," he snaps, stone still, his jaw clenched tight.

I heave a deliberate sigh. He's being impossible. "Don't what? Try and talk to you?"

He pushes off the kennel and pulls on his neck. "This isn't talking. This is sharing, and I'm not doing that with you anymore."

My eyes sting, and I feel the loss of him so severely, I want to rip my hair out. "So we can't even be friends?"

"No, Darcy. We can't. That's not how I work." A frustrated breath hisses through his teeth. "There's only one person who gets to know me intimately, the person I plan to be with forever. I thought maybe that could be you, but now that's not going to happen. So no. We can't be friends, because unlike you, I don't see a line. I look at you and it's still all there, so honestly, being around you sucks for me. But that's life, and I'll deal with it. But do me a favor and stop, okay? Stop trying to create something new between us, because—" His voice breaks and he curses, turning toward the pasture. "Why won't that blasted dog stop barking?"

The sound comes slowly, my mind so wrapped up in Bryson's words that I'd shut out the world around us. Louie's bark isn't just loud and continuous; it's manic and higher pitched than I've ever heard from him. "Something's wrong." I listen closer, the hair on my arms rising. "Louie's panicked."

The frantic dog runs toward us and then rushes back to the same spot, his head leaning down, his eyes fixated on something in the grass. His barking grows louder and louder. "What is he looking at?"

"It could be a snake. Where's Charlie?" Bryson looks around, but he's nowhere to be seen.

We take a hesitant step closer, then another, until we both see a color that makes the world stop moving. Shock rips through me, and right on its heels, gutting fear. "Charlie!" I scream, his bright orange hunter's vest barely visible through the long grass. Bryson takes off in a full sprint, sliding to the ground the second he gets to Charlie's motionless body. Bryson jumps right into CPR, pressing on Charlie's chest in quick, rhythmic movements.

"Don't you do this!" I hear him yell. "Don't you leave me, too."

Sobs rack my chest, yet I fight them off. I have to think. . . . *911. I have to call 911.* Though my entire body's trembling, I somehow find a way to function and take off running. Sweat pours down my forehead, my eyes stinging as I stumble across the path to my truck. I tug open the door, grab my phone so quickly it falls from my hand. I drop to the ground, retrieve it, and somehow punch in the number.

"911. What's your emergency?"

"My friend is unconscious. I don't know how long, minutes or seconds." I rattle off Charlie's address as fear crawls up my throat. We're in the middle of nowhere. Miles from any hospital. "Please, please hurry."

"We've contacted a volunteer fire department in Venus. They aren't far. Maybe five or ten minutes." Her words give some relief, but even that short amount of time could be fatal.

I stay on the line and run to the road, listening for sirens, my hands shaking as I watch each minute tick away on my phone. A lifetime passes before there's a distant echo. Flashes of red appear, and I wave my arms frantically so they don't waste any time finding us.

Two trucks barrel down the highway in a line, one big, one small, and slow when they see me. I take off running again after they turn, follow the kicked-up dust, and start down the long driveway.

"He's in the back field," I gasp when they exit the vehicles. "CPR. My friend. Is doing CPR. I don't know if it worked. He was unconscious." I lean over with my hands on my knees, not sure if my winded state is from exertion or shock. *Pull yourself together,* I scream inside my head. *You have to keep moving.*

I fight for control as the firefighters grab the medical supplies they need and follow me around the house. My heart pounds with every step we take, Bryson and Louie getting closer and closer, but with each clearer image, my hope turns into panic.

Bryson's hands pump frantically, his body ready to collapse from exhaustion. Sweat drips from his hair, his black shirt soaked completely through, and his hands are stark white as if they've lost all feeling. Maybe they have because the firemen have to fight to pull him off Charlie. As soon as they pry Bryson away, he lunges forward, trying to finish what he started.

I block his path, pushing my hands against his shoulders in opposite momentum. "Stop. They're EMTs. They're his only chance."

Bryson looks down at me, his eyes wild, his chest heaving, gasping for breath. And then he collapses to his knees, my arms barely making it around him to try to break the fall. "He can't die. He can't." His breath is labored, his words short. I see the terror in his eyes and my throat turns thick and achy.

"He's going be okay." I rub Bryson's arms, trying to get his shivering under control while the firemen pump oxygen into the mask around Charlie's nose and mouth and lift him from the ground onto a stretcher.

"I'm going!" Bryson yells, shoving me off him. "Don't try to stop me."

"I'm not. I promise. Just let me help you." I wrap my arm around his waist and pull him to his feet. He teeters, blinks through the haze of shock, but manages to take a step. Then another until he's strong enough to walk on his own. We reach the truck just as they lift Charlie inside.

"Can he ride with him?" I all but beg the older fireman who seems to be in command.

He attaches a radio to his belt and stands face to face with Bryson. A flashlight appears and it only takes two swipes across Bryson's eyes for the man to nod. "Yeah. He probably needs to."

The man helps Bryson into the back, his legs so shaky that he nearly falls out of the truck twice. When he's safely inside, I rush to the driver's side window. "Which hospital?"

"Baylor, Scott in Waxahachie."

I back away and watch the trucks leave, holding two of the most important people in my life. Sobs fight to come again, but I can't let them. I have to be strong right now. I have to get Louie put up, Macey brought to Sheila's, and I have to be there for Bryson.

Yet with each step, my legs grow weaker and weaker, until I find myself on my knees, the gravel crushing into my bare legs. My entire life I've been taught to pray. Pray when you're sad, pray when you're scared. Pray when all seems lost.

I did, for months, when my parents split up. Did it even more the first two days after my trip got canceled. And then my prayers became shouts until I stopped altogether because it felt like a lie. Nothing changed. Nothing went back to how it was supposed to be. Like Louie, I've been yelling and yelling, trying to get God to see how disappointed I am with this life He forced on me. How afraid I am to trust Him again. And He's been patiently waiting, pushing me past boundaries, asking me to be vulnerable, testing me with new challenges, all to help me see that His way is better and perfect and it's okay that it doesn't always make sense.

My chin lowers as my clenched hands rise to my forehead. "Save him, please," I cry, letting the tears come in long streams. "But if your will is not his life, then I beg you, give me strength I don't have. I can't do this anymore without you."

⁓

I find Bryson in a small waiting room on the cardiac floor after asking at least five nurses where to go. He's hunched over in his chair, elbows on his knees, head down. In the corner sits an older lady with a long string she methodically crochets into a scarf, but other than her, the area is eerily empty.

As I get closer, I can see the fallout from Bryson's quick response. There's a rip in his pants at his left knee, and his shirt has multiple white salt lines running across the back. The sweat has dried in his hair, leaving it in wild curls around his ears.

I ease down quietly into the chair next to his, and though he must see me or at least hear me, he doesn't move, doesn't nod, doesn't say anything. "How is he?" I ask tentatively. The nurses wouldn't give me any details, but considering we're in a surgical waiting room, I'm almost certain Charlie didn't die on the way here.

Bryson blows out a long, harrowing breath, and it feels like the first time he's breathed since I walked in. "It was a massive heart attack." The words come out stiff and robotic. "They took him straight to the OR and told me to wait here."

I rest my hand on his back, unable to listen to the hurt in his voice and not touch him. The cotton feels coarse against my palm and is still slightly damp. "Charlie is going to be okay." I rub in a large circle, offering whatever small measure of comfort I can. "He's far too stubborn not to be."

Bryson doesn't move except to get rigid under my touch. I don't care. He can hate it, fight it, resent me for it, but I know he needs this right now. I continue to rub his back, across his neck, down his arm until I'm practically hugging him. I feel his heartbeat, his breaths, his worries, his brokenness.

"I can't lose him." He trembles beneath my hand and I move in closer, squeezing him against me in an attempt to give him any strength I might have left.

"You won't." I don't know if that's true, but it's what I'm choosing to believe right now. And if the worst happens, I'll find better words to say then. But for now, he needs to believe in a miracle as much as I do.

We stay that way for long enough that my arm gets a cramp, and not once does Bryson look at me or at anything for that matter. Not until a nurse steps near his chair and looks down at her paperwork.

"Mr. Katsaros?"

I cringe at how she butchers the pronunciation, but Bryson couldn't care less.

"Right here," he says immediately and rises to his feet, forcing me to let go of my grip around him. "Is Charlie okay?"

"He's still in surgery," she says slightly apologetically. I glance at the stack of papers in her hands and realize she's not here to deliver news. "I have you down as Mr. Honza's emergency contact?"

"Yes, I am," he says confidently enough that it's obvious this news isn't a surprise to him like it is to me. I knew he and Charlie were close, but typically that kind of designation is for children or at least immediate family.

"If you wouldn't mind, I'd like to go over some information with you." She glances at me. "It won't take long." A nice way to say I can't go with them, but that's fine.

"No problem." I take Bryson's hand and squeeze it. His fingers are ice cold, and he makes no effort to return my hold. "I'll be here when you get back."

Bryson glances down at my hand around his, then back at the nurse. "Can you give us one second?" She nods and heads to the exit to wait for him. When she's clearly out of hearing range, Bryson eases his hand from mine. "Thank you for coming," he says gently, but not in a way that implies he wants me to stay. "I'll text you the minute I hear anything."

The words slice my already fractured heart. "Bryson, I'm not going anywhere. I want to be here for you. For Charlie."

He kneads his eyes with his fist as if he's reached the limit of what he can handle. "I know you do. And that's what makes you . . . you." He swallows, and for the first time since he walked the path to Charlie's backyard, I see the man I fell for. The soft, vulnerable, loving man who needs me right now.

"I can pick up your truck. Bring you some clean clothes." They're all small things, but in a crisis, it's the little things that become significant.

"It's really nice of you to offer, but right now, what I really need is to focus on Charlie." He blows out a shaky breath. "And I can't do that with you here. It's too hard to be near you and not be . . . us. The *us* we used to be." Hurt pours out of his eyes, and my stomach clenches. My being here is causing him more pain, not helping him.

"Okay." I'm worn out. Physically, mentally, and emotionally, but I dig for the strength it's going to take to walk away. "If that's really what you want."

"I gave up the hope of getting what I want a long time ago. This is what I need."

Bryson has asked me for only one thing—to choose him. I didn't do that before, and I won't make that mistake again.

I nod, holding back the plea I want to make to give me another chance. "If you change your mind, I'm just a phone call away."

"Thank you." He walks past me then, and I have no choice but to turn and watch him leave with a woman in blue scrubs who has no idea that Bryson is bleeding inside.

I've never quite understood heartbreak. I thought I did when my father left my mom, and again when my trip was canceled, but those were different. They were losses completely outside of my control. But as I watch Bryson disappear with the nurse through the glass double doors, that's when I know this pain in my chest is greater than all the others.

Bryson's leaving is my fault. I pushed him away because I was too afraid to let go and love him the way he needed me to. I did to him the very thing his mom did. I chose someone else, and regardless of what I do now, it doesn't matter. I lost him the minute I walked out his door.

THIRTY-FOUR

I'm in my truck, staring at my apartment building for five minutes before finally cutting the engine. Cameron called me twice while sitting here, and both times I let it go to voicemail. For as long as I can remember, he would be the first person I'd seek out when feeling like my world is ending, but not anymore. His admission changed things between us, just like it had when we were in high school. It took a month to get back to normal then; I have no idea how long it will take this time.

The air is hot and sticky when I open the door, and the heat elevates my already frazzled emotions. I need a shower and a time machine to make this horrific day go away. My pace to the stairs is slow, but it's the best I can do when feeling like a collapse is imminent.

"So, you are avoiding me."

I glance up the minute I hear his voice, and anxiety fires through my veins. Cameron's sitting on the stairs, waiting for me, and the expression on his face mirrors my balled-up and twisted insides. "I can't do this with you right now."

He stands and waits for me to get to the top step. "I'm not

leaving until we talk." Dark circles mar his eyes, and he fidgets the way he always does when nervous.

I push past him and head to my apartment. He follows down the hall, into the alcove, and through the door right behind me. I'm grateful for the blast of air conditioning that hits when we enter; maybe it will calm down the rising heat in my chest. Piper barks and runs to greet me for only a second before running back to the kitchen. Zoe's in there cooking, and Piper is obviously reaping the benefits.

"Hey, I tried to call you. Cameron's been by here twice. He's all messed up about some—" She quits talking when she steps into the living room, where both of us still stand by the now-closed door. "Oh, I see you found her."

"We need a minute." Cameron grabs my arm and pulls me toward the bedroom in a move that's far more Neanderthal than I appreciate. This isn't how we operate. We don't demand conversation and impose our wills on the other. He lets go the second we're inside and shuts the door with bottled aggression. "Why won't you talk to me?" he barks. "I've been out of my mind wondering what you're thinking or doing." He runs both hands through his hair and grabs the strands like he needs to pull them out. "I can't play onstage tomorrow feeling like this. You have to give me something."

"I can't." I cross my arms, trying to find the compassion I've always had for him, yet nothing but bitterness remains. I resent him. Resent him for loving me the wrong way. Resent him for convincing me that he was all I needed. Resent him because I chose him, and I shouldn't have.

"You can't what? Answer my phone call? Take two seconds to put my mind at ease?"

"No, because all of those require me telling you what you

don't want to hear." The words fly out harsher than I meant them to, and I rub my temples trying to make sense of this entire mess. "I'm sorry."

He stares at me, and it feels like my world is caving in. This was my worst nightmare. Hurting Cam. Losing my best friend. But I can't pretend something is possible when I know it's not. Maybe if I hadn't known Bryson, then I could have convinced myself that what Cameron and I share is enough, but I know now what love—true, romantic, spend-your-lives-together love—feels like. And it's not this.

"You're sorry?" He stares at the ceiling now as if that might change my words. "Well, I can't go back to just being your friend. Not anymore." He looks at me as though I'm to blame for putting us in this position. "You opened Pandora's box, and my feelings are not going back inside."

"I know that." I swallow down the ache. "I know things between us have to change now."

He shakes his head, bewildered. "Why? Just give me one good reason why you and I aren't perfect for each other?"

I duck my head because I can't verbalize it.

He rushes to me and cups my face, his eyes pleading into mine. "You love me, don't you?"

Tears assault my eyes. I can see how this ends even if he can't yet. "You know I do."

"And I love you," he says with a ferocity that tears my heart in half. "Don't you see? This is our moment. You were leaving, and by some miracle you stayed, and I don't think it's coincidence. I think it's providence that we are here together right now." He leans forward, touches his forehead to mine. "This is the beginning of our love story, Darcy. If you would just stop being afraid . . ."

"I'm not afraid, Cameron." I pull his hands away and put

more space between us. "That's just it. For the first time in years, I'm completely at peace with where God has me."

"Then help me understand why you won't even try. We are soulmates. You know it. I know it. Our families know it." He throws out his arms. "Even Bryson knows it! Why do you think he forced you to choose?"

"He didn't make me choose for him. He did it for me." I rub my eyes, only just now recognizing that truth. Bryson knew I was caged by fear. That's why he couldn't waver. Why he couldn't let me have both. "You and I don't thrive together, Cameron. Don't you see that? Every time one of us starts to move and try something new, the other one keeps us stuck right here."

His breath hitches like I've slapped him. "You feel stuck with me?"

"No. Not just me. I've done it to you, too. We live safe and we live trapped and I don't want to live that way anymore." He takes a step back, the hurt so dark in his eyes I swear they change colors. "You know I'm right. You've called me fifteen times in the past four days. You couldn't even play your concert tomorrow without seeing me. That is not healthy. *We* are not healthy, Cam."

"This isn't you talking. This is Bryson. You've been pushing me away since the minute you two became involved with each other."

"Bryson's not why I've pushed you away." Though I almost wish he were the reason, because then I wouldn't have to admit the darkest truth to myself or to my best friend. "I think I've known for a long time that you and I . . ." I shake my head, unable to speak the words out loud. How do you break up with your best friend? How do you say goodbye to the one person you thought would always be there?

His jaw tenses as he reads the anxiety I'm emoting. "What do you mean you've known? Known what?"

Tears lodge in my throat. I can't say it. Can't say what I've only just now accepted. But I have to, because if I don't, I'll cave to him. I always do. Bryson's right. I've spent so much time clinging to Cameron, I've ignored the fact that I'm terrified to take a step on my own.

He comes to me again, gentler this time, my hesitation giving him hope that I don't know how I feel when really I just don't know how to tell him. "This is you and me, Darcy. We don't have secrets between us. I love you. And whatever is stopping you from taking this step, you can talk to me about it. We'll get through it together." His gaze remains fixed on me and I ache with his want, ache with what I can't give him. "Tell me. What have you known?"

"How you feel. I just didn't want to accept it." His eyes soften, and I duck my head, unable to look at him and see the agony I'm about to unleash. "I think part of why I wanted that mission trip so bad was to see what life looked like without you. And to give you time to let go of me."

The air immediately turns cold between us, and even though I knew this reaction was coming, it still sickens me when Cameron shoves himself away. "You wanted to get away from me?"

"You and I have been entangled my entire life. So much so that I don't even make decisions without first considering the impact on you. I've been Cameron Lee's best friend for so long that somewhere along the way, I stopped knowing who I am without you." I look up, bracing myself for what's to come. "A year away was my chance to find me again."

He chuckles and it's a horrific sound. "You're telling me

that you went through all of that work of trying to be a missionary just to get me out of your life?"

"That's not what I said." I did want to be a missionary, at first. Then it became more about leaving than actually what I was going to do. God was right to stop me. My heart wasn't where it needed to be. "This isn't about you, Cameron. It's about me and what I've had to learn through all the pain this past year."

"So now I'm a lesson?" He takes two more steps away, as if he doesn't trust me not to plunge a spear into his chest. "A lesson in what? How to hurt people? How to betray a twenty-nine-year friendship? Bravo, Darcy. You learned it well."

"Cameron." I move toward him, but he raises his hand.

"I heard you. Loud and clear. You want to know what your life looks like without me in it?" He smiles but it's not sweet. It's quite possibly the nastiest look I've seen him give anyone. "Your wish is granted. You're about to find out." He leaves then, slamming both my door and the front door on his way out.

The sound hits me like a wrecking ball, the gut punch so severe I have to lean over to brace myself.

He's gone. It echoes in my head, in my trembling body.

My best friend is gone. And this time, there won't be a make-up call weeks or months later. I know the difference. This is the kind of break that stays permanent.

I collapse to my knees, the sobs coming so fast and hard that my room becomes a blob of color around me.

A soft knock comes at the door. "Darcy, are you okay? Do you want to talk about it?"

"Not now, Zoe," I manage to squeak out. As much as I appreciate her effort, she's not who I need. I need my mom. I need her caring touch and her unconditional love. But mostly, I need her to tell me it's all going to be okay.

I'm still a blubbering mess when I reach out and press my mom's doorbell. I don't even remember what time it is or when Mom usually gets home from work. I only hope that Michael's parked SUV means that she's here and hopefully still willing to talk.

The door opens after my second press to the ringer, and her mouth opens in surprise. "Darcy?" Her eyes trail my pathetic state—the bloodshot eyes, scuffed knees, disheveled hair—and she immediately pulls me into her arms. "Baby, what happened?"

I break down, sobbing into her embrace like a little girl. I hear Mom mumble something about getting the door and feel myself being slowly moved to a more private location. I recover enough to recognize I'm in the living room, close to the couch. Michael stands in the doorway, fidgeting, while Mom uses her palms to brush the tear-soaked hair from my eyes. "Are you hurt? Did someone do something to you?" She's gone to the worst conclusion, and I shake my head to ease her fears.

"No. Cam and I had a fight." My breath shakes as I try to talk through the tears. "He's gone. He hates me. Bryson hates me. Charlie's in surgery." I break down again as Mom eases me down onto the couch.

Michael clears his throat. "I'm going to . . . um, go somewhere else."

I lay my forehead in my hands and start to laugh. Michael is truly the most socially awkward person I've ever met.

Mom runs her hand along the back of my hair. "Do you want some water?"

I sit up, the hysteria finally under control. "No, thank you. I'm better now." It's amazing how just being here helps. How even though I'm nearly thirty and long past adolescence, her touch can still heal a million hurts.

"Do you want to talk about what happened?"

I fall back against the couch cushion and look toward the woman who raised me. "Cameron wanted more from our relationship. I couldn't give it to him." My chest seizes, my mind still struggling to accept his final words to me. "You don't look surprised," I add when my mom shows no visual reaction.

"You're my daughter, so I can read you pretty well, and Cameron, well, he kind of wears his heart on his sleeve."

I look at the ceiling and shake my head. "How did I miss it for so long?"

"We see what we want to see, especially when we love someone. You probably knew this would be the result if the issue ever got pressed."

As usual, my mom is right. "What do I do now?"

"Are you willing to go where he wants you to?" When I shake my head, she sighs apologetically. "Then you can't really do anything. When and if he's ever ready, he'll come back. Until then, it's only fair you give him the space he needs to fall out of love with you." She touches my cheek and brushes hair from my eyes. "Considering how amazing you are, that may take him some time."

It's in that moment I realize how very much I missed her these past several weeks. "I'm sorry I haven't called you back." She folds her hands in her lap and looks down. "I didn't know how to be happy for you and still be sad for me."

She nods like she understands. "I've thought a lot about

what you said the other day. I've even written you three ridiculously long emails that I didn't send, because you asked me to give you time, and Michael convinced me I needed to respect that request even though I didn't like it."

Score one for Michael. Dad would have made her push. And like it did with Cam, pushing would have only led to words that couldn't be taken back.

"I should have talked about how I was feeling earlier," I admit. "I shouldn't have waited until I was that angry to unload on you."

"Well, if I'm being honest, I didn't exactly want to hear it. I wanted to move on, to keep going and looking forward so I didn't have to deal with the whys and the hows." We smile at each other, both cut from the same cloth in that respect. "I've been unfair. I've expected you to comfort me like my friend, while still expecting the blind support of a little girl." Her words nearly bring the tears again, because for the first time she truly does seem to understand my struggle. "But you're an adult now, and it's only fair that you be given the courtesy of my listening instead of assuming." Her voice shakes from nerves. "I know that for you, our divorce was a shock. We've never wanted you kids to stress about the two of us, and I guess we got a little too good at hiding our issues." She takes a stabilizing breath, then releases it. "I don't know what's crossing the line for you. How much you want or need to know, but I'll give you whatever information you ask for . . . even if I don't necessarily want to."

I pull out my ponytail holder and pull my hair back into a fresh tail, tired of the strands sticking to my face. There are so many questions I've been too afraid to ask. Too afraid to get answers for. And some of those still linger in my mind.

Were there other women? Were there other men? How long had they been unhappy? Was our Partridge family growing up a lie or was it real? But none of those questions will change the outcome; they'd only change my feelings toward my mom and dad. And if this summer has taught me anything, it's taught me to let go. My parents' marriage and divorce is not my problem to solve. It's their journey and their choices. Not mine.

"Do you remember when I was a kid and you'd make your special night-night concoction for me when I was scared at bedtime?" I later learned it was tea, hot milk, and some honey, but it never tastes the same when I make it. "Could you make me some now?"

She sighs in relief as if she realizes exactly what I have decided, that I'm not going to live in the wreckage of what's lost anymore. "Only if afterward you promise to tell me who Bryson and Charlie are." Sadness descends on me like a heavy cloud, and my mom sees it right away. Her face turns pensive, ready for me to dump all my burdens onto her. "Unless you don't want to," she amends.

No, I need to, but not until I do this first. I scoot over and wrap my arms around her. "I love you, Mom."

She presses her cheek against mine. "I love you, too, sweetheart."

~

Bryson's text comes three hours later, long after my mom soothed away my pain and helped me reconcile my choices. We ended the night with a long hug goodbye and a promise to never again go so long without speaking.

I sit up in bed, preparing myself for what his text might tell me. I don't think it's possible to cry any more than I have in the last twenty-four hours, nor can I fathom a world without Charlie in it. Carefully, I swipe up to see the full message.

Charlie is out of surgery. Critical but stable.

I hold the phone to my chest and look up at the ceiling, the enormous relief enough to liquefy every muscle. "Thank you, Lord."

Answered prayers come in many different forms, most of which we don't recognize. This one, though, came exactly how I'd hoped.

THIRTY-FIVE

I'm beginning to see the cycle in my roommate's dating ritual. It starts with phone calls, and then her mood picks up and she practically dances through the apartment. Calls turn into dates, which turn into Zoe disappearing because she's a big fan of the overnight stay. Days or weeks later, she's back, her heart slightly bruised, until new calls start the process all over again.

We're in the giddy stage right now.

"How's Charlie doing?" she asks, plopping on the couch next to me, nail polish in one hand and her phone in the other.

"Better. He's still in ICU, so they won't let me see him yet since I'm not family. I'm going to try again tomorrow."

"That's good." She leans over and carefully puts a foam separator between her toes. "Got any big plans for tonight?"

"You mean besides watching TV and going to bed early? No." Which I have a feeling will be the new normal in my life. Cameron has been radio silent since he stormed out, and Bryson's truck was gone when I went to check on Louie this morning. I guess he called someone else to take him home from the hospital, someone he obviously prefers more than

344

me right now. Probably Jay or Harrison. After all, the biggest break of their career is happening tonight.

Turns out there was one more option besides my choosing between a best friend and a boyfriend. Me . . . all alone.

I brush off the sadness, refusing to fall back into the depressive state I've been in most of the summer. Charlie is alive. Everything else in my life is inconsequential comparatively. "What about you?" Though based on the freshly shaved legs and bright polish, I'm sure her plans are not the same as mine.

"The hottie from your dad's party is taking me out." She winks. "Thanks, by the way."

I think back to the barbecue, trying to figure out the appeal. Sure, he was nice to look at shirtless, but he was also inconsiderate to my dad and definitely not the brightest bear in the clan. "That guy is a waste of your time."

Her head pops up, and she genuinely looks confused. "What do you mean?"

"All he talked about was biking and running and mountain climbing."

"So?"

"So . . . your idea of working out is shopping for the best booty-shaping leggings. You two have nothing in common."

Zoe snickers. "I guarantee he'll like the leggings as much as I do."

I groan. Sometimes it's like talking to a wall. "I'm being serious." I pull my right leg up onto the couch so I can fully turn and look at her. "You always know exactly what these guys want in a girl and try for however long you can stand it to be that person. But have you ever stopped to consider what *you* want in a partner?"

Her hand freezes mid-stroke of painting red on her second toe. "Not really."

"Well, maybe that's what we need to do first. Give me three things, besides their looks, that you would find attractive."

Zoe stays quiet, but I can tell she's at least trying to come up with an answer. I guess it makes sense that she doesn't know right away. She's probably never bothered to ask. "Cooking, I suppose. It would be nice if the guy liked to cook."

"Okay. That's something." Not quite as deep as I was hoping for, but a start. "What about the guy's character?"

"I don't know. I mean, I hope he's a good guy." She laughs, embarrassed. "What do you want? Like, what was it about Bryson that made you finally say yes?"

Pain seizes my chest, but it's a fair question and brings an easy answer. "He's loyal and dedicated. To Charlie and to you. He loves passionately, even though he's spent most of his life not being loved back. He has integrity. He says what he feels and doesn't play games." I blink back a new round of tears and look down at my fingers. "I liked that he challenged me and pushed me out of my comfort zone. And yeah, Bryson has always been easy on the eyes, but when he's soft and vulnerable, I think he's quite possibly the most beautiful man I've ever seen."

I stop, even though there are pages more I could give her. But to continue means I'll have to relive yesterday over again, because the image of him begging me to leave him alone is now what's lodged in my mind.

"Anyway . . ." I look back at Zoe and force a smile. She's abandoned her nail polish and is now listening with focused attention. I don't miss the opportunity. "The point is that you need to stop letting these guys choose you as if you're lucky to have them. Zoe, you are kind and generous and beautiful—in

346

here." I point to my heart. "You are special. You are a catch, and you need to start choosing someone of equal value to be a part of that. And trust me, it's not going to be some dim-witted jock who had to ask me my name three times."

"You're right," she says with conviction, and in a way I've never heard her express. "We both deserve to be with men who love and appreciate us." She gets up and texts something on her phone. "Done. Date's canceled."

Wow. She actually took my advice. "That's great, Zoe. Good for you."

"And now that I'm available again, we're going out."

I should have known there would be a catch. "I'm in no mood. Really. Yesterday was literally the worst day of my life. And considering the year I've had, that is saying a lot."

"Too bad. You owe me." She raises her brows, and it's clear I'm not getting out of this. "I went to your dad's party when I wanted to sulk, and now because of your little motivational speech there, I have nothing to do on a Friday night. So, get dressed. We're going out."

"Zoe, I don—"

"Wear a cute dress!" She's down the hall and gone before I can argue more.

I drop my head to my knees and put my hands over my neck like we used to do in tornado drills. When will I ever learn to keep my mouth shut?

~

I don't realize where she's taking me until the car is parked and we're standing outside the club. In bright letters, the sign reads *Firesight, Friday, 9:00 p.m.* Underneath, in a smaller font, is the name that's practically branded into my soul: *Black Carousel, Friday, 7:30 p.m.*

It's 7:55.

My feet are planted on the sidewalk. "I can't go in there."

"Yes, you can." She tugs on my arm, but I don't move. "And more than anything, you need to."

"No, I don't. This is the last place I should be." I shake my head. "Cameron despises me, and Bryson has made it clear he wants me to stay away."

"Do you really think that?" She sets her fists on her tiny, jeweled waistband and lectures like my seventh-grade teacher did when Cameron and I would text in her class. "After all you know about my brother now, do you really believe he meant it when he said he didn't want you there?"

"Yes, I do." I swallow down the panic of what she is asking me to do. "This is their shot, Zoe. There are managers in there. Record executives. If I distract them or mess this up in any way for them . . . I'd never forgive myself."

"This venue is huge and sold out. I only have tickets because Bryson sent them to me four days ago, which he has never done in the history of ever. So that alone tells you he wants the people he cares about to see him play tonight. The guys won't be able to see us. I promise. And we'll leave the minute you say so." When I still don't move, Zoe comes closer, her voice more a plea than a demand. "If this concert is really his big opportunity, then he deserves to have you in there supporting him. Even if you and I are the only ones who know you did."

I wet my lips and try to keep my legs from trembling. "You're right. He does deserve that." I take in a stabilizing breath. "Okay, I'll go in . . . for a few songs."

"Good, because I really didn't want to cause the kind of scene we'd make by me swinging you over my shoulder." I chuckle at the visual of her size-two frame even trying to do that. "I know my brother." Her tone turns serious. "Actions mean everything. And your being here will matter more than you'll ever know."

I glance up at her, and a rush of appreciation surges through me. "When did you get so wise?"

She rolls her eyes, but it's accompanied with a smile. "I have this really annoying roommate who must be rubbing off on me."

"Thank you."

"Whatever. You know I'm here for the cute boys." Her arm links through mine, and she guides me to the front door and to a very burly-looking man taking tickets.

He clicks her phone when she offers him her screen. "These are VIP. You have reserved seats down front." He grabs a flashlight from the table next to him. "I'll take you."

"No thanks," Zoe says easily and flips back her hair. He follows it, slightly mesmerized. "We like the back. That won't be a problem, will it?"

He shrugs and sets the flashlight back down. "Suit yourself, but it's standing room only." Arm out, he backs up until the door swings in and darkness faces us.

Zoe walks inside first, pulling me behind her. The place is crowded, the air sour with alcohol and adrenaline. We push through sweaty bodies dancing until we make it to the back, far enough that there's no way the band could possibly make out individual faces.

"Does this work?" Zoe yells in my ear.

My eyes zero in on Bryson, and everything in me melts. Zoe was right. I needed to be here. "Yeah. This is perfect."

"Good. Then I'm going to get us a drink." True to her nature, Zoe's gone a heartbeat later.

It takes only two songs for me to realize I've once again

come full circle. Here I am, standing next to a bar, a drink in hand, watching Bryson and Cameron light up the stage in front of me. Only this time, the drink is water and it's not my best friend up there. He's someone completely different. Wild, angry, and working the crowd to a frenzy.

"We love you, Dallas!" Cam rips open his buttoned shirt and spreads his arms, his chest exposed under the lights. The screams from a line of girls are deafening. They love him right back.

Zoe leans into me. "It's kind of weird. I feel like I'm watching my brother and Cameron become celebrities tonight."

"You are. I have no doubt Black Carousel will soon be a household name." Any fear I had of Bryson and Cameron surviving our little love triangle is gone now. They're perfect. Not one beat off, not one line dropped. And if I didn't know better, I would believe they loved each other like brothers up there.

Cameron once told me that the true art of performance is giving the crowd the illusion they want. Bryson and Cam are both proving their artistry tonight, and they deserve every great thing this next tour is going to give them.

Bryson shoves his hair out of his eyes and leans into the microphone. "We have something special for you. A song I wrote, and it's the first time it's ever been performed."

The crowd screams, and my breath freezes in my lungs. Bryson's song. He finished it.

He drags over a stool, much like the one he had onstage in the youth room, and trades out his electric guitar for an acoustic one.

Zoe watches the scene unfold with wide eyes. "What is he doing?"

"I don't know."

Black Carousel doesn't do ballads. Maybe that's why Cameron backs away, why Jay sets down his bass guitar, and Harrison holds his drumsticks in his lap.

Bryson swallows. "This song is for someone who's incredibly special to me. I hope you like it. It's called 'A Decade of Love.'" He begins slowly, his fingers plucking away at the melody I first heard in his backyard. But it isn't until the lyrics flow through the hushed room that I realize exactly what the song is about.

My throat burns as I try to hold back the emotion pummeling through every inch of my body. His beautiful, touching words fall over me as a powerful, rushing warmth invades my bloodstream. It's the first time I've seen *my* Bryson onstage. The sweet, loving man who in an incredibly short period of time changed my entire outlook on life. His voice aches of pain, taking each one of us through the journey he faced, the prison of the anger, the pain of overcoming his weaknesses, and the beauty of finding peace in the arms of the one person who saw who he could be from the very beginning.

It's an epic love song. The kind that catapults artists to the top of the charts.

Zoe turns to me, her eyes watery. "He wrote about you."

"No." I shake my head, nearly too overcome to speak. "That song isn't for me. It's for Charlie."

Bryson's voice fades as he ends the song, and silence lingers for a fraction of a second while we all recover. Then pandemonium strikes. The crowd is hungry for more, dying to get their hands on whatever force invaded the building just now.

I cover my ears, the sound deafening. Black Carousel begins gearing up for their final song, and then comes the headliner. But all of us know that nothing else tonight will top what just took place on that stage.

"It's time to go," I tell Zoe, my chest aching from the vibration and from the black hole that's taken residence inside.

"Okay. I just need to hit the ladies' room real fast."

I nod and point to the door. "I'll be outside." Desperate to escape before I fall apart, I push my way through the crowd. Hot bodies press and pull me until I finally reach the exit, my lungs gasping for any air, even the hot Texas air hovering over the concrete outside. I fall back against the brick building, my eyes swollen and my hands shaking as I pull out my phone.

I press on his name and wait for voicemail. It comes in two rings, smooth and fluid.

"Hey . . . it's me." I press the phone closer to my ear and turn away from the busy street. "I just wanted you to know that you were amazing tonight. Well, amazing now since you're still onstage." I wrestle to find the right words. "Your song was perfect. I know Charlie will be so honored by the things you wrote, and I know how hard that must have been to get up there and sing something so vulnerable." A tear falls, then another. "You were right about everything." I swallow because my voice begins to crack. "I was afraid to let go. Afraid of being disappointed again. Afraid to trust you with my future. Just . . . stupidly afraid. So thank you—thank you for showing me what it looks like to be brave." My voice breaks again, and this time I can't stop it. "I . . . I love you, Bry—"

The phone beeps before I can finish, but I said what I needed to. Now I can let him live out his dream with no regrets. He'll know he is loved, even if I ruined any chance of his loving me back.

THIRTY-SIX

I was up at dawn even though I didn't sleep well. My heart kept hoping I would hear something back from Bryson: a call, a text, some kind of acknowledgment at all, but there has been nothing. For all I know, he and Cameron are on a bus together, heading off to fame and fortune.

At least I can call the day productive, even if my mind has been teetering between accepting my reality and clinging to the fantasy that Bryson will come back. The dog fair was remarkable. Penny got adopted within the first twenty minutes by an elderly woman who had just lost her longtime companion—a white Jack Russell terrier who could have been a twin to Penny. I know this because she showed me at least fifteen pictures. The adoption probably would have happened in ten minutes, but I spent an equal amount of time detailing all of Penny's hang-ups. The lady assured me Penny would not be alone or crated and there were no other dogs to compete with. Plus, I have to give that little dog credit; she knows a good thing when she sees it and was on her absolute best behavior.

But as happy as I am that Penny found a home when only

weeks ago she was terrifyingly close to being euthanized, her quick adoption leaves me an entire Saturday alone to try to forget the aching mess that is my broken heart. Maybe that's why I'm back at Charlie's farm. Who would have thought that one large Great Dane would become my closest friend?

Louie trots around his cage when he sees me coming and howls a hello to me.

I open the kennel, give him room to come outside, and hug on him. Though I can only stand it for about a second.

"You smell awful," I moan, pushing him away. "Did you get into a fight with a skunk last night?"

Louie sits, his mouth hanging open, a proud, satisfied look on his cute doggie face. I'm guessing that's a yes. I don't think he got sprayed, the smell isn't that horrific, but he definitely picked up some residual scent.

"Okay. Let's get you bathed." I take him over to the hose and clip him to the door. Unlike Sam, Louie loves the water, so this task will not be nearly as daunting as it was that first week on the job.

My mouth quirks up when I think back to that original adoption fair and Bryson squatting down to show Jacob the harmonica. That was the day that changed our relationship. His façade was completely gone, and we got to see each other for probably the first time since we were kids.

"How could I have doubted him?" I ask the canine, who has no idea what I'm saying. So many of our decisions in life are based on baggage and perceptions we've obtained. Bryson had asked me to look past all of those and see the real him. Unfortunately, by the time I managed to do so, it was too late.

I let the cool water run over Louie's back, soaking his fur. He leans into me, leaving wet hairy marks on my shorts, but I don't care. He's showing his love for me and

I'm caring for him. That's the way it's supposed to be. I scrub the soap, giving him lots of scratches, and finally rinse him off. My attempt at towel drying only lasts about a minute before he escapes to the yard, running in quick, excited circles.

He ducks his head and rubs it in the grass, somersaulting to his back.

"Really?" I ask, wetter than he is. "I just cleaned you."

He continues to use the ground as a back scratcher while I work to clean up the mess we made. A faint buzz stops me as I'm rolling up the hose, and I sprint to the steps where I deposited my phone for safekeeping.

"Hello," I say, breathless, having no idea who's calling since the sun's reflection made my screen too dark to decipher. Though if my stomach has anything to say about it, I can assume the sudden butterflies are directly related to my hopes that Bryson is on the other line.

"Darcy?"

I try not to deflate at the female voice on the other end. "Yes, this is she."

"Hi, this is Miranda Elledge from the rescue society."

"Oh yes, hey." I press my cheek to my shoulder to hold the phone while I wipe my hands dry. "I was going to call later today and let you know Penny was adopted. That just leaves Macey, and I fully expect her to stay here with Charlie, and then Louie, and I'll probably hold off on taking him to the fair until the end of the summer." Truth is, he could probably go now, but I'm not sure I'm willing to give him up. My new apartment will allow two pets; I just need to get a waiver about his size.

"Yes, actually that is what I wanted to discuss with you. We found Louie's original owners."

My heart sputters, and I ease myself onto the concrete steps. "The ones who abandoned him?"

"No. The ones who bought him." She pauses, and I wipe my palms on my shorts. I'm sweating and it's not from the heat. "Do you remember when you asked me to look into his past so that you could best know how to work with him?"

I nod my head. "Yes."

"Well, I kept digging, mostly because I wanted the breeder to know that he sold a dog to the kind of owner who abuses and abandons animals. The breeder just got back to me yesterday after contacting her clients. Louie was stolen out of their backyard six months after they brought him home. After all this time, they thought he was gone for good."

"Wow. That's . . . wonderful." I practically choke on the word, which makes me a horrible person because I should be happy. "Are they wanting him back?"

"They're not sure. I explained what all he's gone through, and they're obviously a little hesitant. They have two kids: a nine-year-old girl and a six-year-old boy. They want to make sure he's safe first."

"Of course. What do you need me to do?"

"Well, if you aren't busy, could you meet me there today?"

"Today?" A pain presses against my chest as I internally plead with God not to take another thing from me. I glance at Louie, who's now sunbathing on his side, his legs stretched way out. "Um, yes." I swallow down the *No!* I want to scream. Despite my own needs, I have to do what's best for him. "I can bring him there this afternoon."

"Wonderful. I'll text you the address, and we'll plan for one o'clock."

I end the call, my hand numb. I was supposed to have more time, and yet somehow I know this is just another step

God is forcing me to take. To trust Him, even when nothing
is how I want it to be.

～๑

The drive out to Louie's owners is a beautiful one. They
live in Ennis, nestled in a small neighborhood with large
homes and even larger lots. Across the street is a park with
walking trails and exercise stations. A perfect place for Louie
to run around, I surmise, trying to squelch the small part of
me that still hopes he comes back to Charlie's with me today.

The GPS signals to turn left, and I reach for the passenger
seat to pet Louie's head. He's great in the truck. Hops right
in and sits like an adult in the seat. I roll down the window
when we slow to fifteen miles an hour and let him hang his
head outside.

"Almost there, big guy. Just three more houses."

But Louie is no longer listening to me. Hair stands on his
back, but his tensing isn't fear like I'm used to. He's excited.
So excited that he's trying to climb out the window in a space
that barely fits his head.

I grab his collar and hold him back while parking the car,
afraid he's going to break the glass. Louie barks frantically
and follows me out the driver's door, practically pushing me
over in his eagerness. I grab the leash and holler out commands, but it's no use. He knows this house, and if I had
any question whether the memories are positive, his thrill of
being home answers them.

Two children sit on the front steps, waiting, and make
a run for us the minute we appear from around the truck.
Louie stands on his back legs and surges headfirst, pulling
me forward until I either bust my chin on the ground or accept the onward motion he's demanding.

A lady hurries from the house, calling her children's names. "Lilly, Jaxon, wait!"

Her commands are as effective as mine, and the two kids and their long-lost puppy reunite halfway up the paved walk. They hug his neck, the little girl in tears. Louie howls like he's crying right along with her.

"I knew you would come home, Zeus. I just knew it!" she cries, kissing his long snout. Louie licks her face and nearly pushes her over trying to lean into her tiny body.

"Zeus?" I ask, kneeling between Louie and the kids, just in case. Their mom reaches us about the same time. "Is that his name?"

"I homeschool, and we were studying Greek mythology. They were quite fascinated," she says, winded and understandably worried.

"We picked the name because Zeus was the grandest dog of all of them!" Lilly says in a cheer. She reaches out for his leash. "Can I take him inside?"

I look toward her mother and wait for confirmation.

She assesses him nervously. Her hesitation is fair. Louie has likely tripled in size since they last saw him. "What do you think? Is he trustworthy?"

"Louie . . . I mean, Zeus, has never shown any aggression. He was recently attacked by a small dog, and even then, he defended himself without hurting her. You can never say concretely with an animal, but I believe he's extraordinarily gentle."

She bites her lip, then seems to make a decision. "Jaxon, go get your dad and tell him to meet us in the backyard. Lilly, take Zeus through the gate."

The kids both say, "Yes, ma'am," which leaves me no choice but to turn him over.

"Can I have just a second with him?" I ask, tears already filling my eyes.

"Sure." Her voice is compassionate, and she guides Lilly away by the shoulders to give us some privacy.

I squat down in front of Louie and scratch his ears the way he loves. "Well, I guess this is goodbye for you and me." He nudges me with his cold nose, and I try to laugh through my tears. "All this time, you had a home just waiting for you. And I can tell, they are going to love you even more than I do." I wrap my arms around his big neck and hug him. "Fear has deprived us of so much. Let's make a pact that from now on, we embrace whatever path God has for us." I pull back and put out my hand, palm up. Louie lifts his paw into mine, and we shake on it. "Good boy." It feels impossible, but I find a way to stand and walk back over to the little girl and her mother. "Here you go. Take good care of him, okay?"

She nods very seriously. "Oh, I will. I know how to change his water and feed him, and Mom got us a new brush today to use on him."

"Sounds like he's in good hands." I smile, and this time I really mean it. Louie deserves a best friend; Lilly will make a fine one.

I show her how to properly hold the leash and tell her to keep him on her left side. She concentrates on every word of advice and does very well considering his massive size.

"I think you have a future dog trainer there," I tell her mom.

"Yes, she wants to be a veterinarian when she grows up."

I chuckle at God's sense of humor. Life. Full circle. Once again.

"Thank you for bringing him here and for taking such good care of him." She glances at the house and back again. "My kids were devastated when he disappeared. I still can't believe we found him."

Silence falls, and the anxiety it brings forces me to fill it. "I'm not sure if he's still housebroken. He's only been kept outside."

"Okay."

"And if you have any issues at all, please call me. I'd be happy to come help train him for you or work on any behavioral issues." I pull out my phone. "If you give me your cell number, I'll text you my info."

We're in the middle of exchanging contacts when a black sedan pulls in behind my truck. A woman I assume is Miranda exits and waves at us. She's more polished than I expect. Black pencil skirt, button-up blouse, and three-inch heels. Obviously, she isn't the one handling the animals.

"Well, I seem to be late to the party." She quickly shakes my hand, her grip far stronger than her thin figure implies. "Darcy, it's so nice to meet you. And, Linda, how are you feeling about everything?"

Linda sighs. "A little better now that I've seen him with the kids. He's certainly beautiful."

"The name Zeus fits him. He's grand, as your daughter put it, even by Great Dane standards." I turn to Miranda. She has a large hardback folder in her hand. "Do we need to fill out any paperwork?"

"No, we do not. Since the Walkers were Louie's original owners, this is a return, not an adoption. My favorite kind of case." Her smile is bright and warm despite her corporate vibe. "Do you have any questions for me?" Her offer is to Linda, not me, so I wait to see if there's more she wants to discuss.

"No. I should probably get out back and see what havoc

has started." She goes to leave but then turns back and wraps me in a tight hug. "You are an answer to prayer. One my kids have prayed every night for a year." Her eyes are as glassy as mine when she pulls away. "Thank you."

"It was my pleasure." And God's providence that brought us to this moment. Of that I have no doubt.

Miranda and I watch as Linda disappears inside. She turns to face me a beat later.

"Well, this turned out to be a great start to the day." She flips open her folder and pulls out a stapled stack of paperwork. "Here's hoping you can make it even better."

Confusion furrows my brow. Didn't she just say we didn't need to file anything?

"I'm sure Charlie spoke to you about our conversation a couple of days ago," she continues, also pulling out a pen.

"No, I'm sorry. He didn't." But this is probably what he was referring to before his heart attack. "Is everything okay?"

"I'm hoping it will be." She smiles again, bright and inviting. Miranda must be the fundraising guru. She has an innate ability to make you want to say yes to whatever it is she needs. "We'd like to offer you a position with the foundation." She extends the stack she's holding to me, but I'm too stunned to take it.

"A job? Doing what?"

"It's all right here." She pushes the papers closer, and I finally take them from her. "And ignore the date. I've been in a rush since Charlie's call. But don't worry, the final documents will all be correct."

I flip up the first page and read the job title: Foster Coordinator and Trainer. Underneath are more details like work hours, pay, benefits. All of which are more than I need. "I don't understand. Charlie's call?" I close the packet and look at her.

"Yes. He told us that he hasn't seen someone this talented with animals since Sue Ann." Her voice falters a little, and I can tell there's still grief there. "And that he wholeheartedly approved you for the position."

I'm nearly too blown away to speak. "Why would he need to approve anything?"

"Well, because our new facility is going to be built on Charlie's land." She pulls out a surveyor's map. I recognize the road. It's the same address as Charlie's. "Before Sue Ann died, she donated the funds for us to build indoor/outdoor kennels and a training course. She also leased two acres to us for one dollar a year for the next ten years."

Miranda hands me the plans. It's the two acres of land between Charlie's house and Sheila's covered in beautiful hardwood trees.

"We expect the facility to be up and running by early November. Assuming you agree to take the job." Her smile falters a little. "A stipulation in the lease was that Sue Ann and Charlie had to approve our hire. Sue Ann didn't want someone they didn't like so close to their home." Her voice turns soft. "Charlie has rejected every résumé we've sent."

I stare at her and back down at the plans. How is this even possible? It's not just a great paying job, but it's my dream job, and I'll be doing something I'm totally passionate about.

She gently touches my arm. "There's a lot of Louies out there waiting to be saved. Will you at least consider the offer?"

"I don't have to consider it." I drop my hands to my sides, still slightly in shock. "Yes. I absolutely would be honored to work for your foundation."

Miranda's face lights up. "Excellent!" She points to the business card clipped to my application. "Look over everything and come see me Monday morning at nine. I very much look forward to getting to know you." She briskly shakes my hand.

"Yes. Me too." All this time I thought God had forgotten me. That He had left me purposeless and broken. But He was here the whole time, and like Louie, I just had to find my way home.

THIRTY-SEVEN

On Sunday, Charlie calls, ornery as ever, and tells me I better come visit him before he's forced to break free of all the coddling the hospital staff are doing. I'm so thrilled to hear from him, I rush to Waxahachie, barely taking the time to brush my teeth and throw my hair in a ponytail.

The nurses point out his room, which is thankfully no longer in ICU, and I try to prepare myself for what I might see. My grandfather was in the hospital when I was fourteen, and in only two days, he seemed to age ten years.

Charlie, thankfully, looks better than I expect, though still pale and weak.

"It's about time," he says when I enter his room. "I was beginning to think you'd forgotten me."

"As I told you on the phone, they wouldn't let me in to see you. ICU policy." I set my keys down on the nightstand and lean over to hug him quickly and carefully, or so I thought. Instead, the minute I feel his arms wrap around me, I break down and hold on until the tears stop. "I'm so glad you're okay." I pull back and use hospital-grade tissues to wipe my eyes.

"Eh. This old ticker just needed an oil change. Nothing a few bypasses couldn't fix."

I chuckle at the way he downplays his brush with death. "Is that what they did?"

"Yep. Cut open my chest and then had the gall to force me to try to walk across the hall this morning."

"I'm sure they know what they're doing." I pull over a chair and sit next to his bed. "Are you in much pain?"

"I'll live," he says gruffly, which means he is. Considering Charlie's history with addiction, I can only assume he's limiting taking pain medicine. "Tell me how it went with Penny."

"Great. She got adopted, and Louie went home." His brow furrows, and I give him the details of my crazy day yesterday. "And thank you for the job. I don't even know what to say."

"Say you'll hike yourself down to my door and come visit me and Macey as often as you can."

I smile at the image, wishing it included the one person neither of us has mentioned. "Absolutely."

He sighs and looks at the ceiling. "I heard that dog saved my life. I guess I should be glad you talked me out of getting rid of him."

"Louie certainly helped, but Bryson saved your life. I've never seen anyone fight the way he did." My eyes fill, but I push back the tears. This isn't the time to cry for lost loves. It's the time to celebrate the gift of life. I squeeze his hand, the lyrics from Bryson's song echoing in my mind. "You should be really proud of the man he's become. You had an enormous amount to do with it."

Charlie smiles at me, and his own eyes get watery, a rare and beautiful thing for him.

"Have you, um, heard from him since the concert?" I know I shouldn't ask, but I can't stand not knowing.

"Yeah. The boy's head is so big he's practically floating in the air."

"They got the tour, then?"

Charlie's expression turns apologetic. "And a record deal. A pretty sweet one from what I understand."

"Wow." I suck in a breath, having no idea why his confirmation punched me in the gut. This isn't a surprise. I knew they were that good. I knew it that night. But knowing something and *knowing* something are two very different things.

The door in his room swings open, and we both turn our attention that way, expecting a nurse's intrusion.

My heart plummets into my stomach. "Bryson." His name slips out in a breathy whisper. He's wearing a blue shirt, and I don't know what's worse, the fact that he waited until we broke up to finally ditch the black, or that the enhanced color makes his skin golden and his eyes a stunning array of greens and browns.

"Oh, I forgot you were coming by." Charlie's singsong voice tells me he didn't forget in the slightest. "Well, since we're all here . . ."

Bryson scowls at the old man, though as usual there's a hint of humor underneath. "You couldn't let me do it my way, even this once."

Charlie shrugs. "Your way was taking too long."

I look between the two men and suddenly feel completely out of place. "I'll let you guys have some time together." After all, Bryson is leaving soon. I stand, scooting back the chair, and squeeze Charlie's hand before I go. "I'll come see you soon."

"You better."

I focus on the floor as I walk by, no longer able to stand the sight of Bryson so relaxed and . . . joyful. That's what hurts the most. Here I am, devastated, while he's the happi-est I've ever seen him.

His hand gently wraps around my arm as I slide past him. "Can we talk?"

I dare to glance up at him, though it's nearly my undoing. "Um, sure." I continue into the hallway and walk toward the end where there's a small nook and at least the ap-pearance of some privacy. He doesn't come right away, so I stand there trying to get my nerves to settle and my mind wrapped around saying goodbye for what feels like the fourth time. Only this moment feels permanent because there won't be accidental run-ins at the farm or concerts for me to crash.

He finally comes out of the room and looks the other di-rection before turning my way and seeing me. A smile comes a second later, and it's so reminiscent of the ones he used to give me that my stomach whirls with a sudden hope that maybe, just maybe . . . I watch as he approaches, his eyes never leaving mine and his smile growing with each step, and just when I'm sure my chest might explode from anticipation, he's in front of me, way too close for a man who has asked me to keep my distance.

"Bryson, I'm—"

His fingers tunnel through my hair as hot, eager lips swal-low the words I'm attempting to say. I wrap my arms around his neck, ignoring the fact that we're in a hospital hallway and just one door over there's a steady beat of someone's heart monitor. His hand slips behind me, bringing me closer. I press in, the yearning of days without him burning, the fear I'd lost him dissolving.

The release comes slow, neither of us wanting to let go. He touches his forehead to mine. "I love you, too."

Relief courses through every electrified nerve. "You got my message."

"Yeah. I got your message." He pulls back and his smile melts into my skin. "Though I'd planned on telling you in a much more romantic setting. Obviously, Charlie had other ideas."

My cheeks warm, embarrassment catching up with me. "I'm glad. The last couple of days have been really hard . . . you know, wondering."

"I'm sorry." He brushes my hair away from my face. "I promise I wasn't avoiding you. There were just some things that needed to happen first."

And that's the cruelest reality of all. Our second chance comes on the eve of his new tour.

"When will you be leaving?" I ask, trying to sound happy for him.

He smirks at me, his brow lifting in that arrogant peak I've learned is all part of his charm. "Cameron, Jay, and Harrison are leaving tonight at seven. I, however, am staying right here."

I back away, struck by what he's saying. "What do you mean, you're staying? Charlie said you got a record deal."

"Black Carousel got a record deal. I'm just no longer a part of the band."

I can't process what he's telling me. "How? I mean, what label would sign a band that has no lead singer? It doesn't make sense."

"You and I both know Cameron was never meant to play backup to anyone. He'll carry the band without me just fine. And the label, well, they weren't happy about it, but money talks, and I made them an offer they couldn't refuse."

"What could you possibly have given them?"

"Not given them," he clarifies. "I sold the rights to my songs, all of them, with the caveat that Cameron sings lead. Including 'A Decade of Love.'"

My heart seizes in my chest. "No. You didn't. Bryson, that song is going to sell a million copies. It's a guaranteed hit."

"Let's hope so, because I'm banking on a really fat royalty check." He chuckles, and I cover my face with my hands. It's not possible. No one gives up this kind of opportunity. Bryson lifts my fingers away, and my eyes plead into his for this not to be true. "You seem very distraught over my staying. Call me crazy, but your voicemail sort of implied you wanted me to." And now he's teasing me.

"This isn't a joke, Bryson. I can't let you walk away from your dream."

"Black Carousel has never been my dream. Not even close." He takes my hand and sweetly kisses my knuckles. "Do you know why I picked that name? Because I was surrounded by darkness, stuck on a constant loop of anger and rebellion. It was me; it was my music. It was the only expression I had of my pain. Darcy, that's not who I am anymore."

I desperately want to believe him. "Are you sure? Because I don't want you to wake up one day and resent me for keeping you here." I won't replace my dependency on Cameron with a new one on Bryson. It isn't fair to anyone. "You don't have to stay for me. I'll wait. Gladly."

"And I love you for saying that." He leans down and kisses me, soft and gentle. "But do you really think I would even consider leaving with Charlie lying in a hospital bed only two days out from open-heart surgery?" I shake my head, and he rubs the pad of his thumb across my cheek. "'A Decade of Love' is my swan song. When I stepped onstage Friday night, I knew it was for the very last time." He winks at me.

"Getting the call that the love of my life loves me back, well, that was just a nice bonus."

I throw myself into his arms and laugh. A dazed laugh. I feel weightless and lightheaded from the shock of it all.

Bryson chuckles as he kisses my hair. "You going to be okay?"

I nod, my face pressed into his chest, and pull myself together. "Yes, for the first time in a long time, I think I'm going to be just fine."

Our arms stay wrapped around each other as we walk back down to Charlie's room, Bryson no more eager to let go than I am. "Best to tell him the good news slowly. I don't want his heart rate to spike all of a sudden. The guy's been a mess since I told him we broke up."

I squeeze his waist and glance up at him. "He's not the only one."

Tenderness fills his eyes. "Yeah, I didn't much care for it myself." We stop in the doorway, Bryson blocking my entrance. "Is your mom still doing Sunday night dinners?"

I nod, confused by the sudden shift in conversation. "Tonight was going to be my first one back, but I can postpone the reunion."

"Actually, I was thinking you could add a plus one. I mean . . ." He shrugs, and it's adorably insecure. "You've met Charlie and Zoe. Seems only fair I'd get to meet your family, too."

I don't miss his underlying request. Am I ready to give him everything this time? No holding back parts of my life. If we do this, we do it all the way. I lift on my tiptoes and kiss his cheek. "I'd love for you to meet my family. But be warned. They're sort of wacky right now."

"Yeah, well, whose isn't?"

As if on cue, Charlie grumbles from his bed. "Are you two going to stand there making out all day or come in here and talk to me?"

We both burst out laughing and walk inside to let Charlie know his little matchmaking scheme worked.

THIRTY-EIGHT

Sunday night dinners have become more than a family ritual confined to two parents and two kids. They now include Bryson, Michael, often Zoe, and even Charlie has been coerced into joining us on occasion.

It's been three months since the first time Bryson walked into my childhood home, quickly overwhelmed by the lavish affection my mom is known for. Now he's the one who initiates hugs and starts fights with her over guests doing the dishes.

I lean back in the reclining chair by the pool. It's a beautiful October day, hot enough for shorts, yet cool enough that by evening we'll all need a light sweater.

Michael is by the grill, a new one he bought a couple of months ago. It's happened slowly, but I now see all the wonderful traits my mom saw so early on. He still isn't charming and is quite possibly one of the most awkward small-talk initiators in the universe, but he listens well. He truly cares about people and is completely selfless with his time and energy.

Bryson comes over with a platter full of marinated chicken and takes up the space next to the man I'm currently analyzing. "Liz says she needs a ten-minute heads-up for the asparagus."

"No problem." He uses tongs to place each piece of chicken on the hot grill. "How's the new class going? Any luck getting the grant you applied for?"

Bryson took a full-time position as the music director at the elementary school by his house, and I swear he's the most dedicated teacher I've ever met. In only a few months, he's revitalized the practically nonexistent music program, and if the grant comes through, he'll have instruments for all the kids.

"Not yet. We're hoping to hear something by Thanksgiving. Meanwhile, those recorders we got have been game changers. They love playing them."

"Oh, that's great news."

Bryson winks at me, because we both know exactly who supplied the recorders.

That's the other thing about Michael. He's very generous. If that's because he has money to toss around, I don't know. Michael never talks about business or income or status like my dad always did, but if a concern comes up in conversation, it's a guarantee that a few days later, an anonymous gift will find its way into the hands of those who need it. In this case, a shipment of a thousand brand-new recorders addressed in care of Bryson Katsaros. A gift Michael denies he had anything to do with, though I stumbled upon the receipt in one of Mom's drawers days afterward.

Michael closes the lid to the grill and says something to Bryson I can't hear but assume it's related to me, because Bryson quickly catches my eye and then looks away. He nods and takes Michael's place as chef.

I sit up, as it's obvious something is going on. Michael is walking my way and biting his nail.

"I was wondering if I could talk to you for a minute?" he asks, blocking the sun.

I stand, and his face comes out of the shadows. "Yeah, sure." We've come to the point in our relationship where there's mutual respect, but deep, private conversations haven't really been established yet.

"Could we go into the living room?"

I nod, feeling an even wider pit growing in my stomach. Michael takes the lead, holding the glass door open for me when we enter. I can hear Mom when we pass by the kitchen, stirring something on the stove and listening to her favorite music station.

Michael walks over to the love seat and pulls out a box from under the cushion.

I blow out a breath because it's the kind of box that holds diamond rings, often worn on a very important finger.

He sits nervously, and I join him, feeling exactly the same way. "I know you and I had a slower start, but I hope these past few months have let you see how much I truly do love your mother."

"Yes. I can tell you do." He adores her, dotes on her, listens to her, and jumps from his seat the minute she needs something. I reach out my hand. "Can I see it?" He gives me the box, and I open it slowly, knowing that doing so will once again change the life I've gotten used to. Inside is a ring that feels very much like Michael and my mom. It's a simple gold band with a traditional cut diamond in the center. No frills, no excess. I close the lid and hand it back to him. "She's going to love it."

"I know it's a lot to ask for your blessing, but I don't want to walk into a new marriage with any dissent. Relationships are hard enough without inviting fractures early on." He stuffs the box back in its hiding place, and I wonder how long it's been there. "So, if you want me to wait, I can."

I'm assuming, since it's down to me, that the others involved are on board. No surprise there. Dexter has loved Michael since the beginning, and based on Mom's replay of meeting Michael's daughter, he's not the only one who adores her. I take another deep breath before I answer. It's a lot of pressure, his question, yet I also respect him for it. He could have just as easily proposed without my input or agreement. And maybe that's why I don't hesitate.

"You have my blessing, Michael. Completely."

He exhales as if he's been holding his breath. "Thank you. I promise I'll love her more than my own life."

I smile at him. Somehow, I know that he will.

Michael stands, though I remain planted since I don't want to engage in some weird congratulatory hug. "I'm going to check on the chicken." He steps around my legs and past the couch.

"Hey, Michael." He pauses and turns back to me. "When are you going to ask her?"

His eyes get that dreamy lovestruck look. "Wednesday. On her birthday."

"Good choice."

He remains standing there until the air grows awkward and then excuses himself again.

I stand and walk to the mantel covered in family pictures that long ago quit showcasing my father. Soon Michael will be up here. Probably his daughter, as well. A whole new life. I stop in front of the 8x10 photo of Cameron and me that has to be at least ten years old. We're in the backyard, his arm slung over my shoulder, and we're laughing.

Hands sneak around my waist, and I lean back into Bryson, welcoming the warmth and security I feel in his arms.

He kisses my neck and squeezes me closer. "You okay?" He must have known before I did what was going down in here.

"Yeah. I think so. Michael's a good man."

"Yes, he is."

We stay there silent for more than a few minutes, and I love that we don't have to fill the room with words. Cameron's face stares out at me, his eyes squinted, his dimples deep. It's been three months since our fight in Zoe's apartment. Three months of pure silence. But even though we aren't speaking, I still think of him. Wonder if he's doing okay and if he's pleased with the life he's chosen. Mostly I wonder if there will ever be a day when we can be friends once again.

"What's on your mind?" Bryson asks like he knows. And maybe he does. My eyes haven't moved from staring at the picture of me and Cameron together.

"I'm just wondering if he's happy."

Bryson turns me around so we're facing each other. "Of course he is. He's living out his dream." He smiles at me tenderly, and I want to melt into the hardwood floor at my feet. "And I'm living out mine."

I lift my eyes to the man whose face I see in every picture of my future. "No regrets?"

"Not even one." Bryson wraps me in a hug and kisses my forehead. "You, me, a family one day. Kids jumping on Charlie's back and calling him Papa. Maybe even a big house like this one where we'll host our own Sunday night dinners, with I'm sure a dozen rambunctious dogs barking in the background." He chuckles, and happy tears spring to my eyes. "That is my dream, Darcy. Don't ever doubt it."

I place my palms on his cheeks and once again thank God for this amazing, loyal, kindhearted man whom I never would have known if I'd gotten everything I asked for.

Somehow, against all odds, my worst-case scenario has turned into a bright, wonderful future.

ACKNOWLEDGMENTS

I'm not sure if it was coincidence or providence that I wrote and edited this book during the height of the COVID-19 pandemic. In a flash, our world was completely upended, and fear gripped me in ways I never expected. The church my husband and I work at closed its doors for the first time ever and went strictly online, myself and my husband both got sick, his reaction especially hard and lingering for weeks, my children suddenly required virtual school assistance and dealt with their own anxiety about school closing, and I watched as too many of my dearest friends buried their loved ones. Worst-case scenario was suddenly alive and right in front of me. But like Darcy, it was in those hard moments when God did His greatest work on my heart.

I pray you saw the beauty in Darcy's story. How with each dog she saved, God was right there, saving and loving her in the exact same way. Thank you to all who read these words I poured my heart into. And I especially want to thank those who made this book, maybe even my most favorite one to date, possible:

To Raela Schoenherr and all the Bethany House editors and staff, thank you for your guidance and push for excellence. Darcy's story would have been significantly less without your feedback and direction.

To my former agent, Jessica Kirkland, thank you for helping me sort out the right place to start this story and for all you've done along the way. I know your time as an agent has ended, but I will forever be grateful you were once a part of my writing journey.

To my amazing writing partners—Connilyn Cossette, Christy Barritt, Nicole Deese, and Amy Matayo—thank you for walking through so many iterations of this story. And for the weekend-long phone conversations as I plotted and replotted and replotted again. You pushed me to trust my instincts and I'm so very grateful.

Finally, to the most important people in the world, my family. This one was hard on all of us. Thank you for allowing me to disappear for entire weekends as I struggled to get words on paper. To my husband especially, thank you for carrying the burden of life on those days when there was already so much on your very strong shoulders. You are my rock, my best friend, and I love you so very much.

Tammy L. Gray lives in the Dallas area with her family, and they love all things Texas. Her many modern and true-to-life contemporary romance novels include *Love and a Little White Lie* and the 2017 RITA Award–winning *My Hope Next Door*, showing her unending quest to write culturally relevant stories with relatable characters. When not taxiing her three kids to various school and sporting events, Tammy can be spotted crunching numbers as the financial administrator at her hometown church. Learn more at www.tammylgray.com.

Sign Up for Tammy's Newsletter

Keep up to date with Tammy's news on book releases and events by signing up for her email list at tammylgray.com.

More from Tammy L. Gray

After hitting rock bottom, January decides she has nothing to lose in working at her aunt's church—while hiding a lack of faith. A minor deception until she meets the church's guitarist and sparks fly. Can she avoid disaster—especially when a handsome landscape architect has an annoying ability to push her to deal with feelings she'd rather keep buried?

Love and a Little White Lie • STATE OF GRACE

You May Also Like . . .

When pediatric heart surgeon Sebastian Grant meets Leah Montgomery, his fast-spinning world comes to a sudden stop. And when Leah receives surprising news while assembling a family tree, he helps her comb through old hospital records to learn more. But will attaining their deepest desires require more sacrifices than they imagined?

Let It Be Me by Becky Wade
A MISTY RIVER ROMANCE
beckywade.com

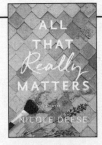

Molly McKenzie has made social media influencing a lucrative career, but nailing a TV show means proving she's as good in real life as she is online. So she volunteers with a youth program. Challenged at every turn by the program director, Silas, and the kids' struggles, she's surprised by her growing attachment. Has her perfect life been imperfectly built?

All That Really Matters by Nicole Deese
nicoledeese.com

Zara Mahoney was enjoying newlywed bliss until her life is upended by her estranged sister, Eve, and Zara must take custody of her children. Eve's struggles lead her to Tiff Bradley, who's determined to help despite the past hurts the relationship triggers. Can these women find the hope they—and those they love—desperately need?

The Way It Should Be by Christina Suzann Nelson
christinasuzannnelson.com

⬥ BETHANYHOUSE

More from Bethany House

In 1929, a spark forms between Eliza, a talented watercolorist, and a young man whose family has a longstanding feud with hers over a missing treasure. Decades later, after inheriting Eliza's house and all its secrets from a mysterious patron, Lucy is determined to preserve the property, not only for history's sake, but also for her own.

Paint and Nectar by Ashley Clark
HEIRLOOM SECRETS
ashleyclarkbooks.com

In the midst of WWII, Jane Linder pours all of her dreams for a family into her career at the Toronto Children's Aid Society. Garrett Wilder has been hired to overhaul operations at the society and hopes to earn the vacant director's position. But when feelings begin to blossom and they come to a crossroads, can they discern the path to true happiness?

To Find Her Place by Susan Anne Mason
REDEMPTION'S LIGHT #2
susanannemason.net

Few are pleased Sophie Deiner has returned to her Amish community, but a sudden illness leaves her no choice. She befriends a group of migrant workers but is appalled by their living conditions. She soon finds her advocacy for change opposed by her ex, the farm foreman, and that her efforts only makes things worse. Has she chosen a fight she can't win?

A Patchwork Past by Leslie Gould
PLAIN PATTERNS #2
lesliegould.com

BETHANY HOUSE